Now a Terrifying Motion Picture!

ALSO BY JAMES F. BRODERICK
AND FROM MCFARLAND

*The Literary Galaxy of Star Trek:
An Analysis of References and Themes
in the Television Series and Films* (2006)

Now a Terrifying Motion Picture!

Twenty-Five Classic Works of Horror Adapted from Book to Film

James F. Broderick

McFarland & Company, Inc., Publishers
Jefferson, North Carolina, and London

LIBRARY OF CONGRESS CATALOGUING-IN-PUBLICATION DATA

Broderick, James F., 1963–
    Now a terrifying motion picture! : twenty-five classic works of horror adapted from book to film / James F. Broderick.
    p.   cm.
    Includes bibliographical references and index.

    ISBN 978-0-7864-4763-3
    softcover : acid free paper ∞

    1. Film adaptations — History and criticism. 2. Horror films — History and criticism. 3. Horror tales, American — Film adaptations. 4. Horror tales, English — Film adaptations. 5. Motion pictures and literature. I. Title.
PN1997.85B75 2012
791.43'6 — dc23
                                            2012008468

BRITISH LIBRARY CATALOGUING DATA ARE AVAILABLE

© 2012 James F. Broderick. All rights reserved

No part of this book may be reproduced or transmitted in any form or by any means, electronic or mechanical, including photocopying or recording, or by any information storage and retrieval system, without permission in writing from the publisher.

Front cover design by David K. Landis (Shake It Loose Graphics)

Manufactured in the United States of America

McFarland & Company, Inc., Publishers
  Box 611, Jefferson, North Carolina 28640
    www.mcfarlandpub.com

Acknowledgments

This book about horror was really a pleasure to write, largely due to the following, whose contributions made the book better and my work much easier: Barry Harding offered several helpful and detailed critiques of individual chapters, and I look forward to the continuation of our online correspondence. My NJCU colleague Katherine D'Alessandro also generously shared her thoughts on several chapters (and during her sabbatical, no less). The Park Tavern Writers — Carlos, Ron, John, Vinny and Raul — provided the necessary dose of inspiration, and they reminded me why any of us writes in the first place. And Adam Philips proved once again not only to be a good guy but also a valued sounding board.

Undertaking a book project without the steadying advice of my prolific colleague Bruce Chadwick is almost unthinkable and I remain grateful for his counsel on all book-related matters, large and small. The staff at the Glen Ridge Library always came through. I especially thank Helen Beckert — who can find anything, I've discovered. When the going gets tough, I'm always grateful to have fellow writer Darren Miller in my corner. And my friend Gordon Osmond never fails to inspire with his wit and his humanity. Every writer should be so lucky to have such ready access to such a gifted teacher, memoirist and wordsmith par excellence.

My parents continue to offer long-distance fortification. My father reads more books in a month than most people read in a year, and he's always willing to share his insights and wisdom. My mother is the philosopher, wise and witty and warm-hearted. There is much of them in all my work. My daughters Olivia and Maddy inspire me daily with their eclectic reading tastes and their unique perspective on many works of literature and pop culture. Whenever my energy lagged, they gave me the inspiration I needed to get back to work. With diligent study, I hope one day to know a fraction of what they do about musical theater. And what my wife Miri provides on a daily basis can't be listed here in a brief acknowledgment.

Acknowledgments

But a short list would include her writerly insights, wondrously quirky perspective, smart and savvy editing, and unconditional love.

Finally, in the early 1980s, a group of thespians in Terre Haute, Indiana, used to dress up and perform along with *The Rocky Horror Picture Show* at the midnight showing at the Indiana Theater. Every Friday night they greeted moviegoers in the lobby, decked out in their *Rocky Horror*–inspired garb, handing out the latest edition of their newsletter. It was a wonderful and bizarre ritual. The Indiana Theater hasn't shown *Rocky Horror* for many years now, but I'll never forget those Friday nights.

This book is dedicated to those iconoclasts, wherever time and fortune have taken them.

Table of Contents

Acknowledgments v
Introduction 1

Altered States 5
The Amityville Horror 13
The Birds 21
Dead Ringers 29
Dr. Jekyll and Mr. Hyde 37
The Exorcist 45
The Fly 54
Frankenstein 61
Freaks 70
From Hell 78
Ghost Story 86
The Hound of the Baskervilles 94
Jaws 102
The Masque of the Red Death 110
The Night Stalker 118
The Ninth Gate 126
Nosferatu 134

Table of Contents

The Phantom of the Opera 143
Psycho 152
Re-Animator 161
The Serpent and the Rainbow 170
The Shining 178
Sleepy Hollow 186
The Thing from Another World 195
Village of the Damned 203

Notes   211
Bibliography   221
Index   223

Introduction

The next time you're in a movie theater watching the latest horror flick, fiercely clutching the arm of the chair (or person) next to you, glancing at the screen through a protective mask of fingers, heart beating in anticipation of the next cinematic jolt, take a moment to reflect on the contributions of a 3,000-year-old Greek writer.

Okay, that's not likely to happen. But it really should, for it was an eighth-century B.C.E. work, *The Odyssey*, by the Greek writer known as Homer, that helped make your time at the movies so frighteningly rewarding. Homer's work (which your tenth-grade high school English teacher reveled in reminding you was *the beginning* of all of Western literature) established a number of motifs that would come to characterize the horror genre throughout its rich, lengthy, and mutating development over the centuries: the threat of darkness and the unknown; the presence of violent brutes waiting to prey upon the unsuspecting; disturbing, surrealistic dreams and omens of foreboding; and hideous, disfigured monsters who cruelly tease and taunt humanity.

Although many other elements would eventually leach into the horror canon — first on the page, and then through the magic of cinema — the very beginnings of Western literature already find a ready litany of terrors awaiting the listener-reader. As one critic has noted, "The Ancient Greeks had the horrors of war and political upheaval. The plays of Sophocles, Euripedes, and their peers included gruesome doings, such as a mother feeding a pie stuffed with children to her husband, or an incestuous son gouging his eyes out for what he did to mommy and daddy."[1]

How's that for a curtain raiser?

After such frights, where could a spinner of scary stories go? Lots of places, it turns out. Horror writers were just getting started. The Greeks, and then the Romans, offered stories of angry gods tormenting humans for their transgressions — or even their political beliefs. The writers of the Bible gave us apocalyptic visions, literally; "the Good Book" is filled with demons, serpents, murder, man-eating creatures, and sword-wielding archangels. Medieval scribes gave us cold-blooded tales of terror, from Beowulf's slaughter of the monstrous Grendel to questing knights battling for their lives against evil giants and shape-shifting murderers.

By the early nineteenth century, horror writing and its consumption was a full-blown social phenomenon, with names like E.T.A. Hoffman and Mary Shelley popularizing tales of the grotesque for an eager, expanding readership. When Edgar Allan Poe came along in the mid–nineteenth century, the tradition of the horror story was well pedigreed in Western literature. And by the time Bram Stoker penned his paean to the persistent, folk-borne fears of East European peasantry, horror tales were fully conventional — even becoming a bit clichéd.

Just when it appeared that horror had no new place to inhabit, a monstrously popular innovation arose to breathe new life into this body of work: the medium of film. And from that time, one of the most fruitful collaborations in Western art was born: the close, creative synergy between the written word and cinema. The film industry, in fact, was built largely on the foundation of Western literature. Thousands of stories that already existed on the page were about to burst onto the big screen, and thousands more were being commissioned by the new power brokers of this path-breaking entertainment.

Although Hollywood would become the center of the film industry for most of its 100-plus years, the first significant excursions in the genre (many of which were based on horror literature) came from abroad. France, Germany, and Japan all produced filmmakers whose visions led to the first cinematic stirrings of the horror corpus. The seminal figure in early cinema was French film pioneer Georges Méliès, who made more than 200 short films in the late 1890s, including *La Manoir du Diable* (*The House of the Devil*), which is often credited as the first horror movie.[2]

These early experiments were, of course, crude and often barely watchable: poorly lit, wildly overacted, and with little attempt to mimic realism. Still, the genre developed rapidly. No less a technician than Thomas Edison added his expertise to the development of the horror film, shooting a one-reel version of *Frankenstein* in 1910.[3] While Méliès, who built his own studio, continued churning out short films with such titles as *The Man with Four Heads* and *The Laboratory of Mephistopheles*, other filmmakers in Europe, especially Germany, incorporated avant-garde elements in the nascent art form.

Introduction

By 1922, when F.W. Murnau made his classic silent film *Nosferatu*—a retelling of the Dracula story—the vocabulary of film had begun codifying into a near-universal cinematic language. Close-ups, tracking shots, back lighting, and of course "special effects" had become the universal tools for filmmakers. It would be more than a decade until the one-two punch of Hollywood's *Dracula* and *Frankenstein* (both released in 1931) launched the American film industry's all-out assault on the horror fan, but the trail had been blazed and the recipe set for getting a rise out of the audience: a popular horror tale adapted for film, a dark theater, an audience eager to be frightened, and flickering images of a misshapen creature, phantom, or alien threatening life as we know it.

The source material has remained much the same as well. Horror films continue to rely on written fiction (film adaptations of Stephen King's work alone come dangerously close to constituting a subgenre of horror films). This book explores the dynamic, sometimes fractious but often-inspired result of bringing together these two modes of fright: books and film. I'm aware, of course, that there are people who will always prefer the book to the movie (these people call themselves "bibliophiles"; others, less charitably, call them "snobs"), and there are many horror film buffs who've never turned a page of such compelling works as Gaston Leroux's *Phantom of the Opera*, Mary Shelley's *Frankenstein*, or Peter Benchley's *Jaws*. To them, the movie version *is* the definitive version.

This book, then, is an attempt to bridge that gap; to explore the interaction between some classic, scary, and thrilling reads, and the films they inspired; to celebrate the irreplaceable quality of each genre and what happens when the best of those qualities are brought together; and to acquaint casual fans of horror with some works they might have unjustly neglected. It's not uncommon for moviegoers to utter such phrases as "The book was much better," or "I didn't like the book nearly as much as I liked the movie." That's a defensible response—though some might argue that one really can't directly compare these two art forms, derived from largely different sets of rules governing their creation. But at least such a judgment acknowledges the collaboration: Every great book-based film owes something of its power to its source material. It's also true that every great movie version of a novel changes forever the way we think of that book, highlighting themes and illuminating plot points that the reader might have overlooked in a first, often hasty or unremembered reading.

A word about how the works in this book were selected. Obviously, there are some brilliant works of horror fiction that have never been made into a movie, and literally thousands of horror films (many of them masterful) that weren't based on a book or short story. So, as much as I would have loved to write about some of them, they didn't make the cut. It's not a film's popularity but its provenance that was a qualifying factor. In each chapter, I carefully consider both the literary and cinematic aspects of the work in question, and how they inform each other. And as much as fans of the horror genre love to argue among themselves regarding what is and isn't properly considered "horror," I admitted some books and films that are more arguably classed as "science fiction," "mystery," or "drama"—provided they exhibit clear elements of horror. (I grant that many stimulating hours could probably be spent trying to strictly classify such disparate titles as *Jaws*, *The Night Stalker*, and *Dead Ringers*. I've included them all as "horror"—let the arguments begin!) Though arranged alphabetically, the chapters can be read in any order. And in those few instances where there was a difference between the book title and the movie it inspired (such as *Nosferatu* and *Dracula*), I went with the movie title. The endnotes for each chapter provide detailed information about the source material I consulted, from primary materials (book, movie) to secondary sources.

Horror fiction, whether on the page or the soundstage, shows no sign of fading away. Bestseller lists—and lines snaking around movie houses and shopping mall theaters—testify to the enduring appeal of temperature-controlled fright. From the earliest oral legends of ogres, ghosts, and ghouls to shaky images of caped marauders and damsels in distress, to the modern slasher film, horror's hold on the public imagination is undeniable and irresistible. As these words are being read, someone, somewhere is hunched over a laptop or legal pad, writing a scary and suspenseful story that exists, for the moment, in just that person's head. But one day, some filmmaker may find in that tale the stuff of blockbusters and the cycle will continue, the collaboration between literature and movies affirmed and renewed, ensuring plenty of arm-clutching for future fans of the genre.

Altered States

When the hinged door closes over you, there is total darkness and total silence. You float, as if magically, almost on top of the water (which is heated to match one's body temperature: 98.6 degrees). The 10 percent saline solution ensures you'll stay afloat, arms and legs adrift. But it's the mind, not the body, that's the real beneficiary. Removed from any sort of stimulus, the conscious mind is free to retreat inward, undisturbed by the phenomenal world and the intrusion of the senses. So you lie in the darkness and the silence, heart rate and breathing slowed, wide awake but immobile, suspended in a state of total isolation. With the present, external world cut off, the mind turns back towards the past, replicating a kind of waking dream, excavating the layers of that past, slowly, slowly. Private memories flicker across your consciousness until something farther back, strange yet familiar, intrudes. You are no longer traveling the corridors of your own mind but the mind of humanity, tapping into primitive memories, ancient experiences trapped in the deepest recesses of the human brain, a repository of our collective past. In the warm, quiet, damp embrace of the womb-like enclosure, one disappears into psychic regions untrammeled by human visitation.

Or something like that.

In the mid-1960s, isolation tanks — also known as sensory deprivation tanks — became something of a fad among those who were seeking to alter their consciousness. Once the province of a small group of neuro-scientists and psychological researchers (led by Dr. John Lilly, a sort of cult figure among those looking for new ways to "drop out"), the widespread use of isolation tanks soon faded like so many other '60s fads. The movement yielded a few controversial, unorthodox scientific articles detailing the mind-altering effect of regular sensory deprivation and a couple of book-length studies chronicling the mind-expanding benefits of such immersion. But mostly the movement faded, and the isolation tanks went into storage.

Not all of them, however. From that early enthusiasm grew a small subculture of sensory deprivation advocates, many of whom now run for-profit businesses that offer the experience to stressed-out business people and harried suburban parents. For a small fee, you can book time for a regular dip into the isolation tank (on your lunch hour, say), and then head back into the rat race, soothed and serene. "There is nothing to learn, nothing to do. Upon being in the floating environment, the body relaxes completely, the mind releases, and the consciousness is free to be in its original state, like a clear sky," promises one such facility that offers dips into the darkness in the course of your workday.[1]

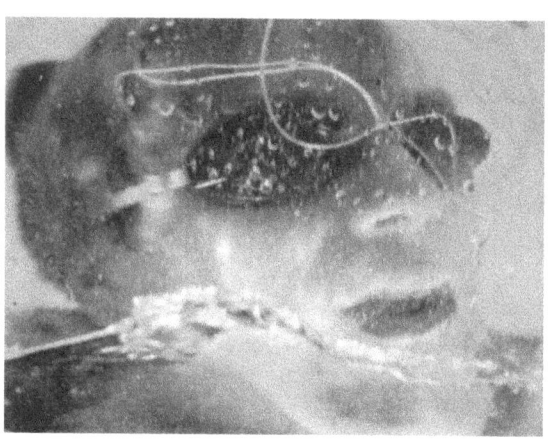

William Hurt descends into a sensory deprivation tank—and into a primitive world—in the disorienting *Altered States*.

Okay, so it helps clear the mind and reduce stress. No one would argue against that. But what if a trip into the isolation tank really was a trip back into the repressed memory bank of human history, a portal into our ancient past? Would that be a good thing? How far back would you want to go? What if you couldn't control how far back you went? And what if you combined the isolation tank experience with psychedelic drugs to heighten the experience?

Those are the questions at the heart of *Altered States*, the 1978 suspense-horror novel by the renowned Paddy Chayefsky. The book's premise—despite an abundance of scientific jargon—is simple and compelling: What if one could take a drug that helps unlock that dormant part of the brain that contains the ancient, passed-down memories of our primitive ancestors? Further, in the right setting (e.g., an isolation tank), that trip down humanity's Memory Lane would also be accompanied by a *physiological* change, taking us back to our ape-like origins, the mind crudely primitive, the physical body simian. You would then be able to witness, and participate in, mankind's evolution at the dawn of civilization:

> I'm in some kind of primeval timespace ... Cenozoic, latter Tertiary, I'm in an edge area—utter tranquility, but alive, life in the trees, life in the sedge, paradise, the garden of Eden, oh my God! The birth of man! That's it! The birth of man![2]

Chayefsky has written a sort of time travel book, but he's made his job a lot easier by making the journey one that is largely interior. Instead of having to explain away the difficulties in actual physical time travel (as in the rather cumbersome exposition found in books such as H.G. Wells' *The Time Machine*), Chayefsky locates the journey in the human brain. In the novel, the ancient past is already there, ingrained in us, locked away in our subconscious mind. But it can be unlocked by the combination of hallucinogenic drugs and sensory deprivation. And when that ancient memory is unlocked, the mind sends the body the message to come along, and the inevitable psychological changes occur:

> Sometime before half-past nine, he raised the hinged lid and climbed out of the tank with some effort, because when he clambered over the side into the subdued brownish-yellow light of the tank room, he was a finely furred creature barely four feet tall, bipedal if perhaps a bit sloping in the shoulders, with definable human features except for a massive projecting ridge of bone above his eyebrows....[3]

Presto—time travel!

Chayefsky is not known as a writer of horror or suspense stories. One of the most acclaimed writers of television's "golden era" in the 1950s, he helped elevate the hour-long television drama into a work of art with teleplays such as "Marty" and "Hospital." His best-known work is the screenplay for the Academy Award–winning movie *Network*.

Altered States is the only novel he ever wrote, and despite the gripping conceit that drives the story, Chayefsky often comes off in his prose as much more of a script writer than a novelist. His scenes are extraordinarily "talky," with characters regularly making long speeches to each other that seem, in the context of a novel, forced and unnatural. His character development is thin, and he seems willing to sacrifice well-rounded portrayals for his story. But what a story.

The novel focuses on 28-year-old Edward Jessup, a "psychophysiologist" who spends his time scrounging grant money to study the brain chemistry of schizophrenics. He has a girlfriend (later wife) named Emily, but throughout most of the novel, she serves almost exclusively as a sounding board and a prompt for Jessup's long speeches about his work.

After a working vacation to Mexico, where Jessup falls in with a group of indigenous people who make a kind of peyote–LSD hybrid out of plants, herbs, and human blood, he returns convinced that the drug can unlock hidden chambers of the mind. (While he's with this tribe, he takes the potion and has a wild trip, reverting to a semi-primitive state and devouring a lizard.)

Jessup decides to wed his previous research involving sensory deprivation with the mind-altering Mexican designer drug and see where it will lead. The novel increasingly begins to read like a kind of modern-day *Frankenstein*, with Jessup trying to convince a couple of his more sober and orthodox scientific colleagues of the validity of his research. There are the usual protestations about venturing into areas that are unfit for mankind, and Jessup's equally indignant replies that he's on the verge of the biggest discovery since Newton and Einstein.

Of course, Jessup prevails — and there's no way to stop him, really, since he's experimenting on himself. All he asks is for his colleagues to record his vital signs, and his dialogue, while he's in the tank. But of course they all end up getting more than they bargained for; it's a staple of sci-fi–horror that when a scientist plays God, he usually ends up with devilish results. So there's Jessup, taking the drug and then taking off his clothes, climbing into the tank while his fellow scientists attach electrodes to his body and hit the record button on the tape player. ("Parrish had never seen an isolation tank before, and it looked to him very much like a plain coffin."[4]) At first, his ramblings while he's under the twin influence of psychedelic drugs and total sensory deprivation are garden-variety, trippy babbling; he sees bright lights, landscapes, and faces, and hears indistinct voices and howling. But then things get truly weird.

Jessup begins to narrate a voyage back into time, where he witnesses volcanic eruptions, tar pits, and prehistoric creatures savagely battling each other. At least, that's what they're able to get down on tape before Jessup's narrative degenerates into first a series of indecipherable grunts, and then simply, a throaty series of clicks. When his friends decide to "rescue" him from his trip, they pry open the lid and notice that he's undergone some physiological changes around his neck, and that he can no longer speak. Sufficiently spooked by what they take to be a seizure, his colleagues decide to have nothing more to do with the experiment. But Jessup is in too deep. So a few days after he recovers, he climbs back in again — and this time, at the end of his journey through time, he climbs out in full ape-like state, bursting out of the lab after attacking a security guard and heading to the local zoo to devour a gazelle and run with a pack of wild wolves.

Of course, when guards later discovered Jessup sleeping naked among the antelopes, his wife and colleagues conclude that he has lost his mind. Jessup tries to tell them that he spent the night roaming through the world as his primitive, beastly self but they have a hard time swallowing the story.

In the best parts of the book, Jessup is in the tank, where we can't see him, where his colleagues can't see him, where the only record of what's going on is the bizarre and convulsive monologue issuing forth from the closed contraption. Chayefsky is a master monologist, and it's in these parts of the book that he plays to his strength. We get pages and pages of a modern mind's descent through time, a scientist groping for the irregular vocabulary necessary to translate the oddity, wonder, and terror of the primitive past. The scenes *Chayefsky* would likely say are the best in the book involve Jessup's numerous digressions on theology and the human need to believe in an external God. The thoughts are lofty, to be sure, but Chayefsky's book actually drags a bit when he gropes for sociological significance. All the action is, ironically, in the closed, coffin-like tank.

With his reputation as a master screenwriter, and an undeniably intriguing concept that encompasses drama, horror, and sci-fi, Chayefsky's story was destined for the big screen. Despite what became a problem-plagued production (the original director quit; the special effects guy quit; Chayefsky himself took his name off the final product), *Altered States* finally made it to the cineplex in 1980 with its weird charms and hypnotic, mesmerizing style intact.

The director who was eventually handed this project, the experimental and visionary Ken Russell, brought refreshing ocular brio to Chayefsky's chatty, thought-soaked screenplay. It's a perfect marriage of words and pictures — and *what* pictures! When this film was released, the special effects dazzled critics and audiences alike (with several critics quipping that they were the only worthwhile part of the film).

The film follows the book closely, but the lead character, Jessup, is much more engaging on film, largely because of the brilliant breakthrough performance of William Hurt (in his first major role). On the page, Jessup tends to come across as either something of a scientific bore or, in his enthusiasms, something of a crazy person. But Hurt conveys the dangerous excitement of a man seized by a radical idea; he tempers it by radiating a boyish glee as he spells out his ideas, getting excited as he overhears himself.

And there is real chemistry with his girlfriend-wife Emily (played by Blair Brown) — a character who's rather flat and one-dimensional in the book.

The movie effectively captures the pomposity and self-involvement — but also the sense of possibility — that awaits a bunch of young and gifted eggheads with grant money to spend and beds to tumble in. The viewer gets a pretty good sense of just how intense and, well, far-out Jessup is as we are privy to his hallucinations during sex, where he tells Emily he sees visions of angels, Christ, and God. (She has sensed that his mind is, often, elsewhere. "I feel like I'm being harpooned by a monk in the act of receiving God," she tells him.[5])

But that's nothing compared to the trips he takes in the isolation tank, where he sees himself hanging on a cross, wearing the heads of various animals, and seeing dead relatives uprooted from their eternal rest. In the book these are trips into the reader's imagination, since they are being narrated by the time-traveling Jessup, and we have to piece together the visions from the fragments he's selectively feeding us. But Russell lays out a buffet and then declares a food fight (visually speaking), assaulting the screen with a barrage of bizarre and engrossing tableaux, mostly dealing with explosive geological upheaval and the perilous, uncertain creatures that inhabit the Earth of our distant past. The impact is unsettling, but effective, as the viewer feels he or she is taking a journey along with the buoyant scientist.

The promise of a visually compelling film is suggested in the first few frames, where the camera lingers on what looks to be some sort of weird metal aquarium with a glass portal. Then, slowly, something rises up from the tank, and we can make out a human figure wearing what appears to be a breathing bubble around his head, dark protective glasses, and some sort of wires that appear to be connected to him. We hear breathing, and see him sloshing around in there, but we can't tell what he's doing. It's a strange and beautiful scene, and Russell holds the image patiently, only slowly pulling back to finally reveal that's it's a large, oval-shaped isolation tank in the middle of a laboratory, and it's being watched closely by some fellow taking notes and sipping coffee. (In the book, and in reality, isolation tanks are horizontal, like bathtubs with hinged tops, and one lies down on his back and floats; in the movie, they are vertical, like miniaturized grain silos, and one floats upright, almost as if you were standing.) The scientist Arthur Rosenberg (played by character actor Bob Balaban), monitoring the experiment, provides the requisite voice-over explaining what the tank is and who is currently floating in it (Jessup). We're witnessing Jessup's first immersion, but his enthusiastic plea to his colleague to schedule another session immediately confirms that he's going to be going back in for many more dips.

Though a sort of science geek, Jessup is not without his social skills. The scenes where he and Emily walk around New York City, with Jessup babbling excitedly about his work and Emily offering her perspectives as an anthropologist, seem unforced and genuine. Hurt and Brown make a nice screen couple — which is all the more tragic because (this being a horror–sci-fi film) their love will be tested to the limit, and likely beyond.

But the scenes most viewers remember are the frenetic and thrilling hallucinations experienced by Jessup while under the influence of his Mexican wonder drug — sometimes while in the tank, other times outside of it. Not only do his trips become more intense, but he starts bringing back souvenirs: a pair of ape's feet instead of his own, the windpipe and larynx of a gorilla, blood smears from an animal he killed while roaming the primitive plains. A scientist began by going ape over his theories, and now the transformation appears to be on track to become total.

Jessup spends much of the second half of the movie trying to convince his wife, his fellow scientists, and even the witnesses of his partial transformations that something *big* is happening when he climbs into that tank. Unable to garner the support he feels his work merits, he decides to continue the experiments himself. The news is both good and bad: He gets the results he was hoping for, but that's also the bad part, because now he *is* an ape. (Just why that's bad is made clear to the janitor who comes across Jessup-Ape.) Victor Frankenstein has become his own creature, and we're fairly certain that this creature will also leave a Frankenstein's Monster–like wake of destruction.

The film frequently teeters on the verge of devolving into an over-the-top scientific satire, but the sheer energy of the filmmaking and the sincerity with which the actors embrace the conceit redeem even the campiest moments (as when Jessup-Ape finds himself in the zoo, dodging rhinos, fighting for space at the elephants' watering hole, and, in a truly silly moment, encountering an electrified fence). You're so caught up and engaged in this visual carnival about this serious scientist who appears to have turned into an ape that you don't really mind spending a few more moments amid the noise and irrationality of the story.

What keeps it all together is Hurt. The challenge of his performance is to continually convince us that what we're watching makes some kind of sense. Every time he "reconstitutes" from ape back to man, he's more determined than ever to get someone to pay attention to what's been happening to him, and to think about what it could mean to science — as well as metaphysics. Jessup's apparent passion for going forward, despite his own increasing worries about what's happening to him on the inside, is mesmerizing to watch.

And Russell keeps the pressure on, right through the end of the film. At times, the final reel devolves into a windy, frenetic, and just plain weird experience — shades of *2001— A Space Odyssey*, with a dash of a high school filmstrip on cell mitosis, *Star Trek: The Motion Picture*, and your cousin Edna's 16mm home movies. But it's never boring, and despite the noise and the funk, you still care what happens to these characters. Ultimately, no truths are learned, no theologies upended, but their connection — to each other — *is* affirmed. At the very end of the film, Hurt, who has been searching his whole life for communion with the eternal, seems to sacrifice it for a chance to return to the flesh-and-blood love of his life, Emily, and all those things that make human life worth cherishing, to live in a state altered only by the daily challenges of the here-and-now.

The Amityville Horror

Fans of the horror genre are rabidly communal. That is, they love to share their recommendations about their favorite movie, book, TV show, or website with other fans. There are dozens of well-regarded works of horror that only achieved success after a robust word-of-mouth campaign among aficionados of dark entertainment. Some horror fans see themselves as members of some sort of secret cult, sharing arcane knowledge and passing on recommendations in a specialized, jargon-filled vocabulary. Countless authors of horror fiction and independent horror filmmakers owe a debt of gratitude to this legion of watchful, discerning connoisseurs.

But it can happen the other way, too: a work of horror first being thrust onto the general public at large and only later receiving the scrutiny and critique of the close-knit horror clan. Denied an opportunity to weigh in with an initial judgment, the horror community then becomes a kind of arbiter of value, answering the question "Is it worthy of all the hype?" In one of the most celebrated instances of this reverse word-of-mouth campaigns, the horror community eventually weighed in — and the verdict was not laudatory.

> To this day, the fact that *The Amityville Horror* story was an admitted hoax is still not widely known — as we often say, the truth never stands in the way of a good story.[1]
> It was a story that seemed almost too frightening to be true ... and the reason for that? Likely because it was![2]
> It is not an evil that goes "bump" in the night, but rather an evil that lives in the hearts of men. Greed, lies, corruption, abuse, betrayal, and finally murder. These are the plot elements to the real Amityville story. The house is not haunted by the supernatural, but it is damned forever to be an icon of horror.[3]

Similar disdain has continued to mark much of the commentary by critics in the horror field about the best-selling book *The Amityville Horror* (originally subtitled *A True Story*), published in 1977 and turned into a popular

Hollywood film two years later. Most readers, however, were hooked from the beginning, and many mainstream critics were left breathless by the book's account of a series of hair-raising horrors during a 28-day stay at the fabled house in Long Island, New York, by a family of five. The incidents described in the book are truly mind-boggling. Assured of the veracity of events by the book's cover — and some complimentary blurbs by major media outlets — *The Amityville Horror* became a national sensation.

And then the skeptics arrived, spectrographs and reporter's notepads in hand. And some — eventually most — of what was chronicled in the book began to be seriously questioned. Some investigators have gone so far as to label the book a total hoax, baseless and born of a lawyer's goading and a homeowner's greed. Other critics have been less harsh, choosing to focus on only some of the more remarkable charges made in the book (human levitation, the regular appearance of a large, black, talking, spectral pig with red glowing eyes, ghostly marching bands parading through the home in the middle of the night, a rivulet of slime on the walls and the stairs, to name just some of the more celebrated otherworldly incursions).

The problem with writing a non-fiction horror book is that the rules of horror are markedly different than if you're writing fiction. Readers aren't likely to complain at all if you're writing a novel that contains the most outrageous events (in fact, that might be what attracts them to your work). We aren't bothered by the fantastical in fiction. Through a magical quality called "suspension of disbelief," we are all able to enjoy books that portray talking animals, lovable ghosts, demonic appliances and even time travel. But in a work of non-fiction, readers will feel cheated — or angry — if the accounts of supernatural events prove to be specious.

So encountering the book today is a different experience than it was in 1977, when the story was still viewed as highly credible. However, the book still has its defenders, and both the author (who died in 1980) and the homeowner at the center of the story (who died in 2006) maintained publicly that the events described were factual, not fictional. And some people still believe.

The book begins with a strange and none-too-helpful preface by the Reverend John Nicola, whose connection to the case is not made clear. Rev. Nicola argues (or rather, decrees) that a reasonable person must accept the following account as true. He arrives at this conclusion by dividing humanity into three groups: the superstitious (too gullible); the scientific and rational (too distrustful of what they can't verify); and "the balanced

The Amityville Horror

What happens when your dream house becomes a nightmare? That's the question that bedevils James Brolin and Margot Kidder in *The Amityville Horror*, the story of the most notorious haunted house in American history.

person of faith" — to whom, presumably, the book will appeal. "The wise man knows that he does *not* know — and the prudent man respects what he does not control." Take that, skeptics.

The narrative unfolds in a sort of diary style, with each chapter titled by one of the dates of the 28 days the Lutz family lived in the home at 112 Ocean Avenue in Amityville. In the hands of a skilled novelist, the events that comprise the narrative might have generated some genuine involvement and momentum. However, author Jay Anson mostly seems to be aiming for little more than a readable transcription of the approximately 50 hours of tape recorded reminiscences provided by George and Kathy Lutz. Unfortunately, those times when Anson actually intrudes, trying to enhance the account with a writerly flourish, the book degenerates into sophomoric slop. Anson's prose style can strike one as juvenile, often sounding as if his target audience is a junior high library browser:

> Handy with his tools and equipment, George made good progress on many interior projects. Now and then, pressed for time, he got his hopeful projects confused with his musts. He soon dropped everything to clean the chimney,

then the fireplace. After all, Christmas was coming up.... George burned some now-empty cardboard cartons in the fireplace, making a merry blaze.[4]

Later, that sing-songy style gets wedded to another time-tested means of conveying genuine horror — the exclamation point!

> He looked up in shock and whirled about. His eyes widened in astonishment. The command had come from directly behind him, but he was alone in the room. Who or whatever had spoken was nowhere to be seen![5]

Two pages later:

> On the Van Wyck Expressway in Queens he found his car was literally being forced onto the right shoulder. He looked around quickly. There was no other vehicle within fifty feet of him![6]

And then on the very next page, in George Lutz's own voice we learn:

> The windshield wipers, they began to fly back and forth like crazy! I couldn't stop them! I never turned them on![7]

Fortunately for Anson — and the reader — the events chronicled in *The Amityville Horror* eventually do rise to the level of exclamation point-worthy. The terrors are somewhat subtle at first, small frights of questionable origin: a chilly draft on the back of one's neck, a phone rings but no one is on the line, a dog barking frantically at an unseen intruder. But by the end of the first couple of weeks in the new home, all sorts of first-class spooky behavior is underway at 112 Ocean Avenue, including levitation of sleeping family members, a plague of houseflies (in the middle of winter), doors inexplicably being ripped off their hinges, and the sound of a military marching band parading through the living room, blaring away at 3 A.M. Probably the single most celebrated instance of haunting in the book is the appearance of a large black pig with red glowing eyes, which the Lutzes can see outside their window at night and with whom their youngest daughter has repeatedly conversed (the pig's name is Jody, she tells them).

It gets worse. Green slime has begun oozing from the walls, demonic faces are singed into the brick work of the fireplace, and Kathy Lutz is afflicted by a mysterious, burning rash across her torso that disappears as quickly as it appears. Enough is enough, the family decides, and less than a month after moving in, they move out — though the demonic forces that have tormented them apparently don't want them to go; the Lutzes' car won't start, a fierce storm blows in, and even after they escape, the slime follows them to their next residence. Yikes!

Woven throughout the book is the suggestion that the menacing spirits are a direct result of a horrific (and, in this case, 100 percent factual) incident that took place two years before the Lutzes bought the house. On November 13, 1974, a disturbed 23-year-old named Ronald DeFeo shot and killed his parents, two brothers, and two sisters while they were sleeping in the Ocean Avenue home. DeFeo's attorney, William Weber, claimed his client heard voices driving him to kill. Could these same voices have been the ones tormenting the Lutzes?

Well, for many fans of the book — and movie — that question was answered by Weber in an interview he gave to *People* magazine in September 1979 in which he admitted that he and George Lutz concocted the whole idea that the house was haunted. In later interviews, Weber described an evening of heavy drinking during which he and Lutz came up with a bunch of horrors they could attribute to spirits in the house. Lutz, however, continued to claim until his death that the house was haunted, and that some of the things chronicled in the book really happened (though he also admitted that Anson embellished some of the events for dramatic impact).

True or not, it was simply too good for Hollywood to pass up, and in 1979, the best-seller became a blockbuster movie starring James Brolin and Margot Kidder as the tormented homeowners.

Anson's screenplay was rejected by the producers of the film, who opted to go with veteran television and film writer Sandor Stern's version. The original plan to film the movie at the actual location had to be scrapped after Amityville officials rejected the idea. Subsequently, a home in Tom's River, New Jersey, was used as a stand-in for the Ocean Avenue residence.[8] Originally conceived as a made-for-TV movie, the theatrical film went on to become one of the highest grossing independent productions of all time.

And while questions still dog Anson's account, the film continues to make many critics' lists of the best horror films of all time.[9] Director Stuart Rosenberg crafted an effective horror movie that succeeds largely because the performers take the over-the-top material seriously. Especially effective is Rod Steiger's tormented priest, Father Delaney. The film is taut, tense, and filled with the bizarre, unsettling events chronicled in the book.

The movie opens with an exterior long shot that exploits the now-famous façade of the Ocean Avenue house, with its triangular attic windows glowing like the eyes of some possessed jack-o'-lantern. As the backlighting shifts from dusk to midnight to dawn, Lalo Schifrin's score features a children's choir singing a lullaby set against the mournful, tense

Now a Terrifying Motion Picture!

cello strains of a *Jaws*-like theme (and a touch of thunder, purely for effect). It's a strange and haunting juxtaposition, and it effectively sets the mood for the central dramatic tension in the movie: dream house vs. hell house.

The thunder gives way to what sounds like gunshots, and we discover we're hearing a re-enactment of the DeFeo murders (with fleeting glimpses of a shotgun barrel and a quick pan of the blood-splattered bed of his parents). Police arrive, bodies are removed and, in a quick exchange between detectives, we learn the grisly nature of the crime and the time of its occurrence (3:15 A.M.). Then it's "One Year Later," George and Kathy Lutz are seen touring the house — and the critical connection is made. The efficient opening has the viewers right where the filmmaker wants them: still reeling from the dark and deadly opening, wishing we could warn the Lutzes about what they are getting into.

As the real estate agent shows the Lutzes around, the film provides quick and violent flashbacks to the DeFeo murders. But the Lutzes love the place, and see it as a potential idyllic residence, boathouse and all. One thing, though: "I only wish all those people hadn't died here," Margot Kidder's Kathy Lutz says, almost rhetorically. Yep, the viewer thinks. You're onto something, lady. But James Brolin's George Lutz — played here as a rather unfeeling and emotionally distant character — assures his wife, "Houses don't have memories."[10] Uh huh.

Even before the deal is closed — as the real estate agent is preparing the paperwork in the home's kitchen — strange things start to happen. A breeze blows through the closed kitchen, scattering the real estate contract. The agent looks concerned (and she doesn't even have to live there).

A priest arrives to bless the house, which he finds empty. He enters and — guess what? — he hears strange voices, a sort of cry or moan, from an upstairs bedroom. He goes in, Bible in hand, and prepares to bless the home. But the door slams, locking him in. He sees the family outside, playing on the lawn, but he can't open the window. A huge swarm of flies begins buzzing around *inside* the sealed room, and as the priest tries vainly to swat them away, a threatening voice shouts, "Get out!" He finally staggers to his car, doubled over in pain, vomiting, and staring up at the house with genuine dread. So it begins.

And so it continues. Drafts are felt, strange noises are heard, doors slam, rocking chairs rock on their own. Rosenberg knows the vocabulary of the thriller. His film is filled with lots of slow pans, long tracking shots, and silence. Eschewing the more frenetic style that was soon to dominate the horror film, his film is a throwback to the psychological chillers of Hitchcock. Which is appropriate, as the film is as much about the crack-up of the Lutzes — specifically George, who seems to be retreating into his own world of silence and paranoia — as it is about external events. (Brolin has said he wasn't offered a part for two years after the movie because his George Lutz was such an awful person.[11])

But who can blame George Lutz? Black sludge bubbles up from the toilets, blood oozes down the walls, and the annoying, spectral pig keeps peering through the window. His wife has screaming nightmares, his kids get locked in closets or cellars, or fall down the stairs, and he spends all of his time chopping wood because he can't ever get the house warm enough to offset the chill he feels running through his body. The flies continue to re-appear, and he keeps waking up precisely at 3:15 A.M. — the time of the DeFeo murders.

At his wit's end, George confides about his problems with a friend, whose girlfriend happens to be psychic. She visits the house and confirms George's worst fears: the presence of demonic spirits. In fact, in a scene that owes much to *The Exorcist*, the demons speak through the medium in a tortured, raspy voice. All the while these things are happening, the priest who blessed the house has been battling his own demons. He hears voices of his own, has his car taken over by evil spirits as he driving, and suffers bouts of bleeding wounds and severe flu.

The locals think George Lutz is crazy. Father Delaney's superiors think *he's* crazy. And the spirits who possess the Lutz house really *are* crazy. It's a standoff, with George digging in his heels and screaming aloud at the forces tormenting him, "This is *my* house!" George has a moment right out of Stanley Kubrick's *The Shining*, where he takes an ax to the bathroom door where his children are cowering for safety. The final night in the house is an over-the-top carnival of horror: blood on the walls, disembodied screams, a raging storm, doors that won't open, cars that won't start, a crash landing through a flight of stairs into a hidden well filled with black goo, and a near-fatal attack on George by Harry, the formerly faithful family dog. By this point, the film bears little resemblance to the book. Stop after stop is being pulled out before our eyes. The Lutzes escape, barely, and as they feverishly drive through the wind, rain, and thunder of a howling storm, the following words are projected onto the screen: "George and Kathleen Lutz and their family never reclaimed their house or their personal belongings. Today they live in another state."

The movie ends on that fever pitch, an intense, action-packed, wrenching scene of devastation. There's no coda, no scene of "One Year Later," nothing to resolve the tension of the cinematic experience. It's a breathtaking and harrowing end to a film that has worked on the viewer's nerves slowly, slowly, culminating in a wild festival of raucous and nightmarish images.

The real Lutzes always maintained that though the movie overdramatized things, the strange occurrences that they described to Jay Anson did happen. The court of public opinion has not seen it that way (even James Brolin and Margot Kidder were skeptics about the story[12]). In the 35 years since the book was first published, and more than three decades since the movie was released, most horror fans and critics have come to regard the entire incident as fiction. Professional researchers, independent spirit sleuths, and skeptics have all pointed out that none of the subsequent residents of the house have ever reported experiencing anything unusual. Amid the wrangling over where the truth lies, Anson's book spawned not only the 1979 movie, but several film and book sequels, turning *The Amityville Horror* into a bankable horror franchise. Though Amityville officials have officially changed the address of the house to discourage gawkers and sight-seeing thrill seekers, the interest in the events of December 1975 at 112 Ocean Avenue has clearly taken on a life of its own.

The Birds

Bird-watching — the familiar term for the more impressive-sounding branch of science called ornithology — is one of the most popular pastimes on the planet. In any region of the world, avid bird gazers can find like-minded souls to join them on pre-dawn tromps through the forest, prairie, or savannah. To the uninitiated, these avian enthusiasts, with their pith helmets and binoculars, might seem as cuckoo as a Swiss clock's sentry. But there's no doubt that this army of amateur bird connoisseurs has contributed mightily to the science of ornithology. To quote the *Encyclopedia Britannica*, "Ornithology is one of the few scientific fields in which non-professionals make substantial contributions. Much research is carried out at universities and museums.... Field research, on the other hand, is conducted by both professionals and amateurs, the latter providing valuable information on behavior, ecology, distribution, and migration."[1]

Paying attention to the habits and migratory patterns of our feathered friends is, apparently, quite useful to the world of science. It's also proved to be a boon to the artistic world. John J. Audubon's sketches of wild birds fetch a small fortune among art collectors, and Edgar Allan Poe's most famous single moment of bird-watching has been immortalized in one of the world's most beloved poems, "The Raven."

Perhaps the most famous artistic tandem to engage the winged contingent of creation is the British writer Daphne du Maurier and the famed suspense film director Alfred Hitchcock. Du Maurier's short story "The Birds," published as part of a larger collection of short stories in 1952, provided Hitchcock with some of his weirdest and most effective raw material, which he turned into a film that remains unsettling and every bit as spine-tingling today as when it was released in 1963.

Part of the appeal of both the short story and the movie might reside in the unexpected source of the terror. While ghosts, witches, devils, and psychopaths make obvious villains for creators in the horror genre, birds don't seem particularly, well, scary. Or at least they didn't until du Maurier's flight of imagination. Sure, there was Poe's famous Raven and his one-word mantra, unnerving the narrator on literature's ultimate dark and stormy night. But the bird in that situation wasn't itself frightening. (Actually, he was the most passive of characters.) Throughout most of Western literature, birds have been celebrated for their beauty, their innocence, and their song.[2] And then comes Daphne du Maurier, who grew up among the wrens, gulls, and rooks of Cornwall. Her effort to immortalize the fowl of her family estate resulted in one of the most harrowing of horror tales, and anyone who has read the story will never look at a flock of birds the same way.

"The Birds" wasn't du Maurier's first attempt at horror. In fact, by the time the short story appeared in the collection *The Green Apple*, she was a well-known writer of suspense novels and stories. She is best known for her novel *Rebecca* (which was also turned into a popular film by Hitchcock). Critically, du Maurier's stock never traded at a premium

Actress Tippi Hedren has her hands — and hair — full as she fends off an avian attack in Alfred Hitchcock's ***The Birds.***

during her life (she was considered a "popular" writer, but not a "serious" one), but since her death in 1989 she's undergone something of a rediscovery by the literary community, which has cone to recognize her naturalistic writing style, her gift for evoking a sense of place, and her debts to writers such as Jane Austen and Robert Louis Stevenson, whom she read as a home-schooled young girl.

Signs of du Maurier's literary artistry can be seen even throughout the brief first paragraph of the story:

> On December the third, the wind changed overnight and it was winter. Until then, the autumn had been mellow, soft. The leaves had lingered on the trees, golden red, and the hedgerows were still green. The earth was rich where the plough had turned it.[3]

For such a short paragraph, there's a lot going on there, stylistically. The first sentence prepares the reader for a story of abrupt changes. The simple, declarative sentence roots the narrative in nature, right from the start, establishing nature as the protagonist of this story. And that last sentence, "The earth was rich where the plough had turned it" is a nice, unobtrusive way of establishing the story's agricultural setting. Before the first page is done, we'll get our first glimpse of the story's title characters, but not just a physical description. Du Maurier gets into the heads of her birds, providing a psychological profile of the flock:

> In autumn those that had not migrated overseas but remained to pass the winter were caught up in the same driving urge, but because migration was denied them followed a pattern of their own. Great flocks of them came to the peninsula, restless, uneasy, spending themselves in motion; now wheeling, circling in the sky, now settling to feed on the rich new-turned soil, but even when they fed it was as though they did so without hunger, without desire. Restlessness drove them to the skies again.[4]

Building on that theme of restlessness, du Maurier links the change in seasons to the change in the birds' behavior in sentences that glow like falling leaves in the late October sun: "The restless urge of autumn, unsatisfying, sad, had put a spell upon them and they must flock, and wheel, and cry; they must spill themselves of motion before winter came."[5]

But this is no paean to pastoral life. These "restless" birds are about to turn violent. Du Maurier builds narrative momentum by giving the reader glimpses of the birds' increasingly bizarre and menacing behavior: a bird tapping menacingly at the window of a sleepy cottage, then a small flock flying into a bedroom and harassing two sleeping children. Then, swooping at a lone farmer walking through his fields. These isolated incidents soon give way to a full-scale attack.

Much of the story's grip and a good deal of the horror lie in the setting: an isolated coastal village, far from "civilization" (here, mid-century London). We know that if these farmers and country folk run into serious problems, there won't be anyone to help them: firefighters, police, civil servants. Their only link to the larger, modern world is the "wireless," which they gather around every four hours for news bulletins from the BBC. The family at the heart of the story — farmer Nat, his wife, and their two small children — barricades themselves in their cottage-like home, boarding up the windows and waiting anxiously for the next news broadcast (the plague of attacks has spread to London, they hear, and a national emergency has been declared).

The birds are undaunted, and they crash into the boarded-up windows, peck at the planks, and dive bomb the chimney. As the family huddles anxiously in the kitchen near the fireplace, they hear the reassuring roar of airplanes, presumably sent by the military to combat the gathering felonious flocks that are headed inland. Their hopes spiked, they listen anxiously to each of the planes roar, sputter, and then finally crash, birds flying into the planes' propellers and dooming their missions.

Food, water and candle supplies are running out, so during a lull in the bird attacks, the family visits a neighboring farmhouse in hopes of borrowing some foodstuffs and fuel. What they find is a grim reminder of how dire the situation is: "Jim's body lay in the yard ... what was left of it. When the birds had finished, the cows trampled him. His gun was beside him."[6]

So that's it. It's every man, woman and child for himself or herself against the birds. The family gathers what they can from their mauled neighbors' home, and head back to their cottage to fortify their home against future attacks. They hope the siege will end. But it doesn't. The birds come again, scratching at their door, pecking at the cracks, braving the flames of the fireplace. The family huddles together for safety, cut off from the outside world, listening to the maddening, gruesome thud of bird after bird, sacrificing their bodies like kamikaze pilots, targeting this Cornish family. The father tries to calm the children, but they know what's happening. His "stiff upper lip" approach doesn't seem adequate to the circumstances, but it's all he has. The story does not end hopefully:

> Nat listened to the tearing sound of splintering wood, and wondered how many million years of memory were stored in those little brains, behind the

stabbing beaks, the piercing eyes, now giving them this instinct to destroy mankind with all the deft precision of machines.

"I'll smoke that last fag," he said to his wife. "Stupid of me, it was the one thing I forgot to bring back from the farm."

He reached for it, switched on the silent wireless. He threw the empty packet on the fire, and watched it burn.[7]

Who will triumph, bird or human? That sense of lingering suspense might have been what attracted Hitchcock to du Maurier's story, resulting in a film that many rank among the director's very best.

It's impossible to talk about the movie *The Birds* without discussing the considerable technical challenges Hitchcock faced. In a film in which the birds would actually star, the difficulties of manipulating so many types of birds in so many circumstances are almost incalculably daunting. Du Maurier had only to put into words the homicidal habits of her gathering bird horde. Hitchcock had *to show* these birds in action. He did this through a variety of ways, involving mechanical birds, specially trained birds, and simply gathering and filming "regular" birds that were flying around the location at Bodega Bay, in Northern California, where the movie was partially filmed.

Hitchcock was determined to pull it off, and he used every means at his disposal during the arduous film shoot including state-of-the-art "blue screen" technology (where actors, or birds, can be filmed in front of a screen, with the background to be filled in later with stock footage or matte paintings), the use of wire pulleys with weighted, mechanical birds attached, tying living birds' feet to elastic in the actors' wardrobes, and even putting little magnets on the feet of crows to keep them from flying off set props. He put seeds in the hair of his actors to induce bird attacks and placed meat on top of the camera to encourage gulls to swoop in for close-up attacks. But it wasn't all hi-tech; in the climactic attack scene (which took five days to film and left actress Tippi Hedren so exhausted and overwrought that she had to be hospitalized for a week), Hitchcock simply hired bird handlers to hurl birds at the trapped actress, flapping and squawking as they pummeled her face and hands in a paroxysm of feathery chaos.

The attack scenes work superbly. Despite a screenplay by Evan Hunter (who would go on to write a series of detective novels under the pen name Ed McBain) that tries to wrest a movie's worth of drama from a short story, it's the bird attacks one remembers. Readers of du Maurier's story would be hard-pressed to find much of the source material actually in the movie. Hitchcock and his screenwriter changed almost everything, transporting the action from a small English coastal town to Northern California. The movie focuses on the Tippi Hedren character, a total invention for the film. Du Maurier's story is claustrophobia-inducing in its focus on the small farmhouse under siege, and the family's desperate efforts to withstand the physical and psychological pressure. Hitchcock's version is far more elaborate, more sweeping, more panoramic. Really, the only link that survives the transformation is the sense of impending doom and the unrelenting, inexplicable attacks by the birds.

Hitchcock originally purchased the rights to the short story for his television anthology series *Alfred Hitchcock Presents*, but then life imitated art in a series of bird attacks in the early 1960s, which caught the director's attention. "After he read of real bird attacks taking place across the country, he thought it [du Maurier's story] had cinematic potential," said production designer Robert Boyle.[8] Screenwriter Hunter recalls Hitchcock "showing us a lot of newspaper articles about unexplained bird attacks, as a reminder that these things do happen, that we weren't just dealing with fantasy."[9]

But that's how the movie begins, as a kind of romantic fantasy, with the kind of verbal jousting and flirty back-and-forth of a 1940s screwball comedy, between attorney Mitch Brenner (played by Rod Taylor) and Melanie Daniels (played by Hedren). Melanie runs into Mitch in a pet store, where he's shopping for lovebirds for his 11-year-old sister's birthday. He pretends to mistake her for a store clerk, and she plays along—until she unwittingly releases a bird in the store, creating havoc. It turns out that Mitch knew Melanie from a court appearance involving a practical joke she had played that backfired, and he was trying to show her what it was like to be on the other end of a prank. He leaves the store, but Melanie decides to pursue the smug-but-lovable Mitch to his weekend getaway at Bodega Bay, and it's on her surprise visit to his shore home that the first attack takes place, and the tone of the movie begins to shift from a featherweight romantic romp to its darker, more mysterious tone. While Mitch waits on the dock for Melanie's boat, a lone seagull swoops down and appears to purposefully attack her, beaking her on the head and drawing blood.

Mitch takes Melanie to a local diner and treats her wounds. Clearly, a romance is developing, which is not going to sit well with some of the other women in Mitch's life, including his steely, protective mother (played by veteran stage and screen actress Jessica Tandy, a Hitchcock favorite) and local schoolteacher Annie Hayworth who was once involved with Mitch. We get glimpses into all of their lives, and learn a little bit about each character. The first half of the movie is as much drama as horror. Though filled with interesting characters, the movie tends to drag during the first hour. There are some nice moments (the closeup of the two lovebirds leaning to and fro in the car, suggesting the winding California coastal highway, or Jessica Tandy's icy look when she first meets Melanie), but overall, the film lacks narrative momentum. It's only the occasional bird attack that keeps us interested.

From a flock of sparrows swooping down a chimney, disrupting a quiet family dinner, to the perturbed sea gulls who menace a children's birthday party, the scenes of bird-borne devastation live up to the billing. With each subsequent attack, the birds become more threatening and more powerful, their victims more confused and more terrified about what's going on. As in du Maurier's short story, the movie never tries to explain what's behind the bird's attacks. "We decided it would be more unsettling if we never knew why," Hunter said.[10]

And he's right. Hitchcock apparently wasn't interested in appropriating some of the screenwriting tricks from his brethren in the sci-fi community. These were not radioactive birds, or birds from an alien planet that hatched overnight, or even birds that had been exposed to experimental bird seed being developed by the military. They were simply your average, neighborhood birds, which meant that everyone watching the film faced the same threat as the characters in the movie.

Melanie calls her father, a San Francisco newspaper publisher, and tells him about the birds' remarkably bad behavior. He's disbelieving, but she agrees to stay in Bodega Bay as a kind of correspondent. In the meantime, the local townspeople begin to gossip about what's been happening, with some dismissing the stories of bird attacks as pure fantasy and others claiming the assaults herald the Biblically foretold end of the world. Meanwhile, the birds continue their onslaught, attacking individuals, groups, buildings, cars, pretty much anything they can get their talons on. (One of the best scenes in the movie has Melanie trapped in a phone booth, trying to call for help, as the gulls, one after another, smash into the glass.)

The body count continues to rise — even Annie Hayworth, the schoolteacher, gets pecked to death. Mitch and Melanie, now firmly a couple (brought together by their desperate circumstances), work to reinforce Mitch's house, while Mitch's high-strung mother continues freaking out and sister Cathy keeps asking, "Why are the birds doing this? Why are they trying to kill us?" There are impressive aerial shots of huge flocks of birds swarming over and around Bodega Bay as Mitch props furniture against the doors and windows of his house. We suspect that there will be one more attack (at least), and that intrepid Melanie will soon be at the mercy of Hitchcock's over-the-top evil genius. And sure enough, the birds do come.

Mitch does his best to defend the household, but he's got his own problems, as the birds keep busting through the downstairs window, pecking him on the hand as he tries to secure the shutters. Now it's Tippi Hedren's turn. During a lull in the attacks, she takes a flashlight and decides to climb the stairs (one can imagine the original theater audience screaming at her to turn back!). She gets to the top of the staircase, opens a bedroom door, shines the light on a crossbeam, and right on cue, a flock of angry birds descends wildly upon her, ripping her clothes to shreds and causing her to collapse. The screaming and high-pitched shrieks bring Mitch to the room, and he fights with the birds to drag her body away. She's bloody and battered and unconscious, and Mitch concludes he must get her to a hospital, even if it means having to face the birds. He slowly wades through the birds who cover his driveway and makes his way to the garage, starting his car, where he hears a radio report of the extensive damage the birds have caused. As he exits the car, we get the tensest scene in the movie, with Mitch moving gingerly among the birds, who are everywhere: on his roof, in his driveway, on his lawn, watching him, waiting, almost silently. He takes the frightened, zombie-like Melanie, walks her to the car, and then he, his mother, Cathy, and Melanie drive away as the camera pulls back to reveal an army of birds as far as the eye can see, swarming over the hills, sagging the telephone wires, stalking the road on which the desperate travelers slowly roll toward the horizon.

Will they make it? Hitchcock didn't want the words "The End" to be shown on the screen because he didn't want to suggest any kind of finality to the situation. So we get the car, the birds, and a fade to black, and that's it, a chilling and marvelous end to a nerve-wracking episode in the human-bird relationship. "It's a movie about complacency," the director Peter Bogdanovich once said about *The Birds*. "We all take birds for granted."

Not after this movie.

Dead Ringers

A great deal of horror fiction revolves around the conflict between the individual and larger forces arrayed against him or her: someone walking alone down a darkened alleyway at night, or walking up a set of creaky stairs by herself in a haunted mansion. A lone swimmer, or a small girl walking a trail to her grandmother's house in the woods. There's something about being utterly alone, both physically and psychologically, that triggers a reflex response of fear.

But for a small group of people, that feeling is modified, for they are never really alone. There's always another, an exact replica of themselves, a living, breathing reminder of their lack of individuality: the identical twin.

Is it comforting — or disconcerting — to come face to face with one's own face? Physicians, psychologists, and poets have all weighed in on the subject of identical twins, with Shakespeare having used the idea regularly in his comedies. And while the potential for comic premises with lookalikes come easily to mind, there is also a darker and more tragic aspect of the experience, one that often expresses itself in real-life identical twins in depression, insecurity, resentment, and even violence.

So it should be no surprise that a best-selling book and a riveting (though controversial) movie were spawned by the case of a pair of identical twins, both highly respected doctors, who rose to prominence in New York City in the 1970s and then, tragically, died under mysterious, even salacious, circumstances. The case combined all those compelling elements about identical twins that have always fascinated the public with a genuine mystery — inviting all manner of psychological speculation. The story has long faded from the headlines, but because of the work of some thoughtful journalists, a pair of novelists, and a mold-shattering director, the incident continues to fascinate.

Stewart and Cyril Marcus were highly successful gynecologists, renowned for their work as fertility specialists at Cornell University and its affiliate New York Hospital in the early 1970s. They were also identical twins whose lives tracked as closely as their appearances: same schools, same hospitals during their medical residency, same apartment, and, rather creepily, often the same woman (they apparently delighted in switching women in mid-double date, with their companions none the wiser). But to the women who sought their professional services, the Marcus brothers were not identical; they were special, gifted, possessed of some wondrous ability lacking in their peers:

> They called themselves infertility specialists, but in the eyes of many of their grateful patients they were nothing more than fertility gods.... In almost all cultures, anyone who has the touch, the divine inspiration, or whatever it takes to induce conception, is regarded as a holy man. The Marcus brothers were secularized heirs of this tradition, pioneers in the use of a whole repertoire of medical techniques — hormones, surgery, fertility drugs — to accomplish the magic that shamans had performed in the past.
> "They were like gods," said one woman who had gone to several gynecologists and had endured years of hopelessness before treatment by the Marcus brothers helped her conceive and give birth to her first child. "They were miracle workers," said another woman. "It was like magic," said a third.[1]

But the Marcus brothers would have most likely remained a highly localized phenomenon, largely unknown to the general public if not for their made-for-the-tabloids tragic ending in which they were discovered in their luxury apartment undressed, dead, and surrounded by weeks' worth of garbage, old newspapers, empty drug vials, and the remnants of several apparent binges on cookies, cakes, soda pop and ice cream. Despite a flurry of tabloid headlines that announced their deaths in July 1975, it would take the journalists Ron Rosenbaum and Susan Edmiston to offer the first extended look at the lives and deaths of the Marcus brother in their March 1976 piece in *Esquire* magazine entitled "Dead Ringers." Their investigations revealed a sordid and bizarre world of drinking, drug addiction, voyeurism, sexual pranks and what proved to be a macabre interdependence. The article is a model of long-form journalism, integrating hard-boiled investigation into novelistic narrative to paint a picture of the brothers' professional and personal exploits.

But for all of the authors' investigations and informed speculation, the exact cause of death was never firmly established — though it was certainly drug-related (perhaps the result of severe withdrawal from barbiturate addiction). As the *Esquire* piece revealed, the Marcus brothers' life and

Dead Ringers

In David Cronenberg's *Dead Ringers*, Jeremy Irons and Genevieve Bujold share a rare moment of intimacy amid the creepy, clinical world of two drug-addicted identical twins.

death was fraught with incapacitating emotional baggage, professional brilliance and chicanery, and undeclared psychological warfare. It was the stuff every fiction writer dreams of. For novelists Bari Wood and Jack Geasland, the story of the Marcus brothers proved impossible to resist, and the journalistic story "Dead Ringers" became the seed of their novel *Twins*, a bestseller that seeks to fill in the many blanks in the dossier of the dashing, doomed pair.

Twins borrows most of the known details of the Marcus brothers' lives to ground its narrative in the facts of the case, many of which are none too controversial: the expected early instances of sibling rivalry, prestigious medical educations, highly attractive physical appearance and the apparent inability to deal with long-term separation from each other. Into that mix, authors Wood and Geasland introduce an element of eroticism that the record only hints at. The authors portray a nascent homoerotic curiosity dating from the twins' boyhood, which eventually manifests itself as full-fledged homosexual intimacy between them. Wedged between the bookends of these encounters are scores of indiscriminate hetero- and homosexual encounters with friends, strangers, wives, girlfriends, and often combinations of the above. *Twins* carries more than a faint whiff of the late 1970s Manhattan dance-and-social-club pheromone dispersion. The novel features sex in bathrooms, kitchens, abandoned apartments, and doctors' offices, and at several turns threatens to degenerate into a soft-porn gloss on the happy-go-lucky hookups of the disco era.

But what gives the book its substance, and maintains reader interest to the end, is its exploration of the psychological bond that exists between identical twins, exposing a kind of horror of connectedness that most "un-identical" siblings likely can't imagine. Early in the novel, the twins as young boys are taken to a neighbor's apartment, where a dying old man has asked to see them so that he might offer them a perplexing, harrowing prophecy. After questioning both boys, and then babbling to himself in Yiddish, he turns to Michael, the minutes-younger and less psychologically secure of the two:

> The old man smiled but Michael knew he didn't mean it. "And when you grow up, will you marry the same woman?" David had started to nod again, but then he stopped, uncertain; the old man went on relentlessly. "And will you both live in the same house and father the same children?" Then, in the same tone of voice, still staring at Michael as if David weren't there, the old man said, "Get away — you must get away from each other. Do you hear me?"[2]

The old man goes on to explain, "In the old country, they say twins are cursed ... not one person, but less than two."[3] The two boys return to their parents' apartment suitably shaken by the encounter. As they grow to maturity, attend medical school, and enter a gynecological practice together, the old man's warning becomes prescient, as each twin takes his ill-fated turn at achieving independence. Michael goes so far as getting married and having a child, but his relationship with his wife is superficial and unsatisfying, ending badly. David, after an impressive-seeming but stultifying string of sexual encounters, ends up in a serious relationship with another man — a relationship that is also fated to end badly. Ultimately, the twins keep circling each other, critiquing each other's lifestyle choices, arguing, reconciling, vacationing together, and eventually setting up a gynecological practice in Manhattan. As their various relationships crumble, they turn increasingly to drugs — and each other. The beginning of the end comes when the receptionist for their medical office finds the brothers on the floor of their office, having sex with each other. She resigns, rumors spread, the drug use escalates, licenses are revoked, and the two seek refuge in a well-appointed family-owned luxury apartment in Manhattan, where they are discovered semi-nude and surrounded by drug paraphernalia and cookie trays.

Wood and Geasland hit their stride in the final chapters of the book, when the decline is inevitable and the brothers' desperation palpable. Each twin is tortured by the thought of being without his *doppelganger*, but equally anxious about the suffocating nature of their lifelong entwining. Locked in a spiral of drugs, failed relationships, and mutual dependence, the Ross twins hit bottom together, with neither able to rescue the other. Their situation becomes unbearable. Pass the barbiturates. Pass the Twinkies.

Twins isn't a great novel. The writing often lapses into melodramatic cliché, and character development is perfunctory. But the book's overheated prose style is just the right temperature to incubate the fear of separation that torments the twins, as well as the terror of their discovery that they also can't live autonomous lives.

Twins is important for another reason, however: It's a source (very loosely adapted) of one of the best and creepiest films in the last couple of decades, a chilling cinematic realization of psychological dependence that also features one of the best performances in any horror-suspense film ever.

"The idea of twins has always seemed so provocative to me," said David Cronenberg, the director of *Dead Ringers* and veteran of several modern cult classics in the horror genre, such as the 1986 remake of *The Fly*, *The Dead Zone*, and *Videodrome*. "As I envisage it, the essence of the relationship is one in which identities become confused, or suffocating, but which are unrelenting and cannot be broken, not at any rate this side of death."[4]

The film represents a slightly askew entry in the overall oeuvre of Cronenberg, focusing much more on the subtleties of characterization than on shock, gore, or explicit violence. But don't be fooled: the movie is a real creeper, including some grimace-inducing scenes of gynecological "innovation" (the twin brothers design cutting-edge gynecological instruments and utilize the prototypes on their trusting, unwitting patients). *Dead Ringers* is the most unsettling and effective film in Cronenberg's catalog largely because he focuses more on internal, psychological torment than on physical discomfort. But that's not how some of the critics saw it.

"*Dead Ringers* has the appeal of tabloid headlines. Watching it is like slowing down to look at a traffic accident, afraid you might see something," said *Washington Post* critic Rita Kempley. "It's really sordid stuff that becomes ridiculous, painful, unbelievable and tedious when the [twins] hit bottom, sharing needles and putting their faces in sponge cake in their squalid offices."[5] Okay, it's not an easy film to watch. So why should you?

Aside from being the work of a visionary, envelope-pushing filmmaker, *Dead Ringers* features a performance by Jeremy Irons that is so good, you almost forget the technical challenges he's being asked to surmount throughout the film. Irons plays both twins, identical in appearance but with subtle-but-significant personality differences. And these differences become critical as the film wends its way through a psychological labyrinth and a descending spiral staircase of drug abuse and sexual longing. Even people who hated the movie — a lot of people hated this film — acknowledge Irons' bravura performance as the twins (here named Beverly and Elliot Mantle). Re-watching the film, knowing that Irons was often acting with *no one* (that is, that he was performing one twin's dialogue while only pretending to see the other, who he would then portray in a subsequent take doing the same scene), one can only marvel at the focus, intensity, and, well, *seamless* portrayal. It stands up as one of the great performances in modern cinema.

The opening credit sequence begins with a series of graphic medical drawings one might find in an eighteenth century anatomy textbook, as well as a parade of odd-shaped medical instruments. All of this amid a swelling, romantic musical score. It's an unsettling juxtaposition — but intriguing.

The movie begins in Toronto in 1954, where we see the young, school-aged identical twins walking down the street, nonchalantly discussing the mechanics of sexual congress. Again, the content is jarringly at odds with the context. The scene ends with a cherubic-faced young girl smilingly sitting on her front steps, telling the boys to "fuck off."[6] This tension between the familiar and the threatening is one of the keynote themes of *Dead Ringers*, a film which never gives the viewer a moment of pure relief even though it frequently teases the viewer with dollops of apparent normalcy.

The action shifts to Cambridge, Massachusetts, in 1967, to a teaching hospital and a lab with earnest students working away on cadavers. The twins are performing some sort of procedure on a body when their professor notices they are using a piece of surgical equipment he's never seen. "Where did you get that?" he asks. "We had it made for us,"[7] one of the twins tells him. The doctors' technological innovation throughout the film is a creation of screenwriters Cronenberg and Norman Snider. Even though the credits proclaim that the film is "based on the novel *Twins*," *Dead Ringers* borrows only the most fundamental elements from the book, namely the identical twin doctors and their eventual decline. Most of the movie plot is original to the screenplay, with the biggest difference between the book and the movie involving the love story that dominates Cronenberg's version.

An actress, Claire Niveau (played by Genevieve Bujold), comes to their office for a medical exam. During the examination, Beverly discovers that Claire has an abnormal reproductive system (he says she's a "trifurcate," possessing in essence three different wombs). Beverly, in the course of treating and counseling her, also falls in love with her (only after his brother Elliot has bedded her, pretending to be Beverly), but it spells the beginning of the end for him—and his brother. Elliot begins to resent Beverly for reaping the benefits of what he, Elliot, started, and Beverly becomes defensive and protective about his relationship with Claire, even as they continue to "share" her.

In *Dead Ringers*, Cronenberg seems to really love tweaking the viewer's expectations. Into the sterile and clinical world of the twins finally comes an attractive, intelligent, available woman. But instead of thawing out the twins' chilly world, she only makes it worse. Beverly's shyness and the insular, protected life he's always shared with his brother make him unable to cope with a complex adult romantic relationship. He begins taking drugs but gets hooked. He starts hallucinating. He claims that something is happening to his patients, that more and more of them are coming in to the office "deformed." In his pharmacologically induced delusional state, he designs a set of bizarre surgical instruments (they are both artistically impressive and frightening looking) to work on "mutant women" such as Claire.

Believing that the only way to save his now–drug-addicted brother is to go down to his level, physically, and then bring him back up, the suave and slightly-more-worldly Elliot begins taking drugs himself. But then he becomes addicted, and they both sink together.

The film divided critics, in some cases quite sharply. Some claimed it was an "instant classic, an Oscar-worthy showcase for Jeremy Irons, and a tightrope ballet over dicey screen material.... A subtle movie—and thus a disturbing one. Like *Vertigo*, *The Night of the Hunter*, *Repulsion* and a few others, it finds beauty in morbidity — then nags you to come back for a second dose."[8] Others were a bit less charitable, with one critic summing up many of her colleagues, calling the movie "[t]rite, weird, ridiculous, uneventful, sick. Cronenberg at his worst."[9]

And while some critics blasted the scenes of women enduring gynecological exams by the drugged-up brothers, with their new-fangled and frightening medical instruments, as simply beyond the pale of entertaining cinema, it's the brothers' simultaneous decline that is really the hardest thing to watch. But Irons is terrific in his utterly un-self-conscious portrayal of a couple of junkies who are feeling around for the bottom, afraid to let go of each other but, like drowning swimmers, choking the life out of each other. The final scenes of Beverly and Elliot, totally out of touch with reality, strung out on barbiturates and sleeping pills, binging on cake and orange soda, and making one final attempt to save their lives by separating from each other, are absolutely searing. Irons won numerous awards for his performance, including the New York Film Critics Circle award.

And lurking behind Irons' portrayal, and Wood and Geasland's novel, is the harrowing specter that something like this *really* happened. Those who knew Cyril and Stewart Marcus in real life reported after their death that they knew there was something wrong with the brothers' behavior prior to their expiration, that they exhibited the signs of both drug addiction and drug withdrawal, but that they had always (in the words of some who knew them) been a strange pair, and that their associates had long been conditioned to expect them to act oddly, or in antisocial and unpredictable ways.[10]

It would appear that despite the advantage of good looks, a good education, and good professional reputation, the twins were doomed from the very beginning of their life, bound to each other in a way that almost no one, except themselves, could ever really understand.

Dr. Jekyll and Mr. Hyde

Eighteenth-century Scottish history is probably not the strong suit for most contemporary readers of horror fiction. And even those who know something of the rich and storied past of the Scots might not be familiar with the name William Brodie, or "Deacon" Brodie, as he was more popularly known in his time. In the mid–1700s, this successful carpenter, merchant, and member of the local ruling council in Edinburgh was arrested for a series of high-profile burglaries. It turns out that Brodie was living a double life: prosperous businessman and public servant by day, cat burglar by night. He would install doors and cabinets in the homes of the well-to-do but make wax impressions of their locks and then return to his workshop and make keys from those impressions.

Not exactly William Wallace (of *Braveheart* notoriety) in terms of heroic profile, Brodie nonetheless became a figure of local legend. Almost 100 years after Brodie was finally caught and hanged (at a gallows he designed), a teenage boy, uninspired by his father's career choice for him of engineering, exercised his creative energies by writing a play about William Brodie. This young Scottish lad would eventually go on to renounce both engineering and the study of the law to pursue his true vocation: writing. And though Robert Louis Stevenson would write adventure tales (such as *Treasure Island*) that would go on to worldwide popularity, his masterpiece remains a work that might have been rooted in his early fascination with Deacon Brodie.[1] Stevenson's *The Strange Case of Dr. Jekyll and Mr. Hyde* portrays humanity at its best and its worst, providing the author's grim critique of the interior life of each human being, who harbors a raging, law-scoffing rogue within even the most decorous frame.

Though Brodie never seems to have approached the level of brutality and homicidal zeal that Mr. Hyde — the avatar of humanity's dark side — reaches in the narrative, he nonetheless must have provided a convenient jumping-off point for Stevenson's dissection of the duality of human nature.

Stevenson was definitely on to something, for his book — and its infamous presentation of a schizophrenic split between good and evil — has become shorthand for a century's worth of readers. Popular culture is filled with innumerable references to Jekyll and Hyde–type characters. The very image of a sedate figure ingesting some vile potion from a beaker, only to morph violently into a beastly, snarling sociopath, has become a visual commonplace in our society. That image derives from Stevenson's rather slim novel, a work that sold briskly in both the United Kingdom and the United States upon its publication in 1886, and has remained popular ever since.[2]

But Stevenson's work gave us more than the iconography of a transformation. His novel provides a psychological critique of the duality of personality and within its pages takes quite seriously the notion (to be explored by Freud and others in the coming century) that each human being is not a singular "character," but a conflation of differing, often competing impulses. Stevenson wrote the book quickly and had a finished draft approximately two months after conceiving the story (which reportedly came to the author in a dream). The book represents a departure for the prolific Stevenson, who died at 44 after a lifetime of respiratory illness and vain efforts at treatment but still managed to produce a prodigious amount of travel writing, essays, poetry, historical novels and adventure stories. *Dr. Jekyll and Mr. Hyde* is deeper and darker than any other work in the Stevenson canon.

The book is as much mystery as horror story, and though it tends to lack the more obvious and traditional earmarks of horror fiction, it doesn't shy away from portraying a truly horrifying situation: the knowledge of one's capacity for inhuman acts. Edward Hyde is a bad dude, no doubt, but it's what we learn of his thought processes, not his antisocial acts, that sends shudders down the reader's spine. Hyde is humanity's primitive instincts unleashed, and his glee at experiencing a rush of animal passion is unsettling because it seems so sincere (even if those passions lead him to bash a passerby with a walking stick, or stomp on a small child who happens to be in his way).

There's one other factor that perhaps keeps the story from common consideration as simply a mere "horror" story: The book is beautifully written. Stevenson had Charles Dickens' eye for description and gift for unexpected metaphor, Poe's love of the complex labyrinthine sentence and a poet's ear for the music of the language. He renders both the exterior world of Edinburgh (especially at night) and the interior world of psychological angst lyrically. Stevenson began his writing career as a travel writer, and his apprenticeship shows. He has a keen eye and, like his near-contemporary (and near-countryman) Dickens, he has an aptitude for linking physical traits with personality, as can be seen in the book's very first sentence: "Mr. Utterson the lawyer was a man of rugged countenance, that was never lighted by a smile; cold, scanty and embarrassed in discourse; backward in sentiment; lean, long, dusty, dreary, and yet somehow loveable."[3] The book is filled with the kind of writing that you just want to chew into like you're biting into a steak.

The story's pretty good, too. Utterson, the lawyer, is friends with the highly respectable Dr. Henry Jekyll, and as a respectable man, he is utterly appalled to discover that Jekyll has written a will leaving everything to a mean, vulgar, and thoroughly *dis*reputable man named Edward Hyde. Most of the book follows Utterson's attempts to persuade, or at least understand, why Jekyll would have anything to do with a ruffian like Hyde. Jekyll becomes secretive, than disappears. Meanwhile, Hyde unwittingly becomes involved in a number of public skirmishes, tarnishing his already low reputation and eventually setting off a city-wide manhunt.

Well, that's the shell of the story. But the glories of *Dr. Jekyll and Mr. Hyde* revolve around those nuggets in the narrative where Stevenson takes us into the mind of the good doctor as he undergoes the transformation from decent, upstanding citizen to murderous hooligan. What began as a noble (if wildly misguided) scientific experiment to isolate that violent part of the human personality so that it can be separated from the virtuous part, turns ugly — literally. The original plan: "[That] the unjust might go his way, delivered from the aspirations and remorse of his more upright twin; and the just could walk steadfastly and securely on his upward path, doing the good things in which he found pleasure."[4]

The result, however, is quite different. After Dr. Jekyll ingests his custom-brewed personality-makeover-in-a-beaker, the dark side takes over completely, altering even his physical appearance. Hyde is shorter, hairier, meaner — but filled with a vitality that the doctor-by-day has never felt. It's that unfettered animal energy that is the real intoxicating beverage:

> There was something strange in my sensations, something indescribably new, and, from its very novelty, incredibly sweet. I felt younger, lighter, happier

in body; within I was conscious of a heady recklessness, a current of disordered sensual images running like a mill race in my fancy, a solution of the bonds of obligation, an unknown but not an innocent freedom of the soul. I knew myself, at the first breath of this new life, to be more wicked, tenfold more wicked, sold a slave to my original evil; and the thought, in that moment, braced and delighted me like wine.[5]

There's genuine horror for you — the idea that an upstanding, self-respecting humanitarian like Jekyll would be seduced so thoroughly by his darker side, degenerating into a creature who feels a rush of physical gratification when brutalizing his fellow human beings. As Hyde, he feels reborn, freed from any social contract or obligation to check his virulent impulses. He is Satanic in his violence, Frankensteinian in his disdain for the crowd.[6] And of course, there's the little problem of the former Henry Jekyll, who has been completely taken over by the evil Hyde.

Utterson stays on the case: He pursues Hyde, convinced that he's engaged in foul play with Jekyll, whose disappearance has alarmed his domestic servants. After Jekyll's manservant visits Utterson, begging him to come to the house because someone — or something — has moved into the doctor's secret laboratory and locked himself inside, the lawyer breaks down the laboratory door and discovers the recently expired Hyde in the clothes of Dr. Jekyll: "Right in the midst there lay the body of a man sorely contorted and still twitching.... He was dressed in clothes far too large for him, clothes of the doctor's bigness..."[7]

So expires Edward Hyde, a character of almost undiluted evil. So too expires Henry Jekyll, benefactor of humanity — at least until he gave in to his subconscious lust for deviltry. And so begins a cinematic love affair with the Jekyll and Hyde relationship. More than ten film versions of Stevenson's novel have been produced, beginning with a silent film from 1908 (essentially a filmed version of an 1887 play written by T.R. Sullivan) and including low-budget made-for-TV dramas and musicals. Kirk Douglas, Michael Caine, Spencer Tracy and John Barrymore have all been attracted to the dual role, with its scenery-chewing pedigree and can't-miss shock value. But the best attempt to capture this Manichean melodrama on film is the 1931 version, starring Fredric March in the title role(s). Despite the many liberties taken with Stevenson's original story, the film keenly captures the potency and peril of the dark side's siren song.

The film owes its success to many factors but perhaps most especially the steady directorial hand of Rouben Mamoulian, who had only made two other films but would go on to have a prolific career, working first in horror-suspense and then later, dramas. Mamoulian and cinematographer Karl Struss (who was nominated for an Oscar) fill much of the movie with compelling, unexpected and imaginative shots. Mamoulian might not have been Orson Welles, but his captivating camerawork (beginning with that great opening shot of a pair of hands dancing across an organ keyboard) and masterful special effects (groundbreaking for their time) turned the film into a popular and critical success. March walked away with the Oscar for Best Actor, and more than a dozen years later, when Spencer Tracy starred in the remake, the critics clobbered him, most comparing his performance unfavorably to March's earlier, celebrated turn.

The film adapts the basic plot of Stevenson's story, but integrates a subplot that was first introduced in the 1887 stage version. Jekyll is given a romantic interest in the person of his fiancée, Muriel Carew. But all the passion and real romantic action is generated by Ivy Pearson, a vivacious "working girl" (1931 parlance for prostitute). Ivy's attempt to seduce Jekyll can arguably be blamed for the unleashing of Mr. Hyde. In a conversation with his friend and medical colleague Dr. Lanyon, Jekyll admits to feeling excited by Ivy (whom he met by chance after being summoned to address her injuries at the hands of a "client"). When Lanyon reminds him that he's engaged and that he ought not be thinking of Ivy and her charms, Jekyll coolly tells his friend, "We can control our actions, but not our impulses."[8] But we can rid ourselves of those impulses if we create an entire, separate being to embody them. That line of thinking will lead directly to Hyde.

The film is still quite captivating today, and the fact that it's been overshadowed by both *Frankenstein* and *Dracula* (they were all made within a year of each other) is a shame because *Dr. Jekyll and Mr. Hyde* can certainly stand up to both stylistically, and in terms of the menace posed by its central character. From the opening strains of Bach's Toccata and Fugue in D minor, the film pulses with a dark, repressed energy. (The frequent use of the pipe organ in the soundtrack links the film, musically, to the previous decade's *tour de force* horror spectacle, *The Phantom of the Opera*, a film that shares some of the same themes as *Dr. Jekyll and Mr. Hyde*). We know we're in for a different kind of experience because of the unsettling perspective of the first few scenes, where we appear to be looking through the eyes of Henry Jekyll as he verbally jousts with his butler and walks through the corridors of his spacious, well-furnished home. We're in his head from the beginning, foreshadowing the interiority of Jekyll's coming crack-up.

Finally, we are afforded a quick look at Jekyll, but only in a mirror, where we see him framed and reflected. Then the viewer is right back in Henry's head, looking out at the world, riding a carriage and arriving at the medical college where he works as a lecturer. Mamoulian has found a nice visual motif to help establish the larger themes of the story, that of being entrapped in someone else's body, of inhabiting a physical frame but not the soul, of detachment and isolation. It's a neat trick, and it helps to keep what would otherwise be mere exposition from bogging down the narrative momentum.

Having Jekyll deliver a lecture to a room full of medical students on his theories about the divided nature of mankind is, in some ways, an improvement upon Stevenson, who was forced to deliver the doctor's

It's a bit too late for Frederic March to drink to good health while Holmes Herbert holds a gun in this climactic scene from the 1931 *Dr. Jekyll and Mr. Hyde*.

unorthodox opinions in casual conversation to his friend Utterson. In the movie, we can see students grapple with Jekyll's challenging ideas, muttering to themselves, "Jekyll is in fine form today!"[9]

The only real weak spots in the film come early, in the forced and clichéd conversations that Jekyll and his fiancée have in the garden outside his estate. In a script otherwise filled with innovative and thoughtful adaptations of the dramatic main story, the romantic scenes force March to utter such drivel as "I love you gaily, madly, high-heartedly! I love you so much that I could laugh and sing!"[10] (Fortunately, he does not.)

But the spooning doesn't last long. The film's still rather high stock among film critics derives in part from the famous transformation scene, where Jekyll turns into Hyde. For years, the special effects used to create this scenes remained a mystery (Mamoulian didn't reveal it until the end of his life). Involving a series of different colored makeup applied to March's face, and photographed through special filtered lenses, the shots of Jekyll-becoming-Hyde were revolutionary at the time. But the real transformation was March's acting. Liberated from the strait-jacket persona of Dr. Henry Jekyll, he devours the role of Edward Hyde, grunting, leering, and snarling with abandon. Mamoulian wrests every drop of dramatic potential from the scene where Jekyll takes the plunge. We see long shots of the doctor behind rows and rows of test tubes, and then we see his hands mixing powders and pouring liquids. As he prepares for this descent into the unknown, he pauses long enough to write his fiancée a note, claiming that if he dies, it's okay — he does so "in the interest of science." He grabs the beaker, holds it up, looks at it, paces in front of a mirror, looks at himself, begins to lose his nerve, and then he looks at a skeleton hanging in his lab. That bony reminder of humanity's end seems to embolden Jekyll, who grimly turns towards the camera and gulps down his elixir.

He immediately grabs his throat, begins panting, and starts hallucinating (he has repeated visions of Ivy, removing her stockings and swinging her leg provocatively over the side of her bed). Reborn as Hyde, with sunken eyes, swarthy skin and a pronounced overbite, he views himself in the mirror and laughs aloud, exulting in his nascent condition. He then returns to the lab, drinks the potion to get his old body back, and presto: he's good old respectable Henry Jekyll again. But soon Jekyll gets the itch (his fiancée is out of town, and it's raining, and he's bored, so...), and he takes beaker in hand and again transforms before our very eyes. What follows is one of the best moments in the movie, as Edward Hyde dashes out of Jekyll's lab, and into the rainy night, where he positively exults in the feeling of rain on his body, as if he's feeling rain for the first time. He stands there, looking up, grinning stupidly, laughing in ecstasy while the rain is coming down. It's a joyous, unexpected, and kind of menacing moment.

Of course, he heads to Ivy's. Her sexual energy attracts Hyde's libido like a magnet. He finds her in a dance hall, where he offends the other patrons by, among other things, beating his waiter instead of offering a gratuity. And there's Ivy, all smiles and garter belts, mingling with the crowd. Hyde invites her over, but she doesn't seem too keen to pursue the relationship. They talk, she tries to get away, but he restrains her and professes his love for her — and also tells her he's rich. That must have done it, because a few scenes later, we see them sharing a flat. She is bruised and tentative; he is angry and abusive. It's clear he's keeping her as a kind of prisoner, using his threats of violence to prevent her from even trying to escape.

The rest of the film focuses on Jekyll in his smoking jacket, looking nervous and remorseful and trying to act respectably — even though he now is morphing into Hyde without warning. That body is no longer big enough for the two of them to co-exist within. Hyde has become more violent with each reappearance and it's poor Ivy who pays the price — with her life. Hyde strangles her and races out into the night. Eluding police, he returns to Jekyll's laboratory, and after summoning his colleague Dr. Lanyon, he transforms in front of him, from Hyde to Jekyll. Jekyll vows he'll never take the drug again, and that he will fight the feelings of transformation, that he will never become Hyde again. Fat chance. He can no more control his alter ego than Jekyll could control his feelings of lust for Ivy. Of course, in the end, Hyde goes too far, and this time, the police do get him. At the moment of his death, he transforms back into Jekyll, proving perhaps that no matter how great the threat one faces from his or her baser impulses, you can run but you can't Hyde.

The Exorcist

No single entity has enjoyed as lengthy and celebrated a career in the horror genre as the Devil. Known by various names in most of the world's cultures, the Devil predates film, predates literature, predates even the creation of language, stretching back to the very beginnings of humanity as recorded in legend, lore, and sacred texts. He's famously devious and destructive, an acknowledged source of evil in many quarters of the ancient world and still a potent pariah to many in the modern world; you've got to give him credit for his staying power. Across several millennia, the Devil has appeared with frightening regularity in the recorded history of mankind. The original shape shifter, he's appeared in every guise from lowly serpent to fiery, horned demon.

But he's at his most frightening when he looks just like you.

"The Devil hath power to assume a pleasing shape," Shakespeare tells us in *Hamlet*.[1] The potential narrative value of such a flexible and devious nemesis has not been lost on writers and filmmakers, who over the ages have mined the netherworld for various incarnations of its most famous resident. Most die-hard horror fans have a list in their heads of the best Devil books or movies, but likely near or at the top of most of those lists is the seminal Devil work of modern times, *The Exorcist*.

The novel, and later the film, have become landmarks of the horror genre, almost as familiar to those who have never read the book or seen the movie. Merely the words "The Exorcist" are enough to summon up a variety of disturbing images and, often, darkly mimed melodramatic gestures (heads turning slowly, eyes rolled back into their sockets). It's one of those works that everybody knows even if they don't *really* know it.

Further enhancing the appeal of the story is its roots in reality— albeit a shadowy and oft-disputed reality. The whole area of exorcism is undeniably fascinating. There's a mesmerizing "could it be true?" aura that surrounds this ancient ritualistic practice of casting out demons. And though little is known, definitively, about modern-day exorcisms, there is no doubt that such a practice does occur.[2] *The Exorcist*'s author, William Peter Blatty, is said to have loosely based the work on a 1949 case of an exorcism that he heard about as a student at Georgetown University.

But one doesn't have to be steeped in the intricacies of casting out devils to be jolted by Blatty's narrative. He provides the reader with plenty of background and history about the hoary, hair-raising practice. And, for the strong-minded (with stomachs to match), Blatty shows you exactly what happens during an exorcism. While it might not make for the most pleasant reading experience, it certainly creates an impression.

Before the text proper begins, there are a couple of grim excerpts that prepare the reader — somewhat — for the horrors to come: an excerpt from the New Testament about casting out devils, a transcript of a gleeful conversation between two Mafia henchmen about a guy they hung on a meat hook, and a doctor's testimony about how Communist enforcers tortured a group of Christians. Blatty wants to make clear, apparently, that the Devil casts a pretty wide net, and has "possessed" many a soul over the years.

The opening scene ("Prologue") is effective in setting an eerie, foreboding mood. There's an unnamed older man, a laconic figure, apparently a priest, at an archaeological dig in Northern Iraq, who has intimations that he's about to be summoned away from the site, an "icy conviction that soon he would face an ancient enemy."[3] We later discover that he is Father Merrin, and over his lifetime he's developed a reputation within the church as *the* go-to guy for exorcisms (based largely on his successful, though almost life-draining, battle with a demonic spirit who once possessed a young boy's body in Africa). This opening scene raises more questions than it answers, and as a sort of table-setter for the demonic dinner party to follow, it's very effective.

Then the action shifts to the Georgetown section of Washington, D.C., and the household of successful film actress Chris MacNeil, a divorced mother of eleven-year-old Regan. The MacNeil residence will be Ground Zero for the coming apocalyptic battle, which Blatty warns us of in his slightly overheated first paragraph:

> Like the brief doomed flare of exploding suns that registers dimly on blind men's eyes, the beginning of the horror passed almost unnoticed; in the shriek of what followed, in fact, was forgotten and perhaps not connected to the horror at all. It was difficult to judge.[4]

Blatty's self-conscious literary style can get to be a little grating. The prose often seems to be straining for metaphorical significance: "The child was slender as a fleeting hope"[5] or, describing a room in the house, "the study had a feeling of whispered density."[6] Occasionally, the writing does goes completely over the top: "The burnished rays of the setting sun flamed glory at the clouds of the western sky and shattered in rippling, crimson dapples on the darkening waters of the river."[7] Fortunately, Blatty seems to get as caught up in the story as the reader and these periodic flourishes are less prominent as he lets the tense and terrific plot generate the sparks, rather than the prose.

The main thrust of the story involves Regan's declining physical condition and degenerating mental state, which baffles her mother, her doctors, a psychiatrist and, at first, a local Jesuit priest, Father Karras. Regan's problems are initially presented as the mere behavioral hiccup of a normal young girl, feeling guilty and angry about the divorce of her parents. But then Blatty turns up the temperature on her temper tantrums, and she becomes foul-mouthed and abusive. She also endures a series of wince-inducing physical problems, from bouts of projectile vomiting to foaming-at-the-mouth seizures. Then she begins speaking in a throaty baritone, and adopting all sorts of accents. She curses and laughs shrilly. She starts levitating and evidencing superhuman strength. She can move things with her mind. Secret messages start appearing in reddened welts on her flesh. She can read other people's minds, and she knows things that have happened in other people's pasts. She becomes hideously antisocial, engaging in a variety of sexual and scatological stunts that frighten her mother and shock the reader. This is not the silver-tongued Devil from the Garden of Eden — or Milton. This version knows the coarse and vulgar slang for every body part and sex act, and revels in gross and public inappropriateness (readers will have to judge for themselves whether, for example, the scene of an eleven-year-old girl masturbating giddily with a crucifix is beyond the pale).

Even the skeptical physicians and psychiatrists are willing to concede that something not documented in the medical literature is happening to this young girl. Enter that aged, laconic priest we met in the prologue. He is, as the book title promises, the Exorcist.

Assisted by Father Karras, who has been doing his best to comfort the family, Father Merrin knows exactly what he's getting into. As soon as he enters the MacNeil household, he hears Regan (channeling the Devil) calling out to him, daring him to renew their battles. At this point, the book becomes a psychic action-adventure story, with a truly no-holds-barred battle between the forces of light and the forces of darkness. The scenes of direct confrontation are vigorously wrought, with the Devil speaking through Regan, who, though tied to her bedposts, can still twist her head around, roll her eyes up into her head, roar like a lion, and move objects with her mind. The last 50 pages of the book are a pretty wild ride, with Fathers Merrin and Karras taking turns in a round-the-clock contest of wits with this most belligerent foe. Blatty exploits the natural interest the reader has in super-secret rituals, detailing the litany of prayer and ritual of an exorcism, from the sprinkling of holy water (which is a torment to the flesh of the devil-possessed, of course), to the making the sign of the cross on the possessed's forehead ("[F]rom the taut-stretched O of Regan's mouth came the nerve-shredding lowing of a steer ... tearing at flesh and shivering through bone").[8] As a climax to the steady ratcheting-up of tension regarding what, if anything, could be done to save the poor young girl, the final confrontation is a fitting finale.

When the book is rooted in the rituals of the Catholic Church, as they pertain to the Devil, *The Exorcist* is a fascinating read. Blatty knows the terrain, having been educated at Jesuit schools and Georgetown University. But considered as a novel, the book is hardly a classic. The writing is often melodramatic, and the subplots and minor characters often feel like add-ons, put in simply to swell the narrative (you won't miss their absence in the movie version). Literary critics were widely divided by the book. In a featured review in a major newsweekly magazine, one critic praised the novel as "wonderfully exciting," claiming, "Blatty maintains headlong thrust.... The battle between the Jesuit and Regan's inhabitant's is always alarming."[9] That publication's rival newsweekly saw it differently: "This is a pretentious, tasteless, abominably written, redundant pastiche of superficial theology, comic-book psychology, Grade C movie dialogue, and Grade Z scatology." That reviewer goes on to predict the book's future as "almost certainly a drive-in movie."[10]

Though it might have played in some drive-ins, the film adaptation became much more than simply a B-movie. Its release was something of a cinematic sensation, and on most horror critics' and fans' lists of all-time great films, *The Exorcist* is well represented.

The film was directed by William Friedkin, fresh off the success of his 1971 film *The French Connection*. Blatty wrote the screenplay, adapting his own book for the screen — and winning an Oscar for it. The resulting

The Exorcist

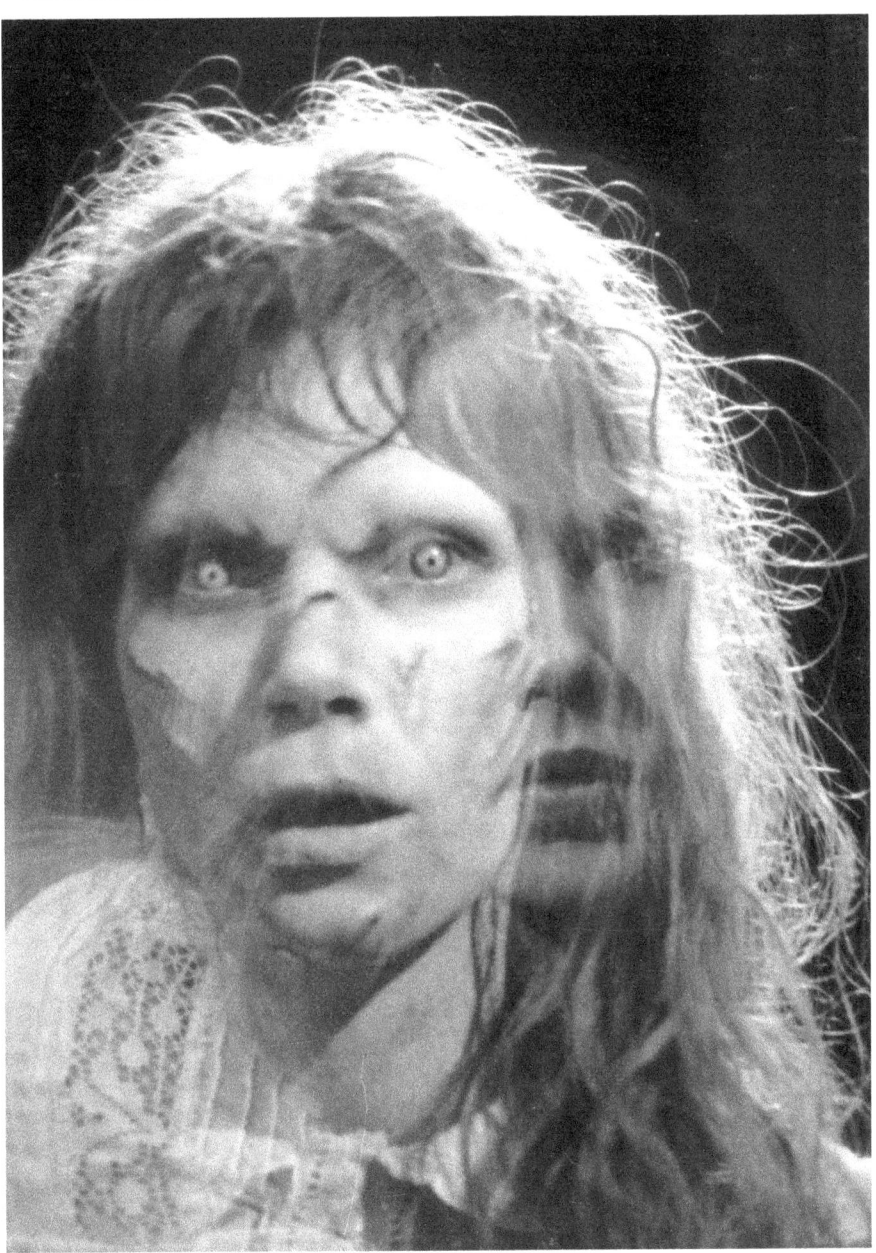

Linda Blair opened eyes and turned heads — including her own — in the film adaptation of William Peter Blatty's novel *The Exorcist*.

film became the highest-grossing horror film of all time. But *The Exorcist* has become a legendary film in many people's minds not because of its box office success but because it is *so thoroughly frightening*. For many moviegoers, it stands at the apex of horror cinema. The movie's combustible combination of a timeless villain, sympathetic victim, mysterious, shadowy ritual, and elegantly simple but chilling plot have brought many a steely-spined viewer to his or her knees. Throw in some quietly effective special effects, as well as some old-fashioned moviemaking magic (pea soup for the projectile vomiting, a refrigerated set to make the breath of the Devil visible) and what resulted was a landmark rendering of the devil incarnate.

The film also touched a nerve among some of its more traditionally religious viewers, who admitted to being disturbed by such a graphic depiction of the rites of exorcism and the blunt face-off between a devil and a priest. As one critic noted, the film "was indeed taken seriously by reverend gentlemen and media personages who talk solemnly about the social and religious phenomenon that the film represented."[11] Subsequent decades of devil-got-my-soul movies have not fully blunted the power of *The Exorcist*. In a genre besotted with cheap imitations, *The Exorcist* remains *sui generis*.

After the title appears in blood red block letters on a black screen, the movie begins where the book does: an archaeological dig in Iraq. A sepia-toned sun blazes in the morning sky until a wide shot reveals a near-desolate stretch of desert, with a few natural rock formations and a large structure that resembles some sort of ancient, dilapidated palace. Dissonant strains of Middle Eastern chanting are heard. The whole mood is one of foreboding mystery, of utter alien-ness. As the camera slowly zooms in to reveal a warren of excavators hard at work, we see a young boy racing to one of the digging pits. In Arabic, he tells an old man, "They've found something."[12] The old man (the estimable Max von Sydow) stops digging, and follows the boy to another part of the dig, where he sees a small stone carved with the face of a demon. His mortified expression lets us know that for the Old Man, Father Merrin, that stone icon is the first in a series of hints that the Devil has found him — and soon, they will find each other again (*Exorcist Two: The Heretic* provides the back story to their previous battles.) This early scene in Iraq is leisurely, mostly wordless, filled with disquietly disturbing images, subtly observed regimens of Arabic culture, and the priest's obvious sense of trepidation. Its laconic pace has the style of a spaghetti western (but von Sydow's bearing suggests that the stakes are much higher than merely avenging some cattle rustling).

The Exorcist

Now the action moves to the well-kept Georgetown home of actress Chris MacNeil, played by Ellen Burstyn. As was the case in the Iraq opening, the first shots here are also of a mysterious occurrence: inexplicable thumps in the night coming from Regan's (Linda Blair) bedroom. The mother investigates, finding nothing unusual, and concludes that the noise must be the result of rats in the attic.

The next few scenes reveal Chris at work on a movie set at Georgetown University, shooting a cheesy movie-of-the-week–type film about a campus uprising, and wandering around her neighborhood past historic brownstones, pausing to observe an argument between two priests in the courtyard of a nearby parish. Then come the obligatory cutesy mother-daughter exchanges between Chris and Regan, teasing each other, chasing each other, laughing together. These scenes seem a bit forced (you can sense the director shouting "cue the domestic bliss!"), but they do serve as a kind of better-days-bookend to the horror that is soon to follow.

Now the thrust becomes the transformation from mommy's little helper to Satan's little mouthpiece. Regan starts to change, morphing from carefree pre-teen to a moody, ouija board–obsessed rebel. Simultaneously, the film offers glimpses of the life and semi-hard times of Father Karras (Jason Miller), a priest at the nearby parish and a man wrestling with theological doubt. These two plots will intertwine, as the priest will find his declining faith put to the test by Regan's descent into Hell.

It's a gradual but painful descent to endure, and to witness. First, Regan's bed starts shaking at night. Then she begins a kind of trance-like sleepwalking. Disrupting a formal dinner party in one of the movie's more remarked-upon scenes, she descends the stairs in her nightgown and brings the party to an uneasy halt as she stands there, peeing on the carpet. The bed shaking becomes more frequent and more severe, along with a severe decline in Regan's physical and mental well-being. Meanwhile, Father Karras is having problems of his own: His mother dies, engendering a sense of guilt that he didn't take better care of her (hey, a priest's salary only goes so far) and his superior at the parish won't relieve him of his duties as the resident psychiatrist, so he has to continue to hear about his fellow priests' lack of faith, compounding his own spiritual crisis.

Regan's mother finds little solace in the clinical, detached attitude of the psychiatrists she consults. They attribute Regan's mood swings to neuro-chemical problems in the brain. (Chris watching her daughter go through sometimes painful medical procedures are some of the most wrenching scenes in the movie.) Even when Regan begins acting like, well, a person possessed, the coolly professional medical men tell Chris it's all in the kid's head. In some ways, *The Exorcist* is as much a film about the horror of a person seeking some sort of rational explanation for aberrant behavior as it is the story of demonic possession.

But demonic possession makes for better cinema, so by the end of the first hour, the film has essentially become a showcase of stupefyingly rude and violent outbursts from Regan. She screams, vomits, croaks crude threats in a throaty baritone, and engages in a variety of supernatural behaviors (moving things with her mind, levitating, hurling grown men around the room). It's as unpleasant as it is compelling. When one of the medicos suggests that perhaps Regan *thinks* she's possessed by the Devil, the mother is persuaded to consider an exorcism.

Father Karras, he of the eternal doubts, gives it a try, but this is clearly a job for a heavy hitter. Father Merrin, the older priest we first saw in the dusty catacombs of Iraq, is summoned, and the battle is joined. And it's an epic battle, one for the ages, good versus evil in a match between a 12-year-old girl (playing the part of Satan) and an aged priest (representing, of course, God Almighty). When it's over, the audience is almost as exhausted as the principal combatants.

The Exorcist went on to receive ten Academy Award nominations (winning two, for sound and adapted screenplay), and to become the highest grossing film of all time. As one fan film website noted:

> *The Exorcist* generated a wave of audience hysteria the likes of which had not been seen since the opening of the 1931 *Frankenstein*, from which patrons ran screaming, causing cinema managers to lay on smelling salts and ambulance crews for the adversely affected. Within weeks of the first public screening of *The Exorcist*, reports were flowing in of fainting, vomiting, heart attacks, and at least one miscarriage. In Berkeley, a male patron received injuries when he threw himself at the screen to "get the demon." Later, the *Toronto Medical Post* reported that four women had been confined to psychiatric care after seeing the film. "There is no way you can sit through that film without receiving some lasting negative or disturbing effects," announced Chicago psychiatrist Dr. Loyis Schlan, whilst Oakbrook theatre manager Frank Kveton was somewhat more down to earth in his assessment: "My janitors are going crazy wiping up the vomit!" he opined ruefully.[13]

While not quite *War of the Worlds*–level mania, the film did unsettle many people, and a quick scroll through film-related websites reveals that many critics still consider it the scariest film they ever saw, almost psychologically scarring, while a smaller group of cinephiles dismisses the film as so much bloviated pseudo-religious nonsense. Friedkin added some fuel to the fire just before the movie's release in 1973 when he revealed that he thought the production itself was "cursed," citing the more than one dozen cast and crew members who were injured during the making of the film, and noting that the entire set burned down during production — on a *Sunday*.[14]

The film spawned two sequels, a prequel, and a made-for-television movie. And of course, the decades since the film's release have seen a hell of a lot of devil-inspired movies. But for all their noise and fury, none comes close to the original, the film some critics have called the "definitive horror masterpiece"[15] and others have been trying to forget for the past four decades.

The Fly

Tucked away within the pages of the June 1957 *Playboy* magazine was an odd piece of fiction from a little-known British writer named George Langelaan. How many readers actually made it through Langelaan's lengthy short story is impossible to estimate (even if you factor in all of those readers who swear they only buy *Playboy* for the articles). But his story was destined to eclipse what surely must have seemed at the time more plausible candidates for lasting public adoration: a photo spread featuring an aspiring red-headed Broadway star named Carrie Radison; an excerpt of a work by French novelist Anatole France; and a meditation on the future of jazz by critic Leonard Feather. In the next fifty years, Langelaan's story would serve as the basis for two groundbreaking and much-talked-about films — and even a critically acclaimed opera. There is perhaps an irony to Langelaan's story's legacy, given that his original work must have been dismissed by some as a flyweight piece of fiction.

"The Fly," which comprised a dozen closely printed pages, provided an obvious stark contrast to the famously photogenic centerfolds for which *Playboy* is famous. There are no illustrations to accompany the story — only a couple of unrelated cartoons pasted onto the page, whose unabashed silliness is awkwardly at odds with the serious tone of Langelaan's story of scientific longing gone terribly awry. (One of the cartoons features a boxer who has just been knocked out, confiding in his manager, "Somebody up there hates me"[1] — a motto perhaps more suitable for Langelaan's story than the cartoon.) But within the world of "The Fly" is a tale of such unexpected originality and professional execution that it's not surprising, in retrospect, that its shelf life and relevance far exceeded that of the larger issue in which it was enfolded.

Langelaan was never a household name, though he was a prolific writer, turning out military history, a memoir, thrillers, and science fiction stories from 1950 to his death in 1972. His best-known story, far and away, is "The Fly," though he also wrote a well-regarded account of his years as a British World War Two spy in which he revealed that he underwent plastic surgery to change his appearance — a necessary consequence of his work, apparently. His impressive range can perhaps be intuited from the titles of his works, from "Zombie Express Train" and "The Collector of Brains" to the more genuinely cerebral *The Masks of War: From Dunkirk to D-Day*.

So if his reputation rests largely on the strength of "The Fly," what should our verdict be, a half-century after its publication? Well, it's certainly a compelling story, by a writer with an awareness of the narrative devices that create suspense and memorable characters. Langelaan is an able craftsman, knowing when to hold his cards and when to show them. He's not afraid to be graphic in the service of his story but more often than not it's his power of suggestion that keeps the reader turning the pages.

"The Fly" tells of a scientist named Andre Delambre who (we learn on the first page) is dead, crushed by an industrial "steam hammer." Trying to puzzle out just how he ended up with his head in such a device becomes the focus of the rest of the story. As a detective probes the case, interrogating Andre's wife and brother, we discover that Delambre was building a teleportation device (called a "disintegrator/re-integrator"). At first, he was able to "transport" inanimate objects through space — putting them in a small chamber in one room and sending them to a receiving chamber in another room. Then, after a mishap with the family cat, he successfully graduates to living creatures. The implications of his discovery are not lost on him:

> He reckoned that the transmission of matter by instantaneous "disintegration-reintegration" would completely change life as we had known it so far. It would mean the end of all means of transport, not only of goods including food, but also of human beings."[2]

As a final test of his device, Delambre decides to transport himself, but when he enters the teleportation chamber he fails to notice a housefly. So although he does, indeed, make it to the receiving chamber, in the process of teleporting he and the fly have merged, and he emerges with a fly's head and arm in place of his own — a situation that requires him to type out messages to his wife, whose frantic pounding on the door is met with hastily written notes slid under the door: "BEFORE YOU COME IN YOU MUST PROMISE TO OBEY ME IMPLICITLY. DO NOT LOOK AT ME AND REMEMBER THAT TALKING IS QUITE USELESS. I CAN'T ANSWER."

Out of context, it seems silly. But Langelaan does a good job of establishing the scientific credibility of his protagonist's quest, and the relationship between Delambre and his wife is well established and full of warm feeling. So the reader can empathize with the horror each feels as the experiment goes awry. When it becomes clear that the experiment can't be undone, his wife agrees to assist in his suicide: death by steam hammer (his laboratory adjoins an industrial factory). She only has to press the button from a protected distance, which she does, reasoning, "It was not difficult. I was not killing my husband. Andre, poor Andre, had gone long ago, years ago it seemed. I was merely carrying out his last wish ... and mine"[3]

In the short story — as with all horror fiction — the fright is suggested, described, but can't actually be shown. The psychological terror of finding one's self changed into a half man–half fly can be articulated on the page, but can it be shown without seeming too, well, absurd? That was the challenge for director Kurt Neumann in the 1958 movie version *The Fly*, starring David Hedison as the scientist-turned-fly, Vincent Price as his earnest but perplexed brother, and Patricia Owens as his suicide-assisting wife.

The movie version (the first of two — both of which are important works in the development of horror–sci-fi cinema) became an unexpected hit. "*The Fly* surprised everyone," Carlos Clarens wrote in his landmark *An Illustrated History of the Horror Film* (1967), "including 20th Century–Fox, its makers, by netting more than three million dollars during the first few years of its release — an unprecedented success."[4] The film only cost $350,000 to make, an amount considered "a minor budget" for a film at the time.[5]

So what made the movie so popular? A number of factors probably contributed to its success. The generally bizarre nature of the story lent itself well to the increasing popularity of big-screen horror–sci-fi hybrids during this time (such as *Invasion of the Body Snatchers* and *Them!*) The performances are noteworthy, especially Hedison as the fly, who must act through the last third of the film with his head shrouded in a black veil. Vincent Price gives a dignified and humane performance, allowing him to register genuine emotion rather than simply exude a chilly evilness as he did throughout much of his career. Throw in the Cold War–era anxieties of a mass audience looking for escapist fare and one can begin to see how *The Fly* became such a crowd pleaser.

Viewed today, the film holds up mostly well. But for a film reputed to be one of the classic horror films of the mid-century, it often comes off as rather staid, even stagey. Some of the dialogue seems forced, and the exposition is a bit clunky (perhaps surprising because the screenplay was written by James Clavell, who would go on to have an impressive career as a best-selling novelist in the next two decades). For instance, in the scene where Andre is explaining how his system of teleportation works, he agrees to demonstrate it, showing his wife an ash tray he intends to send through space. "Remember this?" he asks. "Oh, of course. Our wedding present. From my devoted and very rich Aunt Bess." People in real life who do recognize and remember objects generally don't feel compelled to repeat what is already known about them (unless you've got to get that information to an audience).

Part mystery, part romance, part monster movie, *The Fly* succeeds by ignoring reality and simply positing that such a thing could happen — and then saying to the viewer, "Here's how it would play out." The scenes in the laboratory, after Andre has been hybridized, are genuinely moving. His inability to tell his wife what has happened, her anguish at not knowing what to make of his strange typed messages, and his brother's attempts to shield Andre's young son from the truth give the film its emotional heft, turning the human fly into a character more akin to the pathetic Elephant Man than merely some mutant from the Fox studios makeup department.

Viewers might be forgiven for expecting a less emotionally substantive film as they watched the opening credits — accompanied by an annoying buzzing sound. The opening scene seems to be setting the viewer up for a more straightforward shock-fest, as a factory's night watchman goes to work, only to discover a man partially crushed under a drill press, complete with some streams of blood running down the sides of the machine. But the movie cools off fairly quickly, turning into a sedate episode of "I Married a Government Scientist." There are scenes of the dutiful wife in her post-war world of modern convenience and her husband (who's working for the military) in his basement lab, scribbling away on his chalkboards and putting on his safety goggles. It's a suburban Utopia, with Andre at one point lounging in the backyard with his wife and telling her how grateful he is to be able to continue the scientific progress that has made the world such a wonderful place. (He actually blurts out "I'm just so happy to be alive!"[6]) And now, thanks to the scriptwriter's heavy-handedness, we all know that's about to change.

But hey, that's the price one pays for scientific progress. And for much of the movie, that's what *The Fly* is really about: science. Andre is a man intent on improving the world. As he puts it to his skeptical wife, who wonders just why he wants to send objects — or people — through space: "No need for cars, or railways, or airplanes, even spaceships. We'll just set up matter transmitting-receiving stations throughout the world — and later, the universe!"[7]

At least, that's the plan. And then, to prove it's feasible, he climbs into one of his matter-transmitting boxes and closes the door. But alas, a housefly has also flown in to the box, unseen. (Well, *we* see it, but he doesn't.) The next sign that something has gone wrong is a hand-scrawled note, posted on the laboratory door: "Don't disturb me — I'm working." From here on in, Andre can only communicate by writing. Poor Helene — she doesn't know what the audience knows: that their halcyon days of discoursing in the backyard about the greatness of progress — and swatting flies — is at an end.

The end of the dream arrives far more gradually in the 1986 remake of *The Fly*, directed by the esteemed (and often excoriated) David Cronenberg, and starring Jeff Goldblum and Geena Davis. The basic premise of Langelaan's story remains intact, but the departures from the original source material and the 1958 film are numerous. Also gory. And explicit. And sometimes just plain bizarre. Yet, for all its stomach-churning special effects (which seemed to dominate most reviews of the film), the movie was hailed as a landmark cinematic achievement, with its mix of high-wire directorial flair and scarily-engaged leading man (Goldblum). Really, though, Cronenberg's film did exactly what Langelaan's story did thirty years before: offer a bizarre vision of a scientific experiment gone wrong, using the tools available to shock and unsettle an audience.

And unsettle them it did.

"[*The Fly*] is never easy to watch, yet impossible to turn away from. It will leave you weak in the knees, disturbed and utterly nauseated. It's a sad movie too, because it realizes that those suffering from diseases like AIDS or cancer don't get happy endings. Not even if they're in love,"[8] noted one critic, summing up the mix of admiration and repulsion many felt upon first seeing this film. "Extremely intense, sharply written remake of the 1958 movie that (unfortunately) goes over the line to be gross and disgusting,"[9] commented another.

The remake is a genuine work of cinematic art, with the critically acclaimed Cronenberg (*Videodrome, Scanners*) at the top of his game. The director coaxes deeply felt performances from Goldblum and Davis while

Veteran horror icon Vincent Price and prolific child actor Charles Herbert gaze into a spider's web, whose filaments enwrap a most unexpected victim, in the classic species-transformation movie *The Fly* (1958).

still availing himself of extremely potent makeup (earning the film its only Oscar) and special effects. (One critic remarked, "[T]his flick has some of the squishiest, muckiest, most disgusting FX I've ever seen."[10]) For many viewers, the gross-out factor was simply too much. But for those willing to look beyond the carnival of gore that consumes the film's final reel, the movie remains a devastatingly beautiful and tragic love story. Cronenberg and Goldblum manage to humanize the increasingly non-human Seth Brundle, the scientist who undergoes the near-complete transformation from man to fly. Davis, as the woman who loves him/it, registers the requisite fear and shock as she discovers her lover's predicament (and her own pregnancy, by way of "BrundleFly"— his name for what he has become).

Cronenberg's film jettisons much of the discussion of scientific progress that earmarked its predecessor, emphasizing instead the love story between scientist Goldblum and journalist Davis (she writes for a science magazine). The film's dramatic liability — a love triangle that seems like a late-script revision to justify some of Seth Brundle's brooding as well as the apparent need to supply a villain other than science — is a minor impediment to the film's narrative momentum. The movie captivates from the first frame, with Goldblum's cool-and-confident scientist entrancing Davis, and viewers, with his mix of personal cockiness and coyness about his invention. The scenes in his lab are pure cinema magic, with wide-eyed Davis taking in everything in this chilly, warehouse-like lab populated by these gigantic "pods" which look like overgrown drive-in movie speakers. As with the first film, we get to witness the "teleportation" of objects — first inanimate, then living — leading up to the human trial. And, as with the first film, a fly sneaks into the teleportation pod. But the principal difference — and a clear improvement, dramatically speaking, on both the short story and the original film — is the decision to have Brundle remain *unaware* that a fly has joined him on his journey. So we get the fun (er, sort of) of watching Goldblum gradually become more *fly-like*, both in appearance (a series of thick, sharp hairs that mysteriously sprout on his back) and behavior (his ability to cling to walls). He's baffled by these changes, but unsure what is happening to him. By the time it becomes clear to him that he has begun morphing into a fly at the molecular level, it's too late to do anything about it. This is where the film opts to overcome its dramatic dead end by compensating with buckets of goo. The ugh factor in the final stages of his transformation is off the meter. By the time "Brundle-Fly" is finally "euthanized" (a shotgun blast to what remains of his head), the viewer is probably more relieved for himself or herself than for the poor mutant on the screen. But Cronenberg makes it all so very watchable that it's impossible to look away, though you certainly will want to.

In its way, the 1986 remake brings some closure to Langelaan's original concept, and offers some insights the author only hinted at. In the short story and the 1958 film, the transformation from robust human being to man-fly is so abrupt that there's no time to adjust to the idea of a cross-species mutation. Can you love someone who is only partly human? Probably not if they show up one day at your door with a fly's head on top of their human body. But what if the change is gradual, giving you time to adapt to each new non-human "quirk"? At what point does love turn to repulsion? When physical integrity elides into inevitable decline, even deformity, when is it okay to look away? Goldblum makes BrundleFly's dilemma the tragedy of everyone whose descent and decline is inevitable. Which is to say, everyone.

Frankenstein

Has there ever been a character lifted from the pages of a work of fiction that is more immediately recognizable than the iconic, bolt-necked, green-skinned behemoth known as "Frankenstein"? He's perennial, blundering through cheaply produced cinematic rehashes and lumbering up stoops and driveways coast to coast on Halloween night. And yet all those Frankenstein imitators probably don't realize that the original Frankenstein's Monster (1) isn't really bolt-necked; (2) doesn't have green skin; and (3) isn't even named Frankenstein. But hey, when you've got the kind of worldwide recognition that allows you to simply raise your arms, grunt, walk haltingly, and anyone anywhere would recognize you, why worry about a few details?

So it's probably best just to play along and call this gangly, square-headed creature "Frankenstein," even though the book in which he originates never names him (he is only "The Creature"); the medical student who creates him is named Victor Frankenstein. Calling the creature "Frankenstein" makes no more sense than calling a light bulb an "Edison." But no matter — to millions, he is Frankenstein. The monster has thus been christened — with the blessing and encouragement of Hollywood.

As well as, of course, his fans. Frankenstein has proved to be one of *the* more bankable movie characters. He was among the first film icons, and his screen presence is so compelling that he's reappeared more than a hundred times, not only breaking out of his stony dungeon but also the confines of the horror genre, showing up in comedies and Broadway musicals as well as the standard, scream-in-the-dark fare for which he remains best known.

But once upon a time, this menacing giant lived only in the mind of an 18-year-old girl named Mary. Though her vision was very different from what you might see ambling up to your door on October 31 with a half-filled candy sack, she remains the real creator of the creature, and the work she published remains a monstrously original and unsettling exploration of how society treats those who are different — *really* different. The book explores lots of other themes and issues as well, some tied closely to the Romantic era in which it was composed, and others that continue to resonate today (a true definition of a "classic" — a work that transcends its time). No doubt countless English majors have found lots of things in this book that were not consciously intended by the book's young author, yet the work's elasticity of interpretation has helped ensure that it remains one of the most taught, analyzed, and debated works of English literature. And to think (here comes a cliché that happens, in this case, to be true), it all started with a dream.

Mary Shelley, author of *Frankenstein*, had a childhood that naturally inclined her to literature and an adult romantic relationship that supplied the necessary tumult and vision to foment her envelope-pushing masterpiece. Her parents were well-known intellectuals — radicals, actually — in the England of the late 1700s. Proponents of such concepts as women's rights and "free love," William Godwin and Mary Wollstonecraft raised Mary in an intellectual milieu that featured frequent visits from other English radicals, such as the poet Percy Bysshe Shelley, who found himself so enamored by the eloquent yet soft-spoken Mary Godwin that he subsequently abandoned his wife and escaped with Mary to the Continent, beginning their peripatetic and passionate love affair (which would, after Shelley's wife's suicide, become marriage).

Frankenstein is probably the most famous work of art ever created on a dare. The novel owes its existence to a storytelling contest that was proposed during one suitably stormy weekend at the poet Lord Byron's castle near Geneva, Switzerland. As the author herself explained in a preface to a reprint of the novel in 1831, "It was commenced partly as a source of amusement.... I passed the summer of 1816 in the environs of Geneva. The season was cold and rainy, and in the evenings we crowded around a blazing wood fire and amused ourselves with some German stories of ghosts.... These tales excited in us a playful desire of imitation."

Someone who's never read the book would very likely be startled at how little of the novel actually concerns the creature, and how much involves the tortured cogitations of the creature's creator, the medical student Victor Frankenstein. People expecting a monster tale find instead a philosophical treatise about the consequences and limits of scientific exploration. It would be wrong to even call Frankenstein's creation a "monster."

True, he's oversized, and possessed of great strength and speed — and he does commit acts of murder — but he also utters some of the most thoughtful and eloquent dialogue of the Romantic era. The creature is highly educated, having been "raised" on European literature and, especially, John Milton's *Paradise Lost*. (His education takes place after he escapes from Victor's apartment-laboratory and finds refuge in an annex attached to a modest home in the woods, where he learns to speak and read.)

The novel details Victor Frankenstein's repulsion with his own creation, his abandonment of his "experiment," and the creature's subsequent quest to get Victor to create a mate for him. Not unexpectedly, everywhere the creature goes, people shriek, run away, or throw things at him. After a couple hundred pages, this begins to take a toll on the sensitive giant. So in his quest for companionship, he begs his creator for at least one soul who won't find him utterly repulsive. Victor gives in, and begins to build a second creature but changes his mind half-way through, causing his original creature to vow to wreak vengeance against Victor. This propels the latter part of the narrative as Victor tries to stay one step ahead of his pursuer.

The book was published anonymously, and the guessing game helped ignite some initial interest, but it was the intricate plot and originality of the story — and its overall effect of *strangeness* — that made the book a bestseller. It was reissued several times during Mary Shelley's life; despite the fact that she went on to write several other novels, nothing she wrote remotely approached the popularity of the product of her 18-year-old imagination.

One of the things that still makes the book such a great read is the exuberance of the storytelling. Romantic-era writers — and, it seems, especially the poets — were an energetic, even exhausting lot. Much of the writing of the period reflects the extreme athleticism of its writers (e.g., Percy Shelley's ocean swimming, William Wordsworth's marathon hiking, Lord Byron's sailing), and *Frankenstein* certainly mirrors that, both in plot and style. The novel reflects a restless intensity: creatures racing through the wilderness, ships churning through the frigid Arctic waters, characters climbing mountains or negotiating raging rivers, dog sleds racing along frozen tundra. The book has lots of exotic locales, and characters who act intensely, even when staying put; Victor Frankenstein spends most of the book in a state of frenetic agitation, and the creature he creates is forever on the move.

Now a Terrifying Motion Picture!

The most recognizable monster in all of horror, the iconic creature portrayed by Boris Karloff in 1931's *Frankenstein*.

So it's got narrative energy. And a page-turning narrative. But is it scary?

Well, there are moments of real suspense: The creature stalking Victor through the countryside, Victor trying to keep from revealing the truth of what he's done while his family theorizes about his strange behavior, and the creature's appearance on Victor's wedding night. But Shelley probably undercut her ability to write a genuinely scary story when she made her giant so emotionally gentle, so well spoken. After spending 50 pages with the creature as he presses his ear to the wall of a hut, trying to learn French and reading Milton's *Paradise Lost*, we're not likely to get many Freddy Krueger moments.

There's also a good deal of moralizing in the book (an aspect of Shelley's creation that the movie versions have almost completely done away with). Countless undergrads have been asked to discuss whether the book condemns or endorses mankind's attempt to "play God," and the book provides no shortage of material for such cogitations. There's also a strong message about the need to take responsibility for one's actions. The creature is not born violent, but made violent by the cruelty of society and the cold shoulder of his creator. So it's got the whole nature-nurture debate going on amid the plot machinations.[1]

In the final analysis, *Frankenstein* succeeds as a novel because of, well, the novelty of its premise — an accident of timing as much as anything else. At the time of the writing, the question of whether life could be generated scientifically in a lab (a theory called "galvanism") was just gaining steam in intellectual circles, and was soon to capture the public's imagination.[2] Shelley put a face on the debate, albeit one that most of us wouldn't want to see peering though our windows. It wouldn't be long, however, until Frankenstein's creature would be literally peering at his English contemporaries, striding the boards of early Victorian theaters, losing his philosophical insights and gradually turning into the monster that would make his cinematic bow almost 100 years after his birth.

But few people except literature purists have ever complained about the radical "dumbing down" of Shelley's masterpiece into the classic 1931 film version, with a stiff-limbed Boris Karloff groaning his way through a very bad first week of life. Karloff himself seemed to embrace the role of the grunting, bolt-necked behemoth, both on screen and in life: "I always saw my monster as something inarticulate, helpless, and tragic. To him, Frankenstein was God."[3] Well, that vision of the creature owes as much to Peggy Webling, a British playwright, whose 1927 drama encapsulated many of the changes which had been made in the previous century, beginning with the version of the story as retold by Richard Brinsley Peake. In 1823, *Presumption, or the Fate of Frankenstein*, Peake's stage version of the novel, would serve as a basic transcription of the novel for future playwrights, with a dangerous, non-communicative monster threatening creator and village right from the start. When *Dracula* became a hit in early 1931, the studio heads at Universal raced to bring out a film with a similar pedigree. *Frankenstein* seemed like a ready-made success, being rooted in the Gothic tradition that had worked so well in *Dracula* and also coming off a successful theatrical run.

"The novel was radically different from the countless dramatizations which followed on stage and screen, [but] the adaptability of the story to the theater was recognized immediately," said film historian Rudy Behlmer.[4] And though the "monster" Frankenstein has continued to display an impressive adaptability, he will forever be embedded in most people's minds as the menacing, gangly-armed interloper in that nameless village of pitchfork-wielding peasants.

So why does a film that is only loosely based on Mary Shelley's original, and features some wild overacting, extremely campy dialogue, and an implausible plot remain so popular? And what would have been the fate of the film if Universal Studios had gotten its first choice to play the monster — Bela Lugosi, fresh off the phenomenal success of the cinematic *Dracula*? (Lugosi intended to play the part; he was screen-tested in makeup as the monster, but then objected to being completely unrecognizable. He reportedly also objected to not having any dialogue, merely grunts, and he pulled out at the last minute.) It's impossible to know, of course, but history has decreed that William Henry Pratt — who acted under the name Boris Karloff — would become known as the most popular movie monster ever. British director James Whale had enjoyed a considerable critical reputation directing for the British stage and also had some early success in his first few forays into cinema. *Frankenstein* would prove to be a breakthrough for him, earning more than $12 million in its initial release — a remarkable sum in 1931, and leading to a successful career whose culmination would be reached with the 1935 *Bride of Frankenstein*, which most critics regard as his masterpiece.

But many viewers give the vote to the first go-round of the square-headed one, a film undimmed by time and the advent of special effects (without which most horror films today simply couldn't survive). The film has certainly earned our respect for its staying power, but a closer look reveals that there are some wonderful touches — large and small — that deserve our aesthetic admiration as well. Watched again with a critical eye — and a desire to understand its enduring appeal — *Frankenstein* provides many genuine pleasure associated with sophisticated "cinema," all the while retaining its gut-level appeal as a somewhat campy horror romp.

The movie begins in a thoroughly unexpected way — with a personal disclaimer. A man wearing a tuxedo steps out from behind the curtains and directly addresses the audience. The man — actually, actor Edward Van Sloan, who appears later in the movie as Dr. Waldman — delivers a cautionary message to those who would, by now, be seated comfortably awaiting the first few frames of the movie. He tells them (us), in sober tones, "Mr. Carl Laemmle [the film's producer] feels it would be a bit unkind to present this picture without a word of friendly warning."[5]

So warn us he does, in stentorian tones worthy of the judicious doctor he will soon play (in makeup that renders him unrecognizable from his current, elegant appearance). The film might frighten us, he says. Might shock us, as well. "It might even horrify you,"[6] he adds. What a captivating way to open a horror movie: obviously manipulative but nonetheless effective. The seed has been planted. No turning back now. It's like seeing that sign that reads "Keep your hands inside the ride at all times!" just after you've been locked into your rollercoaster car and are headed up the first, foreboding hill.

The first actual scene in the movie proper is not from either the book or any of the previous dramatizations, but it's a highly effective stage setter. As the scene opens, the camera slowly pans across a group of somber mourners at a graveside burial — solemn souls who don't realize they are being watched from hiding by Henry Frankenstein (as he's called in the movie) and his assistant Fritz, who are merely waiting for the service to end so they can dig up the fresh corpse and strip it for parts (the addled-brained Fritz was Hollywood's first "repo man"). As the camera finishes its leisurely sweep of the mourners, it focuses on a statue of the Grim Reaper, who is also slyly observing the whole scene. This efficient opening immediately communicates solemnity, and alerts us to the close presence of an other-worldly creature who represents death. It also brings the audience into a subtle communion with the protagonists. We — along with the Grim Reaper, Henry Frankenstein and Fritz — are observers, spying on the action, each from our privileged vantage point that the mourners can't detect.[7]

A pretty dark opening, but it gets even darker — and right away. After Henry and Fritz dig up the body, they cart it away — but stop when they come across a hanged man dangling from the gallows. Seeing the opportunity for some quick organ harvesting, Henry orders a frightened Fritz to climb the gallows and cut the rope. Which he does, after a few tense moments in which the camera focuses uncomfortably on the assistant as he gingerly eases out on the gallows' crossbeam. And after what we've just witnessed, we hardly need be told in the next scene, in genteel, drawing-room dialogue between Elizabeth (Henry's fiancée) and Victor (her good friend — who would like to be *more* than a good friend), that Henry's "work" is beginning to create some anxiety in the family.

We've now been prepared for everything that will unfold: Frankenstein's macabre frame of mind, Elizabeth's naïve embrace of Henry and his eccentric work habits, and the outside world's contempt for Frankenstein's modus operandi. All we need now to complete the picture is the creature himself, who comes to life in one of the most unforgettable — and parodied — scenes in the history of cinema.

On a dark and stormy night, amid flashes of lightning, Henry brings his creation to life — with melodramatic cries of "It's alive!" to accompany the creature's halting first movements. This scene — also not in the novel — is one of the most cinematically satisfying in the whole movie, with close-ups of waiting, anxious faces amid the cavernous laboratory, illuminated by flashes of lightning and filled with hi-tech gizmos. It's drama on a grand scale.

But it's the drama on a small scale that ultimately makes this movie so effective, and most of those moments involve Karloff's genius for communicating emotion beneath the mask of monstrosity: the creature reaching out plaintively toward a shaft of sunlight, or smiling wanly as he tosses daisy petals into a lake. There is the jarring, even heartbreaking scene of a grieving father carrying his limp daughter's body through a village festival, and Henry Frankenstein's horror when he encounters his creation on a mountainside, realizing for the first time the consequences of his unchecked scientific hubris.

Essentially, it's a collection of disparate moments, held together by audience anxiety and directorial verve. The film generates a weird energy, bouncing back and forth between scenes built upon the presumption of domestic normalcy (featuring Elizabeth, Victor, and Henry's father) and wild, surreal scenes with the creature. One of this movie's primary contributions to the genre of horror films is the abolition of the emotional middle. We're either relaxing in a Victorian drawing room, drinking brandy and making intellectual small-talk, or fleeing for our lives. It's a movie that succeeds at the extremes.

And in that, it honors the spirit of Mary Shelley's original creation, a novel thoroughly steeped in the Romantic era's embrace of extreme states of emotion: ambition, fear, desire, remorse. The story of *Frankenstein* is the story of what happens when the extreme is introduced into the mundane. That's why we shudder when the creature first pulsates with life. Something alien among us now threatens to upend our normal lives. It's a threat, and we react almost instinctively to the danger. To maintain our normal lives, the creature must be destroyed — but not before a thrilling 70 minutes and a rollercoaster cinematic ride.

Freaks

Can a movie be considered a "classic" horror film when it was panned by critics, reviled by audiences, and banned for decades from even being shown? When even the studio that produced it didn't stand behind it, and the director's career was ruined after the film's release? When the stars of the film are not actors at all but rather real-life circus freaks, including armless and legless people, as well as a bearded woman and "the pin-headed lady"? And when many critics and fans of the horror genre don't even consider the film to be part of that category, classifying it instead as a sort of docu-drama?

You hardly have the makings of a "classic" and yet, that's exactly what *Freaks* is — a masterpiece of horror, an unsettling story about the treachery and torment that can be a part of the human conditions — for *some* humans, anyway.

The story of the film goes far beyond the actual "plot" of the movie, and involves a movie studio eager to cash in on the horror film "craze," a celebrated director looking to make a different kind of film that drew on his personal involvement in the carnival circuit, and an audience that had demonstrated a perverse interest in human oddities. But of course, there was also an actual "story" on which the film was (very loosely) based, a short work of fiction called "Spurs" which is, in its way, even more bizarre and horrific than the film which it spawned.

The name Tod Robbins doesn't mean much to readers today. But Clarence Aaron "Tod" Robbins was part of that group of writers of horror and supernatural fiction who helped develop their genres and contribute to the popularity of their fields by publishing short stories in the pulp magazines of the early to mid–twentieth century. Robbins also wrote novels and had the distinction of having one of his books made into a movie twice — both versions starring Lon Chaney, the famed actor who was billed as "The Man of a Thousand Faces." (One was a silent film, the other

Chaney's only talkie, both titled *The Unholy Three*.) His work is often accompanied by the words "strange," "twisted," and "bizarre," and in fact, his work is populated by characters who exist on the very fringes of society, often living a fairy-tale-from-Hell kind of existence. Robbins' own life followed something of this pattern. Born in 1888 to prominent members of New York society, he caused a scandal when he eloped with Edith Norman Hyde (who would go on to win the first Miss America crown in 1919). The marriage wouldn't last — a pattern that would recur — though he seemed to have finally found some happiness with his fourth wife, noted British tennis player Nellie Anderson. He emigrated from New York to the French Riviera, but refused to leave France after the German invasion. He spent most of the war in an internment camp, but survived. After the war's end, he wrote a final novel, *Close Their Eyes Tenderly*, published in 1947. He died in 1949.[1] Except for hardcore fans of pulp horror fiction, Robbins has drifted into literary obscurity — save for his short story "Spurs."

The story revolves around a midget named Jacques Courbe, part of a traveling French circus, and a fellow performer he falls in love with, "a tall, blonde woman of the amazon type"[2] named Jeanne Marie. Jacques, who rides a large dog in the circus behind a train of regular-sized horsemen, may be diminutive, but his desires are painted in larger-than-life terms. He's a kind of Don Quixote type, a character who lives in his own fanciful world, protected by imagination from the rigors of harsh reality. "What matter that he had no lady, and that his daring deeds were severely curtailed to a mimicry of the bareback riders who preceded him? What mattered all these things to the tiny man who lived in dreams, and who resolutely closed his shoe-button eyes to the drab realities of life?" Unlike Quixote, however, Jacques' heart is not inclined toward goodness and forgiveness, but rather revenge against those who would mock him.

So Jacques decides to proclaim his love to Jeanne Marie — who is herself enamored of the charms of the circus strongman, Simon. When Jacques shows up at Jeanne Marie's dressing room one night to declare his intentions, the scene is a nauseating and tragic-comic mess. Jacques has a huge melodramatic streak to offset his tiny stature. He kneels to her, not kissing her hand but instead "he went and pressed his lips to her red-slippered foot." She is shocked, repulsed, and then deeply amused, and she mocks him.

The whole story, like this one early scene, is extremely weird. The tale has a surreal, nightmarish quality, like a Salvador Dali painting, or a

The real-life circus attractions from Tod Browning's disturbing 1932 masterpiece *Freaks*.

Twilight Zone episode. There's no attempt to establish a fixed, believable reality — a quality Robbins reinforces by his extremely prolific use of exclamation points. Everything in this story is heightened, extreme, pumped-up. There are no oases of rationality here. We're in a freak show, and Robbins' over-the-top prose style is oddly apposite to the world he's presenting.

Though she laughs off his proposal, she soon changes her mind when she learns the dwarf has just inherited an estate and a large sum of money. She now imagines herself "a proud lady, ruling over a country estate." Plus, she reasons, "these pygmies are a puny lot. They die young!" So they get married, and the wedding reception degenerates into a violent farce, with their fellow freaks arguing about who is the most popular attraction — a debate that results in an all-out brawl. The "wolf-lady" takes a bite out of the juggler's hand, prompting the circus' owner to chime in: "Ah, my children, my children! This is no way to behave! Calm yourselves, I pray you! Mademoiselle Lupa, remember that you are a lady, as well as a wolf!" True enough.

The beefy Simon steps in to restore order. He picks up Jacques and places him upon his new wife's shoulders—a big mistake, as we'll soon discover, because she decides to return to their farmhouse with her new husband still perched on her. Simon bets her a bottle of Burgundy that she can't carry him all the way home, and she replies, "I swear that I could carry my little ape from one end of France to the other!"

The scene ends, a year passes, and Simon hears a knock on his dressing room door. It's a female visitor, "a tall, gaunt woman dressed like a peasant." It's Jeanne Marie and she tells him about the hellish year she's endured with her midget husband: "There are no ignominies which he has not made me suffer."

"To whom do you refer?" he asks. "Surely you cannot mean that pocket edition husband of yours."

Well, yes, that's exactly who she means. It turns out that he's been forcing her to keep her vow—of carrying him on her shoulders everywhere they go, until she has covered the equivalent distance of traversing France. "If I so much as slacken my pace, if I falter, he goads me with cruel little golden spurs, while at the same time, St. Eustice [his large, vicious dog] nips my ankles."

The estate in which they live is isolated, and there's no place to escape, no one to help her. Every night, Marie is exhausted and in pain, her boots worn down to the bare souls, her body stopped and weakened; her husband then leaps off her shoulders and writes down the tally of how far they've walked. He insists that she carry him until they reach the distance she bragged about in her drunken and insulting diatribe at their reception: "from one end of France to the other." To get out of her plight, she would gladly poison her husband, or his devil dog, but she is forced to first take a bite out of all the food that is prepared for both man and beast.

Now that the traveling circus is back in town, she's raced to Simon while her husband is sleeping to seek his protection from her tormenter. No sooner has she revealed her plight than Jacques, riding upon St. Eustice, bursts in. Simon scoffs at them, daring them to attack. They do, the dog ripping apart the strong man's oiled biceps and the midget plunging a sword into his gut. He dies ingloriously on the floor in a pool of blood. Jacques's wife, thoroughly downtrodden, assumes the position, picks up Jacques, places him on her shoulders, and trudges home in utter desolation and total defeat. As they depart, the circus owner sees them, as he muses ironically: "Can it be? ... Yes, it is. Three old friends. And Jeanne carries him! Ah, but she should not poke fun at M. Jacques Courbe. He is so sensitive; but alas, they are the kind that are the most henpecked."

Thus ends "Spurs," a story of misery, revenge, murder, and deformity, an illustration of how fickle cruel fate can be. The story juxtaposes odd comic bits with dark, distressing facets of human existence. There are no heroes. Everyone is either vain and superficial, angry, disillusioned, or simply waiting for the wheel to turn. Inescapable horrors await the gifted as well as the maimed.

Tod Browning, the director of the silent *The Unholy Three* and 1931's landmark horror breakthrough *Dracula*, was the logical choice for the film version of "Spurs." Not only was his reputation as a director at its zenith but also Browning had spent some years actually working the carnival circuit, and he was familiar with the life, such as it is, of a troupe of real-life circus freaks. The resulting film is often hailed as his real masterpiece, and one of the most moving and unsettling films ever made. In its way, *Freaks* is every bit as bizarre and surreal as "Spurs"—yet it conveys a humanity, a genuine pathos, totally absent in the short story. The most important change to the story includes the "victimization" of the dwarf character, who emerges sympathetically as a character. He is the subject of a murder plot by his new bride, a money-chasing opportunist in league with the circus strongman. In "Spurs," the dwarf's revenge was grossly disproportionate to his wife's insensitive slight. In *Freaks*, the ante is upped. The crime of the wife is much greater—though so is her punishment

Browning's directorial sympathies clearly lie with the circus freaks. He uses his camera to show us the varying ways of looking at these "freaks" (and leaves no doubt as to how *he* sees them). Yet Browning is no dewy-eyed sentimentalist—this is, after all, a movie that turns coldly horrifying. His freaks are truly freakish—so much so that preview audiences found the film exceedingly distasteful to watch.[3] But for those who can get past their initial discomfort with these avatars of nature's malignity, "fascinated revulsion turns into tender comprehension."[4]

The movie begins with a carnival barker talking up the "living, breathing monstrosities" to a crowd gathered on a circus midway. The barker's diatribe suggests the overall sympathetic tone the film will take in its presentation of these freaks: "But for an accident of birth," he tells the crowd, "you might have been as they are."[5] He urges the crowd to come forward to a lighted pen, where he promises them the "most astounding living monstrosity of all time!" We see the skeptical looks on the faces of the listeners turn to sheer horror as they gaze upon someone who "was once a beautiful woman ... she was known as the 'Peacock of the Air.'" The crowd registers their absolute revulsion — and the movie dissolves into a flashback, where a beautiful trapeze artist, Cleopatra (the prolific silent-screen actress Olga Baclanova), is seen swinging above the big top, as Hans, a dwarf (played by diminutive screen veteran Harry Earles) looks up at her, admiringly. During a break in her act, Hans strikes up a conversation with Cleopatra, and we see how lovestruck he is.

Suddenly, the film moves from the world of the circus to a wooded estate, as a gamekeeper animatedly tells the landowner of some "horrible, twisted things" that he's seen in a nearby clearing. As they head toward the clearing, the camera leads down the path, to a frolicsome gathering of circus freaks, dancing, laughing, playing. The gamekeeper is aghast, but the matronly Madame Tetrallini among the freaks explains who they are, and that she was only looking to give them a chance to "play in the sunshine." The landowner obliges them, smiling warmly, telling her they may all remain as long as they wish. Thus, the two ways of seeing the freaks: as monsters to be shooed away, or as human beings merely seeking a little comfort and joy.

Back to the circus, and lots of behind-the-scenes vignettes of the performers interacting with each other (Hans tells Cleopatra he'll be visiting her later that night). We also get glimpses of Hercules, the strongman, an abusive and obtuse character who argues with Cleopatra before she storms out of his tent. There are also scenes with the half-man half-woman, the stuttering clown, the dwarves, the bearded lady, Siamese twins, the "human torso," and various other performers. As a director, Browning takes his time, lingering behind the scenes, revealing the rich, interwoven fabric of carnival life, helping the viewer to see all the performers as complicated individuals as they exist *outside* the spotlight of the big top. The scene that best coveys the humanity of the circus freaks involves a mad dash to the tent of the bearded lady — who has just given birth. Her fellow freaks all assemble lovingly around her bedside to welcome the new addition (a girl, we're told, "and it's gonna have a beard!").

Hans continues his wooing of Cleopatra, amid champagne and declarations of his love. She appears bemused but is obviously only feigning interest. Meanwhile, a former girlfriend of Hans, the dwarf Frieda, comes by his tent to warn him that Cleopatra couldn't possibly love him, that she's just stringing him along because he brings her expensive gifts. Hans tells her Cleopatra makes him genuinely happy, and he will continue his pursuit of her. So Frieda takes her concerns to Cleopatra, warning her not to toy with Hans — but she mistakenly blurts out that Hans has recently inherited a fortune. Cleopatra and Hercules hatch a plan to have her marry Hans for his money — and then do away with the little man.

Then comes the wedding feast. Each of the various members of the circus entourage performs, or makes a toast, and there's lots of laughing, fire eating and champagne drinking. The freaks agree to make Cleopatra "one of us," and they pass a "loving cup" of champagne around the table, each drinking and chanting, "We accept her! We accept her! One of us! One of us!" The viewer knows how unworthy she is to be accepted so lovingly by the freaks. She angrily chastises the well-wishers, telling them how insulted she is to be called one of them. She tells them to get out, and insults her husband for allowing the chant to have started in the first place. Alone, she tells Hans the wedding was "only a joke."

Throughout these scenes of the lovelorn Hans and his sincere-but-naive attempts to win Cleopatra's heart — and the gatherings of the freaks at the bedside of the bearded lady and the wedding celebration — the film creates a climate of warmth and support among these human outcasts. They might not have much, but they have each other. And when around each other, they are noble, compassionate, supportive, and deeply committed to their community and its welfare. That's what makes the climax of the film so problematic.

After Cleopatra and Hercules' plot to poison Hans is discovered by a doctor who treats the stricken dwarf (they spiked the wine at his wedding), the freaks decide to avenge themselves on the scheming pair. A week passes, and covertly, they move against the duo. There are lots of tense moments as we see the small, disfigured bodies, watching, waiting for the moment to take their truly vicious revenge. As rain falls and thunder rumbles, and the caravan rolls through the French countryside at night on their way to the next town, the freaks strike. Cleopatra is stunned to find two of the freaks at Hans' bedside (where she has been giving him his "medicine" for the last week — a mixture of the poison that didn't finish him off at the wedding). They pull a knife and a gun on her. Meanwhile, the rest of the freaks come after Hercules, crawling through the mud in one of the most eerie and menacing stalking sequences in cinema history.

The viewer doesn't see what the freaks do to them — not at that moment. It seems pretty clear that Hercules was about to be knifed to death (each of the freaks was holding a knife in their tiny little mouths as they made their way on all fours towards Hercules). As for Cleopatra, the one-time "Peacock of the Air"—well, the viewer finally sees what the stunned and sickened onlookers saw at the beginning of the film: She's been mutilated (her legs amputated) and given a stumpy, feathered tail; her fore-shortened arms are also covered with feathers and her vocal chords cut so she can only utter a grating, hen-like "bok-bok-bok" when she tries to speak. She's become a grotesque hen-woman.

The jarring image of the lovely Cleopatra, deformed and imprisoned in her avian body, is unsettling, and will perhaps change the way some viewers have felt about the placid, good-natured community of circus freaks we've seen throughout the film. Did Cleopatra deserve it? Can the freaks' behavior be justified? Is Browning making a statement about justice and vigilante violence—and if so, is he condemning it, or justifying it? That's left open to each viewer's interpretation. Either way, it's a thought-provoking, if horrifying, end to a film about human nature in its most extreme states.

From Hell

There's no name in the history of horror — real or imagined — that evokes more terror than the casual, caustic moniker "Jack the Ripper." Its overtones of both the snidely playful and grotesque testify in some measure to the somewhat inexplicable grip he's exercised on the public imagination for more than a century. In the pageant of traumatic human history, there have certainly been figures whose evil acts have wrought more destruction, anguish, and long-term suffering. Yet there's something about Jack the Ripper that clings to, and even excites, the imagination. He seems much more a character from fiction than reality, though much of what we think we know of him is conjecture. Perhaps he endures in popular consciousness because of the fortuitous (for writers, anyway) junction of several factors: the mystery of his identity, the animal severity of his crimes, the squalid melodrama of his victims' daily lives, and the heroic-but-doomed struggle of the police to solve the crime and prevent future killings. His world is the gaslit slum common to Dickens and Conan Doyle, misty and mysterious, with menace threatening your every step as you stumble from the public house, edging your way through whores, drunks, and thugs. In an unsettling way, the lore and lure of Jack the Ripper cannot be denied. He represents the triumph of the dark side, Satan defying the archangels, the snarky gloating of a Mr. Hyde.

There's no getting around it: Jack the Ripper is a hot commodity. Almost from his first strike, he has inspired a remarkable range of art: ballads and folk tales, paintings, short stories and novels, book-length re-examinations, plays, poems, and even opera. You can find comic books dedicated to his brief, horrifying reign of terror and spend countless hours watching the dozens of movies and television specials dedicated to his crimes. For the serious-minded, there is the discipline of "Ripperology,"[1] — a special sect of sleuthing dedicated to identifying just who Jack the Ripper really was. People today are as likely to know his name as they were when he burst onto the scene in Victorian England. Sophisticated websites share detailed historical and biographical information and debate the Ripper's identity, and online book sites boast dozens of recently published books on the topic.

It's not at all certain that the killer's name was Jack. That was simply how one particular letter writer signed his name in a missive sent to the police in the midst of the killing spree, daring investigators to stop him before he killed again. It's also not clear just how many murders the culprit known as Jack the Ripper might have committed. Between April 1888 and February 1891, eleven women were murdered in London's East End, in a neighborhood known as Whitechapel. But only five of those murders (each of which occurred between August and November of 1888) are generally thought to be the work of the Ripper. Experts vary somewhat in this area, but most serious investigators have concluded that the five murdered between August and November, the so-called "canonical five," were Jack's victims. "Most experts point to deep throat slashes, abdominal and genital-area mutilation, removal of internal organs, and progressive facial mutilations as the distinctive features of Jack the Ripper's *modus operandi*."[2]

Jack the Ripper's work, then, was distinguished from the typical murderer of the time by its savagery and surgical acumen. From the beginning, it appeared to police that the murderer was expert with a knife. He worked quickly, often apparently in public, and was able to remove selected organs from his victims after slashing their throats. In fact, the police actually received a half of a human kidney from someone claiming to be the murderer; experts concluded the kidney probably did come from one of the victims. All of the victims were women, and each was involved in prostitution — a remarkably common and available vocation in the overcrowded and poverty-stricken Whitechapel neighborhood. The crimes took place at night or in the early morning, and those few eyewitness accounts that have been deemed credible offer no clear description and often contradict each other. Though the London police formed a special task force and enlisted the top investigators of Scotland Yard, the killer was never caught. Dozens of suspects were questioned but released, and in the intervening century, more than a hundred names have been put forward as the killer. The crime is now considered insoluble, due to the passage of time and lack of forensic evidence (which, of course, has kept open the floodgates for everyone from credentialed investigators to rank amateurs).

Among the handful of suspects who continue to attract attention is

William Gull, a physician in service to the queen at the time. His notoriety as a surgeon and his closeness to the throne has made him the favorite of conspiracy theorists who have argued that the killings were done to silence a group of prostitutes who were trying to blackmail the royal family. The theory, originally put forward in a BBC docu-drama in the 1970s and later in a book, suggests that the queen ordered Gull to silence the women, who had knowledge that the queen's grandson, Prince Edward, had fathered a child with a "common" shop girl named Annie Crook. Most historians dismiss the theory as absurd — even the man who served as the primary source of the story later recanted, claiming he'd made it all up — but it remains one of the more dramatically compelling theories. The theory finds its fullest and most powerful expression in a graphic novel titled *From Hell*, written by Alan Moore and illustrated by Eddie Campbell.

The term "graphic novel" has gained quite a bit of currency in the past decade. Most bookstores have shelves dedicated to the genre, and some high-profile graphic novels have been reviewed and endorsed by "serious" literary critics — despite the format's humble roots (a graphic novel is, really, just a long comic book). But writers such as Moore, whose works include *The Watchmen*, *The League of Extraordinary Gentlemen*, and *V for Vendetta*, have helped raise the level of critical acceptance of the graphic novel. In the hands of a writer who understands the potential of the genre, a graphic novel can be as moving and powerful a reading experience as any "traditional" novel.

Such is definitely the case with *From Hell: Being a Melodrama in Sixteen Parts*. Each of the parts, or chapters, was published separately over a period of years in the early 1990s in various comic book collections, and brought together as a graphic novel of more than 500 pages, with an appendix and copious, detailed notes. Any reader coming to the work expecting a typical "comic book" is in for quite a shock. The work is philosophical, and dauntingly detailed. It delves deeply into the dark corners of Victorian society — its poverty, squalor, violence, and sense of social dislocation — as well as truly heady subjects such as architecture as civic metaphor and the theological consequences of the shift from a matriarchal to a patriarchal society.

And, of course, there's Jack the Ripper. *From Hell* gives us the words and gruesome images that one thinks of when recalling the crimes of the infamous, unknown murderer. But in the case of *From Hell*, he *is* known: Dr. William Gull, surgeon, Freemason, and loyal servant of the queen (head of the royal conspiracy to do away with the five "canonical" prostitutes).

The novel offers memorably rich characterizations of Gull, the prostitutes, and several of the investigators who vainly pursued the Ripper. One of the things a graphic novel can do even more effectively than a traditional prose narrative is juxtapose scenes for ironic effect. For instance, there's an early scene where Gull's mother is talking to a private school tutor, asking him to take William as a student. While his mother goes on about how inquisitive a child William is, the scene is intercut with visual vignettes of young William wandering around the tutor's garden, capturing a rodent, and gutting it with a pocket knife without the slightest trepidation. Thus, the reader gets multiple glimpses of the future Ripper as both gifted intellect and cruel, callow schoolboy. There are lots of such instances, such as when Moore and Campbell provide near-simultaneous glimpses of well-heeled London aristocracy dining and dancing while lower-class "working girls" are seen turning tricks in dingy alleys and darkened doorways.

Peppered among the plotlines are multiple digressions on the history and mystery of the rites of Freemasonry; an extended architectural tour of London and environs; the historical relationship between Jesus Christ and the Sun Gods who preceded him, the demographics of English slums in the 1880s; an inquiry into "esoterica" and mystical beliefs; an undercover exploration of police procedures; an exposé of abuse in mental hospitals; and even a moving and memorable scene where Gull meets the infamous, tragic Elephant Man, John Merrick. *From Hell* is a wildly ambitious work that succeeds in presenting a fully realized portrait of a time and a place where the dark impulses of humanity play out against a lustrous and somber backdrop of a once-grand but now decayed and morally rotted empire.

In his introduction to the series that became the book, Moore wrote, "It's my belief that if you cut into a thing deeply enough, if your incisions are precise and persistent and conducted methodically, then you may reveal not only that thing's inner workings, but also the meaning behind those workings.... *From Hell* is a post-mortem of a historical occurrence, using fiction as a scalpel."[3] And wield that scalpel he does. The book, though illustrated with black-and-white sketches, is awash in the colors of despair. The Ripper is remembered, in part, because of the horrifying nature of his crimes. And in that respect, the book really is a "graphic" novel. The reader is treated to explicitly drawn carnal collisions in alleys, bars, and cheap rooming houses, as well as the Ripper's slice-and-dice *modus operandi*, and the subsequent autopsies of the eviscerated victims.

But what remains in the reader's mind isn't so much the gruesomeness as the gravitas of the narrative. Moore's work is the product of years of prodigious research, which he chronicles in a series of scholarly endnotes that runs almost 50 pages. And though Moore declaims against believing the conspiracy theory he has just taken 500 pages to advance, the reader is left with a wealth of conjecture that cannot fail to impress. The theory that the surgeon committed these crimes at the direction of the queen holds almost no credence among informed Ripperologists today. Gull is remembered primarily for his contributions to medical literature (he was the doctor who came up with the term "Anorexia Nervosa"). But Gull's entry into the narrative opens the door to lots of other compelling subplots, such as the role of Freemasonry in the crimes (he was once thought to be a high-ranking Freemason, a claim never substantiated), Victorian royalty, and the mistreatment of the criminally insane. Gull might be merely a convenient fictional scapegoat, but given the gaps in the actual police record he fits as well into the blank space of Jack's identity as any other suspect bequeathed by posterity.

Gull's reputation as a potential Jack the Ripper was reinforced by the 2001 film version of Moore and Campbell's novel, also titled *From Hell*, starring Johnny Depp as Inspector Frederick Abberline (who was in charge of the investigation) and British actor Ian Holm as Gull.

Directed by the twin brothers Allen and Albert Hughes, who are probably best known for their breakthrough urban drama *Menace II Society*, their *From Hell* retains the gritty realism of their earlier films but goes much further in the level of physical and psychological violence on screen. While that might not seem surprising for a film about Jack the Ripper, many previous Ripper films damped down the intensity of the actual killings, focusing more on the police investigations. The Hughes brothers offer up a Jack the Ripper that's not for the squeamish.

Yet the movie is stylishly presented. This is no mere splatter-fest. The art direction is impressive, the shadows of Whitechapel and its dark and ghostly spires and serpentine roadways creepily showcased. Whoever he was, Jack the Ripper was a creature of the night, and the Hugheses created a suitable cinematic world in which to highlight his nocturnal madness.

The first few frames signal the intensity and the fury that is to come.

Johnny Depp is a frustrated detective trying to match wits with the notorious Jack the Ripper in the darkly memorable *From Hell*.

The red of blood and fire fill the screen. The very first image is of a flame, followed shortly by the slums of Victorian England, smoky at twilight against a blood-red sky. The camera pans down slowly in a revealing crane shot worthy of Orson Welles, providing a glimpse of all the various gradations of squalor in each successive floor of a decrepit, crowded tenement building and then moving lower and lower, down to the filthy, Dante-esque cobblestone passages at street level, filled with desperate-looking stragglers. In a long tracking shot, the camera moves tentatively through this human flotsam, showing it all: drunkards congregating in an alley, brawling and hurling abusive epithets; dissolute prostitutes trolling brazenly for customers; and a bottle-wielding ruffian urinating at a busy corner amid the hardened, oblivious poor.

And then, suddenly, there's a focal point: a prostitute with blazing red hair, Mary Kelly, whom we watch as she wends her way through the alleyways until she's accosted by her pimp, a charming fellow who slowly slices the buttons off her skirt with a dagger to remind her that she and her fellow prostitutes had better pay up, "or this friend I have here [brandishing the knife at eye-level] will be your next customer."[4]

Okay, so it's not Shakespeare. But it's all done so stylishly, and with great verve by the actors, that the somewhat ham-handed script doesn't interfere with the genuine sense of suspense — and repulsion — as the reels (and Jack's victims) unspool.

The movie develops along the traditional lines of a murder mystery. Depp plays Inspector Abberline as a kind of low-key cross between Sherlock Holmes and Hunter S. Thompson (in his opium-induced trances, he has visions of the crimes being committed, and teasing glimpses of the perpetrator). The performance is another typically solid effort from the talented Depp (who doesn't deserve the scorn that some critics heaped on his Cockney accent; it's really not too distracting once you get accustomed to it). If Depp's performance takes a bit of getting used to, his co-star Ian Holm is pitch perfect from his first moments as the queen's physician and trusted confidant. Holm is highly effective as Dr. Gull, a surgeon of apparent compassion and deep humanity, who's hiding a dark, horrible secret. But much of the horror of *From Hell* derives not from the murderer on the loose but rather the portrayal of the real-life horrors that plagued the poor in 1888. Some of these scenes are as hard to watch as the murders: women washing themselves every morning in the rancid waters of the public fountains; mentally ill patients left to rot in asylums (or worse, being lobotomized with crude implements to relieve their "hysteria"); the homeless, chained-up every night to "sleeping benches" (they are chained so they don't fall forward and wake themselves when they smack the pavement). These scenes are based on the historical reality of slum dwelling in the nineteenth and early twentieth century in neighborhoods such as Whitechapel.

The surgical skill with which Jack the Ripper goes about his killings convinces Abberline that the culprit must be a man with medical training. His superiors find that hard to swallow and urge him to pursue a more convenient suspect: "It must have been a Jew butcher. Or a Jew tailor. There's plenty of *them* in Whitechapel."[5] (Virulent anti–Semitism was also one of the social horrors of slum existence in 1888 London.) But Abberline remains convinced that no mere "tradesman" could be committing the crimes. As he interviews prostitutes who are, quite naturally, fearing for their very lives each time they duck with a "John" behind a fence or into a darkened doorway, he uncovers the threads of a frightening, high-ranking conspiracy that gives both the book and movie their dramatic momentum.

Critical opinion of the movie is sharply divided. Even among horror fans, who are accustomed to darker fare, the word on *From Hell* is mixed. "The film suffers from being overly long, with weak plot lines.... A thriller that's not very thrilling,"[6] warns one popular movie site for fans of the dark side. But other critics found in the Hughes Brothers' vision a touchstone for the presence of evil in the contemporary world: "*From Hell* depicts a crusade of messianic evil, yet it never exploits that horror. It sends you out, instead, haunted by the calculated extremes of malevolence that are the sinister shadow of the modern age."[7]

Perhaps the ambivalence about *From Hell* is reflective of the ambivalence about the Ripper case in general. He's compelling, but repulsive. Murder ought not be so entertaining, and such gruesome murders ought never happen at all. They should be beyond the realm of human possibility. It's perhaps better not to think of such things. But as you read this, somewhere there sits an intrepid researcher, re-assembling notes under a desk lamp or re-arranging paragraphs on a laptop for yet another book that will promise the "final answer" to the riddle of Jack the Ripper. And the community of Ripperologists will rip into that book too, dissecting its pages for new clues in the enduring mystery of Jack's identity. It's horrible, yes, but we can't seem to avert our eyes.

Ghost Story

"Thump!"

A mysterious noise in the night. The wind, howling through the eaves. Stairs creaking, leaves rustling, branches tapping rhythmically against the window pane. Was that a scream in the distance? And that movement in the shadows — an animal? Or ... something else?

Stories of things unseen wreaking havoc in the physical world have always been popular with storytellers — and their audiences. Anthropologists theorize that the first stories humans told each other were ghostly in character: visitations of the dead, angels appearing before disbelieving loved ones, evil spirits issuing warnings across the chasm between this world and the next. Every culture has its own iterations of a "ghost story," every generation re-inventing the template for its own amusement and mortification.

When a writer wades into that stream of ideas, he or she already faces a tidal pull of tradition. Every reader (or hearer) of a ghost story brings to the experience the memory of every other ghost story they've ever heard or read. So it's a pretty tall order to announce your intention to tell a ghost story in a book of more than 500 pages — and then call the book, simply, *Ghost Story*. Most writers probably don't fancy competing with every other writer in their chosen genre, but Peter Straub seems to thrive on the association with this touchstone narrative.

Ghost Story, the breakthrough novel that established Straub as a major writer in the horror genre, provides the reader with most of the expected elements of a traditional ghost story: disembodied voices, re-animated corpses, haunted houses, shared nightmares, animal mutilations, pitched battles between good and evil, power outages, mysterious disappearances, werewolves, vampires, shape-shifting creatures, eerie music, a demonic seductress, hunting knives, fog, creaky staircases, and lots of dark and stormy nights. But as comprehensive as that list might seem, it does little justice to the richness — and the satisfying litany of surprises — that Straub is able to weave into his labyrinthine narrative.

In fact, his book is really as much a celebration of narrative as it is a traditional thriller. It's filled with wild stories, told by a variety of characters, but primarily by a group of elderly men who meet regularly in a semi-formal colloquy they call the Chowder Society. The purpose of their meetings: to tell each other stories. So Straub is telling the story of these men who tell stories, and dutifully recording the stories they, and others, tell, which become the fabric of the novel. In fact, *Ghost Story* is really an exploration of the complex relationship between the made-up stories we tell each other and the "reality" we face.

The book anoints the sacredness of stories — and the undeniably compelling appeal of a spooky tale — from its intriguing opening:

> *"What was the worst thing you've ever done?"*
> *"I won't tell you that, but I'll tell you the worst thing that ever happened to me ... the most dreadful thing..."*[1]

And for the next 500 pages, Straub lays out some pretty dreadful things. The book's plot revolves around the reminiscences of the Chowder Society — lifelong friends in a small, upstate New York town who lead, by all appearances, highly respectable lives. But as readers slowly discover, the Chowder Society has its secrets — or, more accurately, one huge secret that they've all agreed to ignore until circumstances force them into confronting their past.

That's another major theme in Straub's book — the inescapability of the past. And in plumbing that idea, his novel suggests that everyone's life is really a composite of ghost stories — that we're all haunted by the events of our past. The Chowder Society merely has a more *malevolent* ghost in its past. Okay, a *lot* more malevolent. But the equation still holds: If character is destiny, our character is formed by the events of our past, ghostly echoes we can pretend to tune out but never completely banish.

Straub eavesdrops on the Chowder Society's meetings but then follows them home as they deal with the dark residue of their mutual scare sessions. As the story unfolds, certain coincidences begin to trouble the members of the group. Each of them starts to have the same recurring nightmare. Then they each begin to hear voices, and see dim apparitions, and to have unsettling premonitions of evil on the horizon. Amid their uneasy stirrings, actual, troubling events begin to agitate their world. A series of unexplained animal mutilations are reported on farms on the outskirts of their town.

An attractive, highly mysterious woman moves into town, lodging at the only hotel and going for 2 A.M. walks. And a member of their society commits suicide — a real head-scratcher since the victim was the town's doctor and the picture of civic respectability. What's going on here? Straub gets us wondering — though he makes clear that the remaining members of the society know exactly what's going on: retribution for a crime unwittingly committed forty years earlier.

But it's not until an outsider arrives to help the Chowder Society — a novelist who takes seriously their premonitions, haunted dreams, and forebodings — that the group summons the confidence to act (mostly out of a desire for self-preservation, rather than atonement). The novelist had recently been involved with a mesmerizing woman who challenged his fixed notions of what is and isn't possible. He is still somewhat under her spell. As he explains,

> [S]he suggested a world in which advisory ghosts and men who were disguised wolves could exist. I know of no other way to put this. I do not mean that she made me believe in the paraphernalia of the supernatural; but she suggested that such things might be fluttering invisibly about us. You step on a solid-looking piece of ground and it falls away under your shoe; you look down, and instead of seeing grass, earth, the solidity you had expected, you are looking at a very deep cavern where crawling things scurry to get out of the light. Well, so here is a cavern, a chasm of sorts, you say; how far does it go? Does it underlie everything, and is the solid earth merely a bridge over it?[2]

He joins forces with the Chowder Society as they face an all-out assault on the town from an entity that is as gorgeous and alluring on the outside as she is evil on the inside. She is a shape-shifter, or to use the term Straub prefers, a *nightwatcher*. Assisted by minions who resemble other supernaturally recognizable creatures, such as a sneering, sunglasses-wearing werewolf (part James Dean and part Travis Bickle) and a small, illiterate, gnome-like farm boy, this she-devil comes a-calling. After dispatching several minor characters, she sets her sights on the Chowder Society and a duel for the ages ensues, ranging from a local haunted house (and the scene of the society's earlier, unforgiven crime) to a magnificently rendered scene in a movie theater, where a battle between minions and their human prey climaxes in a movie theater showing the film *Night of the Living Dead*, over and over again.

Straub writes about unimaginably wild occurrences, the stuff of surrealist visions, yet the prose never becomes overheated. His linguistic control of this monstrous orgy of evil is most impressive. The difference between Straub and many other "mainstream" horror writers is the literary quality of his prose. Straub writes beautifully about horrific stuff. His style is similar to novelists such as John Irving and Saul Bellow. At its best moments, *Ghost Story* is genuinely eloquent and moving. There's little blood, and almost none of what could be called the "gross-out" component of horror fiction. Straub is often closer to Henry James than he is to Stephen King (although King and Straub have collaborated on two successful books, with a third reportedly being planned).

Ghost Story lifted Straub from relative literary obscurity (he had written two previous novels) into the limelight. The work garnered mostly positive reviews from the critical community, and was made into a motion picture two years after publication. The *New York Times* called the book "a quite sophisticated literary entertainment," though it lamented its "glacial" pace.[3] *Newsweek* lauded Straub's "considerable technical skill," but also noted that "the story takes too long getting into stride."[4] Praise for the writing, with a few caveats about Straub's exposition, and the perceived delay until the "real action" starts, were a common feature of most reviews. But the attack on his pacing is really unfair. What Straub did was write an *intellectual* horror story, as much as a traditional rattling-chains and flying specters kind of tale. The thoughtful exposition establishes a milieu against which the page-turning dissimulation will take place. Much of the action in the book unfolds only in various characters' minds, so the charge that little happens early on is inaccurate, and fails to appreciate how thoroughly Straub has softened the ground for his firecracker finale. First he unsettles you by assaulting the unseen world of the mind, and then he goes for the kill by making manifest what had only been dreamt of. It is a thinking person's horror story.

With so much of the book's dark charm relying on interior horror, the creators of 1981's *Ghost Story* movie faced a real challenge. Whether or not they succeeded remains an open question among film critics. (The reviewers were divided, sometimes sharply, about whether the movie was an engrossing psychological thriller or an overwrought and melodramatic plod.) English director John Irvin might have had his work cut out for him due to the complexity and depth of Straub's novel, but he was also working in a genre that stretches back to the very beginnings of cinema. As director Curtis Harrington noted, "The ability of the camera to present hallucinatory or supernatural phenomena was one of the first discoveries

Now a Terrifying Motion Picture!

The men of the Chowder Society—now and then—maintain a dark secret that comes back to haunt them in the film adaptation of Peter Straub's *Ghost Story*. ("Now" actors: Douglas Fairbanks, Jr., John Houseman, Fred Astaire, Melvyn Douglas; "Then" actors: Kurt Johnson, Ken Olin, Tim Choates, Mark Chamberlin.)

made by the earliest creators of cinema."⁵ Ghost stories have been popular with filmmakers since the French pioneer director Georges Méliès first presented his "magically arranged scenes" at the turn of the century.

Ghost Story the movie participates in many of those time-honored cinematic traditions associated with the genre. And several of its stars bring that sense of tradition with them, as the film boasts performances by a notably eminent (a polite word for "aged') cast: John Houseman, Melvyn Douglas, Fred Astaire (in a decidedly non–singing or dancing role) and, in his last film appearance, Douglas Fairbanks, Jr. These *are* your father's movie stars. And together they make up the Chowder Society — and, for some viewers, the principal reason to watch *Ghost Story*.

The film takes almost innumerable liberties with Straub's original — so much so that it's almost hard to think of the film version as being based on the book. And that might be the key to enjoying the movie, which is different in tone, theme and plot from the original. Viewed as an almost independent film, unmoored to Straub's complex narrative, the movie succeeds in parts. At times, it is genuinely creepy, and it does have moments of character development that hold a viewer's interest.

Like the book, the story unfolds in the winter, and there are some brief, lovely scenes of Milburn, New York, the fictional town where the story takes place. The film begins with intriguing vignettes: an idyllic outdoor winter setting at night, unspoiled and silent, save for a dog barking in the distance; an elderly man in a smoking jacket, listening to opera in his library and drinking brandy; and two other unidentified elderly men tossing and turning, lost in nightmares. A view of the moon, but distorted, as if viewed from underwater. Then we're thrown right into the world of the Chowder Society, with Sears James, a lawyer (played by the stentorian John Houseman), narrating a story for his chums about a man who's been buried alive, trying to claw his way out of his box. And before any of these images have time to register, we're in an apartment building, or hotel, where a man is interrogating a naked woman (whose face is hidden from the camera, and the man) in his bed:

MAN: "Who are you?"
WOMAN: "I am you."

Then she turns to him, and she's grotesque, a death mask on a woman's body. In revulsion, he stumbles backwards, falls through a window, and plunges several stories to his death.

Pretty good start. Unfortunately, the film's sense of foreboding and all-encompassing mystery that these first few scenes generate fail to carry over to the rest of the movie, which brings these pieces together but in a way that does little to create genuine suspense or fear. The screenwriter (Lawrence D. Cohen, who also adapted Stephen King's *Carrie* for the big screen) makes a few curious choices with his retelling of Straub's narrative, the most puzzling one being to limit the scope of evil that the mysterious woman (the one who was naked in bed) represents. In the book, the shape-shifting villainess is allied with the demonic, a permanent and massive force of dark magic and pervasive evil that terrorizes and kills dozens of innocent victims (including farm animals) in the town of Milburn before eventually going after the entire town and everyone in it. Straub's nemesis is Biblical in stature. But the movie turns her into merely a wronged woman who wants to settle a score with a few elderly men who acted boorish towards her fifty years ago.

Much of the fun, and fright, of the book comes from trying to discover what the crime was that the Chowder Society committed, and who will escape the wrath of the avenger. Straub gives us flashbacks that reveal a group of callow young men who were dumbstruck with lust and awe at a woman named Eva Galli, a mysterious stranger who swept into Milburn and swept the young Chowder Society off their feet. In the novel, she's alluring, but mostly she's *dangerous*. She pushes the envelope of social decorum, drinking and dancing and holding wild late-night parties. Her attempts to seduce the group into joining her in her celebration of personal abandon frighten the Chowder Society, whose members liked to pretend they were worldly but in fact were painfully naïve. In their resistance of her — which turns physically violent — they unwittingly commit the crime that would haunt them for half a century.

In the movie, Eva Galli is an older woman, sexually confident, yes, but not dangerous — not even pushy. She likes the attention of the young men, but she does little to hasten their initiation into the mysteries of life. And in a critical scene, where one of the group attempts to bed her (but experiences an ill-timed bout of impotence), Eva is sensitive to his plight, supportive, and nothing like the dominating seductress of the book. When she meets her untimely end, it's hard to believe she'd wreak vengeance for what is, clearly, an accident. Without that feeling of an awesome evil presence rising up to seek revenge, *Ghost Story* the movie falls as flat as Eva's ill-fated suitor.

And since the ghost of Eva Galli, or her restless spirit, or evil *doppelganger*, or whatever she is, doesn't seem interested in anything larger than settling a personal vendetta, the remaining Chowder Society members who finally decide to seek her out before she gets them lack the dimension of heroism which animated the final chapters of Straub's book. They're not trying to confront genuine evil — as in the novel, where Eva Galli is laying waste to half the town, including lots of people who had nothing to do with her fifty years ago. Here, the Chowderites are only interested in saving their own skins, which makes for a far less compelling showdown.

Still, the movie does offer some genuine pleasures. The evil spirit, known as Eva Galli and, later, Alma Mobley, is played by Australian actress Alice Krige with warmth and genuineness. She's the most realistic character in the film — more heart than heat, though. (It would be a few years before she would convey truly bone-chilling evil in her knock-out performance as the maniacal Borg Queen in the movie *Star Trek: First Contact*.) John Houseman gives another of his thoroughly wonderful unthawed performances, and Fred Astaire is believably skittish throughout the ordeal. The brilliant and brave actor Craig Wasson, whose work is always impressive, shines as Alma Mobley's former lover. And the musical score, by Philippe Sarde, is suitably bizarre and enhances the effectiveness of those few scenes that really do exude a creepy mood.

The film, which was nominated for a Saturn Award by the Academy of Science Fiction, Fantasy, and Horror Films, divided critics. Roger Ebert gave it three stars, noting, "The movie is told with style. It goes without saying that style is the most important single element in every ghost story, since without it even the most ominous events disintegrate into silliness. And *Ghost Story*, perhaps aware that if characters talk too much they disperse the tension, adopts a very economical story-telling approach. Dialogue comes in short, straightforward sentences. Background is provided without being allowed to distract from the main event. The characters are established with quick, subtle strokes. This is a good movie."[6] The *New York Times'* Vincent Canby had a different reaction: "[As] *Ghost Story* goes on, and though the complications increase, the mystery becomes less and less mysterious until, during the final six or seven minutes, you may want to hurl a sharp instrument at the screen. You've been had. So has Mr. Straub, but I assume he was handsomely paid."[7]

Ghost stories, like beauty, are apparently in the eye (or ear) of the beholder.

The Hound of the Baskervilles

Though hardly the first detective in literary history, Sherlock Holmes is certainly the best known. For more than a century, readers worldwide have enjoyed the adventures of the British sleuth and his friend and chronicler Dr. Watson. He is one of those rare characters that has transcended his literary origins and become firmly ensconced in popular culture. Holmes's iconic get-up — his deerstalker cap, curved meerschaum pipe, and Inverness cape — is a perennial costume-party favorite, and his image can be seen on everything from movie theater screens to coffee mugs, televisions to cigarette lighters, paperback novels to lunch boxes.

When one thinks of Sherlock Holmes, the picture that comes to mind is often the genteel "private consulting detective" in deep thought behind the desk at his lodgings at 221B Baker Street, London. Holmes' famous paucity of passion makes him the perfect problem-solver, unaffected by emotion, incapable of being distracted once his mind has turned to solving a case. Holmes is the epitome of equanimity.

What's often forgotten, however, is that the flipside to Holmes' composure and decorous demeanor can also be found in the stories which make up the Sherlock Holmes canon: violence, fear, madness, and horror. Creator Arthur Conan Doyle gave his famed fictional cogitator some really terrifying cases to deal with, mysteries involving homicidal lunatics, bloodthirsty marauders, and even supernatural malefactors. While it's not wrong to remember Holmes as a figure of steadfast composure, it must be remembered that his detachment is memorable because of the chaos and evil that surround him. Conan Doyle wrote what are some of literature's greatest stories of macabre horror and brutal suspense.

Take, for example, his 1901 novel *The Hound of the Baskervilles*. The work is a favorite among Sherlockians for several reasons, not the least of which is it resurrected Holmes from an almost-decade-long hiatus. Conan Doyle, a doctor who began writing the Holmes stories to fill the empty hours in his practice while awaiting patients, had achieved great success with some early Holmes stories, which had been serialized in the British magazine *The Strand*. But he was interested in doing other writing, especially historical novels, and he felt Holmes had become something of an artistic albatross. So he appeared to kill off Holmes in a story called "The Final Problem" (1893) and didn't write another Holmes story for eight years. Eventually bowing to public pressure (and immense financial incentives from *The Strand*), he agreed to pen another tale of his super sleuth, but he placed it earlier in time, before Holmes' death, a sort of "prequel." (Conan Doyle called it "a reminiscence.")

The reaction was euphoric among the English reading public, as "eager readers lined up outside the magazine's London offices, waiting for each installment as it was published"[1] between August 1901 and April 1902. Its success was so great that Conan Doyle was persuaded to bring Holmes back, ingeniously explaining away his apparent "death" at the Falls of Reichenbach in the story "The Empty House." For the next two decades, Conan Doyle continued to write Holmes stories.

Critics and fans continue to rate *The Hound of the Baskervilles* as perhaps the greatest Holmes adventure. It's a dark and dastardly tale of murder, greed, deception, and supernatural horror. What makes the novel so much fun to read is not simply Holmes' appearance (in fact, for about a third of the book, from chapters five to eleven, Holmes is absent from the book, as Watson conducts the investigation and sends dispatches back to Holmes), but the overall story. It was based on a legend Conan Doyle had heard about a monstrous dog that patrolled the deserted, windswept Devonshire moors; he marshaled all of his storytelling skills in the service of a tightly knit tale of a family that is cursed and a small village that is terrorized by a ghostly, spectral hound. It's the perfect world in which to plant an ultra-skeptical character like Sherlock Holmes. The conflict between Holmes' cool intellectualizing and the locals' widespread embrace of lurid legends helps propel the narrative through the murky nights and fog-shrouded moors of the story.

The book begins with a scene immediately familiar to any fan of the Holmes stories, with Dr. Watson dropping by Holmes' lodgings and finding the detective in a playful, intellectually combative mood. Holmes challenges Watson to deduce, using Holmes' methods, what he can of a rugged and well-worn walking stick that had been left in Holmes' apartment by a visitor who had missed the detective. After Watson makes several logical-sounding guesses, Holmes compliments his friend's deductive faculties—

and then tells him he's all wrong. But Watson's guesses have helped Holmes determine who actually owns the stick because Watson's logic was so off the mark. In typical Holmesian style, he both belittles and praises Watson: "It may be that you are a conductor of light. Some people without possessing genius have a remarkable power of stimulating it."[2]

The stick's owner comes by (and confirms all of Holmes' deductions), seeking the detective's help in an urgent matter. The visitor, Dr. James Mortimer, says he is worried about the welfare of a man about to take over the Baskerville estate, a centuries-old property nestled in the moors of Devonshire. Why is he worried? Because of the legend, of course, which he relates by reading from an eighteenth century document detailing the horrific legacy, which began with the loutish Hugo Baskerville, kidnapper, drunk and would-be rapist, who was discovered dead on the moors in pursuit of one of his female escapees:

> But it was not the sight of her body, nor yet was it that of the body of Hugo Baskerville lying near her, which raised the hair upon the head ... it was that, standing over Hugo, and plucking at his throat, there stood a foul thing, a great black beast, shaped like a hound yet larger than any hound that ever mortal eye has rested upon. And even as they looked the thing tore the throat out of Hugo Baskerville, on which, as it turned its blazing eyes and dripping jaws upon them, the three [companions of Hugo Baskerville] shrieked with fear and rode for dear life, still screaming, across the moor. One, it is said, died that very night of by what he had seen, and the other twain were but broken men for the rest of their days.[3]

If the legend were a product of the past, Dr. Mortimer's concerns could be dismissed as so much superstitious nonsense, but he informs Holmes that the most recent resident of Baskerville Hall turned up dead two weeks ago — with a grotesque, contorted look of frozen fear on his face amid the paw prints of a gigantic beast. Intrigued, Holmes takes the case, and the rest of the novel involves the investigation of the murder as the newest Baskerville tries to make himself at home.

Conan Doyle gave his avid fans lots of scenes they had been salivating for in the great detective's comeback vehicle: Holmes as master of disguise (he hides out on the moors dressed as a tramp), Watson soberly collecting the facts of the case, the ghostly moors and Gothic-style Baskerville manor under the full moon, and the thrill of the chase. Despite the presence of Holmes, Conan Doyle keeps the story pretty dark. In the midst of his investigations of this one murder, there are further diabolical doings on

The Hound of Baskervilles

the moors, with the expected assortment of suspicious, threatening characters, including ex-cons, drunken gypsies, secretive butlers, murderous naturalists, and an oversized hound with a shiny coat — courtesy of a phosphorescent dye. And he makes credible, for as long as possible, the supernatural aspect of the story. But this being a Holmes story, logic triumphs. *The Hound of the Baskervilles* is not only a thrilling tale of suspense but also the pre-eminent example of one of Conan Doyle's favorite themes: superstition versus science, faith versus fact. Holmes never gets sucked into the world of fanciful belief that engulfed many of his Victorian contemporaries.[4]

Conan Doyle, an avid reader, world traveler, and writer of historical and "speculative" fiction, recognized the elements that make up a good story. In Sherlock Holmes, he had a credible, sober, but entertaining vehicle to explore the shadowy world of legend and folklore, and in the real-life legend on which he based *Hound*, he had all the components of page-turning fiction: murder, mysterious characters, exotic settings, and a ghostly protagonist. But in no other story does Conan Doyle exploit so fully the established conventions of nineteenth century horror fiction. Many of the subsequent Holmes stories take place exclusively in London, or in more genteel Victorian environs, but in *The Hound of the Baskervilles* Conan Doyle embraced a world of fog, folk tales, and fearful howls in the night, milking it for all it's worth. Most of the Holmes stories are classified as detective fiction but in *Hound*, Conan Doyle transcended his previous limits and discovered the artistic possibilities that lurk in the darkness. "Where there is no imagination, there is no horror,"[5] Holmes once said, a lesson learned by his creator.

As beloved as Holmes was during Conan Doyle's lifetime, even his creator could not have deduced that the detective would become one of *the* most popular fictional creations.[6] Contrary to being slavish copies of Conan Doyle's blueprint, there have been some radical reinterpretations of Holmes in print, on television, and at the cinema. Holmes has been portrayed as a drug addict (with some support from the original texts), as well as illiterate, gay, and even as a woman. He's been transported to more modern times (in a few films, he takes on the Nazis), and as recently as 2009, he was the subject of a Hollywood blockbuster in which he spent a good deal of the film with his shirt off, either in a boxing ring or a bedroom. (Holmes as a romantic lead? For some purists, that's simply going too far.)

Different Holmes fans have different favorite interpreters, of course, but on any one's short list of the most definitive and effective players must surely appear the actor Basil Rathbone, who (along with Nigel Bruce as Watson) played Holmes in 14 films. They were always good together, but they were never better than they were in their first outing, the 1939 *The Hound of the Baskervilles*. There had been several filmed version of *Hound*, beginning with a 1914 German film, and including several silent shorts. The first sound version of the classic was produced by the British studio Gainsborough Pictures in 1931. According to Hollywood legend, Darryl F. Zanuck, head of 20th Century–Fox, bumped into Rathbone at a cocktail party and told him he'd be perfect as Sherlock Holmes.[7] Fourteen films later, many Holmes fans would certainly agree.

The 1939 version, directed by Sidney Lanfield and adapted for the screen by Ernest Pascal, begins with the following words superimposed over a shadowy, craggy backdrop: "In all England there is no district more dismal than that vast expanse of primitive wasteland, the moors of Dartmoor in Devonshire."[8] There follows a haunting glimpse of an aged manor house, and then a quick cut to a well-dressed man, racing across the moors in obvious fright, as the baying of a hound is heard in the background. The man collapses, and the scene switches to a coroner's inquest where many of the details which Conan Doyle provides in Dr. Mortimer's visit to Holmes are here provided first hand, and where the key figures in the story, such as Stapleton, the naturalist, are introduced.

The next scene brings us back to 221B Baker Street, where Holmes and Watson puzzle over the walking stick left behind by Dr. Mortimer, and from there, the story mostly follows the original version. Rathbone maintains the bearing of superior intellect and dismissive certainty one expects in Holmes. His lanky physique and angular features offer a remarkable approximation of the image of Holmes in the stories, drawn by artist Sidney Paget. Watson, embodied by Bruce, is a bit more of a stretch, and to some Holmes' enthusiasts, his portrayal is the principal drawback of this and subsequent films with Rathbone. In the original stories, Watson is an accomplished medical man with a perceptive, analytical mind — not quite up to Holmes' standard, of course, but then again, no one is. Still, he's insightful and quick-thinking, courageous and highly reliable. (As the ostensible writer of the Holmes' stories, his intellect is apparent.) But the screenplay in *Hound* and the other 13 Rathbone-Bruce films makes Watson a bit of a bumbler, occasionally slow-witted, more a comic foil for Holmes than an equal partner. It's a choice that yields some dramatic satisfaction,

Sherlock Holmes matches wits with his most menacing rival in Basil Rathbone's first go-round as the super sleuth in *The Hound of the Baskervilles*.

creating more of an "odd couple" pairing — though to some Sherlockian purists it diminishes the seriousness of the canon.

As Mortimer reads the legend to Holmes, we are treated to a vivid flashback scene of Sir Hugo racing across the moor to recover the girl he had imprisoned in his manor house, and encountering the snarling hound that was said to have killed him.

Since the moor is where all the action — and answers — seem to be, that's where the movie shifts. Holmes says he's too busy to make it, so he sends Watson in his stead. (Holmes, of course, was planning to go all along, but incognito, dressed as a tramp, so he could see what *really* happens on the moor.)

From the time Watson arrives at Baskerville, things get creepy. The domestic staff, a husband and wife of longtime service, seem distant and secretive, and the husband (here called "Barryman," and played icily by the great John Carradine) is caught in the middle of the night holding a candle at a window, signaling to some shadowy figure prowling the moor. The film embraces most of the conventions of Gothic fiction that give the Conan Doyle story its appeal: an isolated mansion, a suspicious-acting domestic staff, eccentric locals, ancient ruins, a convicted murderer roaming at large, a séance, a collection of skulls in the drawing room, the persistent, blood-curdling howling from the moors, and the widespread folk belief in the legend of a homicidal hound.

The movie isn't without its lighter moments, as when Holmes dressed as a tramp confronts Watson on the moor, and demands to know who he is and why he's asking so many questions. Watson tells him, "I'm Sherlock Holmes," to which the real Holmes, removing his disguise, retorts, "Then I must be Watson!"[9] (Director Lanfield was well versed in such light moments, having directed a number of Bob Hope films in the 1930s.) However, the comic mood doesn't last long as Holmes and Watson's reunion is interrupted by the howling of the hound and the discovery of another dead body on the moor. Now that Holmes is on the scent, it's clear that the murderous business of the Baskervilles will soon be sorted out — but not before a breathless chase on the moor and a life-threatening climax.

The Hound of the Baskervilles offers lots of satisfaction to both the horror and mystery fan. Holmes' unusual deductive instincts are engagingly displayed throughout the film, and there are some wonderfully atmospheric scenes among the ancient ruins on the moor. The few scenes involving the hound, as when it mauls Sir Charles Baskerville almost to pieces until

Holmes and Watson intervene, are genuinely exciting, and the climax, featuring Holmes escaping from a locked underground crypt, emerging just in time to identify the man behind the Baskerville "legend," is a textbook murder mystery resolution.

The film was unexpectedly popular, spawning a profitable franchise for Twentieth Century–Fox and a providing a career-making turn for Rathbone, who for generations has defined the iconic detective. As one film historian has noted:

> There are moments in cinema history when there is a magical pairing of actor and role which leaves an indelible mark on screen history. One thinks of Clark Gable as Rhett Butler, Humphrey Bogart as Rick Blaine in *Casablanca*, Gloria Swanson as Norma Desmond, Charles Laughton as Quasimodo, and of course, Basil Rathbone as Sherlock Holmes.[10]

Many other actors have portrayed Holmes, from notable stage turns featuring Charlton Heston and Christopher Plummer to Nicol Williamson's much-admired, drug-dependent sleuth in the 1977 film *The Seven Percent Solution* and the critically lauded portrait of Holmes by Jeremy Brett in the series of BBC television films spanning several seasons in the 1980s. Holmes' malleability is due in part to his creator's ingenuity, giving him enough peculiarities (cocaine habit, violin playing, pipe smoking, etc.) to allow individual interpretations but rooting the character in his mesmerizing, never-wavering, iron-clad logic. Everyone would like to *be* Holmes — at least in terms of intellect. But Holmes' popularity is also due to the compelling nature of the stories in which he showcases his gifts. Many of those tales feature the dark side of humanity: addiction, jealousy, violence, murder. Perhaps it's not entirely coincidental that Holmes' popularity coincided with the real-life terrors inflicted upon the Victorian public by the serial killer Jack the Ripper. Conan Doyle knew what terrified his audience, and he knew also what gave them hope.

And in *The Hound of the Baskervilles*, he put it all together masterfully. Linking the public's rising interest in the supernatural with the rational fear of a marauding murderer, applying the tried-and-true tenants of Gothic fiction and providing a forward-looking detective (Scotland Yard reportedly appropriated many of Holmes' methods of detection), Conan Doyle ensured that the legend of a hellish hound would not disappear with the passing of the last of the Baskervilles but would instead endure as long as there were readers who craved powerfully told tales of evil and its opponents.

Jaws

One of the great appeals of the horror genre is the opportunity to face perils in fiction that one would likely never face in real life: vengeful ghosts, demonic possessions, etc. It's fun to battle, vicariously, the forces of evil that exist only in the realm of the imagination.

But in certain cases, horror writers have been able to tap into genuine, innate fears of those things that do exist in our world, and no writer has been more adept at this than Peter Benchley, whose magnum opus *Jaws* scared a generation away from the ocean. Benchley's novel was modestly successful, in terms of sales, when it was published in 1974 but director Steven Spielberg turned *Jaws* into a national phenomenon, generating hair-raising book sales figures (more than nine million copies sold in paperback after the movie was released[1]) and inaugurating the era of the "summer blockbuster" movie.

Probably because of the movie, *Jaws* has become one of the most referenced fictions in popular culture, its mix of primitivism and perennialism keeping it afloat in the public's imagination. You can be assured that any time a newspaper or website in a coastal region runs a story about a shark sighting, a reference to *Jaws* is about to surface. For Benchley, and for Spielberg, *Jaws* was a career maker. Both had been somewhat successful in their respective fields, but *Jaws* represented a breakout for each that made them household words — and a lot of money.[2]

Critically, however, there is a pretty big gap between the book and the movie. While Spielberg's film is routinely touted as one of the greatest ever made, the novel never really acquired anything more than a reputation as a competent page-turner, an ironically dubbed "beach read" that pushes the right buttons but never threatens to veer into "serious" literature. Most people know the *Jaws* story through the movie, rather than the book — which is something of a pity because the book does offer some satisfactions overlooked, or changed, by the film. And if Benchley's pride was ever wounded by the corps of reviewers who found his work more fit for the beach than the college literature syllabus, it's likely the steady string of best-selling *Jaws*-like titles he was able to build a career on (*The Deep*, *Beast*, etc.) must have offered some high-priced balm to soothe his artistic wounds.

Like the shark at the center of its story, *Jaws* the novel crosses lots of boundaries. It's got elements of horror in it; what could be more horror-inducing than being chomped to death by a great white shark? It's also a drama, with the usual pot-boiling domestic upheavals, like adulterous affairs and a cadre of murderous crooks involved in shady real estate deals. It's a suspense/thriller, featuring a mad chase against time for a rogue killer (albeit a 20-foot, two-ton perpetual-motion killer). And it's in part a work of non-fiction, with a large amount of information about the evolutionary biology and habits of the shark. Benchley himself has suggested that the work grew out of actual instances of human-shark encounters, and that the idea of a shark book had long been on the struggling writer's mind:

> I was very lucky to have a literary agent. As a favor to my father [novelist and playwright Nathaniel Benchley], one of his agents ... had taken me on when I was sixteen. [She] encouraged me to have lunch with editors from publishing houses. I kept two ideas ready for those lunches. One idea was for a non-fiction book, a history of pirates, who had always interested me. The other was for a fictional book about a great white shark that terrorizes a resort community. Folded in my wallet was a yellowed 1964 clipping from the *New York Daily News* that reported the capture of a 4,550-pound great white shark off Long Island. I would show it at the first hint of disbelief that such an animal could exist, let alone that it might attack boats and eat people.[3]

Benchley has also spoken about the influence his boyhood summers had on the germination of his shark book: "When I was a boy, I spent my summers on the island of Nantucket, whose waters were well populated by sharks.... [O]n hot and windless days, the Atlantic Ocean surround-ing Nantucket sprouted shark fins like asparagus spears. To me, they spoke of the unknown, the mysterious, of menace and adventure."[4] Another influence on the genesis of *Jaws* is a series of real-life shark attacks that took place off the Jersey Shore in the summer of 1916, stunning the country and creating a mini-frenzy — an episode that is mentioned in the novel.

The plot of the book is simple: A summer resort town, "Amity" finds its seasonal business threatened by the appearance of a man-eating shark who devours a couple of swimmers. The town authorizes a curmudgeonly old sea captain to undertake to bag the beast and he sets out with the police chief and a young shark expert as his mates. Those who know only the *Jaws* story through the movie version might be surprised to discover that much of the book's drama takes place on shore. The novel devotes a lot of narrative energy to the marriage of Police Chief Brody and his wife Ellen, permanent residents of Amity. Unfortunately, the couple (soon to be a trio, of sorts, as Ellen and the young shark scientist Matt Hooper start making waves) must constantly compete with the shark for the reader's attention. It's not really a fair fight. The scenes involving the shark are usually pulse-poundingly rendered and imaginatively written, while the *Peyton Place*-style antics of the bored middle-aged couple often limp along in a melodramatic, "romantic novel" style: "Summers were bad times for Ellen Brody, for in summer she was tortured by thoughts she didn't want to think — thoughts of chances missed and lives that could have been."[5] Or here, in a passage that could have been cribbed from Jacqueline Susann: "There was a full length mirror in the bedroom and she stood before it, examining herself. Were the goods good enough? Would the offer be accepted? She could not bear the thought of rejection."[6]

Fortunately, the shark refuses to be upstaged, so the reader is regularly plunged back into the realm of "The Great Fish [that] moved silently through the waters, propelled by short sweeps of its crescent tail."[7] The narrative really ramps up when the story becomes, simply, a man-against-beast fable. Or, in this case, men against beast; Benchley has a trio of characters go after the mighty and meaty great white. And it's in the last third of the book that we finally get to meet the irascible veteran of many a fish fight, the crotchety old salt Quint, a character with more than a few similarities to another famous literary captain chasing another great white beast of the sea.

The echoes of Ahab resound throughout the quest to catch the shark. On board the *Orca* are Quint, Brody, and Hooper. Under the sea (though sometimes surfacing simply to fill the onlookers with awe) is the great white. Those who remember their "American literature of the nineteenth century" seminars will already have figured out what will happen to poor Quint when he exchanges his taciturn manner for a monomania to catch the shark, uttering such epithets as "Come up, you Devil! You prick!" or "I am going to kill that fish," adding in an aside to a startled Brody, "We have no choice." So Quint/Ahab is engaged in a battle with the fish ascribed by fate, while Brody/Ishmael can only stand idly by and hope for the best. (We sense Hooper's fate also is sealed once his main function in the narrative — as Ellen's lover — ceases to have any relevance on board the *Orca*.)

Wisely, Benchley doesn't overplay his hand by trying to invest the narrative with lots of Melville-esque philosophical significance. Nothing wrong with reminding readers of *Moby Dick* to add a little intellectual heft but best to know when you're in the shallows and when you're in the deep, and Benchley isn't looking to write the great American novel of his generation. His fish goes deep, but the author stays mostly above the literary water line, focusing on the thrill of the chase and the scenery-chewing (literally) finale.

Critics were all over the map when *Jaws* came out. Some loved it, some hated it, some were indifferent. C.J. Bergman, writing in the *New York Times Book Review*, complained, "Briney connections, occasional florid or sentimental lapses, [and] stark manipulations impair the narrative.... Even for a fish story, *Jaws* may be a mite malodorous."[8] *Library Journal* found the work "taut and exciting."[9]

It's not really accurate to say the book suffers in comparison to the movie, because if it hadn't been for the movie, the book would have surely dropped off the radar as just another potboiler with an exotic villain (or hero, depending on your perspective). So the book owes its second life to the movie — an irony Benchley once addressed.

> I called [my agent] and told her the title. "That's terrible," she said.
> "What's it mean?"
> "Beats me," I replied. "But it sure is short."
> Though no one liked it much, no one had a better idea, so no one protested.
> After all ... what we have here is a first novel, and nobody reads first novels, anyway. Besides, it's a first novel about a fish, for God's sake, and who cares? At least it's done.
> Furthermore, there wasn't a chance that anybody would ever make a movie out of the book. I knew it was impossible to catch and train a great white shark. Everybody else knew that Hollywood's special-effects technology was nowhere near sophisticated enough to make a believable model of a great white shark."[10]

In little over a year after publication, millions of moviegoers around the world would beg to differ.

The naturalist E.O. Wilson once said, "We don't fear our predators.

Now a Terrifying Motion Picture!

It's man (Robert Shaw) vs. shark in the teeth-clenching film adaptation of Peter Benchley's best-seller *Jaws*.

We are transfixed by them."[11] That might help explain the phenomenon that *Jaws* became: a national fixation and cinematic blockbuster. Coinciding with a couple of much-hyped shark attacks in the summer of 1975, and splashed across the cover of *Time* magazine, *Jaws* the movie became *Jaws* the sensation. The movie's box office take when adjusted for inflation exceeds $1 billion. That's the easy part to quantify. Far less quantifiable is the impact the movie made on the psyches of a generation of summer moviegoers who still think twice before wading into the water. An awful lot of ink has been spilled by critics and sociologists trying to account for its popularity. The credit is generally split between two main factors: (1) the primitive allure of the shark, a creature as at home in the depths of the human imagination as in the depths of its actual habitat; and (2) a brilliantly crafted film that benefited from some inspired casting, state of the art (for then) special effects, and a visionary genius behind the camera.

Many great films have made it to the screen trailed by tales of behind-the-scenes disasters and budget-busting filmmaking: *The Wizard of Oz* endured a change of directors in mid-shoot, *Casablanca* was being rewritten daily, with actors unsure what lines they'd be uttering as they showed up on the set, and *Apocalypse Now* was wildly over-budget even as lead actor Martin Sheen had a heart attack during jungle filming. *Jaws* belongs in that storied pantheon of troubled films, with the producers constantly expecting the studio to pull the plug because of cost over-runs and the technical crew constantly torpedoed by a series of mechanical sharks that refused to behave on cue.[12]

Yet it all came together in the final cut, and the only disasters that the viewer is mindful of are the ones taking place on screen, as the shark destroys a town's economy, several unfortunate swimmers, a crusty sea captain and a full-sized fishing boat.

The screenplay by Benchley and Carl Gottlieb retains the heart of Benchley's novel but tosses overboard much of the domestic drama, such as Ellen's affair with Hooper and the Amity mayor's nefarious dealings with underworld figures. The film opens as the book does, with a midnight swim by a young woman whose lover is too inebriated to join her. Good thing for him — all he has to deal with is a killer hangover. She gets the killer shark.

That first scene is still one of the most vivid and compelling openings in cinema history, accompanied by John Williams' haunting *Jaws* theme — a steady, alternating two-note riff that pounds like an increasingly accelerated heartbeat as the shark gets closer to its human prey. Spielberg used a series of ropes attached to the swimmer's body to help replicate the jerking motions and spastic movement that would occur in a real shark attack (and the young woman in the scene reportedly broke a rib during the filming, adding genuine distress to her screams for assistance).[13] After watching her swim leisurely, freely in the water, enjoying a moment of meditative languor, she (and the viewer) is jerked violently, repeatedly, underwater until that stunning final plunge from which she does not emerge. Then, once again, absolute stillness.

The script moves efficiently through Chief Brody's (Roy Scheider) campaign to close the beach amid the strong objections of the town fathers, led by Amity's mayor (played by Murray Hamilton throughout like a man in dire need of a drink and a cigarette). Brody is aided by Matt Hooper (Richard Dreyfuss, in his breakthrough role), whose zeal to spot a great white is counter-balanced with his respect for the damage such a beast can inflict. Catching the shark proves to be too big a job for any garden-variety fisherman, so the town agrees to the exorbitant fee ($10,000) of Quint, a cantankerous figure who pledges to catch and kill the beast. In a movie filled with terrific and memorable performances, Robert Shaw's Quint stands out. Shaw gives one of the greatest performances ever recorded on celluloid. His Quint has the requisite distance to remain mysterious but reveals flashes of sadism, mania, and just enough human warmth to make us care about him. The sophisticated British actor did fine work in a number of other excellent films (*The Sting, The Taking of Pelham One Two Three*), but nothing in his body of work prepares one for the searing authenticity of his obsessive and unsettling Quint. It is a performance for the ages (his recitation about the sinking of the U.S.S. *Indianapolis* is one of the finest monologues in movie history — re-written by the actor himself, who was also a novelist and a playwright).

Spielberg has made a remarkably human film about a shark. There are dozens of wonderful moments of warmth, humor, and fear that the director has coaxed from this horror story. The dinner scene when Hooper joins the Brodys (Ellen's memorable line "My husband tells me you're in sharks") is a great example of how Spielberg can invest even the smallest moments with narrative significance. We see at their dinner table what we'll see in the climactic moments: Brody's neurosis perpetually battling his sense of duty; Hooper's idealism in conflict with the real world; Ellen's ambivalence about her husband's profession, a lifetime of worry over a law enforcement spouse bubbling to the surface in the face of this crisis; and the mystery and power of the shark, already casting a pall over a quiet evening on shore like the shadows that darken the chief's furrowed brow. Spielberg's tight focus on the small, numerous human moments (like Brody's childlike expression of glee at finally learning how to tie a sheepshank knot) keep this from simply being a "monster movie" and turn it into something that illuminates the human condition. As one critic noted, "*Jaws*, while clearly proud of its B-movie roots, isn't merely a movie about a giant killer shark, it's about people struggling against this beast and what it does to their lives."[14]

Yet the great white shark at the center of this film is a monster, and *Jaws* is an incredibly suspenseful film, pushing all the buttons that taut and well-crafted horror films do. Spielberg comes at the viewer from so many angles that even repeated viewings do little to prepare one fully for the shocks along the way. We're underwater, watching a shark's tooth being pulled from the hull of a boat when the severed head of the boat's captain startlingly tumbles forward. We're on the beach, watching from the shore as a plume of blood and spray emanate from a young boy's inflatable life raft adrift in the water (with the real horror of the moment coming from the dolly shot that rapidly closes in on Brody's stricken expression). We're on deck of a boat, drifting quietly, ladling chum overboard when the shark's gaping maw menacingly emerges from the blue stillness. And we're in a shark cage, watching helplessly, waiting, scanning the watery depths for telltale signs of the two-ton man-eater. Spielberg's previous work on the suspense film *Duel* (about a mysterious, menacing truck driver) taught him a few tricks about creating tension, but his work on *Jaws* is absolutely *sui generis*, with no clear precedent for the wide variety and effectiveness of *Jaws'* arsenal of scare-inducers.

For a movie that was so identified with a particular time and place — the mid-1970s and an island off the Eastern Seaboard — *Jaws* has aged remarkably well. There's nothing in the film today that seems dated (with the exception, perhaps, of Murray Hamilton's plaid, double-breasted suits). *Psycho* kept some people from ever feeling comfortable in the shower. *The Shining* made some people think twice before booking a room at a lodge in the middle of winter. And *Jaws* is no doubt firmly in the minds of many beachgoers whose summer escapades have forever been tainted by Benchley and Spielberg's plunge into the imaginative depths.

The Masque of the Red Death

To borrow a hypothetical situation from the world of science fiction, imagine that a Martian has landed on Earth with the intention of learning about humanity's interest in something called "horror fiction." How should this Martian begin his education?

There are lots of ways to answer that, but perhaps there is only one author whose works might emerge as the consensus choice, a troubled and tormented genius whose writing has shocked and entertained readers for almost two centuries.

"From Childhood's hour, I have not been as others were, I have not seen as others saw, I could not bring my passions from a common spring"[1] once wrote the visionary short story writer, poet, and critic Edgar Allan Poe.

To the fan of horror, whether in print or on film, Poe's name looms like a haunted hilltop mansion on the landscape of modern terror. His work in the early to mid–nineteenth century established many of the conventions that governed the "popular tale" for more than a century. He is considered one of the founding fathers of the short story, the inventor of the detective story, and the originator of a number of horror motifs that still inform modern fiction. His work limned the psychic caverns of mankind, and his dark imaginings exploded from his pen like detonations of some horrific, repressed memory. Many of Poe's contemporaries thought him mad, and there are critics today who assess Poe's work as more the product of derangement than conscientious art.

But Poe was the consummate craftsman, building his eerie oeuvre brick by blackened brick. His artistry is all too easy to dismiss because of the bleak, fantastical nature of his stories. Few readers pay much attention to Poe's craft, gaping instead at the monstrous and tortured souls who populate his "Tales of Mystery and Imagination." Poe's extraordinary linguistic virtuosity often gets overlooked in the darkened pits, among the rats, in the crypt, or buried in the walled sepulcher of his stories. He often takes his characters' breath away, right before our eyes, and we experience something of the same sensation. It's a thrill to read Poe at his best — and a great relief when the story ends. Few writers exert such a tight grip on their readers' hearts and minds. Generations of horror writers have credited Poe with making them want to write fiction in the first place, and he remains wildly popular today, a standard in college literature courses and the first choice for many readers on dark and stormy nights.

So, back to our friend, the Martian. Which of Poe's works should he be given first? "The Tell-Tale Heart" is probably his most anthologized story, blending black humor with suspense and homicide. Then there's "The Pit and the Pendulum," which elevates sensory deprivation to skin-crawling aesthetic heights (or depths, as the case may be). "The Fall of the House of Usher" shows Poe at his most psychologically rich. "The Black Cat" is full of the supernatural — and no small measure of grotesqueness. And, for purists, the poem "The Raven" might be the prototypical Poe production: a stormy night, a mysterious visitor, a tribute to enduring love and the overactive imagination, a melding of dream and reality. They're all great choices.

But I'd hand that Martian a copy of "The Masque of the Red Death."

"Masque" not only showcases most of Poe's gifts, it's also a singular story in a canon that often cannibalizes itself. It contains some moments, themes, and writing that stand out as truly different from anything Poe had ever done, and its compression (one of the shorter of his classic tales) is a marvel of swift efficacy. Poe never surpassed this short masterpiece, and there's not much to compare it to in the whole of American literature, though it borrows freely from several American and European traditions.[2]

"The Masque of the Red Death" was composed in 1842, as Poe was entering the most productive phase of his writing life, having just published "The Murders in the Rue Morgue" and working on "The Pit and the Pendulum," "The Tell-Tale Heart," "The Black Cat," and "The Gold-Bug," each of which would soon be published. "Masque" appeared in three different magazines between April and June of 1842 (it was common for writers to sell the same story to multiple publications) and has remained among the most popular stories by the macabre master storyteller.

The plot is simple, even by Poe's standards. (Poe was always much more interested in effect and mood than plot.) The rich Prince Prospero has decided to retreat from a deadly pestilence that's ravaging his dominions, so he gathers 1,000 of his fellow aristocrats and relocates to an abbey on his property, "an extensive and magnificent structure, the creation of the prince's own eccentric yet august taste. A strong and lofty wall girdled it in."[3] These "hale and light-hearted" guests are treated to a masqued ball in a garishly decorated suite of rooms, with bizarre lighting and exotic music, and the everpresent and disquieting chiming of a huge ebony clock. Amid the revelry, with the plague seemingly locked outside the walls of the abbey, a guest suddenly appears at midnight, dressed as a corpse and moving silently about the party, unnerving first the other guests and then, finally, the host, who is offput by this figure, "tall and gaunt, and shrouded from head to foot in the habiliments of the grave."[4]

The prince demands to know who this interloper is, but his face remains hidden behind a mask "which concealed the visage made so nearly to resemble the countenance of a stiffened corpse that the closest scrutiny must have difficulty in detecting the cheat."[5] But the prince will not be disobeyed. After he orders his subjects to unmask the man — they don't, however, because they're struck dumb with fright — he draws a dagger and prepares to lunge at the mystery figure, who has walked away from the prince, oblivious to his threats. But the figure turns suddenly and faces the prince. "There was a sharp cry — and the dagger dropped gleaming upon the sable carpet, upon which, instantly afterwards, fell prostrate in death the Prince Prospero."[6] As well as his guests, who begin falling one by one until "Darkness and Decay and the Red Death held illimitable dominion over all."[7]

On its surface, it's got most of what readers who love horror stories seek in a scary tale: weird settings, exotic characters, the threat of violence, a supernatural element, and a mysterious, all-powerful villain. It's also one of Poe's most visually arresting stories. His descriptions of each of the chambers in the abbey, the costumes and masques of the attendees, the candle-lit effects on the walls, and even the music filtering through the suites go well beyond the garden-variety descriptions the hasty writer often employed in his stories. Poe seems to have taken extra care in this story to help the reader *see* what he's describing. Some critics have pointed to "Masque" as Poe's most "cinematic" story.

And despite the apparent mystery of the figure who brings the party to a screeching halt, Poe's villain here is not a supernatural figure at all, but rather the inescapable presence of Death. Poe hasn't written a tale about ghosts, haunted houses, homicidal maniacs or vengeful zombies rising from the grave—his stock in trade, up to this time—but rather the villain we all must confront. The prince and his guests try to wall themselves up in a sanctuary where Death has no dominion—an effort that earns the Reaper's mockery and disdain. Despite the raging pestilence outside, the revelers laugh, drink, and dance, wholly oblivious until the hourly chiming of the clock, which dampens their moods for a moment. But when the echo of the clock's chimes "fully cease, a light laughter at once" pervades the gathering, and thoughts of darkness are banished from the scene—until the arrival of Death himself.

This combination of cinematic-style description of the scene (in fact, the whole story is almost *all* description) and the timeless theme of death's final victory over human life makes "The Masque of the Red Death" seem like an attractive candidate for translation to the big screen. And when that film was finally produced in 1964, it brought together a director, actor and writer who were perfect for each other. That combination resulted in a film that does justice to the spirit of Poe's masterpiece, as well as standing on its own as a triumph of horror cinema.

In 1960, the independent director Roger Corman began filming what would become a series of profitable films based on Poe's works. Corman, who began his directing career in 1955, quickly established himself as a master of economy—with both budgets and time (he reportedly filmed *The Little Shop of Horrors* in two days). Beginning with *House of Usher* in 1960, Corman worked his way through some of Poe's best known yarns, with 1964's *The Masque of the Red Death* considered by many to be his finest work. But all of Corman's Poe adaptations are worth watching, despite the obvious cost-cutting production values (e.g., the same sets being used for multiple locations, cheesy special effects, formulaic musical scores, etc.). And of course, there's Vincent Price, who acted in over a half-dozen of Corman's Poe films.

One of the things that sets *The Masque of the Red Death* apart from other films in the Corman-Poe series is the budget. American International Pictures, which financed the films, shot it in England to save money. As Corman has explained, "There was an English tax law that took the money from the English distribution of the film and refunded a portion of it to the production company—if the film was shot in England."[8] AIP used some of the savings to extend the shoot from the typical three weeks to five weeks. In addition, the sets from the historical drama *Becket* had become available to Corman, and he and his crew made the most of the elaborate settings, which were just perfect for the Byzantine ball thrown by Prince Prospero. The overall result is a film that captures the lush exoticism of Poe's narrative, filling the screen with as rich a palate of colors as Poe's linguistic tapestry suggests. As one critic noted, "With its lavish-looking production values, *Masque of the Red Death* is one of the most beautiful horror films ever made. Production designer Daniel Haller did his most splendid job on the sets, retooling the existing flats to conform to Poe's story.... English cinematographer Nicolas Roeg used lush color to contrast the form and look of the images with the horrifying content of what the images conveyed."[9]

Corman has said that he considers *Masque* to be the finest of his Poe films, citing the additional time he had to bring the final product more closely in line with his vision of Poe's masterpiece. The film is a showcase for many of Corman's cinematic trademarks, such as his regular use of long tracking shots, his shadowy lighting, his deliberate, measured pacing, and his odd-angle close-ups. "My directing style," he once explained, "is to try to be as innovative as I can without becoming obtrusive.... I like to use a lot of moving camera positions, move the actors, come up with as interesting a composition as I can."[10] Such a technique pays real dividends in *Masque* because so much of the movie takes place in a fixed location. Like Poe, Corman seeks to convey mood over narrative sophistication or complicated plot contrivances, aiming at what the director calls "a certain ominous quality."[11]

In order to flesh out a full-length film from Poe's rather slender story, the *Masque* screenplay grafts a few scenes from Poe's story "Hop-Frog" onto the main story of Prince Prospero's defiant show in the presence of the Red Death. These borrowed scenes feature a dwarfish man, Hop Frog, and his young lover, who entertains the crowd with her exotic dancing. Hop Frog's' diminutive stature adds an air of exoticism to the already-bizarre proceedings, and the revenge he takes on his enemies in Poe's story provides one of the most striking images in the film *Masque*, where he convinces a pompous, cruel nobleman to dress as a gorilla and then sets him aflame in his costume. Another major change to Poe's original includes the introduction of a virtuous young peasant girl named Francesca, who will come to represent unsullied good in the world of privileged corruption. But the film captures the overall surreal sense of partying-amid-plague that makes Poe's story so uncomfortably compelling.

The film opens at night in a deserted, scraggly field. An old beggar

The Masque of the Red Death

woman is gathering sticks. She walks by a hooded figure in red, sitting under a tree, thumbing through a deck of Tarot cards. He hands her a white rose that instantly turns blood red — great visual shorthand for Poe's description of how the Red Death almost instantly corrupts healthy tissue into bloodied viscera. Visually, the scene is striking, with the red robes of Death standing out amid the bleak blues and grays of the desolate field. And in another departure from the original, here the Red Death speaks. When he hands the old woman the rose, he says, in a calm, almost soothing baritone, "Take this to your village. Tell them the day of deliverance is at hand."[12]

The scene then shifts to an ornate carriage carrying Prince Prospero, which stops at a poor peasant village,. The prince invites the villagers to his planned feast, at which they'll be allowed "to eat the discarded scraps" of the well-heeled guests. This engenders some snide comments by a couple of peasants, who the prince orders seized and executed. But the young and

The party gets a little out of hand in Roger Corman's 1964 version of Edgar Allan Poe's classic tale "The Masque of the Red Death."

doe-eyed Francesca intervenes, and asks for mercy. The prince, pretending mercy, tells her to choose which of the two men should be spared — the other is to be promptly killed. This mini-drama is interrupted by a scream from the old woman in the first scene, whose face is scarlet and covered in drops of blood. Fearful of contagion, the prince order the entire village burned, and he seizes Francesca and brings her to his castle for the party. As he departs, the camera lingers over the destruction of the village: scenes of robed peasants afire, and close-ups of burning crucifixes. Prospero, it would appear, is devilishly evil, seeming to take great delight in his ability to destroy. (Our suspicions are confirmed when he orders Francesca to remove the cross from around her neck, and "never wear it again!")

So, unlike the Poe story, where we know almost nothing about the prince, from the outset the viewer is already rooting against him. He's pure villainy. This changes the theme of *Masque* from "In the end, Death gets everyone" to "The evil bring destruction on themselves" (and, as we'll discover by the end of the film, everyone they touch). Corman's film version has added moral weight to Poe's coldly ambiguous tale.

As in the story, there is a magnificent clock that chimes the hour (and in a wonderful bit of innovative set dressing, the swinging pendulum of the clock is an executioner's double-bladed axe — a perfect metaphor for Time, the killer). Throughout the film, Price gives one of his best performances. He exudes the confidence and creepiness necessary to believe he is more Mephistopheles than merely proud potentate. He revels in being the smartest guy in the room, as we see when he humiliates his guests, making them crawl about the marbled dance floor like a pig, or braying jackass, or worm, as he laughs heartily. His failure to corrupt Francesca engenders first confusion, then tight-jawed anger, and his obdurateness about being omnipotent is displaced by profound fear in the presence of the Red Death. In a role that could easily have degenerated into lots of mugging and histrionics, Price gives a nuanced performance, making his villainy genuinely frightening because it's accompanied by such intelligence and suavity.

Price even manages to work in a hint of anger at the fates for having made him the man (or devil) he is. His is not just the blind anger of Satan in *Paradise Lost*, it has a large portion of Macbeth's self-loathing in it. In fact, there is a scene between Prospero and the woman vying for his affection, Juliana (played by Hazel Court) that strongly recalls Macbeth's scenes with Lady Macbeth, as the two discuss their guest Francesca. Like the

The Masque of the Red Death

murdered King Duncan, Francesca also represents decency, honor, and God—all of which are irksome to Prince Prospero, mere impediments to achieving one's true station in life. One of Price's gifts to filmgoers in general, and to fans of the horror genre in particular, is his ability to transmit a kind of Shakespearean pathos in even his thinly drawn characters, often finding a tragic dimension of inevitability in their ruin. Watching *Masque*, one has to continually remind one's self that Price is originating this role, as Poe's prince was little more than a spectator in the original story.

Prospero's attempts to inculcate Francesca into his cult of satanic worship do threaten, at moments, to turn Poe's simple study of the inescapability of death no matter how elaborate our distractions, into a modern morality play. The script occasionally burdens Price with some elementary-sounding proverbs about the death of God and the foolishness of believing in a deity whose presence is belied by a ruthless-appearing world. But Corman has the good sense to stage these didactic "God is dead" lectures amid compelling cinematic stage business (as when Prospero takes Francesca into the courtyard and demonstrates the skills of his resident falcon. He tells her that to train a falcon, you first have to "break its will" by sewing its eyes shut. After that, the bird understands the true value of sight; and Christians, he says, are going through the world with their eyes sewn shut. As this scene proceeds, we get to see the falcon chase down its prey in midair, and bring it back to Prospero, bloodied and subdued.

But *Masque* isn't a "message" movie. Like Poe's original, the film mostly thrives on mesmerizing tableaux: the sight of a reveler in a gorilla suit, hanging from a chandelier, costume aflame; the transfigurations of the party guests in mid-dance from healthy revelers to crimson-skinned victims; and the final scene of many avatars of death, all robed in different colors, recounting their weary night of calling souls to their final destination. In that last image, mythic yet mundane, darkly comic yet cosmic, the film terminates in a manner Poe would surely have endorsed.

The Night Stalker

Imagine you live in a town that's being ravaged by a vampire and that the police and other agencies are unable to protect you from this creature of the night, who operates by his own dark instincts. That's a particular type of horror, yes?

All right, imagine that you alone know that this vampire exists, and despite your evidence, which is considerable and credible, no one in authority takes you seriously? That's a kind of horror, too.

Finally, imagine that your personal and professional life is in shambles, that your once-promising career has degenerated into a second-tier, tenuous existence in your profession and you subsist on too much Scotch whiskey and takeout food and not nearly enough sleep or dry cleaning. There's an aspect of horror in that as well.

Combine all of the above and *voila!*— you've got one of the more entertaining works of horror fiction in the last few decades, the book, movie-of-the-week and television series known as *The Night Stalker*.

Horror and science fiction are famous for their cults and subdivisions of fans who embrace particular authors, monsters, directors, or even formats (such as graphic novels or pulp magazines). These cults help sustain works that might otherwise have fallen into obscurity, and their zeal for their subject matter leads to fanzines, websites, clubs, even conventions. And while there is no accounting for just *why* some of these cultural products attract a devoted following, there's no denying the power of such enthusiasms to sustain interest. From H.P. Lovecraft to F.W. Murnau, from *Star Trek* to *The Rocky Horror Picture Show*, certain artists and works have inspired an affection in the face of often-widespread neglect or even derision.

The Night Stalker can proudly takes its place in that pantheon of works whose continuing appeal might seem lost on all but the most devout. Born of an unpublished novel that by its author's own admission merely aspired to the level of "airport reading," and introduced to the public in a movie-of-the-week that was shot in only 18 days, the *Night Stalker* franchise (a handful of original novels and stories, two TV movies, 20 hour-long television episodes, and an aborted television "re-boot") continues to entertain and inspire certain fans of supernatural entertainment, some of whom consider the series among the best television has ever produced in the horror–sci-fi genre.

It was a meteoric rise and just as quick a descent that initially marked the *Night Stalker* phenomenon. A made-for-television movie, based on the unpublished novel, aired on ABC in 1972 and, shockingly (to the programming honchos at the network), became the highest-rated television movie ever broadcast. That led to a sequel the next year, titled *The Night Strangler* (but featuring the same basic cast of characters and premise as the original). The following year saw the weekly series, which garnered lukewarm critical reviews and even less approval from viewers, making it one of the lowest rated programs of the year. ABC cancelled it in 1975 after 20 episodes.

But like the vampire villain of the original *Night Stalker* movie, the show resisted extinction — if only in the fond reminiscences of its small but loyal followers. But then the series was rerun in various television markets late at night, released on VHS and then DVD, and re-shown on the Sci-Fi channel and the BBC, all the while attracting new viewers. In the course of this extended semi-hibernation, a comic book series dedicated to *The Night Stalker* was started, the original novel was released after almost three decades out of print, new novels were written extending the original premise, short story anthologies dedicated to *The Night Stalker* were published, and a new television incarnation was launched, with more books and graphic novels on the way.[1]

So what is it about the franchise that has made it so beloved and endearing? Well, there's the supernatural element of course, with the original novel featuring a vampiric villain and the television episodes showcasing all manner of supernatural menace. And then there's the theme, generally the same in all the books and episodes: a lone voice shouting in the darkness, trying to get the authorities to take action to stop further bloodshed or mayhem. But mostly, there's one of the most engaging and memorable characters in modern horror literature, a hero who is anything but heroic, an almost-has-been who never quite was, an idealist with a short temper, an empty wallet, a wrinkled suit and a body to match.

Nobody brings more indignation and indigestion to his work—in this case, muckraking journalism—than the inimitable Carl Kolchak.

"He was seedy, gross, aggressive, slightly drunk, and a general hindrance to all of us,"[2] writes Jeff Rice in the prologue to *The Night Stalker*, the novel that gave us Kolchak in his first adventure. Rice sets up the premise that he actually met Kolchak, a disheveled and hard-drinking newspaper reporter on the downside of his career, in Las Vegas, and that Kolchak convinced him to take a look at a cache of notes recording what he claimed was "the story behind the greatest manhunt in the history of Las Vegas."[3] Rice agreed to examine the notes, and what he presents in *The Night Stalker* is reportedly Kolchak's transcription of those notes and tape recordings, along with Rice's occasional editorial insertions and summary of events.

The book begins with the reprint of a letter from Kolchak to Rice, where he entreats Rice to meet with him to go over his material on the case. "While I can remain sober, I am going to try to get it all down on tape and in print. If you don't believe it—OK. If no one else does—also OK. It's no skin off my nose."[4] That's Kolchak—passionate but also aloof, engaged but a loner, craving personal attention but also oblivious to the rest of the world. His contradictory nature, coupled with his self-awareness of his numerous personal failings, make him oddly endearing.

Fortunately for fans of horror fiction, Kolchak really has stumbled upon the story of a lifetime, and it's a pretty gruesome one. Several young, single women — most on the lower rungs of Vegas showgirl life — have disappeared, or been found murdered. What links all of these victims—and what sets Kolchak's newshound instincts into overdrive—is the strange coincidence of each corpse having had its blood drained (coupled with discreet bite marks on every neck). Long before the investigators begin to take seriously the claim that the murders are vampiric in nature, Kolchak sounds the alarm, arguing with the local cops, the coroner, and even the FBI that the killer is one of the army of the undead.

Of course, no one believes him. That becomes the leitmotif of the entire book: Kolchak the sentry, warning those on high of a grim danger and the bureaucrats who run the system turning a deaf ear—or worse, threatening to ban him altogether from covering the story. The book is really a celebration of journalistic inquiry and the great spirit of muckraking. The more Kolchak discovers that confirms his theory, the more the authorities dismiss those ridiculous-sounding theories. Some of the best parts of the book involve Kolchak's protestations against his newspaper publisher's willingness to go along with the police and suppress information about the murders so as not to alarm the public. Kolchak is a real "The public has a right to know" kind of guy, but he keeps bumping up against short-sighted authoritarian figures, like his editor, who tells him, "That's the way it is. Stop trying to change the whole world! Learn to live in it like everyone else."[5]

But Kolchak isn't the only one choosing to live by a different set of rules. The vampire killer, a mysterious "foreign gentleman" named Janos Skorzeny, continues to wreak his campaign of terror in Sin City. In Skorzeny, Rice has constructed a fairly by-the-numbers vampire: super strength, bad breath, chronologically much older than his appearance indicates, a need to feed on human blood and to sleep in a coffin filled with the dirt of his native land. But despite his rather commonplace characteristics (for a vampire, that is), there are some great scenes of Skorzeny being cornered by the police, only to escape in a whirlwind of violence. Skorzeny lifts and throws bodies out of his way, twists necks and arms like he's opening a beer bottle, throttles attack dogs, breaks through doors and fences, and absorbs point-blank bullet fusillades — without breaking a sweat. Rice shows readers the frenzy and anger in the trapped vampire, his utter disregard for human life and his single-minded pursuit of life-giving plasma.

But even vampires have their vulnerable spots, and so Kolchak, armed with wooden stake, holy water, and crucifix, finally confronts Skorzeny in the dawn's early light at his lair on the outskirts of Vegas. "Without thinking, I shoved my crucifix at him and he pulled his hand back with a hiss, shielding his face. As quickly as I could, I dug my tubes of Holy Water out of my coat pocket and emptied them on his head." As Kolchak (and all readers of vampire fiction) knows, that's a pretty combustible mix: "He shrieked and clawed at his face.... Skorzeny started to foam and bubble before our eyes."[6]

It's a satisfying, if predictable, end to the manhunt. *The Night Stalker* is not "serious literature," nor does it pretend to be. As Rice has explained, "All I wanted to do was create a 'good read' of the type I thought I would find entertaining; something for people to use to kill time in airports, on planes, or when stuck overnight in a strange town."[7]

Rice's unpublished novel was sent to an agent, who also happened to represent the veteran television and horror fiction writer Richard Matheson (*Twilight Zone, Star Trek*). The agent interested Matheson in adapting the novel, and then sent it to a programming executive at ABC, who approved

Now a Terrifying Motion Picture!

Darren McGavin unleashes another weapon in the arsenal of the lovably disheveled Carl Kolchak as he faces off against a vampire in *The Night Stalker*.

the deal for a television movie.[8] It's impossible to say if the novel *The Night Stalker*—originally titled *The Kolchak Papers*—would have found an audience without the 1972 television movie (the novel was finally published the following year). But there's no denying that the movie created a genuine, if short-lived, fascination for Carl Kolchak and his dogged, dingy approach to supernatural crime investigation.

The Night Stalker

Though lacking the budget and production values of a major theatrical release, the *Night Stalker* telemovie is a minor masterpiece, a fun, thrilling, scary, and well-acted movie that has proved worthy of its huge initial audience. Many film critics today all but ignore the movie in their rankings of best horror movies of all time, but *The Night Stalker* remains thoroughly enjoyable and satisfying. From the opening frames, where we see McGavin as a wrinkled, unshaved Carl Kolchak in a T-shirt, cracking open a beer and settling in for a late night in his shabby surroundings while a tape recorder spools out the beginnings of his incredible tale, the movie quickly establishes the major characters and conflicts (Kolchak and his bosses at the newspaper, Kolchak and the police, Kolchak and healthy living) and the story never bogs down.

The film showcases the glitz and glamour of the Las Vegas strip, with its brilliant lights and less-than-brilliant population of gamblers, hookers, and transients. After the first attack, which happens about a minute into the film, Kolchak is called back from vacation, and we get to see him and his editor, Vincenzo, cross swords as soon as he walks into the newsroom. (The veteran reporter scoffs at being called back for what he sees as a routine story.)

Yet murder victims keep turning up, and Kolchak does too, taking pictures of the victims and sniffing around the morgue for inside information. His rather sensational accounts of these early murders earn the wrath of Vincenzo (played by Simon Oakland, who turned in a memorable performance as the psychiatrist in *Psycho*), who admonishes him, "I expect you to report, not come up with fairy tales!"[9] Director John Llewellyn Moxley sets all the plates spinning in the first few minutes, efficiently establishing backstory, locale, and the central premise of the film. The rest of the movie simply turns up the temperature, with Kolchak becoming more convinced with every crime that a real vampire is on the loose and the police and the officials of the Fourth Estate trying to squelch him. ("Do you believe in vampires, little boy?"[10] one of Kolchak's FBI sources mockingly asks him.)

The first half-hour of the movie revolves firmly around Kolchak, as embodied by McGavin. The veteran TV actor inhabits the intrepid reporter down to his Scotch-marinated bone marrow and captures the sense of jejune enthusiasm and broken-down careerist that the iconclast Kolchak finds himself to be in his early-middle age. Kolchak is just enough everyman to remain a compelling focal point but also just enough of a gadfly to keep us guessing how far he'll go, or whether he really has the credibility to lead the charge against this avatar of the undead. The tension between Kolchak's noble intentions and his avaricious zeal for a byline provides the dramatic momentum of the first part of the movie.

Soon, though, the dark side takes over and it's the vampire Janos Skorzeny (played by Barry Atwater) who gives the film its grisly appeal, turning the movie from a kind of character study in shabby genteel journalism to creepy creature reconnaissance. The first shot of the suspect is pure vampire mythos: pale skin, red-rimmed eyes, dark, slicked-back hair. He looks every bit the classic vampire. (Kolchak, in yet another argument with his editor, asks, "What do you want, Vincenzo? A testimonial from Count Dracula?")

Threading through the movie is another time-honored film genre, the police procedural. Much of the action in *The Night Stalker* has to do with the nuts-and-bolts work of law enforcement officials, and this movie shows it all: crime scene investigations, interrogations, coroners' inquests, and conference calls with the FBI. And, much more illuminating (and disturbing, coming as the film does at the beginning of the Watergate era), the movie shows the lengths to which police and municipal officials will go to preserve secrets and subvert the public's right to know.

This being a horror film, there is also a great deal of information about vampires and vampiric legend and lore. Kolchak might be a cockeyed idealist, but he's also a veteran journalist, and he does his homework, consulting numerous accounts from fact and fiction about the habits of the vampire (and, for the TV audience's benefit, reading them aloud). Just as Kolchak is finishing up his research, the vampire killer strikes again, this time cleaning out the blood supply of a local hospital — and littering the hallways with the bodies of orderlies and nurses who dared to interrupt his midnight refrigerator raid. But there are now eyewitnesses, and fingerprints, and the dragnet starts to close in on Skorzeny. It's only a matter of time until the police close in — with Kolchak, of course, at the fore (camera and tape recorder at the ready).

The final face-off is a mostly by-the-book vampire extermination. One of Kolchak's street sources discovers where Skorzeny lives, and Kolchak decides to pay the house a visit. The scene is achingly suspenseful, as Kolchak stumbles through a sort of dilapidated mansion in the dark, amid creaking staircases and cobwebbed furniture. Kolchak is no Indiana Jones, but he does have the righteous indignation of any self-respecting newsman.

The Night Stalker

When he finds one of Skorzeny's victim's bound and gagged but still alive — "a human bloodbank!" — he finds the courage and anger he needs to confront the fiend himself. But when Kolchak drops his crucifix, it looks pretty bad for our disheveled hero — until he get the bright idea to shed a little light on the situation. As he pulls the planks from the windows of the mansion, the early-morning sun streams in. Skorzeny writhes on the staircase in agony — until Kolchak finishes him off with a wooden stake through the heart.

And for all his pains and inadvertent heroism, what does Kolchak get? A charge of murder.

He gets called into the D.A.'s office and finds, assembled against him, the very lawmen he's been trying to help catch the killer. In their continuing effort to keep the Las Vegas population from panicking about vampires, they've concocted an "official" story about the suspect's death — whitewashed of any mention at all of the truth about Janos Skorzeny. Kolchak is given an option: stay in town and face murder charges, or keep his mouth shut and get out. (Fortunately for fans of the subsequent series *The Night Stalker*, which is set in Chicago, Kolchak agrees to play ball.)

The success of *The Night Stalker* led to the 1973 follow-up *The Night Strangler* and the one-season 20-episode series *Kolchak: The Night Stalker*. The ABC series aired in 1974 and '75 on Friday nights but it failed to find an audience. Fans of the lamented TV incarnation speculate on why the series never caught on: bad time slot, poor production values, a growing weariness with its "monster of the week" format, a general critical drubbing in the television press. But the show has proved popular in reruns, and Kolchak has been "re-born" in a series of graphic novels and books, plus a much-maligned 2005 remake with an all-new cast (ten episodes were produced, but only six aired). The entire original run is available on DVD.

The Night Stalker started out stalking vampires, but today, it's his fans who stalk the bookstores, cable television listings and on-line video services, just so they can spend a few more hours with their favorite supernatural sleuth and dissolute scribe, Carl Kolchak.

The Ninth Gate

There is a class of "book lover" that extends far beyond the casual book club member or regular patron of the local library. For these rarified souls, it's not only the interaction with an author's ideas that excites them and keep them up nights — it's the actual book, the physical product in all of its bound splendor. The book doesn't merely embody art, it *is* the art itself. These people — sometimes they are "collectors," sometimes "dealers," and sometimes just enthusiastic, amateur connoisseurs — all share a mania for the book as *object* (and usually, the older the book, the better). These devotees of the bound and printed word have been known to go to extremes in pursuit of their passion, from flying around the world to attend antiquarian book fairs to paying exorbitant (to most people, anyway) fees for rare first editions of books whose authors did not last nearly as long as their works.

Because the passions — and the stakes — are so high in the field of book collecting, a cottage industry comprised of book brokers, appraisers, printers, binders, and re-sellers has arisen to service the needs of these (often well-heeled) bibliophiles. And because the books being hunted often date from hundreds of years ago, the whole field has the whiff of antiquity about it, which can be both attractive and daunting to its practitioners. Then there's the uneasy, side-by-side mix of the respectable and the shadowy, the dignified, esteemed gallery owner and the unscrupulous Gutenberg gumshoe trying to swindle an unsuspecting book owner out of a treasure. Plus, the field has no locus: any country, city, even small village can be a Mecca for the book stalker.

It seems logical that such passion, drama, and history as can be found in the world of the rare book market would attract the attention of novel writers looking for ready-made characters and settings in which to set their stories. But even with all of its intrigue and excitement, at least one bestselling author found the formula lacking something.

So he added Satan.

It was just what the shadowy world of rare books needed, apparently, as the result of the artistic alchemy between ol' Lucifer and old books became a global best-seller and inspired a film that brought together two giants of contemporary cinema.

The Club Dumas, a thriller with flashes of supernatural horror, has been gripping readers in Spain since 1993, and in English-speaking countries since it was translated in 1996. The book's author, Arturo Perez-Reverte, is an internationally best-selling writer whose works often revolve around the nexus of history, art, and infamy. Perez-Reverte is a former journalist and war correspondent and his fiction showcases his reporter's eye for detail and a neurotic's obsession with historical arcana. Many readers first discovered Perez-Reverte through *The Flanders Panel*, his novel of deceit and treachery in the world of fine art. He's also written a series of seventeenth century historical thrillers set in Spain, featuring a dashing Spanish hero named Captain Alatriste. And although there are elements of the potboiler serial in *The Club Dumas*, the book hinges upon a darker and more horrific presence than any populist page-turner. The real protagonist of the book originates far further back than the seventeenth century, stretching across the mists of time to the formation of the earth and mankind itself: the Devil.

In this particular work, the Devil is not just a corrupter of souls — he's an author. And *The Club Dumas* revolves around a mercenary book sleuth's quest to find a copy of a book whose illustrations and text derive from the devilish original.

In addition to being a first-rate thriller, the novel is a sort of master's degree course in literature — particularly French literature of the nineteenth century. The Dumas referenced in the title is Alexandre Dumas, author of *The Three Musketeers*, as well as lots of other popular, romantic adventure stories. A working knowledge of Dumas' work isn't necessary — though any literary factoid one can bring to the reading of this book is not likely to be wasted. In addition to the work of Dumas, the book is steeped in references to such estimable classics as *Moby Dick*, several of the Sherlock Holmes stories, Edgar Allan Poe, and Dante, to name but a few. In choosing to set his story in the world of antiquarian book traders, Perez-Reverte committed himself to a tale immersed in the *lingua franca* of the literati. Much of the appeal of reading *The Club Dumas* comes from spending time in the company of the book's protagonist Lucas Corso, a gin-swilling, chain-smoking dissolute mercenary of the book trade, as he expostulates on the minutiae of rare books. He's a rather contradictory sort of fellow, motivated only by money yet possessed of a remarkable literary education. And Corso needs every bit of that knowledge — as well as his street savvy — to survive in the surprisingly cut-throat world of rare books and manuscripts. The dealers for whom he works are

> jackals on the scent of the Gutenberg Bible, antique-fair sharks, auction-room leeches, [who] would sell their grandmothers for a first edition. But they receive their clients in rooms with leather sofas, views of the Duomo or Lake Constance, and they never get their hands — or their consciences — dirty.[1]

As the story begins, Corso is working on a minor mystery: trying to determine if a handwritten manuscript of a chapter of *The Three Musketeers* is authentic or a forgery. But the pursuit of that question leads him to a much larger, and much more dangerous, inquiry, one that will ultimately involve suicide, murder, and devil worship. Corso finds himself on the trail of an exceedingly rare, almost mythic title from the seventeenth century, *Book of the Nine Doors of the Kingdom of Shadows*, a sort of medieval Baedeker to the realm of Hell. Whoever possesses the lone surviving copy — and not one of the alleged three forgeries floating around — will have access to a secret spell that can summon the Devil himself.

Corso knows a lot about books, and in the pursuit of the authentic copy, he learns a lot about the lengths to which certain book fanciers and Satanic ritualists will go for the arcane secrets hidden within its 400-year-old binding. As one would expect from a thriller set in such a secretive and hostile world, there are lots of supporting characters of shadowy background and dubious identity. Corso's principal guide, help-mate and sounding board is a mysterious young woman, maybe 18 or 20, who calls herself Irene Adler (a name familiar to Holmes enthusiasts as his most famous female foil). There are more than a few clues, however, to suggest she is either in league with the Devil or, more likely, the Devil herself.

Perez-Reverte's real triumph in *The Club Dumas* is to keep both the high-end, literary and intellectual mystery intact amid a plot cribbed from a pulp detective magazine or even a breathless made-for-television movie. (One critic called the novel "a cross between Umberto Eco and Anne Rice ... a beach book for intellectuals."[2]) And though the English-language version is a translation of Perez-Reverte's Spanish original, the writing is quite beautiful and engaging, regularly surprising in its choice of metaphors and visually precise, as in this early description of Corso himself:

The Ninth Gate

However fragile the oversized coat made him appear, with his rodent-like incisors and calm expression Corso was as solid as a concrete block. His features were sharp and precise, full of angles. They framed alert eyes always ready to express an innocence dangerous for anyone who was taken in by it. At times, particularly when still, he seemed slower and clumsier than he really was. He looked vulnerable and defenseless: barmen gave him an extra drink on the house, men offered him cigarettes, and women wanted to adopt him on the spot. Later, when you realized what had happened, it was too late to catch him. He was running off in the distance, having scored another victory.[3]

But those victories don't come easily. Corso encounters several real-life horrors in his quest for the mythical, mystical guidebook for summoning Satan. If there is an authentic, original copy of *Nine Doors*, it starts to look more and more like it's better *not* to possess it. The book leaves a trail of corpses in its wake, and Corso himself comes under police scrutiny as the body count rises. Through all of the tumult and adventure that takes them through France, Spain, and Portugal, there is the steadfast Irene Adler (if she baffled Sherlock Holmes, what chance does Corso have?). She guides him through several dangerous situations, tipping him off to threats waiting just around the corner. In the book's most violent scene, she rescues Corso from an assault and pummels his armed assailant — who outweighs her three to one. Yet, she emerges without a scratch. She appears to have superhuman abilities and to know things about the history of the Devil and the way he's been represented in literature that even the erudite Corso doesn't know. Yet it's her kindness and empathy are most disarming and this baffles the hard-boiled book detective.

Perez-Reverte ratchets up the suspense in the final chapters, as well as throwing in a tutorial about numerology (especially the number 666) and the Devil. He also settles the puzzling matter of which of the extant *Nine Doors*—if any—are authentic. And the book's wild final scene, like something out of Poe's "The Fall of the House of Usher," with an insane devil worshiper amid pentagrams, goblets of blood, and a ring of fire, reminds the reader that some people take literature very, very seriously.

With *The Club Dumas*, Perez-Reverte joins a long and distinguished list of authors who have also wrestled with the Devil, including Dante, Milton, Goethe, and C.S. Lewis. And though it's Corso and the creepy, creaky book collectors he deals with that mostly comprise the list of characters we encounter in *The Club Dumas*, it's the Devil himself (or herself), hovering around and over the action, that gives the book its sense of danger and excitement. If Corso were hot on the trail of a rare Shakespeare manuscript, the novel would lose much of its luster. The Devil, as time and literary tradition has proved, always raises the stakes.

Famous (infamous?) director Roman Polanski's film of the book, titled *The Ninth Gate*, is a taut and chilling thriller that eliminates a large portion of the novel in order to focus more clearly on the malevolent shadow cast by Satan. Polanski, who collaborated on the screenplay with John Brownjohn and Enrique Urbizu, jettisons the part of the story that has to do with the Dumas manuscript, and this allows the filmmaker to focus on the more lurid and frightening aspects of Perez-Reverte's tale.

Johnny Depp plays the renamed *Dean* Corso with just the right mix of contemptible con man and sublimated humanitarian. He is more restrained than the book's Lucas Corso, more buttoned-up, less gin-swilling reprobate. The tradeoff is greater credibility. Depp's creation seems like the kind of fellow who really does know that much about antiquarian books and rare historical manuscripts, and it's easy to see how he inspires the trust of his well-heeled and professional clientele (even though as we discover in the first scene, where he dupes a grieving family out of some priceless books, he's all about the money).

Polanski is the perfect director for this material. He's always been a master of setting a mood, of capturing the off-kilter and the menacing behind the mundane and *The Ninth Gate* is full of tableaux that testify to the eerie and demonic aura that surrounds Corso's investigation. Even the opening title sequence, with its labyrinth of mysterious doors and otherworldly music, puts the viewer on edge.

The Dumas subplot is excised, but the movie follows the narrative of the rest of the book fairly closely. Corso is summoned to the home of a rare book collector, Boris Balkan (played by Frank Langella), who owns a rare copy of *The Ninth Gate of the Kingdom of Shadows*. He hires Corso to find any other copies and determine which, if any, are authentic and which are forgeries. The movie follows Corso's pursuits, as he meets with other collectors and fellow book experts, dodges hired thugs (or tries to), and encounters the mysterious muse of his mission, the lovely but devilish character known only as "The Girl" (played with requisite ambiguity by Emmanuel Seigner), who rescues him from danger. Of course, she might also be responsible for creating the danger in the first place.

As with the novel, there are many illuminating and educational scenes of the high-priced world of rare book collecting. Few people have probably

The Ninth Gate

Rare book detective Dean Corso (Johnny Depp) spends most of his time on the run in Roman Polanski's dark thriller *The Ninth Gate*.

ever wondered about that arcane and exclusive club but *The Ninth Gate* makes it an undeniably fascinating world, with its humidity-controlled private libraries and animated, detailed discussions of typography and medieval book illustration. (At one point, Corso gets into an in-depth discussion with two professional book binders about the technical difficulties in forging a work with three-hundred-year-old paper and ink — not the standard stuff of thrillers.) It's all very strange and very compelling. It has to be, because there's not much warmth or comfort to be found in the human characters. Early in the film, Balkan says to Corso: "You don't like me, do you?" Corso tells him, "I don't have to like you. You're a client, and you pay well."[4] That's the chilly reality of Corso's trade and the visual reality of Polanski's film. One doesn't identify with these characters. Rather, you are attracted by their unattractiveness, and the oddity of such cold and abstract people drawn to the humanity and physicality of books.

What drives Balkan is not his love of literature. He wants to acquire an authentic *Ninth Gate* so he'll be able to recite the proper spell to summon the Devil. For all his worldly power and erudition (in our first glimpse of him, he's delivering a lecture on the history of witches), he really seeks only to be a servant of Lucifer and an inhabitant of the realm that is guarded by the nine gates. Langella plays the uber-intelligent Balkan as a powerful, intimidating presence. But nobody intimidates Corso, and the scenes between the two are great fun as we watch the man who lives to command respect getting none from the aloof book sleuth.

Whereas the book offered dozens of pages about the history of Satanic iconography and the medieval scribes' fascination with the Devil, the movie provides lots of scenes of the bleary-eyed Corso in various libraries, taking notes from dusty, leather-bound tomes and comparing engravings from rare manuscripts with the illustrations in *The Ninth Gate*. Corso spends a good part of the film learning about the Devil, and then discovering that the people he's dealing with sometimes act as if they are possessed by a demon spirit. A grieving widow viciously attacks him after a raucous bout of lovemaking; a rich book collector hangs himself; a mysterious man trailing Corso turns out to be an assassin; even a scaffolding nearly collapses on top of him as he emerges from a printer's shop. Everywhere he goes, he encounters people who seem to be hiding something, hiding their past, or their reasons for wanting to see him. And increasingly, their motives appear to be strikingly similar: The Devil made them do it.

Through it all, there is Corso, persistent, cool, smoking his cigarettes, studying the illustrations in old books with a jeweler's eyepiece, leafing though medieval volumes while holding them up to his ear so he can hear if the paper sounds authentic when he flips through the pages. For all his composure and competence, he can't seem to figure out who is after him, and why he seems to be leaving a trail of death in the wake of his investigation. Like Perez-Reverte, Polanski won't show his hand until the final reel, and then he lets loose with a conflagration befitting a mind turned demonic.

Some viewers and critics have assailed the climactic scenes as inappropriately over-the-top, a Luciferian bout of Grand Guignol that seems so strikingly at odds with the chilly and sober feel of the rest of the movie. There's no doubt the climactic ring-of-fire scene is a bit jarring, and wildly theatrical, as well as the sexual congress of Corso and "The Girl" amid the conflagration. But from a purely dramatic standpoint it's undeniably thrilling. Langella's Boris Balkan throws himself into the final scenes with abandon — as befits a man who spent his lifetime seeking communion with the dark forces of the world.

The Ninth Gate remains a visionary treat, a superbly acted and hauntingly filmed thriller that yokes together unusual worlds and somehow makes them compatible. Polanski's patient direction and unflinching embrace of the rare book world (long, slow close-ups of hand-tooled book spines, the camera lingering lovingly over vellum pages and leather-bound tomes cradled in mahogany shelves), and an undeniably compelling premise combine for a highly satisfying film.

So file *The Ninth Gate*, and its source *The Club Dumas*, into that overstuffed but still sometimes-distinguished credenza of "literature of the Devil." It seems that writers from every generation, stretching back to antiquity, have been unable to resist summoning up the dark side of mankind's spiritual yearnings. The thirteenth-century Italian poet Dante, in his first-hand tour of Hell, *The Inferno*, had this to say when he entered the final depths of Lucifer's realm: "How frozen I became and powerless then/ask it not, Reader, for I write it not/Because all language would be insufficient."[5]

Insufficient, perhaps, but as literary posterity has shown, clearly worth the effort.

Nosferatu

He is attractive. Also repulsive. Suave, yet socially inept. High cultured and articulate — or barely literate. Possessed of delicate features. Or brutish. And from all regions of the globe: Russia and the Caucausses, South America, Europe, Africa.

He crosses genres as easily as borders: poetry, novels, screenplays, oral legend, drama. And time, too: The medieval era, Victorian England, antiquity, last week. The future.

The vampire is the most adaptable of creatures. His appeal, perhaps, resides in his mutability. His shadowy origins offer an opportunity for the writer, or actor, to visit upon his dark character qualities and quirks that have come to define him: hatred of sunlight, lack of reflection, even a Hungarian accent. And though he's changed over the decades and centuries, the core of his character remains closely allied to his roots, a figure of the folk imagination once viewed with genuine terror by European peasantry, an avatar of demonic possession, leader of an army of the undead. His exploits have been researched by scientists, anthropologists, authors, and television crews, and enjoyed — or at least observed — by millions of people for decades. The vampire legend is legion.

From the earliest accounts — which far predate movable type[1] — people seem to have always been fascinated by stories of vampiric creatures. The vampire vogue keeps re-igniting, from the eighteenth century, which saw the spread of vampire legends across Europe and the New World, to the nineteenth century, which added the first vampires to the literary mix, and the twentieth century, which gave us films, silent and scream-filled. Once John Polidori, friend of the Romantic poet Lord Byron, penned his short story "The Vampyre" (during the same sojourn where Mary Shelley created her modern Prometheus, *Frankenstein*), there was no putting the genie back in the bottle — or the undead back in the casket.

Polidori's work was published in April 1819 in *New Monthly Magazine*, a landmark literary event that sparked imitative stories, plays, and — two decades later what's considered to be the first vampire novel in English, James Malcolm Rymer's *Varney the Vampire*. Interest in the vampire would percolate throughout the nineteenth century until 1897, when the work of an Irish writer and theater manager propelled the vampire into the pantheon of globally revered literary figures.

Bram Stoker's *Dracula* is one of the best-known horror novels ever published. Turn-of-the-century British readers proved a ready audience for Stoker's mix of supernaturalism and science, Victorian restraint chafing against unbridled sexuality, and the triumph of virtue amid the persistence of primitive evil. The book created a minor sensation, and led almost immediately to several stage adaptations and, shortly thereafter, film versions.

After more than a century of interpretations — some of which hew fairly closely to the vampire of established legend, though many others are ludicrously embellished — the modern reader can be forgiven for being somewhat uncertain as to what Stoker's novel actually says about the infamous count and his dark, Transylvanian culture. (In fact, Dracula himself appears sparingly in the novel; most of the book deals with how those around him — minions as well as foes — react to his presence.)

And for all the schlock that has accompanied so many retellings of Stoker's *Dracula* story, one surprising fact emerges from a re-reading of the novel: *Dracula* is more than a mere thriller. It is a meticulously crafted book, creating maximum suspense while offering a depth of commentary on matters from the mundane to the esoteric (an aspect of the book seldom hinted at by the various cinematic interpretations). The book runs thick with ideas. Those fans of the vampire myth who think they know the novel because they've seen the various film versions probably have little inkling of the superbly well-wrought story and its cast of indelible characters created by the theatrically inclined Stoker. He wrote other novels (*Miss Betty*, 1898; *The Mystery of the Sea*, 1902; *The Jewel of the Seven Stars*, 1903; *The Man*, 1905; and *The Lady of the Shroud*, 1909), as well as nonfiction books (such as *The Personal Reminiscences of Henry Irving*, the actor who gave Stoker his start in theatrical management), but nothing Stoker ever wrote approached the popularity of *Dracula*.

The legend of Dracula was known long before Stoker dramatized the life of the reclusive, demonic count. Scholars acknowledge that Stoker based his fictional creation on a real-life ruler of Wallachia,[2] a fourteenth-century tyrant known to history as Vlad Dracula (sometimes called Vlad the Impaler). As J. Gordon Melton has noted:

> Stoker, it seems, constructed his leading character, at least in part, from the historical Dracula. That Dracula was a prince not of Transylvania, but of the neighboring kingdom of Wallachia. Stoker turned the Wallachian prince into a Transylvanian count. The real Dracula's exploits largely occurred south of the Carpathian Mountains, which divided Wallachia and Transylvania, and he only infrequently ventured into Transylvanian lands. The real Dracula was Romanian, not a Szekely, though given the location chosen by Stoker for Castle Dracula in Szekely, he was correct to think of his main character as a Szekely.[3]

Even though Stoker borrowed his title character from a different era, the novel and its central figure are very much of the author's time. As one critic noted, "He represents an unbridled and illicit sexuality, paganism, superstition, and unheeded immigration. In other words, he represents everything respectable Victorian society was terrified of. For Stoker to bring the two together is, without doubt, a dramatic masterstroke."[4]

The novel is told in a variation of the epistolary style—a story told through letters (epistles) characters write to each other. In *Dracula*, the story unfolds mostly through journal entries, with the occasional letter or newspaper article used as well. The first couple of chapters consist entirely of journal entries from Jonathan Harker, an assistant solicitor who's been asked by his employer to travel to Transylvania to complete a real estate transaction between Harker's firm in Exeter, England, and Count Dracula, who is seeking to buy an estate in London. Stoker wastes no time in establishing the predominant tone of creepiness as the steadfast and sober Harker tries to make sense of his increasingly bizarre host. Even before he—or we—meet the count, the omens are not good. Researching Transylvania in the British Museum, Harker concludes, "Every known superstition in the world is gathered into the horseshoe of the Carpathians, as if it were the centre of some sort of imaginative whirlpool." Harker's reception at a hotel along the way provides little reassurance:

> 4 May: I found that my landlord had got a letter from the count, directing him to secure the best place on the coach for me; but on making enquiries as to details he seemed somewhat reticent, and pretended that he could not understand my German. This could not be true, because up to then he had understood it perfectly; at least, he answered my questions exactly as if he did. He and his wife, the old lady who had received me, looked at each other in a frightened sort of way. He mumbled out that money had been

sent in a letter, and that was all he knew. When I asked him if he knew Count Dracula, and could tell me anything of his castle, both he and his wife crossed themselves, and, saying that they knew nothing at all, simply refused to speak further.[5]

Harker attributes such behavior to mere peasant superstitions, but when he finally reaches Castle Dracula, he discovers the sinister source of their suspicions:

[Dracula] motioned me in with his right hand, with a courtly gesture, saying in excellent English, but with a strange intonation: "Welcome to my house! Enter freely and of your own will." He made no motion of stepping to meet me, but stood like a statue, as though his gesture of welcome had fixed him into stone. The instant, however, that I had stepped over his threshold, he moved impulsively forward, and holding out his hand, grasped mine with a strength that made me wince, an effect which was not lessened by the fact that it seemed as cold as ice — more like the hand of a dead than a living man.[6]

The picture that emerges is not that of the oft-portrayed suave, attractive man, caped and possessed of a gleaming eye and winning smile:

His face was aquiline, with high bridge of the thin nose and peculiarly arched nostrils; with lofty domes forehead, and hair growing scantily round the temples, but profusely elsewhere. His eyes were very massive, almost meeting over the nose, and with bushy hair that seemed to curl in its own profusion. The mouth, so far as I could see it under the heavy moustache, was fixed and rather cruel-looking, with peculiarly sharp white teeth; these protruded over the lips, whose remarkable ruddiness showed astonishing vitality in a man of his years.... [H]is ears were pale and at the tops extremely pointed.[7]

Although most screen portrayals offer a much more attractive countenance for the count, one film in particular got many of the details — aquiline nose, protruding, rat-like teeth, and pointed ears — just right. In fact that film, the 1922 silent *Nosferatu*, can claim to be perhaps the best representation of Stoker's *Dracula* (a claim I shall return to shortly).

Harker spends the next several chapters chronicling the weird goings-on behind the scenes of Dracula's castle, living there as, essentially, a prisoner (Dracula locks all the doors that provide entry into the castle). Harker discloses a nightmarish world of un-reality, concluding in quite sober prose in his journal that he just might be going mad. He sees and hears things that belie logical explanation: the count crawling lizard-like down several stories of smooth stone walls, vampiresses disappearing into mist, and armies of wolves obeying the midnight summons of Dracula. By the end of his month-long stay, he's discovered the count's true intention: to establish himself in London and prey upon its population. The thought horrifies him and provides the impetus for his daring escape:

> This was the being I was helping to transfer to London, where, perhaps, for centuries to come, he might, amongst its teeming millions, satiate his lust for blood, and create a new and ever-widening circle of semi-demons to batten on the helpless. The very thought drives me mad."[8]

Dracula does indeed head to London. Harker escapes but is injured in the attempt and ends up being cared for in a religious hospital for six weeks. Meanwhile, Dracula has moved into his new quarters and had begun preying on the very people he heard about from Harker in some of their midnight discussions at the castle. Dracula has targeted the best friend of Harker's fiancée Lucy Westenra, and then shortly after that source dries up, Harker's fiancée herself, Mina Murray. We don't see much of the count once he flees from Transylvania, but we get lots of glimpses of his handiwork and the terror his nighttime feedings create.

The second half of the book is really a cat-and-mouse contest between Dracula and a doctor–vampire hunter named Van Helsing, who was originally summoned to help treat Lucy Westenra's mysterious sleepwalking habit (she was reporting nightly to the count, though completely unaware of it). Van Helsing joins with the recently returned Harker and a couple of Lucy's former suitors to pursue Dracula—as he pursues *them*. Along the way, Stoker fills his narrative with lots of arguments about the limitations of modern scientific knowledge in an increasingly logical age, and some prescient pre–Freudian philosophizing about the relationship of dreams to the waking state.

Stoker seems at times as interested in mounting a defense for the metaphysical as he is in unfolding a suspenseful story. As Van Helsing points out,

> You are a clever man, friend John; you reason well, and your wit is bold; but you are too prejudiced. You do not let your eyes see nor your ears hear, and that which is outside your daily life is not of account to you. Do you not think that there are things which you cannot understand, and yet which are; that some people see that others can't?

That whole idea of an alternative reality, the strangeness we can't explain, is what really drives the book, and it's what most filmmakers seem to miss when they approach the Dracula story. The menace doesn't come from what we know but what we don't even understand. When directors cast seductive, attractive Draculas, they replace the beating heart of Stoker's story. Dracula isn't a suave, intriguing-small-talk-at-cocktail-parties type — he's a misfit, a monster who can barely contain his murderous impulses and one who wears the patina of respectability barely, uneasily, most awkwardly. What's needed in the successful film adaptation is a Dracula who communicates that sense of unclassifiable otherness. Cool counts (*a la* Bela Lugosi), while charming and fun, lack the requisite unreality. When we meet Dracula, we shouldn't be thinking, "This guy isn't so bad"; we should instead be thinking, "There's definitely something wrong with this guy." The whole novel pulsates with oddity, a sense of nightmarish engagement with a being from a dark and dangerous place.

That's why the best film interpretation remains the 1922 F.W. Murnau–directed classic *Nosferatu*, a slightly changed retelling that stands as a testament to the bizarreness of Stoker's creation in particular and the vampire legend in general. Nosferatu (a word that appears in the text of *Dracula* as a name some cultures have bestowed on the vampire) features Count Orlock (instead of Count Dracula), who would never be mistaken for respectable. He looks like a cross between the model for Edvard Munch's "The Scream" and an emaciated sewer rat. Bald, long-toothed, pointy-eared, his appearance is at once disarming, a reminder of the "unreal" that lurks on the fringes of reality.

Murnau's film is a masterpiece of moodiness. Although Murnau trimmed the storyline, changing character names and eliminating others, the general creepiness survives. Max Schreck, a German stage actor, makes the perfect vampire. He looks, and moves, like someone only mimicking the living, trying to get the gestures just right. Because the film is silent, the emphasis is on the visual. The filmmaker lights each frame for maximum effect, each shadow and sunset marvelously evocative. The scenes of Count Orlock in silhouette are really the stuff of nightmares. No illusion of charm or respectability here — just vengeful bloodlust percolating in a malodorous body.

One critic, writing about the film, noted:

> Murnau's inspired editing, framing, lighting, distorting relations of space and time and his direction of the weirdly jerking figure of Count Orlock, the way he imbues both location and studio shots with an eerily disturbing atmosphere, all combine to make the film the perfect illustration of Jean Cocteau's dictum that cinema is the registration of Death at work.[9]

Now a Terrifying Motion Picture!

Max Schreck as the creepy, malformed central character in the 1922 silent classic *Nosferatu* still has the power to disturb audiences used to more charming and seductive vampires.

The film follows roughly the outline of Stoker's novel, with some notably skin-crawling diversions. *Nosferatu*'s screenplay adds an additional layer of creepiness by linking rat-borne pestilence to the count, who is portrayed as being responsible for bringing a host of plague-infested rats with him from his Carpathian Mountains hideout to menace the (fictional) town of Wisborg. Since he's rat-like himself, it's a nice touch. While it's an invention of the screenwriter, the rat–Orlock connection is in keeping with the spirit of Stoker's book, which features a scene of rats swarming around the count's coffin when it's discovered in a basement in London. The rat–Orlock association also underlies the broader vampire-animal relationship by having Dracula turn into a bat, and a wolf, and having him control the behavior of horses and packs of wild dogs.

Other changes to the original include Count Orlock's death by sunlight. While Dracula himself is not terribly fond of the daylight, he is able to endure it, whereas Orlock dies by exposure to the sun. (Dracula, on the other hand, can't be killed by sunlight: his death can only be brought about by having his head cut off and his heart cut out, simultaneously, at which time his centuries-old body crumbles into dust.)

The greatest liberty Murnau took with Dracula exceeds any individual plot point. His production company failed to get the Stoker estate's permission to film the novel (which is why he made changes in character names and plot points). Stoker's widow sued for copyright infringement, and won, with a British court ordering all copies of the film destroyed. But like its undead predecessor, the film survived in several pirated copies — though it virtually disappeared in its original form. (In 1929, a heavily-edited version was shown to American audiences.)

It would be decades until the film was rediscovered, and now that it is in the public domain, several "restored" versions have become available on DVD. In 1993, *New York Times* film critic Caryn James found a contemporary resonance in the movie: "The enduring power of *Nosferatu* is more than a testament to Murnau. It also suggests the depth and complexity of the vampire myth, which adapts to every genre. The disease-carrying hero can refer to the bubonic plague or to AIDS; his state of eternal unrest holds meaning for the religious and the godless."[10]

So if it's such a great film, why have so many people never seen (or even heard of) *Nosferatu*? There are several reasons. Being a silent film, of course, a large contemporary audience is unlikely. Silent films are a decidedly niche market. The film also has a title that gives little sense of what it's about. (Its original title was *Nosferatu: A Symphony of Horror*— slightly more helpful, but only slightly.) There are a lot of vampire movies out there — even those like Francis Ford Coppola's adaptation, which puts Stoker's name in the title[11] — so a sepia-toned German Expressionist silent film from 1922 probably has too many strikes against it to compete with lesser but more modern competition.

That's a shame — just as it's a shame that so many people think they know *Dracula*, the novel, because they've seen a vampire film on late night television. Both the novel and *Nosferatu* offer stunning visions of originality and embody compelling narratives enhanced by artistry of the highest order. They are genuinely frightening, yes, but also marked by an invasive quality that, vampire-like, gets under one's skin if read or watched in the right frame of mind. As Jonathan Harker wrote in his journal, "I am encompassed about with terrors that I dare not think of," in a story we can't stop thinking about.

The Phantom of the Opera

As of this writing, *The Phantom of the Opera* has surpassed 9,000 performances on Broadway, a record for popularity that shows no signs of abating. In the middle of New York City's Times Square, towering over the tourists and traffic in the busiest intersection in the world, is a massive billboard featuring one of the most iconic images in pop culture: the white mask of the deformed phantom. In cities around the world, the award-winning musical plays to sold-out houses. In art-house theaters and film schools, prints of the 1925 black-and-white film version are screened. In undergraduate classrooms and graduate French literature programs, the now 100-year-old novel, penned by French journalist and author Gaston Leroux, is read and dissected as a "classic."

What is it about this work that has exercised such a grip on the worldwide public's imagination?

Whatever it is, there's more than a touch of irony in the fact that the book was not very popular when it was first published and was all-but-forgotten when the 1925 silent film came out, launching what would become a veritable franchise of films, plays, literary spin-offs, musicals, and a television mini-series. And with each new incarnation, the masked visage of the infamous phantom became more ingrained in the public's consciousness, his secret life under an opera house the stuff of folk belief. "Leroux ha[s] ably blended fact and fiction in a way that increased the reality of the horror," one critic has noted.[1]

Critics who write about literature often talk about the "universality" of a work — that is, what makes something appealing to all people, across different times and cultures. Clearly *Phantom* has something universal in its story of doomed love, revenge, human deformity, regret and — certainly as consequential as all of those aspects — the seductive power of art.

In addition, the phantom that Leroux gives us has that oddly compelling mix of the repulsive and the attractive, putting him in the tradition of such ambivalent, and also universal, creations as Frankenstein's Monster, Dracula, and the Hunchback of Notre Dame. (In much of the critical literature about the book, the phantom is variously referred to as both the "hero" and the "villain" of the story.) The wellspring of compassion and revulsion that Leroux has tapped into makes the work a natural for adaptation into such forms as the highly melodramatic, demonstrative silent film, or the emotionally evocative modern Broadway musical. Yet the roots of Leroux's novel are far more pedestrian than its legacy of worldwide popularity would suggest.

Leroux wasn't even supposed to be a writer. He trained in Paris to be a lawyer, but after completing his studies and earning a law degree in 1898, he opted out of practicing, having lost interest in the field. As a balm for his bored professional soul, he began a spate of writing-related assignments, working first as a court reporter, then as a drama critic and journalist for a couple of French newspapers. The work was highly congenial to him, and he made good use of his journalistic observation in many of his subsequent novels. (One of his articles was about a Paris opera house patron who died after a chandelier's counter-weight fell from the ceiling[2] — an event that, slightly altered, would prove to be a turning point in the plot of *Phantom*.)

Many critics also note that Leroux appears to have been influenced by a long-forgotten (but then popular) novel by fellow Frenchman George du Maurier, titled *Trilby*, about a highly controlling character named Svengali who hypnotizes an Irish working girl and turns her into a great singer. Like many fine writers, Leroux appears to have synthesized much of what he read and what he saw into his own works — including, in the case of *Phantom*, Parisian high society's zeal for classic opera at the turn of the century. The novel is not only about opera, it is, in many ways, operatic itself. The characters are not particularly well-rounded or developed, but they are all highly emotional and intense. The plot involves wild events and exotic settings that would be at home in any grand opera libretto. The dialogue is often exaggerated and highly exclamatory. The story is melodramatic, with tears, tragedy and tension taking their respective turns on the page. The overall impact on most readers is not, one suspects, too different from how they might feel emerging from the rarified, magical world of the opera, with its dramatic upheavals, reversals of fortune, tragically unrequited loves, and fairy tale endings.

And like a fairy tale, *Phantom of the Opera* is a fairly simple story.

And, apropos of a fairy tale, there are lots of elements that challenge the reason and engage the imagination. The story takes place in Paris in the late Victorian period, and centers almost exclusively on the Paris Opera House, an opulent, multi-storied structure whose labyrinthine design and subterranean chambers become almost a character in the novel.[3]

A narrator's prologue informs the reader that the story is all true (of course), and that it has been verified through documentary and personal testimony — though the author concedes that he had to almost given up trying to solve this mystery: "I was within an ace of abandoning a task in which I was exhausting myself in the hopeless pursuit of a vain image. At last, I received the proof that my presentiments had not deceived me, and I was rewarded for all my efforts on the day when I acquired the certainty that the Opera ghost was more than a mere shade."[4]

The reader is plunged immediately into the intrigue, excitement, and egotism of the Parisian opera world. The story begins with an account of an operatic gala celebrating the retirement of the two outgoing directors of the opera house. Taking their place, the two new directors are on hand to greet their employees. During the celebration, one of the members of the ballet company shrieks that she has just seen the Opera Ghost. This specter, who has been credited with sometimes violent mischief-making, has been the subject of rumor and gossip for many years.

The new directors dismiss the idea of a vengeful ghost as theatrical over-imagination — even after a longtime member of the stage crew is found mysteriously hanging from the rafters. Faced with the evidence of this ghost's existence — testimony from several of the stage hands and handwritten notes (signed "O.G.— Opera Ghost") demanding a monthly stipend — they steadfastly refuse to believe. Even after the ghost's threatened mayhem occurs (the famous crashing of a chandelier in the middle of a performance), the directors are still uncertain. As they dawdle, a promising young diva has been receiving vocal lessons — and romantic entreaties — from this ghost, who also calls himself the Angel of Music. His fervor for his protégé reaches such a height that he stages an abduction — *while she's in mid-aria*. He spirits her away to his elaborate lair several stories under the Paris Opera house, a complex network of secret rooms, hidden hallways and trapdoors, and even a secret lake.

The diva has a non-ghostly lover, and his efforts to find and rescue his beloved comprise the bulk of the novel's second half. There is, of course, an inevitable showdown between the suitor and the ghost, a deformed evil genius whose mask covers a countenance that is hideously deformed. The phantom possesses a sublime lyrical voice, a magician's high level of skill at deception, and a vengeful streak to make your typical Parisian opera-goer shudder. And he's designed his underground dwelling to ensure that any unwanted visitors will encounter a variety of traps, treacherous and lethal. The last few chapters feature an *Indiana Jones*–type last-minute escape from what the Phantom calls his "torture chamber"—an inescapable hall of mirrors that can be heated to high temperatures or filled with water to drown any visitor.

There are lots of page-turning set pieces in *Phantom*—due in large part to the book's publication history. It was originally serialized in a French journal, and Leroux was a savvy enough writer and observer of pop culture to know what keeps readers coming back. So he constructed cliffhangers throughout the book and placed the lovers, Christine and Raoul, in exotic locations such as the roof of the Paris Opera, looking out at the city at night (while a bat-like creature stares with red eyes from where the Phantom—just a moment ago!—was perched).

It's easy to roll one's eyes at the melodramatic nature of such plot devices today but Leroux entertainingly captures the spirit of grand opera, with its often-illogical plot twists and Grand Guignol excesses. Readers willing to sacrifice a bit of realism (it is, after all, a *ghost* story) will discover a bizarre and engaging narrative that has captivated readers and theatergoers for a century. And while Francophiles insist that the book *must* be read in its original French to appreciate Leroux's particular type of literary genius, those who know the work only in translation will nonetheless be rewarded with an unforgettable tour of the subterranean levels of the Paris Opera, and also of the human heart.

Such a story seems to cry out for dramatization, reading at times as if it were written directly for the stage or the screen. Its potential theatrical charms were not lost on Carl Laemmle, president of Universal Pictures, who, according to theatrical lore, read the book and was immediately captivated. As the story goes,

> In Paris, Laemmle met Leroux ... and confessed to him how excited he had been gazing at the Opera House from the Place de l'Opera. Leroux, sensing some interest, gave Laemmle a copy of *The Phantom of the Opera* for his bedtime reading. Apparently, that night Laemmle stayed awake, intent on getting through the entire story. By the next morning, he had determined that it should be made into a film.[5]

In a famed career that spanned silent films and the talkies, Lon Chaney was never better than when he played the Phantom in the 1925 silent film *The Phantom of the Opera* with Mary Philbin.

And that film, the 1925 version starring Lon Chaney, became one of the most popular and celebrated silent films ever, a landmark in horror in particular and movies in general.

In the 1920s, there was no bigger star than the self-styled "Man of a Thousand Faces" Lon Chaney. Both of Chaney's parents were deaf and mute, "and from his earliest childhood he had been obliged to signify his feelings through expression and gesture, which was a contributing factor to his success as a silent star."[6] Chaney went through an arduous personal transformation to achieve the famous skull-like look of the Phantom, achieved through celluloid discs inserted inside his cheeks and a wire contraption that pulled his nostrils up, giving him a distorted and disfigured face. And in keeping with the importance of the opera house as a focal point of the story, Universal erected a massive interior set that replicated the opera house; it has been used in many subsequent films and still stands today on the Universal lot. Despite significant "creative differences" between Chaney and the film's original director, Rupert Julian (who was replaced midway through filming), the resulting film is widely acknowledged as a kind of masterpiece.

The movie begins with an eerie, evocative sequence: An unidentified man is carrying a lantern in what appears to be a stony cell, looking for something—or someone. Following behind him, barely glimpsed, is a shadowy figure, caped and clandestine. The man with the lantern reappears, having failed to find his quarry, and he strides away. Then, a quick cut to a scene at the opera house, and a throng of well-dressed Parisians heading up the grand staircase before settling in for the performance, which begins with a corps d'ballet moving impressively in unison across the grand stage. In just these first two scenes, the keynotes of Leroux's novel have been struck: the terror and the beauty of the opera house, the high drama on the stage and the danger of the subterranean caverns beneath. (The musical score also transmutes from the moody and turgid opening strains in the first scene, with lots of cello and plaintive strings, to the lilting balletic whirls and swirls that unfold on the opera's stage, all violins, clarinet and brass.)

The next few scenes take the viewer into the offices of the opera house, where the old managers are grateful (as can be deduced from their broad smiles, robust handshakes, and rapid bowing out of the room) to turn over the management of the opera to the new managers—who laugh off the warning about "the ghost in box five." (Of course, there's no *actual* dialogue; the words are all on title cards, this being a silent film.) The managers investigate, but with an aim only to discover who is pulling their leg. Their jocularity is doused when, upon entering the box, they do indeed see a mysterious, caped figure (who, moments later, vanishes).

The ballerinas, now offstage, race to a stage hand in alarm because they, too, have just seen the Opera Ghost. They decide to consult the scenery changer, Joseph Buquet (who has reportedly seen the Phantom). He leads them through the part of the opera house where the massive sets are stored. Throughout all of these scenes, the viewer gets a glimpse of the almost city-like complexity of the opera house: hidden passages, people popping in and out of trap doors, warrens of dressing rooms and offices, catwalks, and stone caverns. The film does a good job of visually communicating the immensity of the Opera House demesne.

There are the requisite opera scenes, with opulent performances of staged works featuring lavishly gowned divas and audiences clapping their approval. And very quickly, the relationship between singer Christine and her lover, the noble Viscount Raoul, is established (we see them embrace in the dressing room and pledge their love to each other). But then ... enter the Phantom (and cue the dissonant notes in the score). Seen in silhouette, the Phantom warns Christine, "You must forget all worldly things and think only of your career — and your master."[7]

She doesn't, of course. The singer (played by Mary Philbin) continues to stare dreamily into the distance, batting her heavily mascara-ed eyelashes, thinking not of her masked mentor but of Raoul. While we wait for the inevitable showdown, the Phantom continues his behind-the-scenes machinations, sending threatening letters to the opera's directors, demanding that Christine replace the reigning diva, Carlotta, in an upcoming production. Raoul is admiring Christine from his private box when he receives a letter from an usher, written by Christine, telling him that they must not see each other again. While he's puzzling over the letter, the lights flicker, and the Phantom releases the rope holding up a massive chandelier, which comes crashing down on the audience. The scene is clumsily filmed and edited, and the actual falling of the chandelier is nowhere near as exciting as the stampede of opera-goers racing for their lives as they head down the grand staircase.

Christine retreats to her dressing room, but is commanded by the Phantom to "walk through the mirror"— which she does, right into a secret chamber where the Phantom is waiting for her. He takes her down a secret staircase, advising her to "look not on my mask," but to focus instead on his devotion to her. He puts her on a white horse, and we see them traverse the catacomb-like underbelly of the opera house, ending up at an underground canal that leads to the Phantom's lair. The scenes of the Phantom and Christine in the gondola, paddling slowly toward the dark unknown, are mesmerizing. There are no close-ups—only the dimmed candlelight and foreboding music to suggest what must be a look of sheer terror on the soprano's face. (She's not reassured when she stumbles across a coffin, and is told, "That's where I sleep!")

Still masked, the Phantom pours out his heart to Christine, declaring his love for her and admitting that, yes, he's been living down here for years, alone and masked, cut off from humanity. Upon hearing all this she, quite naturally, faints. At this point, the appeal of the film lies in watching Christine try to adapt to her surreal setting, groping for clues to make sense of her transplanted situation. And, of course, to wait for the inevitable unmasking of the Phantom, who spends most of his time playing macabre dirges on the organ while Christine explores her new, hellish home. Unfortunately, she goes a bit too far, sneaking up on the Phantom while he's playing one of his compositions ("Don Juan Triumphant!") and removing his mask from behind. He's aghast, she's agog, he's a ghoul. She recoils in horror as he points accusingly at her. This leads to the best moment in the movie, when he grabs her head and forces her to look closely at him, as he laughs in agony and shame, and utters with murderous intensity "Feast your eyes—glut your soul, on my accursed ugliness!"

Having thus completely unnerved the woman he loves, the Phantom relents a bit, and tells Christine that he loves her so much, he is willing to let her return to the "outside" world—but that she must vow to return to him. She swears it, and that leads to what, for many film historians, is one of the great scenes not only of this movie, but the entire silent era: a masked ball in the grand concourse of the Opera House. Filmed in color (which adds immeasurably to its impact in this otherwise black-and-white movie), the ball features all the gaudy and delightfully excessive costumes one would expect in turn-of-the-century Paris. But guess who else attends the ball? The Phantom, dressed as "The Red Death"—a figure of such striking gruesomeness that all of the other revelers leave a wide path for him. He slowly, dramatically descends the staircase and curses them all for their revelry, claiming it mocks the dead, and then he vanishes. Amid much confusion and speculation about who that was, Christine and Raoul sneak up to the roof of the opera house to plan their elopement after tomorrow night's performance of the opera *Faust*. But the Phantom overhears, and abducts Christine in mid performance of *Faust*. Assisted by Police Inspector Ledoux, who says he has been tracking the Phantom for months, Raoul attempts a rescue. Both pursuers end up in the Phantom's torture chamber, but are saved when the Phantom relents to Christine's pleas for mercy. The scene of their almost-demise is very effective, with lots of quick cuts between the Phantom, Christine, and her would-be rescuers, swelling music, and close-ups of the hideous Phantom's face. It all culminates in the two exhausted men emerging from a flooded chamber by way of a trap door that the Phantom opens, just as they were on the point of drowning.

This being a silent horror film, an angry mob is required, and they show up right on time to chase the Phantom into the Paris streets, pursue him to a bridge, pummel him, and throw his body in the river. What the film lacks in subtlety (in the book, the Phantom expires quietly, mysteriously, on his own dignified terms), it make up for in sheer cinematic brio. Lon Chaney gets the most out of every scene in a remarkably energetic, tortured, yet *humane* performance. He holds the film together, and keeps the waves of melodrama from washing out one of the over-arching themes of Leroux's original story: that loves grows in the heart of all creatures, and that the wounded among us often have the most, and deepest, love to give.

Psycho

Robert Bloch's novel of a lonely and deeply disturbed motel keeper, *Psycho*, is a book that is impossible to read.

That's not an aesthetic judgment of Bloch's writing. His efficient, workmanlike prose, suspenseful plot, and memorable characterizations suit his narrative. The book delivers all the thrills and chills one hopes to get from fiction in the horror genre—even surpassing the boundaries of what was, at the time of its writing, standard scare fare.

Yet it's a book that is impossible to read.

It's extraordinarily unlikely that anyone coming to the book today will truly be able to read it—that is, to see what *Bloch* wanted them to see. Instead, Bloch's vision has been supplanted by that of Alfred Hitchcock, director of the 1960 film version, one of the most famous and revered movies of all time.[1] *Psycho*, the movie, seems to be on every critic's "must see" list of all-time great films, and so if anyone ever does actually get around to reading the novel, it's the characters, mood, and vision of the filmmaker, not the writer, that are likely to be uppermost in his or her mind. And while this is often the case with lots of other books that have been made into movies, few films have left such an indelible imprint on the cultural mental landscape as *Psycho*.

After spending two hours with young, skinny, neurotic Anthony Perkins as he plays Norman Bates and crumbles slowly under the twin pressures of his dead mother's ghost and the investigation into the murder of Marion Crane, can a reader really embrace Bloch's original version of Norman as fat, middle-aged and bespectacled?

And though Bloch takes such great pains to create the illusion that Norman's mother is still alive, controlling her son through her despotic smothering, the reader is forced to nod knowingly long in advance of the revelation of her death, remembering those scenes in the movie where Norman dons her garb and pretends to be his long-deceased mother. While

Bloch's book is an enjoyable read, it's not a masterpiece of fiction. It took the genius of Hitchcock to turn the story of a psychologically scarred recluse into an enduring work of art.

Okay, but you've got to give Bloch points for originality, right? Well, yes and no. He did write the 220-page narrative that became the basis for the movie (and, Norman's physical appearance aside, *Psycho* followed the book extremely closely). However, as is the case with many enduring works of fiction, the story was inspired by a true story, the grisly non-fiction accounts of a psychotic murderer named Ed Gein.

In 1957, police arrested the Plainfield, Wisconsin, resident for murder after they discovered a female victim decapitated and hanging upside down from meat hooks in his garage. It was, tragically, the first of dozens of gruesome discoveries on Gein's property, a tract of farmland he inherited from his domineering, puritanical mother. Subsequent investigations found lots of other bodies — and body parts — strewn throughout the Gein home (severed heads placed on shelves, internal organs in jars on desks, bodies buried around the yard). Many of these body parts came from corpses Gein dug up from various Wisconsin graveyards.

Psychological investigators began to determine the full extent of Gein's monstrously psychotic behavior. Apparently unable to overcome his extreme resentment and simultaneous adoration of his mother after her death, Gein became obsessed with the physical bodies of women his mother's age, often flaying their corpses so he could wrap himself in the skin of these middle-aged women. He would often wear women's clothes, sometimes stuffed with actual female dismembered body parts, and he would talk in his mother's voice in her room — which he left absolutely undisturbed in the years since her death. Investigators say Gein's mother drilled into him a loathing for sexual contact, and when she herself died, Gein slipped over the edge of sanity, pretending to be his mother while also committing unspeakable indiscretions that he knew would rile his mother.[2]

The novelist Bloch lived about 35 miles from Plainfield and filtered the press accounts of the Gein saga into his latest work of fiction. As Bloch has commented, he began the book with "the notion that the man next door may be a monster unsuspected even in the gossip-ridden microcosm of small-town life." Though many of the specific and grisly details of the Gein case were kept out of the press, Bloch admitted later he was surprised when "discovered how closely the imaginary character I'd created resembled the real Ed Gein both in overt act and apparent motivation."[3]

The Master of Suspense, Alfred Hitchcock, used all the means at his disposal—including barring moviegoing latecomers from being admitted to theaters once the film began—to make *Psycho* a national sensation.

This resemblance hits home in the early chapters of *Psycho*, where Bloch really focuses on Norman's mother fixation. While in the movie the twisty relationship between Norman and his mother is something the viewer gradually discovers, the novel provides several early, extended scenes of Norman and his mother having lengthy and uncomfortable debates about his lifestyle and general philosophy. Throughout these chapters, the reader is led to believe that Norman's mother is actually there, in the room with him, a lively and hectoring presence. The only relief he seems to get from this onslaught of personal animus can be found in his reading. Norman collects esoteric volumes of supernatural religious practices and gruesome historical studies. The following passage, inspired by Norman's reading of a book called *The Realm of the Incas* (which details various ritual practices and tortures), provides a glimpse into Norman's perverse curiosity. He has just come across a passage about the "grotesque but effective" procedure of turning an enemy's body into a kind of war tom-tom:

> Norman smiled, then allowed himself the luxury of a comfortable shiver. *Grotesque but effective*— it certainly *must* have been! Imagine flaying a man — alive, probably — and then stretching his belly to use it as a drum! How did they actually go about doing that, curing and preserving the flesh of the corpse to prevent decay? For that matter, what kind of a mentality did it take to conceive of such an idea in the first place?[4]

Norman exhibits an extraordinary amount of patience as his mother criticizes him for his personal weakness, his poor business judgment, and his impure thoughts, though he seldom has a chance to register any impure thoughts. His extremely chaste lifestyle keeps him remote from any actual sources of temptation. Much the same could be said of Mary Crane (as opposed to "Marion," the first name given her in the movie), a woman who seldom had the opportunity to be tempted to do the wrong thing. Bloch provides a psychological backstory that helps make sense of Mary's decision to steal $50,000 from her employer and run off to join her lover, Sam Loomis. In the early sections of the book that deal with Mary, she clearly hears the clock ticking, there's a gnawing sense of desperation, a fear that time to truly *live* is running out. She has been the dutiful daughter, sister, and employee for so long that she has forgotten how to satisfy her own needs. The opportunity to abscond with enough money to bring her and her lover some happiness proves to be too much, and she gives in. Norman Bates and Mary Crane are on a crash course that fate has set them upon, their moments of madness fueled by a lifetime of living up to others' unreasonable expectations. Of course, Norman's attempts to please his controlling and delusional mother yielded far worse results than Mary's mere attempts to adhere to society's norms, and that's where *Psycho* really separates itself from the horde of genre-fiction thrillers familiar to horror readers up to that time. While most horror stories produced before Bloch's

1959 book conjured up a villain from the shop-worn list of *external* bugaboos — aliens, ghosts, vampires, mad scientists, et al. — it was *Psycho* that really put the horrors of the mind front and center. Bloch's work — and Hitchcock's popularization of it — made it possible for writers to begin to mine new terrain for terror: the interior of the human mind.

Even the classic "shower scene" that everyone remembers from the movie is, in Bloch's hands, a psychological horror. The scene takes pages and pages to unfold, and the reader is treated to multiple perspectives: Mary's ("And that's what she was going to do, take a nice, long hot shower. Get the dirt off her hide, just as she was going to get the dirt cleaned out of her insides. *Come clean, Mary. Come clean as snow.*"[5]), Norman's ("He was going to tilt the framed license on the wall and peek through the little hole he had drilled so long ago. Nobody else knew about that hole, not even Mother."[6]) and even Norman's mother ("There was nothing to be afraid of. She'd come to protect him from the bitches. Yes, that was it. She'd come to protect him. Whenever he needed her, mother was there."[7]). Hitchcock regularly gets lauded for his ability to show us the shower attack without actually showing us the knife striking the flesh, but Bloch, arguably, has the even trickier task of showcasing a murderous scene that plays out largely in the minds of his characters.

But it is once again Hitchcock's work that has left generations of film critics gasping for the right words to convey the master's chilly proficiency with Bloch's story. Just why *Psycho* has become one of the most analyzed films in cinematic history is subject to multiple interpretations but there can be no doubt about its impact and influence.

In addition to being a cinematic genius, Hitchcock was also a crafty promoter, and he came up with a marketing idea that helped ensure *Psycho* would make at least a temporary splash at the time of its release. Hitchcock decreed — and theater owners agreed, surprisingly — that no one would be allowed into a showing of the movie once the film began. There were signs in theater lobbies around the country noting that even the president of the United States "will not be admitted after the film begins."[8] Of course, the public responded to this cinematic catnip by lining up for hours before show times, eager to get a seat and be in on the secret.

Early critical reaction to the film was not nearly so enthusiastic — a muted response that some of those involved in the film attributed to Hitchcock's refusal to allow advance critic screenings. "I think the critics didn't want to see it in a theater. That really pissed them off," said Joseph Stefano, the film's screenwriter. "They wanted to see it in a screening room, but Mr. Hitchcock said 'No Previews!' I'm convinced we got a lot of bad reviews because of it."[9]

Those early reviews stand as Exhibit A in the changing fortunes of popular art, as *Psycho* has gone on to become one of the most celebrated and admired films of the modern era. So what makes it such a great film?

The list is well rehearsed, but still apt, and impressive. Start with the performances. Anthony Perkins provides one of the most memorable character turns in movie history. There's the nervous stutter that underlies Norman's apparent nonchalance. There's the personal charm, the warm smile that stands in contradistinction to his homicidal impulse. There's the palpable sense of entrapment, of being like those stuffed birds he collects. And of course, there's the ambivalence about his mother. He apologizes for her eccentricities to the bemused but alarmed Marion Crane, played by Janet Leigh. He defends his mother, explains his mother, resents his mother, itches to be his own man but simultaneously recoils into the scared little boy that engenders viewers' sympathies. One of screenwriter Stefano's first decisions was to rewrite Norman as young, nervous, and shy — giving the audience a much more sympathetic character to wrestle with for the final two-thirds of the movie.[10]

Of course, there's the story — a twisting psychological mystery that entrances viewers no matter how often the movie has been seen. The plot, though based on a real-life killer in Ed Gein, was utterly original and unprecedented. Most horror films to that time relied on a different sort of scar, a monster "out there." *Psycho* is a horror film about the monster in your own mind.

And of course, there's the mastery of Alfred Hitchcock, who fills the black-and-white film with so many compelling and memorable scenes that the movie is a kind of primer on how to create horror without the requisite blood and gore that cheapen so many modern fright films. The shower scene is, of course, the alpha and omega of memorable horror movie scenes, made all the more remarkable because of what the viewer *thinks* he or she sees (we don't see Janet Leigh's breasts, contrary to widespread belief, nor do we ever see the knife piercing her flesh). It took Hitchcock seven days to film the 45 seconds of film that make up the attack. The sound of the knife hacking into Marion was the result of Hitchcock experimenting with several different sound effects, eventually settling on a knife repeatedly plunging into a casaba melon. The traces of "blood" that darken the swirling water as Leigh meets her fate are actually chocolate syrup (movie blood and ketchup having tested as too dark). One third of Leigh's time on the set of *Psycho* was spent standing in the shower, screaming, flesh-colored moleskin clinging tenuously to her waterlogged flesh.

But long before we arrive at the Bates Motel, from the first strains of

Delivering one of the most effective performances in the history of suspense-horror, Anthony Perkins came to be identified for the rest of his career with the deeply disturbed Norman Bates.

Bernard Herrmann's schizophrenic score (all strings, alternating between screeching violins and plaintive, mournful basses), the movie feels different. Just when Hitchcock puts you on edge with his manic opening music and interlocking, abstract title sequence, the film changes pace with an expansive wide shot of a modern cityscape and a slow pan into one of those numberless windows that reveals human life within. In this case, it's two lovers, fresh from a tryst (Marion and her paramour Sam Loomis, played by John Gavin), talking about the future of their relationship, and where it ought to go. Unlike the book, which opens squarely in the world and mind of Norman Bates, this would appear to be a love story in the making, one of the many attempts at misdirection Hitchcock employs to keep the viewer unsettled.

As the film unfolds, it is Marion who is front and center, and her dilemma (whether to abscond with the $50,000 entrusted to her by her boss, and once taken, whether to return it) would seem to be the focal point of the story. Her arrival at the Bates motel appears little more than providential — a narrative (as well as literal) detour that might illuminate her plight and advance her story. The murderous act that claims her life is shocking, not only because of the mix of artistry and butchery but also because of what it does to the viewer's expectations. A leading lady at the heart of a story — played by a star, no less — killed in the first act of the film? What's going on here?

The questions are just beginning, and they keep coming until the final moments, when a psychological expert explains on screen just what we've seen, and what it means, and how it could have happened. But these theories seem more comforting in the abstract than they do when applied to the real live flesh-and-blood Norman Bates, who even in his last few frames manages to convey the indecipherability of the interior of the disturbed human mind.

People responded to Hitchcock's cockeyed view of the psyche, and the film was a huge hit. Perkins continued to work in television and film for decades afterward, but it was his role in this movie that represented the high water mark of his career. He was forever identified with Norman Bates, and in 1983, he gave in after years of pressure to reprise his role as the troubled motel keeper for *Psycho II*, a film that naturally left some critics disappointed. Overall, however, the movie is pretty good and quite suspenseful, and its popular success led to a third installment, also starring Perkins.

Robert Bloch also revisited the Bates Motel for a couple of follow-ups to his best-known product, turning out *Psycho II* (which was unconnected to the movie) and a third volume, *Psycho House*.

In the opinion of many critics, the film *Psycho* changed the way both the audience and filmmakers approached the horror genre, grounding it in the science of psychology and rescuing it from the throes of rubber-suited swamp creatures and mutating alien blobs. Norman Bates, for all his nervous tics and defensive, rambling tirades, could really be the guy next door. Keep your shades down, keep your bathroom door locked. The world had a new villain, the guy who had "issues" with his mother. Bloch and Hitchcock had taken the sacred and made it profane.

The movie is always something of a revelation, no mater how many times one has seen it. Fans of today's horror fare, raised on a steady and desensitizing diet of slashers and hackers who most certainly *do* plunge their cutlery on screen into their victims (who unlike Janet Leigh generally reveal much more than just their limited acting range), really need to revisit *Psycho* for its remarkable power of suggestion. Hitchcock was able to unsettle an entire generation of filmgoers with a little chocolate syrup, a casaba melon, and a few of reels of black-and-white film stock. He didn't need wind machines, special effects, computer-generated graphics, or even 3-D. What makes Norman such a perennial terror, and a character who will live in our imaginations, is not his wild, psychotic attack mode but rather that he's indistinguishable from the people one meets every day, people who are just trying to get through life without losing it. "We all go a little mad sometimes," Norman Bates reminds Marion Crane quietly, a half-smile forming on his lips, as gentle-seeming as a loving son can be.

Re-Animator

The cult of readers that reveres the writer H.P. Lovecraft seems to grow larger with each passing year. Though he never became a darling of academics, like his doppelganger Poe, Lovecraft and his minions have persistently dwelt on the fringes of respectability, due mostly to the writer's "pulp fiction" origins. But there are signs that might be changing, with fan clubs, Lovecraft-inspired websites, and glossy new re-issues of his work becoming *de rigueur* among horror fans — and even "serious" readers. The heavy lifting of his reputation, however, has always fallen to his ardent disciples. Get true devotees talking about Lovecraft, and they will tell you, first, how brilliant he was. They will weigh in with accolades about his labyrinthine prose style and his immersion in English literature of the Neo-classical era. They'll also point out that he was a learned author of scientific papers on astronomy, and a pithy correspondent whose voluminous correspondence is lyrical, insightful, even brilliant.

And he wrote some great zombie stories, too.

At the end of the day, Howard Phillips Lovecraft knew who he was. "There is no field other than the weird in which I have any aptitude or inclination for fictional composition. Life has never interested me so much as the escape from life," he once noted. And so he searched feverishly in his fiction for an escape hatch, an exit from the problem-filled life we all experience. Unfortunately for his protagonists, when they do find the escape hatch, what exists on the other side is worse. Usually much worse.

Lovecraft's works, which languished in near-obscurity at the time of his death at age 46 in 1937, are fraught with the standard horrors that one finds in lots of other scary stories but also much more, and much darker, psychological elements: paranoia, nihilism, existential defeat. In the final analysis, humans are doomed, utterly, in Lovecraft's world. Though it's not actually his world, or ours. The world as we know it is really a plaything for cruel, alien forces who dwarf us in intelligence and revel in visiting misery upon us.[1] Lovecraft has always been a page-turner for fatalists who love literature. As one website dedicated to the author notes, "His works were deeply pessimistic, and cynical, challenging the values of the Enlightenment, Romanticism, and Christian humanism. Lovecraft's protagonists usually achieve the mirror opposite of traditional gnosis and mysticism by momentarily glimpsing the horror of ultimate reality."[2]

A glaring irony in all of this is that one of Lovecraft's better-known works has inspired a classic modern horror movie that is far more campy than creepy, more fun than funereal. The 1985 film *Re-Animator*, based on Lovecraft's early work "Herbert West — Reanimator," is much more darkly humorous than darkly Lovecraftian.

"Herbert West — Reanimator" was one of Lovecraft's first professionally published stories. He wrote six installments for serialization in a magazine run by an acquaintance, who rewarded Lovecraft's efforts with $5 per installment.[3] There's little to indicate how well the stories were received, and Lovecraft himself came to regard the effort as little more than an obligation to a friend. What popularity the story continues to enjoy today is due almost exclusively to the 1985 film adaptation, which dropped the prosaic "Herbert West" from the title but kept the tantalizing "Re-Animator." Lovecraft fans don't usually number "Herbert West — Reanimator" among his finest efforts, yet it does contain much of what would earmark Lovecraft's best work, as well as reveal an artist still groping for a definitive style. It's an unfairly disparaged story, a fun and freaky narrative that offers most of the satisfactions one looks for in horror and suspense literature. It lacks the gravitas of later Lovecraft but makes up for it in narrative verve and sheer kookiness.

The real action of the story happens in the first two of the six parts, and the film wisely focuses on these two installments (though it also appropriates some material from the climactic final installment). The premise is simple: A young medical student at Miskatonic University in Arkham, Massachusetts (an institution and town Lovecraft invented, and would return to again and again in his fiction), has fallen out of favor with his professors because of his unauthorized experiments with recently deceased dogs, cats, and various other animals — whom West believes can be brought back to life, or "re-animated," by the injection of a life-giving serum. In the story, West is assisted by an unnamed student who narrates the tale. The two refuse to let the protestations of the medical faculty keep them from testing this serum, and in fact they ratchet it up a level, seeking recently deceased human corpses for their experimentation.

"Herbert West — Reanimator" succeeds on a number of levels, aided largely by the recurrent, matter-of-fact tone that reassures the readers that we are in the realm of science, not fiction: "[Holding] that the so-called 'soul' is a myth, my friend believed that artificial reanimation of the dead can depend only on the condition of the tissues; and that unless actual decomposition has set in, a corpse fully equipped with organs may with suitable measures be set going again in the peculiar fashion known as life."[4]

This tone is put to use in the service of describing the increasingly macabre experimentation that West and his colleague pursue: "We followed the local death-notices like ghouls, for our specimens demanded particular qualities. What we wanted were corpses interred soon after death and without artificial preservation; preferably free from malforming disease, and certainly with all organs present. Accident victims were our best hope."[5]

That last line — so clinical and abjectly insensitive — points to one of the ways in which this story succeeds. In this horror story, there's an absence of characters who are horrified by these experiments. The medical school officials don't object on ethical grounds, but rather because the experiments fall outside the approved curriculum. The moral tone of "Herbert West — Reanimator" is ice cold. The narrator coolly laments the lack of fresh bodies available to him and his ghoulish co-conspirator because "[t]he college had first choice in every case."[6] Lovecraft playfully exploits this dearth of feeling. After a fresh corpse is dug up in a midnight raid, the narrator notes: "The process of unearthing was slow and sordid — it might have been gruesomely poetical if we had been artists instead of scientists."[7]

That ability to describe horrific behavior in the tone of a clinician would become one of Lovecraft's defining qualities. Yet in this early story we also see the young writer struggling with the ghost of Edgar Allan Poe, whose overwrought prose style and metaphorical richness profoundly impacted Lovecraft. "Herbert West — Reanimator" contains lots of passages that sound like Poe transposed: "Not more unutterable could have been the chaos of hellish sound if the pit itself had opened to release the agony of the damned, for in one inconceivable cacophony was centered all the supernatural terror and unnatural despair of animate nature."[8] In the hands of the not-yet-mature prose stylist Lovecraft, such straining after significance can strike some readers as a bit overheated.

Yet the story still captivates as the narrative moves, however gruesomely, towards the inevitable attempt to reanimate a human corpse. As West and his collaborators race to find a suitable subject for their experiments, Lovecraft adds a complicating factor: a typhoid plague is ravaging Arkham. This might seem to be good news for corpse hunters but it adds some new difficulties to their task. Because the protagonists are both medical men, they are pressed into service to treat victims and attend to the dying, an exhausting regimen that leaves them precious little time to go grave-robbing:

> And then had come the scourge, grinning and lethal, from the nightmare caverns of tartarus. West and I had graduated about the time of its beginning, but had remained for additional work at the summer school, so that we were in Arkham when it broke with full daemonic fury upon the town. Though not as yet licensed physicians, we now had our degrees, and were pressed frantically into public service as the numbers of the stricken grew. The situation was almost past management, and deaths ensued too frequently for the local undertakers fully to handle.... This circumstance was not without effect on West, who thought often of the irony of the situation — so many fresh specimens, yet none for his persecuted researches!"[9]

The very man who "persecuted" West — Dr. Allan Halsey, dean of the Medical School — succumbs to the plague himself, and in another instance of Lovecraftian irony lends his body to the reanimation effort (at least, that's the suggestion, for the corpse West brings to his laboratory three days after Halsey's death bore "an unbelievable resemblance to a learned and self-sacrificing martyr who had been entombed by three days before — the late Dr. Allan Halsey, public benefactor and dean of the medical school of Miskatonic University"[10]).

Not surprisingly, the experiment goes wildly wrong. The corpse does indeed come back to life but in its nascent zombie state, possessed of renewed, chemically enhanced strength but brain damaged from three days of lifelessness, the zombie destroys the laboratory, assaults his reanimators, and leaps out of the window. For three days he runs free in Arkham, engineering a small reign of terror. So vicious are the attacks that a circus manager is questioned to see if any of his exotic creatures had escaped from their cages. The vicious ministrations of the resurrected scourge are much worse than even the typhoid menace stifling the town: "Eight houses were entered by a nameless thing which strewed the red death in its wake — in all, seventeen maimed and shapeless remnants of bodies were left behind by the voiceless, sadistic monster that crept abroad. A few persons had half seen it in the dark, and said it was white and like a malformed ape or an anthropomorphic fiend."[11] A local posse eventually tracks it down and shoots it. Wounded, it is taken to a local insane asylum, "where it beats its head against the wall of a padded cell for sixteen years."[12]

Installments three through six detail West and his partner's continuing efforts to refine their reanimation serum and their subsequent struggles to find suitable subjects for their experimentation. Each newly reanimated corpse suffers from various setbacks or unforeseen side effects of the process, many escaping into the night in their reanimated state. In addition, West expands his experiments to include reanimation efforts on individual body parts, and he even succeeds in reanimating a severed head and its former bodily host.

In a perhaps predictable ending for a series of cliffhanging stories, West meets his end when the legion of reanimated beings convenes and hunts him down. These later installments provided the grist for further *Re-Animator* film sequels, but it's the first and original *Re-Animator* film that has ensured the immortality of this series of stories, which are still widely republished today.

It should be noted that among Lovecraft's gifts as a writer are also found some qualities that continue to bother even some of his most devout fans, especially a tendency to disparage minority figures. Insertions of admittedly racist sentiments — one of the most famous of which occurs in "Herbert West — Reanimator" — are dismissed by some fans as merely indicative of the thinking of the time. Others are less inclined to overlook such passages as this one, where West and his partner are summoned to a boxing match to attend to a fallen fighter:

> The Negro had been knocked out, and a moment's examination shewed us that he would permanently remain so. He was a loathsome, gorilla-like thing, with abnormally long arms which I could not help calling fore legs, and a face that conjured up thoughts of unspeakable Congo secrets and tom-tom poundings under an eerie moon."[13]

Such observations do creep occasionally into his fiction and letters. His critics have acknowledged this unfortunate mental tic. Esteemed Lovecraft biographer S.T. Joshi noted, in an online interview, "It is foolish to deny that racism enters into his fiction at key points — although I might suggest there is a considerable element of humour and parody in that passage [from 'Herbert West']." Many readers would perhaps be inclined to agree that questions of ethnography are secondary in a story like "Herbert West — Reanimator" which is, after all, a campy thriller about zombies.

Now a Terrifying Motion Picture!

The movie version restores this focus, subordinating everything else in the story to the central, gruesome, and oddly compelling reanimation efforts. *Re-Animator* is certainly one of the most gleeful zombie movies ever made, and its deft handling of the darkly comic, the grossly exaggerated, and the straightforward narrative make the film a curiously rewarding viewing experience.

Directed by Stuart Gordon and adapted for the screen by Gordon, Dennis Paoli, and William Norris, it also represents an inversion of the normal book-to-movie conversion. Filmmakers often jettison aspects of character development in the interest of advancing the plot. Characters' backstories don't often survive the adaptation process. In *Re-Animator*, that situation is reversed. Lovecraft provides almost no information about Herbert West; there is some perfunctory physical description (hair color, glasses, etc.), but the reader knows nothing about where West came from, or what makes him tick. Since Lovecraft was writing for the pulp magazine market, he was primarily interested in creating a gripping story, with each installment providing a brief recapitulation of previous action, and then right back into the laboratory for more fun and games. There wasn't time for character development, nor would readers have been well served by a story that was dependent on character traits that might have been detailed in a previous week's story.

Because the filmmakers could only get so much cinematic mileage out of repeated reanimation efforts (make no mistake: they play those scenes for all their worth), it was necessary to create some dramatic tension with character interaction. So West morphs from simply an exceptionally bright but misguided medical student to a mysterious transfer student, whose past work with a reputed European genius in brain physiology prepares the viewer for some of his unorthodox ideas. The movie version also turns West into an obnoxious, smug, and socially inept young man who seems to delight in offending his peers — especially his "superiors" at the medical college. One of the first scenes shows the callow student disrupting one of his professor's lectures by loudly breaking a pencil each time the professor makes a point West disagrees with. So he's brilliant, but annoying.

But who wants to spend two hours in the presence of a gifted jerk? That's where the partner comes in. The movie provides a much more fully developed character who befriends and works with West, replacing the bland and nameless narrator of the history with a student named Dan

Re-Animator

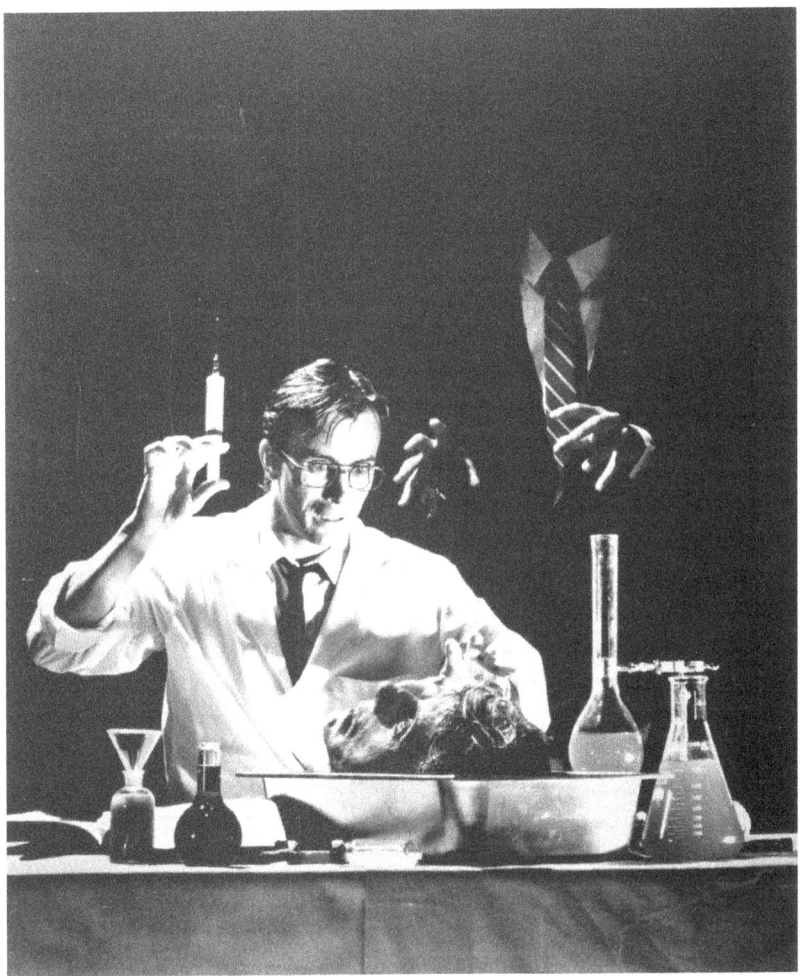

Maniacal medical student Herbert West (Jeffrey Combs) attempts to perfect his life-restoring serum in the cool and campy film *Re-Animator*, based on an H.P. Lovecraft story.

Cain (played by Bruce Abbott). In the movie he has a girlfriend, an apartment, and the requisite doubts and anxiety that any reasonable person would have about West's odd propensities. And their differing personalities — West is brash, unfeeling, and rather prissy while Cain is curious and humane — provides the opportunity for the filmmaker to explore their differing philosophies, and for West to explain to his peer the thinking behind his experimentation: "The theory is really quite simple. All life is a physical and chemical process — correct? It stands to reason then that if one could find extremely fresh specimens and recharge those chemical processes, then, bang! We have reanimation ... we can defeat death!"[14]

Although the film fleshes out the characters more fully, it mostly traffics in cinematic clichés and stereotypes. It vilifies the head of the medical school, Dean Halsey, turning a wise and sympathetic character in the original story into a stereotypically power-hungry and insecure bureaucrat, and it makes one of West's professors an evil schemer who tries to blackmail West to get the formula for his serum.

The movie is also infamous for featuring gore a-plenty. There's lots of blood, severed limbs, decapitated bodies, and other unappetizing screen fare. But the violence and gore are all over-the-top, so campy and cartoonish as to be laughably inoffensive. There are outrageous scenes of a headless body carrying around its former head in a shallow pan, naked reanimated zombies running amok in a hospital, and even a long-deceased cat that comes screaming back to life (though the "special effect" in that scene is clearly nothing more than a mangy, stuffed cat puppet). *Re-Animator* also features one of the all-time creepiest sexual moments in cinema, as a decapitated medical school professor fondles the dean's daughter as she's strapped naked to a gurney, while his decapitated head nearby whispers in her ear, "I've always loved you!"[15]

Such scenes have helped the film earn its reputation as one of the strangest and most arresting horror films in recent decades. It's a bizarre compendium of some time-honored horror film clichés, awash in blood and reanimating serum, and just enough of a compelling, intellectually teasing hook (are such experiments ghoulish descents into madness or legitimate areas for scientific inquiry?) to sustain genuine interest. *Re-Animator* also contains some clever touches that reveal themselves through repeated viewings. For instance, in the early scene where Dan Cain and his girlfriend, the dean's daughter, are in bed, the viewer catches a glimpse of the poster hanging above his headboard: an advertisement for the concert movie *Stop Making Sense* starring the avant-garde rock band Talking Heads. For a zombie movie that degenerates into a carnival of senselessness, it's the perfect avatar of what's to come — including talking heads!

There are lots of small, clever moments throughout. In one early scene, a doctor is seen trying to save a life, refusing to give up hope. Eventually defeated, he wheels the body to the medical school morgue and unlocks the door. A security guard offers what at first seems to be a throwaway line that only later acquires ironic overtones: "Why do they lock the doors of the morgue?" he smirks.[16] By the end of the movie, he'll have his answer.

Re-Animator, clearly, is not for everybody. At the time of its release, it was greeted with groans by some critics who found its manic energy and quirky plot overmatched by its quotient of gore and grotesqueness. And the ending, in which a zombie army rises up in anger, wreaking vengeance on the living, was simply too much for some viewers.

But that ending reinforces one of Lovecraft's prevailing themes: the destruction wrought by an unfettered curiosity. Humanity, in its quest to know and to discover, will eventually get its wish — but at a frightful price. Science will uncover truths that the mind is not capable of embracing. The Herbert Wests among us represent the nadir of human longing for knowledge — and the beginning of our end. As Lovecraft once wrote,

> Life is a hideous thing, and from the background behind what we know of it peer daemoniacal hints of truth which make it sometimes a thousandfold more hideous. Science already oppressive with its shocking revelations, will perhaps be the ultimate exterminator of our human species — if separate species we be — for its reserve of unguessed horrors could never be borne by mortal brains if loosed upon the world.[17]

A horrific prospect, yes, but a great idea for a movie.

The Serpent and the Rainbow

Death is the great leveler. It's inescapable. And while we can't know what lies beyond, we ought to feel reasonably confident assessing the condition itself: lack of heartbeat, cessation of respiratory function, termination of brain function. Pronouncing someone bereft of life really shouldn't be a guessing game. It's the very certainty of death that horror writers and filmmakers exploit when they bring a being back to life. Obviously, there's something startling about confronting someone who had been declared dead, an ex-member of the living, an emissary from the mysterious realm of death.

The name that is often given to such creatures — from fiction, folklore and even legitimate science — is zombie.

For most people, the word is enough to conjure up an image familiar from so many cheaply made horror movies about some army of glassy-eyed, rag-draped creatures with gray skin and stiff limbs, wandering about with hungry looks in their eyes. It's hard not to laugh at the absurdity of the zombie — but there's also something undeniably unnerving about the zombie as well. This particular creature straddles the chasm between the ridiculous and the sublime. What's more preposterous than a walking mannequin, complete with tousled hair, decomposed flesh, and moldering grave clothes, wordless and entranced, stumbling about like a hypnotist's unwitting victim? But what's more frightening than the prospect of being *buried alive*, and having to claw one's way out of the grave back to the world above ground?

Those two notions, so far at odds with each other, give the zombie his special power over us today. Most of us deal with the apparition by simply dismissing it as too bizarre for serious consideration. Thank God zombies don't *really* exist, we console ourselves. Now, if there *were* zombies, that would tilt the balance from a thrilling but harmless fright to a genuine nightmare. Just how do you get your mind around the idea that the dead have actually sprung from their graves? It's too weird to even contemplate.

Weirder still, it's not only been contemplated, it has apparently been proved—by a Harvard-educated scientist, no less.

"We propose to send you to the frontier of death."[1] This was the proposition offered to Wade Davis, a graduate student in ethno-botany at Harvard University, who was urged by his mentor to embark on a journey to Haiti to investigate the phenomenon of, well, zombies. Davis' remarkable account of his time among the living—and otherwise—became the controversial 1985 book *The Serpent and the Rainbow*.

This non-fiction work doesn't fail to live up to the promise in the book's subtitle: *A Harvard Scientist's Astonishing Journey Into the Secret Societies of Haitian Voodoo, Zombies, and Magic*. Astonishing it truly is, but perhaps even more astonishing is how Davis managed to write a book about zombies that is so impressively sober. *The Serpent and the Rainbow* is a work of serious scholarship—never dull or blandly academic, but also never salacious or flip. It would have been easy, one imagines, to engage in overheated prose or hyperbolic exhortations, given the subject matter (few people are indifferent, presumably, on the subject of the threat posed by a corps of the undead shuffling about). But Davis keeps his eye on his work, which he clearly loves: seeking out the source of a mysterious zombification powder that might help explain how these zombies were able to present the symptoms of death though still, technically, be alive.

The book is really a record of Davis' attempts to reconcile science, mysticism, and arcane folk tradition. It focuses on one particular case—a man named Clairvius Narcisse—who had been declared dead by Haitian medical officials only to turn up in his village several years later, alive (though much, much worse for the wear); Davis pieces together a puzzle whose picture ends up looking pretty dark and dangerous. He uncovers a system of Haitian justice that operates in secret and appears to deal with certain "undesirables" by sentencing them to zombification. What this actually means is that these individuals who have violated the norms of their tribal-like communities are "sold" to a voodoo priest or priestess, who arranges to have them dusted with a poisonous powder that creates a catatonic, death-like state after it is ingested or absorbed through the skin. Once they have been "marked" for selection by the voodoo practitioner, they become a pariah in their community, and as a result of their "death," the rest of the village wants them removed as quickly as possible, so as not to anger the spirit world. So, the victim is buried right after the pronouncement of death by the medical establishment. But not being dead, actually, creates a real problem for the victim. Although Davis is somewhat unclear on the specifics of how the body actually makes it back above ground, in most cases of zombification the "resurrected" person is kidnapped at his gravesite, drugged again, and sold into indentured servitude in the hinterlands of rural Haiti, forced to live as a slave and a perpetual pariah. Occasionally, these "zombies" escape and return to their villages where they are greeted like the living dead: with violent scorn and great trepidation.

Davis retains just the right mix of astonishment and scientific demeanor to keep the twin threads of his narrative moving: the specific zombie case he's investigating and the broader exploration of a society whose spiritual reins are held by practitioners of voodoo. Frequently, the threads become intertwined, as when he finally discovers the source of the zombie powder: "The implications of these conclusions were extraordinary. Here was a material basis for the entire zombie phenomenon — a folk poison containing known toxins fully capable of pharmacologically inducing a state of apparent death."[2]

Much of *The Serpent and the Rainbow* has nothing to do with zombies. Davis provides an immense amount of information about Haiti — its history, its people, its geography. Perhaps not unexpectedly from a Ph.D. candidate writing about the flora, fauna and wildlife of the country (the book grew out of his doctoral dissertation), there are whole chapters where the zombie thread is left hanging as we venture into the countryside with Davis on one of his hunter-gatherer outings. But even these are infused with a sense of such childlike wonder that it's hard not to be drawn into Davis' world of the microscope and petri dish. There's even a touch of the poet in the ethno-botanist: "In the damp evenings, sitting awake for long hours while the torrential rains turned the earth to mud, I began to feel like a crystal of sugar on the tongue of a beast, impatiently awaiting dissolution."[3]

Davis' book would have gotten little attention if it had just been a naturalist's study of Haitian life and vegetation. It's the world of the zombie that made the book so popular and controversial (with some scientific authorities questioning Davis' conclusions[4]). And while the author paints a clear picture of a horrible predicament — to be turned into a zombie — is his sociological excavation of Haitian sub-cultures really a fitting source for a horror movie?

Well, it must have seemed so to at least a few people in Hollywood. The film version of *The Serpent and the Rainbow* was directed by one of the most acclaimed and successful horror directors of the last couple of decades, Wes Craven, whose classic *Nightmare on Elm Street* helped revive a subgenre of horror films. But that doesn't necessarily mean that Davis wrote a horror book. In fact, initial readers of Davis' book must have been taken somewhat aback to learn that the book had been turned into a horror film, reading as it does like a sociological treatise, low on the scare factor and high on anthropological conclusions. In fact, Davis not only doesn't condemn the culture of black magic that envelops Haitian society, he offers several eloquent arguments for the *embrace* of this "alternative" religion. Davis' thesis is as much a plea for preserving the old "folk" ways of primitive cultures as it is an excavation of their origins and effects. His subsequent work and writings have revealed a genuine passion to preserve and even revere those modes of living that might strike the Western mind as "backwards."[5]

But moviegoers can be forgiven if they feel less inclined to adopt the ways of the Haitian peasantry — at least as they are presented in Craven's *The Serpent and the Rainbow*, a film "inspired by" Davis' book. Although the basic premise of Davis' investigative work remains intact in the film — that is, the pursuit of the magical powder — Craven opts for a far more dramatic (and, in much of the film, completely invented) presentation of events. The biggest change from the book has to do with the role of Davis (played in the movie by Bill Pullman as Dr. Dennis Alan). In the book, the scientist involves himself in the pursuit of the mysterious zombie powder, but in the movie he goes much further, arousing the interest of a sadistic captain of the Haitian secret police and even suffering a bout of zombification himself. The final half-hour represents the triumph of creative license over original source material, and while not un-entertaining, we've clearly traded the realm of the possible for the terror of the implausible.

Yet, for all of the creative license taken by the makers of the film, the movie emerges as a thoroughly entertaining, moody and even thoughtful exploration of Haiti and its various sub-cultures. What Craven has tried to do in the film is pretty ambitious, given the template that most horror movie makers work from. There's an entertaining and culturally rich subtext that wends its way through the movie. Craven chose to intertwine a narrative of political upheaval — Haiti's political revolution and the deposing of dictator "Baby Doc" Duvalier—amid the voodoo ceremonies and black magic rituals.[6] In an clear departure from the original source material, the film portrays those who are "zombified" as political dissidents who were opposed to the Duvalier regime. So zombification becomes a kind of political payback. Nothing of the sort is suggested in Davis' book, but such a motive does allow the film to address the political situation in a way that seems germane to the plot, rather than arbitrarily tacked on.

There are a lot of reasons to give this film a closer look—despite its flaws (including a very silly ending that somewhat undercuts the entire film). The story is compelling, the script moves briskly, and Craven has given us one of the great movie villains not only in the horror genre, but in all of cinema, a corrupt Haitian police captain who moonlights as a voodoo priest (though it might be the other way around). Played with icy restraint and pitch-perfect creepiness by South African actor Zakes Mokae, the character of Dargent Peytraud deserves to take his place with such cerebral tormenters as Hannibal Lecter from *Silence of the Lambs* and O'Brien from *1984*.

Voodoo is nothing to trifle with, as Bill Pullman will soon discover in Wes Craven's film of the non-fiction book *The Serpent and the Rainbow*.

The Serpent and the Rainbow

The film gets off to a rather unpromising start with the following pseudo-profound words on a black screen: "In the legends of voodoo, the Serpent is the symbol of Earth. The rainbow is a symbol of heaven. Between the two, all creatures must live and die. But because he has a soul, Man can be trapped in a terrible place where death is only the beginning." Cue the shivers! What in Davis' book served as a rather profound and moving creation myth becomes here simply a mantra to remind moviegoers that they've bought a ticket for a horror flick.

Early in the movie, we meet Harvard anthropologist Dennis Alan in full Indiana Jones mode, tromping through the jungle, being chased by a jaguar, coming across the dead body of his helicopter pilot, running for his life, etc. The scenes in the Amazon, and in Haiti, have the full flavor of big-screen adventure — yet the rest of the movie offsets what would otherwise merely be comic-book escapades by its serious consideration of Haitian mores and spiritual practices, which are to most Western observers pretty weird. The whole movie screens like a hybrid between *Raiders of the Lost Ark* and the icily demonic *Angel Heart*, a film by Alan Parker that also deals with voodoo but is consistently darker and much more mysterious. Yet *The Serpent and the Rainbow* holds its own with these two classics, in part on the strength of its directorial verve. Every scene is *alive*. The appealing Bill Pullman throws himself completely into the various uncomfortable postures that Craven puts him in: wrestling with a jaguar, handling a slithering python, letting a tarantula crawl across his face, having a nail being driven through his scrotum, being buried alive, etc. He even becomes the victim of zombie possession at the end, forcing him to flail about and smile dumbly as the film degenerates into "good zombie vs. bad zombie." Still, it's a role that calls for a lot of physical energy and an equal amount of empathy (Dr. Alan is, after all, the everyman who must register for the viewer the extreme puzzlement over the prohibitive weirdness of voodoo culture).

There's a love interest, a wise old mentor — and even a former zombie who hangs around the graveyard, showing up just when needed to rescue Dr. Alan from premature entombment. (Zombies have to stick together, you know.) But it's definitely the villainous character of Dargent Peytraud that makes the film a must-see. Although the role is small by traditional villain standards, actor Zakes Mokae makes even the briefest screen moments resonate with tension. The scene where he attempts to extract information about Alan's reasons for being in Haiti — while the good doctor is strapped into a replica electric chair and about to have his testicles permanently attached to the furniture — is more fun to watch than it is to describe. Peytraud is so confident in his position, and so smart — and so completely *comfortable* in his evil skin — that you have to sort of admire the guy. He never becomes a caricature, a smarmy bad guy from Central Casting. You really believe that this guy thinks he's the baddest dude in Haiti. So we're cheering for Alan, but we're also really eager to see what happens next.

Now, does the fact that none of this actually occurred taint the film? Author Wade Davis has weighed in on the changes wrought by the filmmakers and his verdict is not complimentary: "When I wrote my first book, *The Serpent and the Rainbow*, it was made into one of the worst Hollywood movies in history. I tried to escape the hysteria and the media by going to Borneo."[7]

That might strike some as a rather extreme critical reaction (many people who don't like a movie simply walk out of the theater rather than leave the country). Davis' contempt for the changes clearly kept him from viewing the final product in a more objective light. The irony of his criticism is that the movie is indeed more enjoyable if one has read the book before seeing the film. Notwithstanding the broad creative license taken by the filmmakers, the scenes of peasant life in Haiti and the late-night meetings of Haiti's secret voodoo societies are fleshed out fully in the book, amplifying one's understanding of those scenes in the movie. And some of Davis' larger points — such as how Western ideas of moral purity are incompatible with Haitian thinking — are illustrated in the film, as in the scene where Haitian doctor Marielle Duchamp (the love interest, played by Cathy Tyson) tells Alan, "There is no conflict between our science and our faith. God is not just in Heaven, but in our bodies. Haiti is 85 percent Catholic and 110 percent Voodoo"[8] — a line taken right from Davis' book.

It's not the script's deviations from Davis' serious-minded book that deserve contempt but rather the script's deviation from intelligence that threatens to undermine the film. The ending of what had been, to that point, a bizarre but plausible intellectual mystery-adventure becomes a cheesy effects-laden mess, with Alan destroying Peytraud's voodoo temple and unleashing zombie spirits, good and bad, who inhabit the characters and lead them to — what else — a climactic fistfight amid swirling mists of disembodied spirits. In the melee, Peytraud catches fire and immolates spectacularly — all because Alan broke a few mason jars on an altar containing the trapped souls of the undead. As Davis' book makes clear, voodoo can be easily mocked by those who don't understand it but it does offer a cohesive world view that deserves more respectful treatment than this over-exaggerated meltdown.

Well, at least the good guy wins: As the souls of the trapped are freed by Alan's defeat of Peytraud, the movie gives us scenes of the real Haitian populace storming the governmental buildings and taking back the country from the repressive Duvaliers. The implication is clear: As the veil of black magic is lifted from Haiti, the spirit of freedom re-embraces the populace (rather a stretch, at least as contemporary history has revealed). But in 1988, with the Haitian uprisings still fresh in people's minds, it probably made dramatic sense to turn voodoo into a metaphor.

In voodoo practice, the powder that turns one into a zombie works its special magic after it gets under your skin. The same could be said about this movie.

The Shining

No author, living or deceased, has done more to popularize the horror novel than Stephen King. His more than 50 works — largely novels, but also collections of short stories and non-fiction, too — constitute a "mini-genre" within the overall horror category. His name has become a bankable commodity, his style a brand. When horror fans get together, his name offers a demarcation between styles and types of horror, between likes and dislikes. And within his eye-bulging corpus of work, there are divisions as well: early King, mid-career King, playful King, literary King, serial King. If there is an equivalent in popular literature to the food pyramid, King stands at the apex, his spectacled eyes, flared nostrils, tight thin lips and triangular face peering out like a gargoyle, surreptitiously woven into the wallpaper of horror fans' reading rooms.

For someone who's never read anything by King, the question of where to begin is daunting, but it's also answered in a myriad of places: candid ratings left by customers of online book sellers, reference books about the horror genre, newspaper and magazine reviewers, and King's website, where fans append their comments to the various message boards and proclamations from the man himself. Anybody who's read more than one King work seems to have an opinion about where the best place to start is. And while good arguments could be made for just about any of his books (though not all — some books, such as those in the *Dark Tower* series, must be read in sequence), *The Shining* is perhaps the most appropriate entrée into the King canon.

King said in an introduction written twenty-five years after the book was originally published, "I think that in every writer's career — usually early in it — there comes a 'crossroads novel,' where the writer is presented with a choice: either do what you have done before, or try to reach a little higher.... For me, the crossroads novel was *The Shining*, and I did decide to reach."[1]

The Shining

It apparently paid off. More than 30 years after it was first published, it remains one of King's best-known works — due in large part to a wildly popular 1980 film adaptation as well as a television mini-series in the 1990s. One particular moment from the film has become perhaps the most iconic image of horror in the last 50 years: a demonically grinning Jack Nicholson, showing his face through a hole in a door that he's just bashed with an ax. (In the movie, that memorable image is accompanied by Nicholson's jarringly upbeat "Here's Johnny!")

The Shining is King's spin on the haunted house story, except in this case it's a haunted hotel called the Overlook, a majestic playground for the jet set tucked into a mountainside in Colorado. But even for a fairly simple story such as *The Shining*, that reductive description doesn't do justice to what King is up to in the novel. *The Shining* is about a lot of things, really: the agony of the creative process, the fears that lurk deep within the heart of every parent, the redemptive power of love, and the inescapability of the past. But all of those themes *are* wrapped within a remarkably simple plot for a novel of almost 700 pages.

The story revolves around the Torrance family: Jack, a former schoolteacher and would-be playwright; Wendy, his supportive wife; and Danny, their son, whose psychic gifts, including the ability to read minds and see events from both the past and future, give the book its title. (Danny is told by a knowing, elder character that his ability "to shine" is more common than he might suspect.) A few efficient chapters give us the back story: Jack, a former alcoholic, lost his job as a prep school teacher when he beat up a student he found puncturing his tires in the faculty parking lot. Jack has always had anger management issues, leading to a particularly unpleasant instance when he came home drunk one night and jerked his three-year-old son so hard that he broke his arm. In the meantime, Danny is tormented by dark visions from an "invisible friend" he calls Tony. Trying to keep the family together amid all this emotional turmoil is Wendy, whose character offers King a chance for commentary about the seemingly limitless depths of unconditional love, and the horror that such a commitment often engenders.

King seems to paint himself into a corner, dramatically, very early in the book (much of the fun of reading *The Shining* is trying to deduce how he'll get himself out of his bind). The problem is this: Given Jack's violent history, Danny's bloody visions of the hotel they're moving into, and the hotel's history (recounted by a crass, chatty maintenance man) that involved several gruesome murders, the reader has few delusions about where the story is headed in the next 600 pages. There are too many volatile elements for this to end any way other than tragically, and bloodily. But knowing where a story is headed means there's no real suspense. So how does King manage to keep his narrative afloat? Mostly through sheer inventiveness. He puts so many spins on the traditional haunted house tale that he practically reinvents it. King pulls out the stops — *all* of the stops — as he proceeds to psychologically and physically torture the Torrances in gleefully monstrous ways, from having Danny nearly strangled by a bloated purple corpse that emerges from a blood-filled bathtub, to bringing to surreal life 15-foot hedge bunnies who go on a murderous rampage. But what keeps us glued to the story, really, is Wendy, the character with the least to do and the most like us, a victim of each passing hour's bizarre inversion of normalcy and logic. When her husband finally comes after her with an ax, it's really just another night at the Overlook, where elevators run on their own, hundreds of well-dressed party guests from eras past suddenly show up in the ballroom, clocks feature cute little scenes of little mechanical men beheading each other, and fire hoses turn into menacing, snake-like creatures.

Where did King get the idea for such a nightmarish terror palace? As he explained, the story originated in an actual stay by King and his wife, Tabitha, at a hotel called the Stanley, near Estes Park, Colorado. Checking in on the last night of the tourist season in the fall, King and his wife dined alone in a huge dining room where all the chairs were up on tables, they wandered the vacant corridors, and dealt with a skeleton staff that was busy packing up for the coming off-season months, during which the hotel would be shuttered for the winter. "I mean, it was like God had put me there to hear that and see those things. And by the time I went to bed that night, I had the whole book in my mind."[2]

King is almost as famous for his productivity as for what he produces. He writes really fast, and *The Shining* was reportedly written in four months, with King churning out 3,000 words a day.[3] The book itself is a speedy read, with few digressions to slow down the narrative pacing. King keeps the action coming fast and furious. There's a remarkably small cast of characters for a book of that size, and few scene changes once the action gets underway. He gets maximum mileage from the weird sense of isolation anyone would feel alone in a large luxury hotel, and once the weather begins to turn, the mood of the book darkens.

The Shining

There's been a lot written about King's style, and whether or not his books are "literature." (To his credit, the author seems blissfully unbothered by how he is classified by the critics.) He's never been a writer interested in subtlety. Some critics have labeled his work heavy-handed — and there's no doubt that he sometimes seems to value the gory detail more than the profound insight. His works are viscerally charged, and often feature stomach-churning passages. Yet he has an ability to wring more from a static situation than just about any author. There are pages and pages in this book about household objects such as lamps, radios, newspaper clippings, furnace pipes, clocks, mirrors, and dozens of other mundane things, that in the hands of most other writers would get lost in the woodwork. For King, even the woodwork has tales to tell. His ability to prolong a suspenseful scene is legendary, and deserved. The last 100 pages constitute one long chase scene, but in King's hands, the energy never flags. You can practically hear his fingers flying across the keyboard as the winter storm rages outside the Overlook and Jack Torrance stalks his family in a last, desperate attempt to satisfy the hotel's restless, malevolent ghosts who are whispering "Kill them!" in his psychotic ear. The pacing is masterful, an urgent rush of words whose fury often obscures a genuine lyricism. Those critics who bash King as a mere literary populist grossly underestimate the power of his prose and his ability to be as *moving* as he is frightening.

The ending of the book — and a good deal of the material in the previous 700 pages — was the subject of reconsideration by the acclaimed filmmaker Stanley Kubrick, who co-wrote the screenplay and directed the film version, a landmark cinematic achievement that still shows up regularly on many critics' lists of the greatest films of all time. But the controversial film divides viewers. Many are attracted to Kubrick's highly stylized and cerebral approach to the material. Others find the whole affair too mannered and are put off by its portentous nature, as well as Jack Nicholson's lead performance, which is jarringly at odds with the languid, suggestive tenor of the rest of the film. (Imagine if one of the astronauts in *2001: A Space Odyssey* was played by manic comic actor Jim Carrey, and you get some sense of Nicholson's volcanic approach to Jack Torrance's meltdown.)

There's no doubt that Kubrick, who helmed such cinematic landmarks as *2001: A Space Odyssey, Dr. Strangelove* and *A Clockwork Orange*, turned King's novel into a visually stunning work of awesome beauty and striking vignettes. The Steadicam shots of young Danny riding his tricycle

Now a Terrifying Motion Picture!

"Here's Johnny!" announces a deranged Jack Nicholson, in Stanley Kubrick's film of the classic Stephen King novel *The Shining*.

through the hotel's corridors are powerful visual reminders of the spaciousness, and loneliness, that distinguish the hotel. Kubrick's depiction of Danny's visions of the hotel's former horrors — and especially the regular, spectral appearance of two young twin girls in party dresses, covered in blood, who were slaughtered by their caretaker father — are truly unforgettable. And the director is not afraid to move his camera s-l-o-w-l-y through the deserted hotel and its landscaped environs. But the criticism that Kubrick turned a vibrant and rollercoaster-powered narrative into a chilly, emotionally distant offering aimed at the mind (but not the gut) is not completely off the mark. The movie provides a brooding, memorable ensemble of filmed set pieces that stick in the mind. But the pace, as in many of Kubrick's most noted works, is often glacial.

The movie dispenses with the backstory about the Torrances' home life and history before they take up residence at the Overlook. And it's the hotel that really deserves top billing. Kubrick turns the Overlook into another character, ferrying his camera through the place's large corridors, empty lobby and snow-spackled exteriors. But what gets lost in his visual élan is the sense of humanity that beats like a racing heart through King's manuscript. The hotel is impressively vast, and as Kubrick's cameras linger over its largeness the human characters shrink. In the book, some of the most touching, and scary, scenes are those that involve conversations that unravel and painfully go awry as Wendy, and Danny, try to reach out to the receding Jack. But in the movie, those scenes of failed intimacy are turned into occasions for Nicholson to increase the volume, and ferocity, of his maniacal transformation.

Perhaps because of this, the most effective performance in the film is given by veteran actor "Scatman" Crothers, who plays the cook, Dick Hallorann. Hallorann and Danny (played by the young Daniel Lloyd) share a scene that is the best in the film, in large part because it's the first time Kubrick seems willing to let his characters, rather than his cinematographer, tell the story. It's the first time we get a sense of Danny's fear and pain at his ability to "shine," and the first time the viewer gets a recognizably human character, rather than something closer to caricature. When Hallorann re-enters the story in the final reel, the movie goes from being a disturbing amusement to a genuinely powerful story.

King's story relies on emotionally charged events that leave his characters unsettled, feeling adrift, left ultimately trying to inhabit a psychic space that has not been cleared for landing. Kubrick's style is exactly the opposite, to probe large, inhospitable spaces and, after establishing their relative weirdness, put some people in them and see how they would react. One of the best examples of these two storytellers' respective visions of how to tell the same story can be seen in the treatment of King's hulking, threatening hedge creatures. Many effective scenes in the novel involve these gigantic hedge animals near the entrance to the hotel. In King's narrative, these animals come to vibrant life and terrorize the Torrances. King lets readers participate in the astonishment and visceral fear of his characters as they discover that these leafy adornments are really murderous predators. But in Kubrick's reworking of the story, the hedge animals are replaced by a hedge *maze*. This provides the filmmaker the chance to send his cameras into this labyrinth and shoot from the wanderer's perspective for several minutes, as each hoped-for escape leads to yet another dead end. It's the *setting* that Kubrick exploits, finding in large spaces the source of horror, whereas King focuses more intensely on his characters, and generally uses the setting as an echo chamber to amplify their fears, not to cause them.

The characters in the film version, especially Jack Torrance, are in many ways different from the novel. In the book, Jack has moments of genuine decency and likeability, a man dealing with alcoholism and his lingering anger at authority figures, triggered largely by an abusive father. In the movie, those issues are downplayed. And, as embodied by Nicholson, Jack comes off as a pretty squirrelly character right from the start, with his trademark arched eyebrows and sarcastic grin. King reportedly lobbied strongly against the casting of Nicholson, feeling that audiences would identify the actor with his recent performance as the mental patient McMurphy in *One Flew Over the Cuckoo's Nest*. King is said to have wanted an actor whose descent into madness would be less expected, a character seen as normal rather than halfway to madness, as might be the case with Nicholson.[4]

King's initial dislike of the film (he has since softened his criticisms) was shared by several high-profile critics, such as Roger Ebert (who has also changed his opinion of the film). Some critics slammed Kubrick for the pacing, likening it to *2001: A Space Odyssey* in its languor. Both Kubrick and actress Shelley Duvall were nominated for "Razzies," the equivalent of the Academy Awards but for the *worst* rather than the best. A review in the entertainment trade journal *Variety* pretty much summed up the animus many critics felt toward the film: "With everything to work with, director Stanley Kubrick has teamed with jumpy Jack Nicholson to destroy all that was so terrifying about Stephen King's bestseller...."

The crazier Nicholson gets, the more idiotic he looks. Shelley Duvall transforms the warm sympathetic wife of the book into a simpering, semi-retarded hysteric."[5]

The passage of time has been good to *The Shining*, which has seen its critical stock rise. The film ranked 29th in the 2001 American Film Institute survey "100 years ... 100 thrills," a countdown of the best thrillers of the last 100 years.[6] It's "freshness" ranking on the popular film review website "Rotten Tomatoes" has risen to an impressive 89 percent.[7] Kubrick's painstaking vision (it took almost a year to complete principal photography) has apparently triumphed in the end — though there are still those critics and readers who feel the movie is a poor translation of King's best-seller.

Both views are defensible. Kubrick has made a movie that is impossible to dismiss. His artistry is evident in every shot, announcing itself in the first, marvelous frames, where an aerial camera captures the Torrance VW Beetle tooling along a majestic mountain highway amid spruce-splotched cliffs. The cinematography, by longtime Kubrick lensman John Alcott, is truly breathtaking. Kubrick will spend the next two hours and twenty minutes filling the screen with similarly arresting images.

But there are definitely problems with his translation of the story to film, and for many viewers who read the book, the biggest problem is the final, highly controversial shot: a close-up on a vintage photograph on the wall of the Overlook hotel, taken in the 1920s during a ball in the hotel. As the camera pans in on the photograph, we see, standing in the front of the group, a well-dressed, grinning man who bears an uncanny resemblance to Jack Torrance. The implication seems to be that the Jack Torrance of *The Shining* is really a reincarnated Jack Torrance from a previous era, a ghost from the troubled past of the Overlook, a figure who represents the blood-soaked history of the hotel. In King's novel, there's no such suggestion. Jack Torrance was simply a deeply troubled man whose personal demons found accommodation in the claustrophobic Overlook, a hotel that readers, and viewers, continue to enter imaginatively, despite its fateful legacy.

Sleepy Hollow

During America's Colonial era, the idea of a national literature in the emerging republic was still something of a joke to our forebears in Great Britain. America was considered a land of rough and ready settlers and wild, dangerous Indians — hardly the pedigree required for a nascent literary movement. Since the establishment of the colonies, Americans *had* produced quite a bit of writing — but almost all of it was of a religious or political nature, arguments in favor of the existence of an austere God or a defense of individual liberty in the public sphere. From Cotton Mather to Thomas Paine, eloquent and forceful articulation of ideas found a ready home in the burgeoning republic. But nothing America had produced rivaled the power, prestige, or popularity of the fiction (novels, short stories, poems, plays, even opera librettos) of the European literati. As one critic noted, "During the first decades of the American republic, a great deal of writing was done, but very little of it possessed that mysterious vitality that made it *literature*."[1]

All that changed rather rapidly in the first few decades of the nineteenth century, as a truly "American" literature began to emerge. Writers such as William Cullen Bryant, James Fenimore Cooper and Nathaniel Hawthorne put America on the literary map and staked out the wild and untamed landscape for its fictional possibilities. But the first American writer to do this — and, consequently, the first to be acknowledged as an authentic "man of letters" — was the storyteller and world traveler Washington Irving.[2] His story "The Legend of Sleepy Hollow" is not only an entertaining tale and a deceptively adroit mix of European models and American uniqueness, it is also one of the first literary works to garner the attention of an audience far beyond the country's shores.

Irving (whose given name was chosen in honor of George Washington, a hero to his parents[3]) was hardly a "rough and ready" American. Born of a wealthy family, he trained as a lawyer, but lacked the passion for the practice of law. Instead, he was a natural traveler and writer, wandering through New York's Hudson Valley and collecting folk tales and legends, which he eventually transmuted into his own fictional "tales." Though in later life he became as well known for his travel writing and biographies as for his fiction, it was his early "sketches" such as *Knickerbocker's History of New York* (1809) and his even more famous *Sketch Book of Geoffrey Crayon, Gent.* (1820) that made him a household word. His most famous story, "The Legend of Sleepy Hollow," comes from *Sketch Book*. Now widely anthologized in collections with titles like "Best American Short Stories," or in standard high school literature textbooks, the narrative mixes several genres: the European fairy tale, the adventure story, the British comedy of manners and, most importantly, the horror story, which was just coming into its own. Irving filtered each of these through his literary sieve but he added some characteristic American flavors that give the story its distinctive taste. His protagonist was not well-born or of noble birth — a staple of many European "quest" narratives — but rather a humble character of marginal social importance: a country schoolmaster with the unprepossessing name Ichabod Crane.[4]

The account, we are told, was "Found Among the Papers of the Late Diedrich Knickerbocker"— a bald-faced attempt to add a whiff of folkloric authenticity to the narrative. Irving sets the scene in the first paragraph as the story opens just outside Tarrytown, "one of those spacious coves which indent the Eastern shore of the Hudson" in New York State. The narrator claims the burg got its name because tradesmen from the nearby villages used to visit its pubs and "tarry" before returning to their wives. The specific locale for his tale is an arresting valley near Tarrytown called "Sleepy Hollow," whose strange, soporific appeal is related by the narrator:

> I recollect that, when a stripling, my first exploit in squirrel shooting was in a grove of tall walnut trees that shades one side of the valley. I had wandered into it at noontime, when all nature is peculiarly quiet, and was startled by the roar of my own gun, as it broke the Sabbath stillness around, and was prolonged and reverberated by angry echoes. If ever I should wish for a retreat, whither I might steal from the world and its distractions and dream quietly away the remnant of a troubled life, I know of none more promising than this little valley.[5]

But this idyllic oasis has another side — one that Irving's pastel prose makes seem less menacing than might otherwise be the case: "A drowsy, dreamy influence seems to hang over the land, and to pervade the very atmosphere ... certain it is the place continues under the sway of some witching power that holds a spell under the minds of the good people, causing them to walk in a continued reverie."[6] What we really have here is some sort of zombie-land, where the residents "are given to all kinds of marvelous beliefs, are subject to trances and visions, and frequently see strange sights and hear music and voices in the air."[7] The reader is now (somewhat) prepared for a tale true to this possessed landscape.

Like his contemporaries Cooper, Bryant, and Ralph Waldo Emerson, Irving offers the reader lengthy, descriptive passages of nature. The untamed landscape seemed to fire the imagination of the first generation of great American writers. But unlike his contemporaries, who found in nature a sense of tranquility and even religious grandeur, Irving's scenes of nature are as foreboding as they are majestic. "Sleepy Hollow," with its crackling twigs, menacing shadows, and wraith-like forests, can be said to provide the prototype for contemporary horror's "lost in the woods" motif, usually featuring a group of teenagers who end up staying in a cabin near a lake (cue the dissonant music and wild-eyed, hook-handed maniac!).

Ichabod knows those woods quite well. As an itinerant schoolmaster, he resides in the homes of his students' parents, so he's been all over Sleepy Hollow, trudging from one modest cabin to another. He seems resolved to this rather uninspiring life — until his perambulations bring him to the home of Katrina Van Tassel, a young woman who is as beautiful as her father is rich. Ichabod convinces her father to spring for singing lessons, which he (the schoolmaster) will provide. It doesn't take long for Ichabod to decide that they should be singing duets. He decides to seek her hand in marriage no matter what.

Well, there is one small problem with his plan. Actually, a not-so-small problem in the form of a rival suitor, Brom Bones, as brawny as he is unsophisticated.

Ichabod's dilemma reaches its nadir at a soiree given by Katrina's father. All the local villagers are there, as are the two rivals for Katrina's affection. The young woman plays the coquette for most of the evening and Ichabod finally resolves to state his intentions. But Katrina shoots him down — and the wounded Ichabod "stole forth with the air of one who had been sacking a hen roost rather than a fair lady's heart."[8] But his troubles are just beginning.

The rest of the story details Ichabod's ride back home "during the witching hour" aboard a broken-down plow horse named Gunpowder.

Here's where Irving masterfully brings together all that had come before: the frightening landscape, local superstition, Ichabod's susceptibility to wild flights of imagination, Brom Bones' dominating physique and a master storyteller's use of the devices of horror and suspense. Ichabod ends up in a death race through the woods, with a spectral Headless Horseman riding fast, then slow, then fast again, mimicking Ichabod's pace precisely. The learned, pious schoolmaster concludes that his only chance to survive is to make it to the sanctified land of the nearby churchyard (there's a strong whiff of lingering Puritanism is much nineteenth century American fiction). Urging on poor old Gunpowder, Ichabod races for his life, pursued by the headless rider who, at the climax of his chase, appears to hurl his head (which he had been holding in his lap for safekeeping) at Ichabod. It's one of the great moments in early American literature, a precursor for both the wild adventure yarns of Cooper and, a few years later, the grotesqueries of Poe. Here's the passage that launched a thousand "phantom in the woods" stories:

> Another convulsive kick in the ribs and old Gunpowder sprang upon the bridge; he thundered over the resounding planks; he gained the opposite side; and now Ichabod cast a look behind to see if his pursuer should vanish, according to rule, in a flash of fire and brimstone. Just then he saw the goblin rising in his stirrups, and in the very act of hurling his head at him. Ichabod endeavored to dodge the horrible missile, but too late. It encountered his cranium with a tremendous crash — he was tumbled headlong into the dust, and Gunpowder, the black steed, and the goblin rider, passed by like a whirlwind.[9]

One of the remarkable aspects of Irving's prose is how absolutely *cinematic* it seems, a century before moving pictures would become a viable way of showcasing such pulse-pounding action, violence, and horror. But Irving's story would indeed find its way onto the big screen, beginning with a silent version from 1922 and making regular appearances throughout the century. One of the most compelling versions — which also takes an enormous number of liberties with the story but still manages to communicate the *strangeness* of Irving's tale — is a version from the end of the twentieth century by a visionary filmmaker whose wild and weird cinematic style makes him the perfect director to bring "Sleepy Hollow" to vivid, cinematic life.

Director Tim Burton has made a career out of strangeness. In films such as *Beetlejuice, Edward Scissorhands,* and *Corpse Bride,* Burton's surreal and darkly humorous cinematic posture has elevated mundane, even silly material, into a kind of macabre abstract art. His movies are visually cap-

Now a Terrifying Motion Picture!

Poor Ichabod Crane (Johnny Depp) — little does he know the terror that awaits him in *Sleepy Hollow*, Tim Burton's stylish update of the classic Washington Irving short story.

tivating, translating the spectral into spectacle. He seems to thrive on material that takes as its jumping-off point the actual presence of ghosts and other supernatural entities. That makes him the perfect director for *Sleepy Hollow*, a film that is predicated (like *Hamlet*) on the widespread belief in ghosts.

Fans of Irving's story might have some difficulty adjusting to the central change from the original tale to the screenplay: In the movie, Ichabod Crane is not a rural schoolmaster but a New York City police detective in 1799, called to the village of Sleepy Hollow to help investigate a series of murders in which the victims were decapitated. Now, that sounds like quite a stretch, and arguably, a perversion of Irving's simple story about the allure of local lore. But the screenplay (by Andrew Kevin Walker) actually hews pretty closely to the themes from Irving's story. Crane, in both story and film, remains the voice of reason, a self-declared skeptic and advocate of logic over superstition. Both Irving and Burton present a central character who spans the chasm between faith and science. Crane, like the reader of the story, is immersed in a world in which fanciful legends and menacing ghosts are presumed to be as real as the trees in the forest and the bodies of the victims who have crossed paths with the murderous phantom. His task in both the story and the movie is to try to keep his wits about him in the presence of what seems pretty clear evidence that ghosts *do* exist And in a Tim Burton film, nothing is out of bounds. His *Sleepy Hollow* is a mesmerizing festival of wild images and compelling special effects. If supernatural creatures exist anywhere, it's surely within the frames of this bizarre and darkly beautiful movie.

The opening sequence shows a pair of lovers' hands embracing, and then a will being written on parchment and sealed in blood-red wax. Throughout this wordless introduction, Danny Elfman's attention-getting score, featuring booming brasses and children's choirs, moves through a series of haunting crescendos (the movie is as much fun to listen to as it is to watch). A quick cut to a horse and carriage carrying a well-dressed man, riding through the mist at night, sets the stage for what's to come. The passenger glances out of the carriage window and sees an ominous scarecrow in the distance, with a pumpkin head and a smirking, devilish grin. He then hears the slashing of swords and, terrified, he leans out to see what's happening. That's when he notices the carriage driver has no head. In shock, he leaps out and rolls around the ground, but soon finds himself face to face (well, face to stump) with the headless driver.

The action moves to New York City, where we find Constable Crane (Johnny Depp) fishing a dead body out of the river. His supervisor sees it as a cut-and-dried case ("When you find them in the river, the cause of death is drowning,"[10] he says), but Crane wants to examine the body — a sign of the officer's unshaking belief in science to crack criminal mysteries. He goes so far as to lecture a judge in his courtroom — Christopher Lee in a small but memorable moment of restrained indignation — that police should use the latest scientific investigative tools, not the words of snitches and bottom-feeders, to convict suspects. This belief that science trumps instinct will be thoroughly tested when he's transferred to Sleepy Hollow — the punishment for his presumptive lecture to the judge.

The New York scenes have a gritty and suggestive authenticity about them (despite being filmed in England). But historical verisimilitude soon gives way to surreal lushness when the action moves north to Sleepy Hollow. Burton has created a vivid impressionistic landscape that ideally conveys Irving's original conception of a burg awash in phantasmagoria. The skies undulate with competing shades of chalky white, slate gray, and overripe plum, and the light streams through the forest in diffuse and menacing patterns. The townspeople are as hard to read as the shifting, shadowy landscape but eventually Crane gets acclimated, though he'd like to do more than simply get acclimated with one particular Sleepy Hollow resident, Katrina Van Tassel, played with coy resilience by Christina Ricci.

Most of the dramatic tension derives from Crane's initial certainty that the Headless Horseman (played by Christopher Walken, made up to look like a cross between a punky Dracula and Edward Scissorhands) is the product of a locally overactive imagination. "Murder needs no ghosts to come from the grave," Crane proclaims to the town elders, who have just told him all about the Headless Horseman. "We have murders in New York without benefit of ghouls and goblins." But, as one of the town elders retorts: "You're a long way from New York, constable."[11]

Burton provides lots of action-packed sequences of terrified innocent victims being chased down in the forest by the headless one, with the requisite amplified hoofbeats, over-the-shoulder glance-backs, and ominous thunderclaps punctuating the evil deeds. The gore factor for a modern horror story is stunningly low, though there are some compelling shots of freshly severed heads staring up from the ground, mouths agape, eyes wide in terror, blood tricking from the remains of a neckbone. But even these maimings are done so stylishly, and in keeping with the feel of the rest of the movie as a kind of adult wonderland, that they transcend the normal retch-factor that usually accompanies murderous movie mayhem.

The homicidal moments are leavened by a screenplay that offers many delightful touches of comic relief. There is a wonderful scene shortly after Crane's arrival, when another murder has just taken place. The town elders are all at the scene when the constable arrives, and they are positively baffled when he begins to move about the crime scene like Sherlock Holmes, pacing off the distance between hoof prints and donning a large magnifying eyepiece attached to some sort of bizarre-looking headgear. They look at each other like he's crazy. Depp plays these scenes for all their worth. Crane is too young to command the respect of the baffled onlookers, and too inexperienced to be able to really know how to investigate, so he adopts a kind of defensive bluster, pretending he's more savvy than we know he really is.

But he also plays genuine terror well, as when he himself is stalked by the Headless Horseman and must spur his steed and flee for his life, or when he's "interviewing" a witch in her lair, and she suddenly lashes out at him, revealing a desiccated skull where her face should be. It's a varied performance than never descends into camp, and a mirror of the film's overall tone of serious implausibility.

And this being a Tim Burton film, there are lots of wickedly dopey scenes, such as the Headless Horseman continuing to duel even though he's got a knife in his back and a lance through his chest (cue the Monty Python comparisons!), or Ichabod Crane hacking away at the tree which hides the Horseman's grave, only to be splattered with blood rather than sap. The special effects are superbly well-wrought, and the art direction is a marvel (the movie won the Oscar for art direction and set decoration, and was nominated for cinematography). *Sleepy Hollow* was well received by critics, and was nominated by many specialty critics' groups, such as the International Horror Guild, for best film of the year.

It deserves all of its plaudits, though it's not a perfect film. It bogs down near the ending, as Crane stumbles upon a conspiracy of the town elders, which helps explain the Horseman's anger. There's a subplot involving devil worshiping and demonic possession as well. It all gets a bit chaotic in the last 20 minutes, but even as Crane puts the pieces together (and faces off against a soldier of Satan) it's the arresting visuals and the aura of endearing creepiness that carries the film to its violent and climactic conclusion.

With "The Legend of Sleepy Hollow," Washington Irving put American literature on the map. His sleepy little town along the Hudson River has continued to be a favorite destination of his fellow artists for more than 200 years. There's not a ghost of a chance that will be changing any time soon.

The Thing from Another World

During a period that scholars and fans now recognize as the infancy of popular science fiction (the 1920s and 1930s), pulp magazines dedicated to what was originally called "scientifiction"[1] churned out hundreds of stories, most of which told of some sort of vicious monster from space besieging planet Earth. The invaders might resemble giant bugs, or spider-like, multi-tentacled robots, or simply gelatinous blobs. These creatures were never friendly, almost always destructive, and usually averse to any attempt at communication. The stories that offered these thrilling and dangerous encounters derived their narrative momentum from the simple "us vs. them" dynamic. They were mostly forgettable, but generally entertaining. And once the monster was defeated, the page was turned, and a new story awaited.

Once in a rare while, however, one could have come across a pulp story that focused more on humans than on aliens, exploring the terrain of the mind and psychological terrors rather than simply a by-the-numbers confrontation with a spaced-out nemesis. And it's these stories that are generally the ones remembered (and still read) today. They remind one that there were writers who were aching to break away from the formulaic constraints of the "bad alien, good Earthling" confrontation.

The widely acknowledged force behind this transition from monster-based fiction to more insightful explorations was John W. Campbell, who for decades edited the most influential SF magazine of all time, called (appropriately) *Astounding Science Fiction*. Campbell published and polished the work of seminal sci-fi writers Robert Heinlein, Theodore Sturgeon, Isaac Asimov, et al. Those writers, and dozens of others who came to prominence in mid-century, often cite Campbell in their dedications, and many have written movingly about how this "father-figure" helped shape and guide their careers. In his groundbreaking survey of the history of science fiction, *The Trillion Year Spree*, Brian Aldiss dedicates a chapter to Campbell and his influence: "Unlike many editors before and after, Campbell knew when a story made sense and when it didn't. He argued strongly with his contributors — and his arguments were often well informed and fair. Thus he laid the foundations for what the gentle hearts of fandom call 'The Golden Age.'"[2]

Before Campbell began directing other writers' careers, he was busy establishing himself in the burgeoning world of science fiction. He sold his first story in 1930 at age 19, and for the next five years wrote a number of adventure stories set in space. In the mid 1930s, he married, and began selling stories under the pen name Don A. Stuart (from his wife's name, Dona Stuart). In 1937, he was hired as editor of *Astounding Science Fiction*, and a year later, under the Stuart pen name, he published in the magazine his novella *Who Goes There?*

Though in many ways a groundbreaking story, *Who Goes There?* didn't make a huge splash immediately. Gradually, though, it built momentum. It was reprinted in a few science fiction anthologies throughout the 1940s, and in 1951 it was made into the horror–sci-fi film *The Thing from Another World*. The success of the film, which was placed on the National Film Registry of significant films in 2001, led to a resurgence of interest in Campbell's story in the sci-fi community (the Science Fiction Writers Association placed the work on its list of the best science fiction novellas ever written[3]). A subsequent remake in 1982 by acclaimed horror film director John Carpenter once again thrust the original story back into the spotlight, where it continues to command a cult-like following.

Who Goes There? has aged well — in spots. The qualities that recommend the work to a modern audience include the suspense, the focus on the psychological aspect of the story, its internal rather than external plot machinations, and Campbell's ability to describe a scene in evocative, sensory language. (Think of the opening passage: "The place stank. A queer, mingled stench that only the ice-buried cabins of an Antarctic camp know, compounded of reeking human sweat, and the heavy, fish-oil stench of melted seal blubber."[4])

On the other side of the ledger there are some liabilities that veneration simply can't make disappear: Campbell's characterization is often crude and heavy-handed. He frequently gives his characters physical markers, like a bushy beard, or a bald head, which he feels compelled to refer to, distractingly, throughout the entire book. His dialogue can be clunky and his narrative has a tendency to bog down in the thickets of scientific jargon.

This was, however, the beginning of the Golden Age of Sci-Fi, so by the standards that governed the production of most pulp manuscripts, Campbell's story stands head and shoulders above the rest.

In outline, the story is a fairly simple one. The action begins in — and is entirely limited to — a frozen stretch of unbearably cold and windy Antarctic. Tucked four feet below the surface is a scientific outpost populated by 37 researchers and military men. There is a cramped living quarter, dining quarters, a kind of a bunk house, and some laboratories connected to the main camp.

The reader is thrust into this environment immediately as a meeting of all the camp's personnel is taking place. Its purpose is to discuss and then vote on a proposal put forward by the camp's senior biologist, regarding a blue-greenish, gigantic three-eyed creature that had been recovered several miles away in a crevice in the ice, near a crashed and abandoned alien spacecraft. The debate takes place in the main living quarters and the whole place is rendered rather claustrophobically, with "the fringe of dingy gray underwear hanging from the low ceiling." The men are being asked whether they agree with the scientist's plan to thaw out the creature, whose frozen body is now in their barracks, to take tissue samples.

Some cede to his authority, while others balk, worried about the danger of releasing harmful bacteria from another world. Some even worry that this creature could come back to life. But the biologist assures them it is dead, and has been dead for maybe tens of thousands of years.

The arguments are presented in some depth, giving Campbell a chance to demonstrate his knowledge of biochemistry and physiology. Of course, the reasonable-sounding scientist carries the day, and the creature is thawed out. And guess what happens then?

Okay, so it doesn't take an Antarctic scientist to foretell the results. As the accumulated pounds of ice melt away, the creature is reborn. And, well, he's a little bit angry at having lost the best years of his life chin-deep in Arctic cold storage. So he attacks a guard dog and one of the human members of the research party. Later he's cornered by a search party, and electrocuted. They positively barbecue him. If there was any doubt about whether or not he was alive before, there's no debate now. He's been turned into a interstellar potato chip.

But what's this? As they study his cooked corpse, they notice something strange: Isn't that a dog's leg where his own leg should be? It appears that the creature had the ability to transform into a sort of clone of whatever other living being he had contact with. His brief battle with the guard dog allowed him to absorb enough DNA to begin at least a partial transformation. He also had an unseen but overheard fight with the camp's engineer, a fellow named Connant, who barely escaped. But what if he really killed the engineer and assumed his form (splitting himself, essentially, between his alien self and the engineer). And what if he's living among us now, and he only left this monster corpse behind to fool these gullible humans?

And what if it's not just the engineer? What if he's spreading among us right now, shaking hands, slapping backs, and absorbing enough DNA to replace all the camp members with substitute clones? How does anyone know, for sure, who anyone else really is?

That's where the real power and narrative drive of Campbell's book reside, and that's where the work's title — *Who Goes There?*—derives its irony and resonance. After straining to explain a scientific basis for this shape-shifting (Campbell would have made a good lab technician — he seems to know quite a lot about blood platelets and chromosomes), the book focuses on the distrust and paranoia that now infects the inhabitants of the research ice station.

Who Goes There? is a legitimate piece of horror fiction, but with a twist. Campbell has engaged in one clever act of misdirection. What should have been the generator of horror — what we'd *expect* to frighten us — is a large, ungainly monster from outer space. But what really provides the fright is one's fellow human (maybe) being. It's when the monster disappears that the horror begins.

Of course, filmmakers don't quite have the luxury of presenting internal horrors with the same skin-crawling potency as more traditional, *visible* frights. So it's perhaps not unexpected that the movie made of Campbell's book would focus more on the menace of the thing itself.

As most horror film fans know, there have been *two* successful adaptations of *Who Goes There?* The first version was the 1951 Christian Nyby film, *The Thing from Another World*, and the 1982 remake by John Carpenter, *The Thing*. Both are worth seeing, but as with so many other films that are based on books, the first one remains, for most sci-fi and horror fans, the preferred version. Carpenter's film is flashier and his effects are more visually arresting, but the original better conveys Campbell's focus on the *people* who populate the research camp and struggle with the nascent presence of the Thing. Critical opinion, of course, differs as to which is

Long before he became trusted lawman Matt Dillon on TV's *Gunsmoke*, James Arness portrayed one of the most lawless characters in horror when he menaced an Arctic outpost in 1951's *The Thing from Another World*.

the better version. I think Nyby's film is more fun, and it also captures the claustrophobic spirit and paranoia-tinged political world-view of so many horror films of the 1950s.

The Thing from Another World has achieved, among sci-fi and horror fans, the status of a cult classic. The movie opens ominously with the words THE THING slowly coming into prominence in white shafts of light against a black background, as veteran sci-fi composer Dimitri Tiomkin's thrilling brass-inflected score blares away. Then, as the opening credits continue, the viewer sees a white-out blizzard swirling above some dark, frozen Arctic landscape. (The stark contrasts of the frozen setting benefit from a black-and-white treatment — another reason to prefer the original over the remake.)

In an officer's club, a group of about a dozen men in uniform hang out, looking bored, with a group of three playing poker. A man enters and makes his way to the table. He's a newspaperman named Scotty (who's not in the novella), and he's sniffing around for a story. He learns there's some sort of research team working at an outpost at the North Pole, and when a plane leaves this nondescript (and non-newsworthy) military base to head north to investigate a reported crash landing of some type of airplane, Scotty joins them.

As the plane lands, the team is enswirled in snow, and they head to a small warren of military barracks and low-ceilinged living quarters. The captain of the plane, Patrick Hendry (played by Kenneth Tobey) immediately visits the office where Nikki Nicholson (Margaret Sheridan) works, and it's clear these two have some sort of romantic history. Their banter seems contrived and jarring, considering the context — hey, they're in an Arctic outpost in the middle of nowhere, and they're carrying on like Tracy and Hepburn. It's rather obtrusive, but fortunately, it doesn't last long.

The movie really gets going when we enter Dr. Carrington's lab. Carrington, played with an eerie detachment by veteran television and film actor Robert Cornthwaite, runs things at this research outpost, and his lab is filled with lots of military radar screens and other odd-looking hi-tech gizmos. Dressed in civilian clothes (he looks rather dashing in his blazer and turtleneck), he represents that role that all scientists seemed to play in these kinds of films in the 1950s: the supreme belief in the primacy of science and logic. You know the type: Everything can be explained and understood by the scientific method (a sure cue to the viewer that we're about to find something that *can't* be explained that way).

He informs the captain that there's been some sort of large object crash, creating an electromagnetic "deviation in Sector 19" that sounds at first like something caused by a meteor. But the seismograph, and remote radar sensors detect that the object traveled upward before crashing into the earth — something meteors simply don't do.

A reconnaissance crew sets out in a plane to explore the crash site. As they approach, the compass goes berserk, the Geiger counter clicks feverishly, and they see strange markings on the ground and large swaths of melted ice. The stage is being set for the discovery of something otherworldly. Yet, they forge ahead cheerfully, shouting out to each other once on the ground as they each find other strange, unaccountable clues (such as a piece of metal that is made of a totally unknown alloy). Part of what makes the film so much fun is the giddy sense the crew exudes as the situation gets stranger. There's a great scene where all the crew members stand in the perimeter of a large shape under the ice, trying to figure out what's down there. As they look around, they discover that they are standing in a perfect circle. Whatever landed on this spot is a saucer of some sort, prompting one member of the party to exclaim "Holy cats! We finally found one! A flying saucer!"[5]

The film skillfully exploits the contrast between the initial thrill of discovery and the growing sense of doom as that discovery proves deadly. These are explorers, after all, and when they find what they think is the evidence of a flying saucer, naturally they are ecstatic. But when the reality of the situation eventually hits them, their sense of fear and disillusionment is all the more poignant because we've witnessed their initial euphoria. That's where the film locates its real sense of horror: finding that what we've always dreamed of turns out to be a nightmare.

The crew detects a saucer under a thin layer of ice, and they try to blast it out with explosives. "A few minutes from now we may have the key to the stars,"[6] Dr. Carrington exclaims as the charges are being planted. Unfortunately, the charges aimed at melting the ice ignite the saucer's engine, and the entire spaceship-like structure appears to be destroyed by a fire. Yet, there's still some movement on the Geiger counter — something (or someone) wasn't blown up in the explosion, and is there under the ice.

It's the Thing — a large, frozen creature just under the ice. The crew carves out a large block of ice (with the Thing inside) and puts it on the plane heading back to the research base. On the plane ride back, the crew members theorize what it could be, but there's still no sense of peril associated with the creature — just basic human curiosity. The ice block is stashed in a storeroom on the base. As in Campbell's original story, there's a debate about whether or not to thaw the creature because of some germs he might unleash from whatever world he's come from.

As the ice melts and the crew gets a better look at it, they start freaking out. The Thing is hideously ugly, and nobody wants to stand guard around it. Aside from a brief romantic interlude between Captain Hendry and the comely Nikki (made all the more strange because they are having a playful, flirty conversation while he's sitting in a chair with his hands tied behind his back), the focus is now firmly on the crew's increasingly anxious reaction to the Thing.

One of the men guarding the Thing bursts in to the barracks, shouting frantically about how the creature is now alive, how he shot at it but nothing happened. We get some great, snow-distorted images of the Thing (James Arness) rampaging among the sled dogs as the researchers begin to understand just how perilous their situation is. How do you battle a creature that doesn't seem to follow the known laws of biology, that can absorb bullets with no ill effects, that can exist in a frozen state and when thawed has an animal-like ferocity married to super strength?

As a search party armed with axes fans out across the base to find the Thing, the doctor pleads for restraint. He wants to communicate with it, not destroy it — but the anxious military men have other ideas. The doctor tries to convince them that the creature is merely a frightened foreigner, but the rest of the crew sees a more potent threat, and conclude it *must* be destroyed before doing more damage. (Many critics have found lots of Cold War era symbolism in *The Thing*, with the powerful alien creature apparently representing the U.S.'s Communist enemies.)

After another attack on a crew member, the mere willingness to kill the Thing is replaced with outright zeal and the search party heads off again, axes in hand. They encounter the Thing, who tries to bash his way into the barracks, and the crew manages to hold him off and they board themselves in.

Though the filmmakers take several liberties with the plot of Campbell's *Who Goes There?*, the focus throughout *The Thing* remains firmly on the humans. The atmosphere is increasingly tense — made all the more surprising by the relative absence of the creature throughout most of the movie. James Arness's role is truly a bit part, barely on screen, glimpsed but not glorified. Today's horror film directors could take a cue from *The Thing*, a film ostensibly about an alien that finds all of its drama and terror in the *human* condition.

Village of the Damned

To live in a place where nothing ever happens must be quite an experience. Few of us are even partially insulated from the frenetic pace of the modern world, and with the near-ubiquity of the Internet, cell phones, and cable television, the concept of "isolation" has become more of a harrowing prospect — or at least a personal inconvenience — than a quaint wish. But not long ago, even in the most advanced and "civilized" countries, there were villages and boroughs that were truly isolated from the bustle of modernity, pockets of placid life, leisured and content to live at their own rhythm.

In such places, the events that stirred the populace tended to be local rather than regional or national, and personally involving rather than publicly spectacular: a marriage, a funeral, or, most especially, a birth. What could be greater cause for celebration than the arrival of a new member of a close-knit community? What happens innumerable times throughout the wider world every day — and hence, achieves the patina of the mundane — can be a seminal event in an intimate, isolated village.

But what if birth engendered trepidation and anxiety rather than joy and expectation? And what if that anxiety was multiplied by the number of women who were expecting? And what if *every* woman of child-bearing age in that small, isolated village were to become pregnant at the same time — and have *no idea* how it happened? And finally — to make matters just a bit worse — what if it were discovered that the "instigator" of the pregnancy was a power, alien in nature, and possibly seeking the destruction of the human race?

That'll put a damper on a baby shower.

In this inversion from blessed event to cursed event, it's impossible to predict just how people might react. Would the miracle of birth and its attendant awe trump the fear of the unknown? Would husbands embrace their wives' "situations" — even though they themselves are clearly only spectators, not participants? Would religious and moral considerations impact each woman's decisions about how to proceed? The litany of predictable "oohs" and "ahhs" would be totally re-written, the civic playbook for the annunciation of new life thrown out.

The scenario seems far-fetched on so many fronts, it begs the question: Who would even imagine such a thing?

Britisher John Wyndham Parkes Beynon Lucas Harris (who wrote mostly under the much more manageable moniker John Wyndham) cut his teeth on the detective and sci-fi pulp magazines of the 1920s and '30s. In the '50s, his stock rose with the publication of a number of novels that posited global apocalyptic scenarios that often left only a handful of survivors to deal with the detritus. His most famous work is the terrifying *Day of the Triffids*, about a species of poison-spitting plant that takes over most of the Earth's arable land. Other sci-fi novels featuring various "doomsday scenarios" from the 1950s include *The Kraken Wakes* and *The Chrysalids*, but his 1957 novel *The Midwich Cuckoos* stands as his best written and most involving work.

Wyndham takes what is a fairly preposterous yet frightening notion — alien impregnation — and addresses it in such restrained and mannerly prose that the unrealistic premise dissolves, leaving the reader with an almost matter-of-fact discussion of how a small English town attempts to cope with the situation. What makes *The Midwich Cuckoos* a horror novel isn't the usual apparatuses of terror. Instead, Wyndham has written what must be one of the most stylistically quiet horror novels ever published. He locates the terror in the disruption the event causes in the orderly life of Midwich, an English burg largely undisturbed by the tug and tumult of history. Among the townspeople, many of whom the reader gets to know well, there is growing suspicion, impotent rage, and probing self-examination (one of the characters sees the mass impregnation as "God's judgment" against the sinners of Midwich). Unlike a Poe, Lovecraft, or Stephen King, Wyndham gives us no series of wild and terrifying events that unfold, gradually ratcheting up the terror. There's an initial disquieting event, and then, well, the townspeople are left to sort things out as they will.

The book begins with the narrator, a minor character named Richard Gayford, who happens to live in Midwich, describing the puzzling situation he and his wife encounter as they attempt to return to their village after a night spent celebrating her birthday in a town 20 miles away. The opening pages reinforce how mundane, how nondescript the village of Midwich is. After a constable informs the couple, somewhat cryptically, that there is no way to enter the village ("Tisn't no use tryin',' ma'am. Nobody can't get into Midwich, an' that's a fact"[1]) Gayford muses on Midwich's place as a certified "no-place":

> What made it the more odd was that Midwich was, almost notoriously, a place where things did not happen. Janet and I had lived there just over a year then, and found this to be almost its leading feature. Indeed, had there been posts at the entrances to the village bearing a red triangle and below them a notice: MIDWICH. DO NOT DISTURB, they would have seemed not inappropriate.[2]

What ought to be posted at the entrances is a CANNOT DISTURB sign, because the whole town — animals and birds included — has been rendered unconscious. But we only learn this slowly, as the village is surrounded by an invisible barrier. If anyone steps beyond this invisible curtain, he or she will join the townspeople in unconsciousness. So we get police officers, firefighters, military men, even dogs and birds trying to get into the town — and then their knees buckle, they hit the ground silently, and are completely knocked out (though when pulled out, they revive immediately, with no harmful after-effects).

This invisible cocoon eventually lifts — with the only clue to its origin a fuzzy, high-altitude photograph of some sort of cylinder (alien spacecraft?) located in the center of town. Before further examination can be made, things return to normal — or so they appear. But within a few weeks, both the town doctor and vicar begin to hear from several of Midwich's young women about their suspicions of pregnancy. No one yet realizes that *every* Midwich woman of child-bearing age is now pregnant (the title of the book refers to the cuckoo's habit of laying eggs in other bird's nests). There's a rash of domestic disturbances (husbands berating or even beating their wives, for their presumed infidelity, as well as some tragic, self-administered abortions), and a town meeting is organized to address the crisis. The wife of the town's resident philosopher/author is enlisted to inform women that they are not alone. In a wonderful speech, she acknowledges the extremely fraught nature of the situation, but urges calm and solidarity:

> Fair or unfair, whether we like it or not, we are all of us, married and single alike, in the same boat. If any married woman here is tempted to consider herself more virtuous than her unmarried neighbor, she might do well to consider how, if she were challenged, she could *prove* that the child she now

carries is her husband's child. This is a thing that has happened to all of us. WE must make it bind us together for the good of all.[3]

Wyndham has taken a few hits from critics for the lack of strong female voices in his work—a fair knock, in general. But *The Midwich Cuckoos* isn't interested in maternal psychology as much as mass hysteria and the notion of the healing balm of "community" in the face of a crisis. In fact, that's perhaps its most powerful theme, the idea of a collective response to cataclysm. Midwich endures the situation—and even thrives, it could be argued—because of the collective embrace of a town-wide plan regarding how to proceed. And that plan involved rearing the children—who appeared "practically" normal, save for their golden-hued irises and a faint luminescence about their skin—and then setting up a special boarding school for their education.

The narrator leaves Midwich for almost a decade after the 60 children

Don't let those clean faces and freshly pressed school clothes fool you. These innocent-looking children are really a budding alien attack force, plotting to conquer Earth in *Village of the Damned*.

are born, and then returns, updating the reader on what's happened: not much. The children of the "Dayout" — which is what the period of unconsciousness has come to be called — have lived largely without incident in their private school.

But after a couple of confrontations with the locals — who have never really embraced the children, but rather only accommodated them — the tension increases. We learn more about who they are (though Wyndham resists the urge to explicitly detail anything about their origin, or the strange incident of the "dayout"). In a candid conversation with a town official, a representative of the children confirms that they are part of a superior race that is determined to expand its numbers and establish a dominant presence on Earth.

So the town that gave them life must now wrestle with the moral quandary of what to do with its "children." There are lots of back-and-forth exchanges among the residents as they grope for a solution. The novel becomes a great gloss on the likely debate any civilized society would have if faced with such a thorny situation. As one town elder puts it:

> Their existence here constitutes a challenge to authority which cannot be evaded for long. They cannot be ignored, but any government that tries to deal with them will bring immense political trouble down on itself if it is not successful, and very little less if it is. The Children themselves have no wish to attack, or to be forced to defend themselves.[4]

How will these children's mothers and fathers deal with the threat they pose? Are they part of the community or not? Is there a maternal obligation to these "children"? Wyndham provides lots of good arguments on all sides of a question so dramatic that it was almost inevitable that the book would be made into a film.[5]

Village of the Damned is the dramatic title given to the 1960 film version of Wyndham's novel. German director Wolf Rilla helmed the effort, resulting in a film that has become far better known than the original book. The movie successfully captures the eeriness of the book, while avoiding the trap of cheap sensationalism (though you gotta love those glowing irises in the movie). The film's deliberate pace adds to the tension, and the performances — especially that of the great actor George Sanders as the town's resident wise man — really capture the anxiety and terror of the village's residents. In a film that could have degenerated into melodramatic schlock — always a danger when demonic children are a focal point of the plot — the director focuses instead on the quieter, more subtle and more truly frightening aspects of the children and their unexpected arrival. In fact, not unlike Wyndham's book, this film contains lots of small, quiet moments that are really barometers of communal anxiety. The cool, almost detached feel of the film is at jarring odds with the natural warmth of the subject of maternity and birth. It's an unnerving, and successful, juxtaposition.

The opening scene is of a bucolic little village. Professor George Zellaby (Sanders) is in his comfortable home, at fireside, as he makes a phone call. But in mid-conversation he collapses. His dog has also collapsed. In the field adjoining his house, a tractor continues plowing, its driver slumped over the wheel. There are quick vignettes throughout town of people lying on the ground, tubs overflowing, phonographs spinning, steam irons overheating ... it's all very *Twilight Zone*-ish. Then, the camera's eye view shifts from the small, closely observed details to the panoramic: streets and parks throughout the village, strewn with people and animals lying prostrate. And, as the village clock chimes, the opening credits appear on screen. It's a terrific, mood-setting opening.

The rest of the film follows Wyndham's book quite closely. There are the scenes in the doctor's office, with young women discovering they're pregnant but protesting that it's simply not possible, and scenes with the vicar as he wrestles with the dilemma. And there's a quick but powerful scene of the men in the village, silently sitting around a pub, all sharing an unexpressed anger and resentment, with the camera slowly panning up to one of the men who mutters, "I hope none of them lives."[6] But, for the time being, they all do — healthy, slightly oversized babies who appear normal except for their "strange eyes."

As in the book, the film skips to the point where the children are now eight years old — although they resemble pre-teens more than young children, and now the film exploits its principal advantage over the book: the chilly, detached, almost demonic self-possession of these children, all of them with healthy mops of blonde hair and distant countenances. No wonder the townspeople are so unnerved by their presence, as they wander around in tightly grouped packs, looking and acting nothing like children.

The other big advantage the film has over the book is George Sanders, an actor who specialized in icy, sarcastic roles and uber-intelligent sidemen (he steals his scenes in *All About Eve*, which is truly saying something). Sanders, as the professorial Zellaby, shares some of the best scenes in the movie with his "son," David, one of the "Dayout" children. Because he's not intimidated by the children's super-intelligence and growing kinetic abilities — but also because he's got an intimate connection to the community — he's the only character who's really able to interact with the children meaningfully. They trust him, and he doesn't fear them. This leads to some great moments where Zellaby and the children discuss serious issues as equals — even though they are still, after all, just children. Watching them match wits makes for some entertainingly off-kilter moments.

The movie shifts gradually from a mystery (who are the children and where did they come from?) to a horror film, as the children use their powers of mind control to exact revenge for even minor slights. For instance, a motorist narrowly misses hitting one of the Dayout children as she's crossing a street. The remaining children glare at him as he gets out of the car to see that she's all right. Their eyes start glowing, and he suddenly finds himself in their power: he climbs back into his car as if in a trance, starts the car, and promptly drives at high speed into the nearest brick wall, the car exploding in the wake of the crash. The townspeople are suitably frightened, and a small mob of them grabs torches and head at night to the building in which they all live. But one of the children opens the door and glares at the leader of the mob who, instead of setting fire to the building, sets fire to himself. (The rest of the mob wisely disperses.)

The children realize that they can no longer remain in town, so they direct Zellaby to make arrangements for their safe "dispersal," as they plan the next phase of their infiltration (and conquering) of human society. They tell him that if he doesn't assist them, "more people will be hurt." He tells them he'll give them the details of their removal in a few days. In the meantime, while the rest of the town frets about what's likely to happen next, Zellaby is as cool as a cucumber, calmly reassuring everyone that the situation will be fine. Just why he feels this way becomes clear when we see him pack his valise for the trip to the children's residence: He puts in a time bomb.

As in the book, Zellaby decides to take matters into his own hands and eliminate the danger they represent. And because the children trust him, he's the only one who can get close enough to them to pose a threat (the children are even able to keep military aircraft from flying overhead). But these kids can read minds, remember, and so there are some very tense moments after Zellaby arrives, with the children trying to discover what's in Zellaby's mind and he thinking only of a brick wall (which their kinetic interrogations gradually break down). It's a tense game of mental cat and mouse and it makes for a spectacularly effective ending

So, we return to the original mystery. Who, exactly, are the real "parents" of these children? By what means were they able to knock out the whole town? Why was it necessary to find human hosts for the alien species? And did any of the children survive the cataclysmic climax? But these aren't nagging questions that interfere with a reader's — or viewer's — enjoyment of the work. Rather, they only add to the complexity and richness of this bizarre and memorable excursion into the life of a small village, and the limits of human love.

Notes

Introduction

1. Peter Guttmacher, *Legendary Horror Films* (New York: Metrobooks, 1995), 12.
2. This designation, however, is also subject to critical quibbling. For a thorough review of the genre's development, see Carlos Clarens, *An Illustrated History of the Horror Film* (New York: Capricorn Books, 1967). See the Wikipedia entry for "Horror Films" for a quick overview and for more about Méliès and his role in originating the horror movie.
3. Guttmacher, 12.

Altered States

1. Blue Light Flotation, which is located in New York City and may be found online at www.bluelightflotation.com.
2. Paddy Chayefsky, *Altered States* (New York: Harper & Row, 1978), 78.
3. *Ibid.*, 122.
4. *Ibid.*, 75.
5. *Altered States*, directed by Ken Russell, Warner Bros., 1980.

The Amityville Horror

1. Benjamin Radford's commentary on the entire Amityville saga can be read online at http://www.snopes.com/horrors/ghosts/amityville.asp.
2. Troy Taylor, "Amityville: Horror or Hoax," http://www.prairieghosts.com/amityville.html.
3. Ric Osuna, http://www.amityvillemurders.com.
4. Jay Anson, *The Amityville Horror* (New York: Pocket Books, 2005), 17, 27.
5. *Ibid.*, 22.
6. *Ibid.*, 25.
7. *Ibid.*, 26.
8. For more on the background on the production of the film, see the Wikipedia entry on the 1979 version.
9. The 2005 remake, however, was widely considered a disappointment, both critically and commercially.
10. *The Amityville Horror*, directed by Stuart Rosenberg, American International Pictures, 1979.
11. "The Amityville Horror—1979," www.imdb.com.
12. *Ibid.*

The Birds

1. *Encyclopedia Britannica*, www.brittanica.com.
2. Keats' "Ode to a Nightingale" is probably the most lyrical and well-known of all bird-borne literature.
3. Daphne du Maurier, "The Birds," *The Birds & Other Stories* (London: Virago, 2004), 1.
4. *Ibid.*, 1.
5. *Ibid.*, 2.
6. *Ibid.*, 34.
7. *Ibid.*, 38–9.
8. From the featurette on the making of *The Birds*, from the Universal Studios "Collector's Edition" of the film.
9. *Ibid.*
10. *Ibid.*

Dead Ringers

1. Ron Rosenbaum and Susan Edmiston, "Dead Ringers," *Esquire*, March 1976, reprinted in Rosenbaum's *The Secret Parts of Fortune* (New York: HarperCollins, 2001), 99.
2. Bari Wood and Jack Geasland, *Twins* (New York: Putnam, 1977), 18.
3. *Ibid.*
4. John F. Burns, "Post Mortem on Twin Doctors," *The New York Times*, May 1, 1988. Available online at jeremy-irons.com.
5. Review available online at http://www.washingtonpost.com/wp-srv/style/longterm/movies/videos/deadringersrkempley_a0c9ec.htm.
6. *Dead Ringers*, directed by David Cronenberg, Morgan Creek Productions, 1988.
7. *Ibid.*
8. From the *USA Today* review, available online at http://www.metacritic.com/video/titles/deadringers/.
9. Moira Sullivan's review, for FilmFestivals.com, is excerpted online at http://www.rottentomatoes.com/m/dead_ringers/.
10. For more on this, see Rosenbaum and Edmiston's article in *Esquire*, cited in note 1.

Doctor Jekyll and Mr. Hyde

1. This fascinating figure has inspired books, movies, and works for the stage. A good, concise overview (complete with sketches of his execution) can be found online at www.fortunecity.com/athena/exercise/2492/DEACONBRODIE.
2. More than 40,000 copies were sold in the first six months.
3. Robert Louis Stevenson, *The Strange Case of Dr. Jekyll and Mr. Hyde* (London: Octopus Books, 1984), 645.
4. *Ibid.*, 678.
5. *Ibid.*, 679.
6. In fact, there are many similarities with Mary Shelley's *Frankenstein*, especially the theme of a scientist over-reaching, daring to play God and suffering an inevitable downfall and destruction as punishment.
7. Stevenson, 670.
8. *Dr. Jekyll and Mr. Hyde*, directed by Rouben Mamoulian, Paramount, 1931.
9. *Ibid.*
10. *Ibid.*

The Exorcist

1. Act II, Scene 2.
2. Though exorcism is perhaps popularly thought of as a Catholic ritual, other Christian denominations — as well as other religions, including Judaism and Hinduism — have engaged in the practice. Official documentation of specific exorcisms is often hard to come by, but numerous reference works (e.g., the *Catholic Encyclopedia*) offer more information.
3. William Peter Blatty, *The Exorcist* (New York: Harper & Row, 1971), 7.
4. *Ibid.*, 11.
5. *Ibid.*, 28.
6. *Ibid.*, 30.
7. *Ibid.*, 163.
8. *Ibid.*, 304.
9. P.S. Prescott, *Newsweek*, May 10, 1971, 77.
10. R.Z. Shepeard, *Time*, June 7, 1971, 96.
11. Phil Hardy, ed., *The Encyclopedia of Horror Movies* (New York: Harper & Row, 1986), 274.
12. *The Exorcist*, directed by William Friedkin, Warner Bros., 1973.
13. From "The Exorcist Tribute Zone," http://www.the-exorcist.co.uk/articles/deceptions.htm.
14. See, especially, the article on *The Exorcist* at House of Horrors (www.houseofhorrors.com), which expands on Friedkin's litany of "strange occurrences."
15. Joe Lozito, http://www.bigpicturebigsound.com/article_127.shtml.

The Fly

1. Cartoon signed "A. Erickson," *Playboy*, June 1957, 66.
2. George Langelaan, "The Fly," *Playboy*, June 1957, 38.
3. *Ibid.*, 68.
4. Carlos Clarens, *An Illustrated History of the Horror Film* (New York: Capricorn Books, 1967), 151.
5. *Ibid.*
6. *The Fly*, directed by Kurt Neumann, Twentieth Century-Fox, 1958.
7. *Ibid.*
8. John Kenneth Muir, *Horror Films of the 1980s* (Jefferson, NC: McFarland, 2007), 497.
9. Leonard Maltin, quoted in Muir, 497.
10. MaryAnn Johanson, quoted in Muir, 497.

Frankenstein

1. Many contemporary critics claim to detect a decidedly feminine slant to the text, with its emphasis on nurturing and caregiving and its sympathetic treatment of the abandoned "creature"— an irony given the fact that most critics at the time assumed the anonymously published work to be written by either William Godwin, or his disciple, Percy Shelley.
2. Maurice Hindle, "Introduction," *Frankenstein*, by Mary Shelley (New York: Penguin, 1992).
3. Quoted in Alan Frank, *Horror Movies: Tales of Terror in the Cinema* (London: Octopus, 1974), 15.
4. Audio commentary, *Frankenstein*, "The Legacy Collection," Universal Studios.

Notes

5. All quotations from the film come from *Frankenstein*, directed by James Whale, Universal Studios, 1931.
6. *Ibid.*
7. This is an old theatrical device, opening with a scene where the audience watches the watchers. It's been used countless times, perhaps most effectively in Shakespeare's *Hamlet*, where we also sit in the dark, and watch a couple of watchers (Horatio and Bernardo) do their watching.

Freaks

1. The Internet has lots of biographical scraps about Robbins' life. A good place to start is the entry on Robbins at www.imdb.com.
2. Tod Robbins, "Spurs," reprinted online at www.olgabaclanova.com/spurs.htm. All subsequent quotes are from that version of the story.
3. The history of its reception is discussed in Carlos Clarens, *An Illustrated History of the Horror Film* (New York: Capricorn Books, 1967), 70–71.
4. Tom Milnes and Paul Willermen, *The Encyclopedia of Horror Movies* (New York: Harper & Row, 1986), 51.
5. *Freaks*, directed by Tod Browning, MGM, 1932. All subsequent quotes come from this film.

From Hell

1. The term "Ripperology" was coined by British novelist and true crime writer Colin Wilson in the 1970s to define the vast and growing interest in the study of Jack's true identity. The name has stuck, and several periodicals and groups dedicated to pursuing the case have appropriated some form of the term into their official names.
2. Robert D. Keppel; Joseph G. Weis; Katherine M. Brown; and Kristen Welch, "The Jack the Ripper Murders: *A Modus Operandi* and Signature Analysis of the 1888–1891 Whitechapel Murders," *Journal of Investigative Psychology and Offender Profiling*, vol. 2 (2005), pp. 1–21. Quote attributed in the Wikipedia article on "Jack the Ripper."
3. Quoted in Curt Holman's review of *From Hell* posted on Salon.com, Oct. 26, 1999.
4. *From Hell*, directed by Albert and Allen Hughes, Twentieth Century–Fox, 2001.
5. *Ibid.*
6. Quoted from the review posted at http://www.plume-noire.com/movies/reviews/from hell.html.
7. Quoted from the *Entertainment Weekly* review posted at http://www.ew.com/ew/article/0,,180104-1-0-fromhell,00.html.

Ghost Story

1. Peter Straub, *Ghost Story* (London: Futura, 1979), 11.
2. *Ibid.*, 216.
3. Gene Lyons, *The New York Times Book Review*, April 8, 1979, 14.
4. P.S. Prescott, *Newsweek*, March 26, 1979, 93.
5. Curtis Harrington, "Ghoulies and Ghosties," in *Horror Film Reader*, ed. Alain Silver and James Ursini (New York: Limelight, 2000), 9.
6. Roger Ebert, *Ghost Story*, available online.
7. Vincent Canby, "50-Year-Old Ghost Story Revisited," www.reviews@nytimes.com.

Notes

The Hound of the Baskervilles

1. From the "Introduction" to *The Original Illustrated Sherlock Holmes by Arthur Conan Doyle* (Secaucus: Castle, 1978).
2. *Ibid.*, 343.
3. *Ibid.*, 349.
4. Ironically, Conan Doyle himself embraced certain supernatural beliefs, becoming an avid believer in "spiritualism" late in life, regularly attending séances and writing articles about communicating with the dead.
5. Quoted by Holmes in *A Study in Scarlet*.
6. In fact, Holmes is listed in the *Guinness Book of World Records* as the "most portrayed fictional character" of all time, with more than 75 actors playing him in more than 210 films.
7. Richard Valley, publisher of *Scarlet Street* magazine, relates the anecdote in the liner notes accompanying the 2004 DVD release of the film.
8. *The Hound of the Baskervilles*, directed by Sidney Lanfield, Twentieth Century–Fox, 1939.
9. *Ibid.*
10. Comment offered by author and film historian David Stuart Davis in his audio commentary on the 2004 *Hound* DVD.

Jaws

1. Peter Benchley, *Shark Life* (New York: Delacorte, 2005), 19.
2. According to BoxOfficeMojo.com, *Jaws* is now the seventh top-grossing domestic film of all time (adjusted for inflation).
3. Benchley, *Shark Life*, 15–16.
4. *Ibid.*, 16.
5. Peter Benchley, *Jaws* (New York: Ballantine, 1974), 14.
6. *Ibid.*, 137–38.
7. *Ibid.*, 3.
8. Review excerpted in *Book Review Digest—1974* (New York: H.W. Wilson, 1975), 82.
9. *Ibid.*
10. Benchley, *Shark Life*, 18.
11. Quoted by Peter Benchley in an un-aired British documentary, *In the Teeth of Jaws*, the footage of which is widely available online.
12. For the full story of the behind-the-scenes chaos, see Carl Gottlieb's *The Jaws Log* (New York: Dell, 1975).
13. From *In the Teeth of Jaws*.
14. Quoted by Michael Calia in his review of *Jaws* at www.cynicbytrade.blogspot.com. Considering its brevity, Calia's review is remarkably insightful and perceptive.

The Masque of the Red Death

1. From the poem "Alone," in *Treasury of World Masterpieces: Edgar Allan Poe* (London: Octopus Books, 1981), 782.
2. For a good discussion of Poe's literary debts, see Arthur Hobson Quinn's *Edgar Allan Poe: A Critical Biography* (Baltimore: Johns Hopkins University Press, 1998), Perry Miller's *The Raven and the Whale* (Baltimore: Johns Hopkins University Press, 1997) and Michael Allen's *Poe and the British Magazine Tradition* (New York: Oxford University Press, 1969).
3. E.A. Poe, "The Masque of the Red Death," in *Edgar Allan Poe: Thirty-Two Stories*, ed., intro. and notes Stuart Levine and Susan F. Levine (Indianapolis: Hackett, 2000), 182.

4. *Ibid.*, 185.
5. *Ibid.*
6. *Ibid.*, 186.
7. *Ibid.*, 187.
8. From the "featurette" *Roger Corman Behind the Masque*, included on the DVD release of *The Masque of the Red Death*, directed by Roger Corman, American International Pictures, 1964.
9. Steve Biodrowski, "The Masque of the Red Death — A Retrospective," available on the website of *Cinefantastique*, at www.cinefantastiqueonline.com.
10. From *Roger Corman Behind the Masque*.
11. *Ibid.*
12. Quoted in the film *The Masque of the Red Death*.

The Night Stalker

1. The entire *Night Stalker* saga, with all its permutations in popularity, is charted comprehensively in Mark Dawidziak's *The Night Stalker Companion — A 25th Anniversary Tribute* (Beverly Hills: Pomegranate Press, 1997), a remarkably thorough and well-researched book that is highly recommended for fans of the series — or those simply wondering what all the fuss is about.
2. Jeff Rice, *The Night Stalker* (Calumet City, IL: Moonstone, 1997), 14.
3. *Ibid.*, 12.
4. *Ibid.*
5. *Ibid.*, 112.
6. *Ibid.*, 159.
7. Dawidziak, 27.
8. This is a fairly reductive account of the deal-making behind the movie. The process, in all of its Byzantine complexity, is detailed in Dawidziak's book, pp. 27–29.
9. *The Night Stalker*, directed by John Moxey, American Broadcast Company, 1972.
10. *Ibid.*

The Ninth Gate

1. Arturo Perez-Reverte, *The Club Dumas* (New York: Harcourt, 1993), 6.
2. From the review by the *New York Daily News*, available through their online archive.
3. Perez-Reverte, 9.
4. *The Ninth Gate*, directed by Roman Polanski, Artisan Entertainment, 1999.
5. Dante Alighieri, *The Inferno*, trans. Henry Wadsworth Longfellow (New York: Barnes & Noble, 2003), 175.

Nosferatu

1. For a comprehensive history of the vampire legend, see J. Gordon Melton, *The Vampire Book: The Encyclopedia of the Undead* (Farmington Hills, MI: Visible Ink, 1999), ix–xvii.
2. A summary of Stoker's prodigious research on the Romanian sources of the vampire legend is available in Christopher Frayling's *Vampyres: Lord Byron to Count Dracula* (London: Faber and Faber, 1991), 317–47.
3. Melton, 200.
4. Jonty Claypole, "Afterword," *Dracula* (New York: Barnes & Noble, 2003), 519–26.
5. Bram Stoker, *Dracula* (New York: Barnes & Noble, 2003), 11.

6. *Ibid.*, 27.
7. *Ibid.*, 29.
8. *Ibid.*, 76.
9. Phil Hardy, ed., *The Encyclopedia of Horror Movies* (New York: Harper & Row, 1986), 30.
10. Caryn James, "Critic's Notebook; *Nosferatu*, the Father of All Horror Movies," *The New York Times*, April 2, 1993 (available online at http://nytimes.com/1993/04/02/movies/critic-s-notebook).
11. A well-made and entertaining film, though, as many critics have pointed out, it too takes many liberties with Stoker's original.

Phantom of the Opera

1. Jean-Marc L'Officier, "Le fantome de l'Opera," in *Horror: Another 100 Best Books*, ed. Stephen Jones and Kim Newman (New York: Carroll & Graf, 2005), 47–49.
2. This event, and Leroux's handling of it, is commonly referred to in the critical literature about the novel. A good, brief summary can be found in the "Phantom of the Opera: Facts and Fiction" article at Bookstove.com.
3. The story of the design and construction of the Paris Opera House is as dramatic as any novel. See "The New Opera House" in George Perry's *The Complete Phantom of the Opera* (New York: Henry Holt, 1987), 8–21.
4. Gaston Leroux, *The Phantom of the Opera* (New York: Harper Perennial, 1987), 2.
5. George Perry, *The Complete Phantom of the Opera* (New York: Henry Holt, 1987), 46.
6. *Ibid.*, 50.
7. *Phantom of the Opera*, directed by Rupert Julian, Universal Pictures, 1925. All subsequent quotes from the film derive from this version.

Psycho

1. Almost all critical and popular rankings of 20th century cinema place *Psycho* among the top films of the century. See, for example, *Time* magazine's list at http://205.188.238.181/time/2005/100movies/the_complete_list.html, or the list maintained by AMC at www.filmsite.org.
2. The website House of Horrors (www.houseofhorrors.com) has a useful, comprehensive overview of the Gein saga, including his subsequent incarceration as a reportedly model prisoner.
3. Paula Guran, "Behind the Bates Motel," www.DarkEcho.com.
4. Robert Bloch, *Psycho* (New York: Tor Books, 1959), 11.
5. *Ibid.*, 49.
6. *Ibid.*, 58.
7. *Ibid.*, 61.
8. A fascinating look at the making of the film, and the subsequent public frenzy and critical reaction, is offered by Laurent Bouzereau's "The Making of *Psycho*" as part of Universal Studios' "Collector's Edition" DVD of *Psycho*, released in 1999.
9. *Ibid.*
10. *Ibid.*

Re-Animator

1. This formulation reaches its zenith in Lovecraft's "Cthulhu" stories, a set of related tales that offer frightening glimpses of a controlling, superior alien race. The name "Cthulhu"

represents "a fumbling human attempt to catch the phonetics of an absolutely non-human world," Lovecraft explained.

2. "H.P. Lovecraft," www.wikipedia.org. For more on this strain of Lovecraft's thought — and for a fuller elucidation of all things Lovecraft — interested readers are encouraged to consult the works of S.T. Joshi, the dean of Lovecraft studies. Joshi is without peer, and his biographical and critical studies have done much to revive interest and enthusiasm in Lovecraft.

3. H.P. Lovecraft, *Tales*, ed. Peter Straub (New York: Library of America, 2005), note, p. 287. All subsequent references in this chapter to the story are from that edition.

4. *Ibid.*, 24.
5. *Ibid.*, 26.
6. *Ibid.*
7. *Ibid.*, 27.
8. *Ibid.*, 28.
9. *Ibid.*, 31.
10. *Ibid.*, 34.
11. *Ibid.*, 33.
12. *Ibid.*
13. *Ibid.*, 37.
14. Quoted in *Re-Animator*, directed by Stuart Gordon, Empire Pictures, 1985.
15. *Ibid.*
16. *Ibid.*
17. Lovecraft, "Facts Concerning the Late Arthur Jermyn and His Family."

The Serpent and the Rainbow

1. Wade Davis, *The Serpent and the Rainbow* (New York: Simon & Schuster, 1985), 24.
2. *Ibid.*, 126.
3. *Ibid.*, 20.
4. See Terrence Hines, "Zombies and Tetrodotoxin," *Skeptical Inquirer*, Volume 32, Issue 3 (May-June 2008): 60–62.
5. See Davis' 2002 speech to the Commonwealth Club, available at http://www.commonwealthclub.org/archive/02/02-09davis-speech.html.
6. In fact, according to imdb.com, "due to political strife and civil turmoil" in Haiti, filming was moved during production to the Dominican Republic because Haitian officials couldn't guarantee the safety of the film crew.
7. From the Commonwealth Club speech.
8. From *The Serpent and the Rainbow*, directed by Wes Craven, Universal Studios, 1988.

The Shining

1. Stephen King, "Introduction," *The Shining* (New York: Pocket Books, 2001), xv.
2. George Beahm, *Stephen King: America's Best Loved Boogeyman* (Riverside, NJ: Andrews McMeel, 1998).
3. From the "Introduction."
4. King has discussed his concerns about the film in several published interviews. For an overview of his objections, see the Wikipedia article on the film *The Shining*.
5. *Variety*, Jan. 1, 1980, www.variety.com.
6. That list, and lots of other conversation-provoking movie rankings, can be found archived at the American Film Institute's website at www.afi.com.
7. See the page for *The Shining* at www.rottentomatoes.com.

Sleepy Hollow

1. Elizabeth Ackley, et al., *American Literature* (New York: Scribner's, 1989), 100.
2. *Ibid.*, 104.
3. From the biographical article on Irving available at www.hudsonvalley.org.
4. Irving reportedly knew a man with that name, an acquaintance from Staten Island who was a colonel in the army. For a fuller discussion of the names and source material in the story, see the Wikipedia entry for "The Legend of Sleepy Hollow."
5. Washington Irving, "The Legend of Sleepy Hollow" (published in an edition with "Rip Van Winkle," Watermill Press, 1980), p. 2.
6. *Ibid.*, 3.
7. *Ibid.*
8. *Ibid.*, 39.
9. *Ibid.*, 47.
10. *Sleepy Hollow*, directed by Tim Burton, Paramount Pictures, 1999.
11. *Ibid.*

The Thing

1. The writer-editor Hugo Gernsback is widely credited with coining the term in 1926, simultaneous with the launch of his new magazine *Amazing Stories*.
2. Brian Aldiss, *The Trillion Year Spree* (New York: Atheneum, 1986), 217.
3. See all the other selections at the Association's website, www.SFWA.com.
4. John Campbell, *Who Goes There?* (N.p.: Rocket Ride Books, 2009), 17.
5. *The Thing from Another World*, directed by Christian Nyby, Winchester Pictures, 1951.
6. *Ibid.*

The Village of the Damned

1. John Wyndham, *The Midwich Cuckoos* (New York: Ballantine, 1957), 8.
2. *Ibid.*, 9.
3. *Ibid.*, 72.
4. *Ibid.*, 174.
5. Actually, *two* films. John Carpenter's 1995 remake pales in comparison to the original, though it does up the quotient of violence and sensationalism. In all significant respects, the 1960 version is more faithful — and far creepier — than the remake. A 1964 "semi-sequel" — *Children of the Damned* — bears only an incidental relationship to Wyndham's work.
6. *Village of the Damned*, directed by Wolf Rilla, Metro-Goldwyn-Mayer, 1960.

Bibliography

Aldiss, Brian. *Trillion Year Spree: The History of Science Fiction*. New York: Atheneum, 1986.
Anders, Lou, ed. *Projections: Science Fiction in Literature and Film*. Austin: Monkey Brain Books, 2004.
Augustyn, Michael. *Vlad Dracula: The Dragon Prince*. IUniverse, 2004.
Aylesworth, Thomas G. *Monsters from the Movies*. Philadelphia: J.B. Lippincott, 1972.
Barber, Richard, and Anne Riches. *A Dictionary of Fabulous Beasts*. New York: Walker, 1971.
Belford, Barbara. *Bram Stoker: A Biography of the Author of Dracula*. New York: Knopf, 1996.
Bilstad, T. Allan *The Lovecraft Necronomicon Primer: A Guide to the Cthulhu Mythos*. Woodbury, MN: Llewellyn, 2009.
Blackman, W. Haden. *The Field Guide to North American Monsters*. New York: Three Rivers, 1998.
Clarens, Carlos. *An Illustrated History of the Horror Film*. New York: Capricorn Books, 1967.
Clark, Jerome. *Encyclopedia of Strange and Unexplained Physical Phenomena*. Detroit: Gale Research, 1993.
Davis, Richard, ed. *The Encyclopedia of Horror*. London: Octopus Books, 1981.
Dawidziak, Mark. *The Night Stalker Companion: A 25th Anniversary Tribute*. Beverly Hills: Pomegranate, 1997.
Ellison, Harlan. *The City on the Edge of Forever: The Original Teleplay That Became the Classic Star Trek Episode*. Clarkston, GA: White Wolf, 1995.
Frank, Alan G. *Horror Movies: Tales of Terror in the Cinema*. London: Octopus Books, 1974.
Frost, Brian. *Monster with a Thousand Faces*. Bowling Green: Bowling Green State University Press, 1989.
Gee, Joshua. *Encyclopedia Horrifica: The Terrifying Truth About Vampires, Ghosts, Monsters, and More*. New York: Scholastic, 2007.
Gifford, Denis. *A Pictorial History of Horror Movies*. London: Hamlyn, 1973.
Griffith, Mary. *Three Hundred Years Hence*. Philadelphia: Prime Press, 1950.
Guiley, Rosemary Ellen. *The Encyclopedia of Ghosts and Spirits*. New York: Checkmark Books, 2000.
Gunn, James. *The Science of Science Fiction Writing*. Metuchen, NJ: Scarecrow, 2000.
Hardy, Phil, ed. *The Encyclopedia of Horror Movies*. New York: Harper & Row, 1986.
Harms, Daniel, ed. *The Necronomicon Files: The Truth Behind the Legend*. Boston: Weiser, 2003.

Hill, Douglas. *Return from the Dead*. London: McDonald: 1970.
Hutchings, Peter. *Hammer and Beyond: The British Horror Film*. Manchester: Manchester University Press, 1993.
Jones, Steven Graham, et al. *The Essential Monster Movie Guide: A Century of Creature Features on Film, TV, and Video*. New York: Billboard Books, 2000.
Jones, Stephen, and Kim Newman, eds. *Horror: 100 Best Books*. New York: Carroll & Graf, 1988.
Jones, Stephen, and Kim Newman, eds. *Horror: Another 100 Best Books*. New York: Carroll & Graf, 2005.
Kesterson, David B. *Critics on Poe: Readings in Literary Criticism*. Coral Gables: University of Miami Press, 1973.
King, Stephen. *Danse Macabre*. New York: Berkley, 1981.
King, Stephen. *On Writing: A Memoir of the Craft*. New York: Scribner, 2000.
Maberry, Jonathan. *Vampire Universe: The Dark World of Supernatural Beings That Haunt Us, Hunt Us, and Hunger for Us*. New York: Citadel, 2006.
McCauley, Kirby, ed. *Dark Forces*. New York: Viking, 1980.
Park, Orlando. *The Sherlock Holmes Encyclopedia*. New York: Avenel, 1985.
Perkowski, Jan. *Cats, Bats, and Vampires*. New York: Dracula Press, 1992.
Poe, Edgar Allan. *Essays and Reviews*. New York: Library of America, 1984.
Bogdanovich, Peter, ed. *This Is Orson Welles*. New York: HarperCollins, 1992.
Silver, Alain, and James Ursini. *Horror Film Reader*. Pompton Plains, NJ: Limelight, 2000.
Schwartz, Carol, et al. *Video Hound's Complete Guide to Cult Flicks and Trash Pics*. Detroit: Visible Ink, 1996.
Skal, David. *Dark Carnival: The Secret World of Tod Browning, Hollywood's Master of the Macabre*. New York: Doubleday, 1995.
Summers, Montague. *The Vampire: His Kith and Kin*. London: Trubner, 1928.
Time-Life Books. *Alien Encounters: Mysteries of the Unknown*. Richmond: Time-Life Books, 1992.
Wallace, Amy, et al. *The Book of Lists: Horror*. New York: Harper, 2008.
Waller, Gregory A. *The Living and the Undead: From Stoker's Dracula to Romero's Dawn of the Dead*. Urbana: University of Illinois Press, 1986.

Index

Abbott, Bruce 167
Adler, Irene 128, 129
Ahab 104
Alan, Dennis 173, 175
Alcott, John 185
Aldiss, Brian 195
Alfred Hitchcock Presents 26
All About Eve 208
Altered States 5–12
Amity 103
The Amityville Horror 13–20
Anderson, Nellie 71
Angel Heart 175
Anson, Jay 15
Apocalypse Now 107
Arness, James 199, 202
Asimov, Isaac 195
Astair, Fred 90, 91, 93
Astounding Science Fiction 195, 196
Atwater, Barry 124
Audubon, John J. 21
Austen, Jane 23

Baclanova, Olga 75
Balaban, Bob 10
Balkan, Boris 130, 131, 133
Barryman 100
Barrymore, John 40
Baskerville, Charles 100
Baskerville, Hugo 96, 100
Bates, Norman 152, 154–160
Beast 103
Becket 113
Beetlejuice 189
Behlmer, Rudy 66
Bellow, Saul 89
Benchley, Nathaniel 103
Benchley, Peter 102–106
Beowulf 2
Bergman, C.J. 105
The Bible 1
Bickle, Travis 88

The Birds 21–28
"The Black Cat" 111
Blatty, William Peter 46–48
Blair, Linda 49
Bloch, Robert 152–156
Bogdanovich, Peter 28
Bones, Brom 188, 189
Book of the Nine Doors of the Kingdom of Shadows 128
Boyle, Robert 26
Braveheart 37
Brenner, Mitch 26
Brett, Jeremy 101
Bride of Frankenstein 66
Brodie, William 37
Brody, Ellen 104, 107
Brody, Martin 105, 107–108
Brolin, James 15, 17
Brown, Blair 9
Browning, Tod 72, 74, 77
Brownjohn, John 130
Bruce, Nigel 98
Brundle, Seth 59
Bryant, William Cullen 186, 188
Bujold, Genevieve 31, 35
Buquet, Joseph 149
Burstyn, Ellen 51
Burton, Tim 189–193

Cain, Dan 167, 168
Caine, Michael 40
Campbell, Eddie 80
Campbell, John W. 195–198
Canby, Vincent 93
Captain Alatriste 127
Carew, Muriel 41
Carlotta 149
Carradine, John 100
Carrie 92
Casablanca 107
Chamberlin, Mark 90
Chaney, Lon 70, 147, 148

Index

Chayefsky, Paddy 6
Choates, Tim 90
The Chrysalids 204
Clarens, Carlos 56
Clavell, James 57
Cleopatra 75
A Clockwork Orange 181
Close Their Eyes Tenderly 71
The Club Dumas 127–130
Cohen, Lawrence D. 92
"The Collector of Brains" 55
Conan Doyle, Arthur 78, 94–97
Connant 198
Cooper, James Fenimore 186, 188
Coppola, Francis Ford 142
Corman, Roger 113–117
Cornthwaite, Robert 200
Corpse Bride 189
Corso, Dean 130, 131, 132
Corso, Lucas 127–130
Count Orlock 139, 141
Courbet, Jacques 71
Court, Hazel 116
Crane, Ichabod 187–189
Crane, Marion 152, 155, 159
Crane, Mary 155
Craven, Wes 173–175
Cronenberg, David 33–36, 58–60
Crook, Annie 80
Crothers, "Scatman" 183

Daae, Christine 146, 149–151
Dalí, Salvador 71
Daniels, Melanie 26
Dante 127, 129, 133
The Dark Tower 178
Davis, Geena 58
Davis, Wade 171–177
Day of the Triffids 204
Dead Ringers 29–36
The Dead Zone 33
Dean, James 88
The Deep 103
DeFeo, Ronald 17
Delambre, Andre 55
Depp, Johnny 82, 83, 84, 130, 131, 192, 193
Dickens, Charles 38, 78 173
Dillon, Matt 199
Doctor Carrington 200
Doctor Halsey 164
Dr. Jekyll and Mr. Hyde 37–44
Doctor Mortimer 96, 98
Dr. Strangelove 181
Doctor Waldman 67

Doctor Watson 94, 96
Douglas, Kirk 40
Douglas, Melvin 90, 91
Dracula 3, 4, 41, 66, 74, 135–142, 144, 192
Dreyfus, Richard 107
Duchamp, Marielle 176
Duel 109
Dumas, Alexandre 127
du Maurier, Daphne 21–25
du Maurier, George 144
Duvalier, "Baby Doc" 174, 177
Duvall, Shelley 184

Earles, Harry 75
Ebert, Roger 93, 184
Eco, Umberto 128
Edison, Thomas 2
Edmiston, Susan 30
Edward Scissorhands 189, 192
Elfman, Danny 191
Emerson, Ralph Waldo 188
"The Empty House" 95
Esquire 30
Euripedes 1
The Exorcist 19, 45–53
Exorcist Two: The Heretic 50

Fairbanks, Douglas, Jr. 90, 91
"The Fall of the House of Usher" 111, 129
Father Delaney 17
Father Karras 47
Father Merrin 46
Faust 151
Feather, Leonard 54
"The Final Problem" 95
The Flanders Panel 127
The Fly 33, 54–60
France, Anatole 54
Francesca 114, 116
Frankenstein 2, 3, 8, 41, 52, 61–69, 134, 144
Frankenstein, Henry 67
Frankenstein, Victor 61, 62
Freaks 70–77
The French Connection 48
Frieda 75
Friedkin, William 48, 53
Fritz 67
From Hell 78–85

Galli, Eva 92, 93
Gavin, John 159
Gayford, Richard 204
Geasland, Jack 31
Gein, Ed 153, 157

Index

Ghost Story 86–93
Godwin, William 62
Goethe 129
"The Gold-Bug" 111
Goldblum, Jeff 58
Gordon, Stuart 166
Gottlieb, Carl 107
Grendel 2
Gull, William 80
Gunsmoke 199

Haller, Daniel 114
Hallorann, Dick 183
Halsey, Dean 168
Hamilton, Murray 107, 109
Hamlet 45, 191
Hans 75
Harker, Jonathan 136, 137, 138, 142
Harrington, Curtis 89
Hawthorne, Nathaniel 186
Hayworth, Annie 27
Hedison, David 56
Hedren, Tippi 22, 25 26
Heinlein, Robert 195
Hendry, Patrick 200, 202
Herbert, Charles 59
Herbert, Holmes 42
"Herbert West — Reanimator" 162–165
Hercules 75
Herrmann, Bernard 159
Heston, Charlton 101
Hitchcock, Alfred, 21, 25, 152, 154, 156–160
Hoffman, E.T.A. 2
Holm, Ian 84
Holmes, Sherlock 84, 94–101, 127, 128, 129, 193
Homer 1
Hooper, Matt 104, 107
"Hop-Frog" 114
Hope, Bob 100
Hospital 7
The Hound of the Baskervilles 94–101
House of Usher 113
Houseman, John 90. 91, 93
Hughes, Albert 82
Hughes, Allan 82
Hunchback of Notre Dame 144
Hunter, Evan 25
Hurt, William 6, 9, 11–12
Hyde, Edith Norton 71

An Illustrated History of the Horror Film 56
Indiana Jones 124, 146, 175
The Inferno 133

Inspector Frederick Abberline 82
Inspector Ledoux 151
Invasion of the Body Snatchers 56
Irons, Jeremy 31, 34–36
Irvin, John 89
Irving, John 89
Irving, Washington 186–191, 194

Jack the Ripper 78
James, Caryn 141
James, Henry 89
James, Sears 91
Jaws 102–109
Jessup, Edward 7
The Jewel of the Seven Stars 135
Johnson, Kurt 90
Joshi, S.T. 165
Julian, Rupert 148
Juliana 116

Karloff, Boris 64, 65
Kelly, Mary 84
Kemply, Rita 34
Kidder, Margot 15, 17
King, Stephen 3, 89, 92, 178–185, 204
King, Tabitha 180
King Duncan 117
Knickerbocker's History of New York 187
Kolchak, Carl 120–125
The Kolchak Papers 122
Kolchak: The Night Stalker 125
The Kraken Wakes 204
Krige, Alice 93
Krueger, Freddy 65
Kubrick, Stanley 19, 181–185

The Lady of the Shroud 135
Laemmle, Carl 67, 146
Lanfield, Sidney 98, 100
Langela, Frank 130, 133
Langelaan, George 54
Lanyon, Dr. 41
The League of Extraordinary Gentlemen 80
Lecter, Hannibal 174
Lee, Christopher 192
"The Legend of Sleepy Hollow" 186–191, 194
Leigh, Janet 157, 158
Leroux, Gaston 143–146
Lewis, C.S. 1
Lilly, Dr. John 5
The Little Shop of Horrors 113
Lloyd, Daniel 183
Loomis, Sam 159
Lord Byron 62, 134

Index

Lovecraft, H.P. 118, 161–165, 204
Lugosi, Bela 66, 139
Lutz, George 15
Lutz, Kathy 15

Macbeth 116
MacNeil, Chris 46
MacNeil, Regan 46
Mamoulian, Rouben 40–43
The Man 135
La Manoir du Diable (The House of the Devil) 2
Mantle, Beverly 34
Mantle, Elliot 34
March, Fredric 40, 42
Marcus, Cyril 29
Marcus, Stewart 29
Marie, Jeanne 71
"Marty" 7
The Masks of War 55
The Masque of the Red Death 110–117
Mather, Cotton 186
Matheson, Richard 12
McGavin, Darren 122–1231
McMurphy, Randall P. 184
Méliès, Georges 2, 91
Melton, J. Gordon 136
Menace II Society 82
Merrick, John 81
The Midwich Cuckoos 204–207
Miller, Jason 51
Milton, John 63, 65, 129
Miskatonic University 162, 164
Miss Betty 135
Mobley, Alma 93
Moby Dick 105, 127
Mokae, Zakes 174, 175
Moore, Alan 80
Moxley, John Llewellyn 123
Munch, Edvard 139
"The Murders in the Rue Morgue" 111
Murnau, F.W. 3, 118, 139, 141
Murray, Mina 138
The Mystery of the Sea 135

Narcisse, Clairvius 171
Network 7
Neumann, Kurt 56
Nicholson, Jack 179, 182–185
Nicholson, Nikki 200, 202
Night of the Living Dead 88
The Night Stalker 118–125
The Night Strangler 119, 125
Nightmare on Elm Street 173
Nineteen Eighty-Four 174

The Ninth Gate 126–133.
Niveau, Claire 35
Norris, William 166
Nosferatu 3, 4, 134–142
Nyby, Christian 198, 199

Oakland, Simon 123
O'Brien 174
Odyssey 1
Olin, Ken 90
One Flew Over the Cuckoo's Nest 184
The Overlook Hotel 179, 180, 181, 183, 185
Owens, Patricia 56

Paget, Sidney 98
Paine, Thomas 186
Paoli, Dennis 166
Paradise Lost 63, 65, 116
Parker, Alan 175
Pascal, Ernest 98
Peake, Richard Brinsley 66
Pearson, Ivy 41
Perez-Reverte, Arturo 127
The Personal Reminiscences of Henry Irving 135
Peytraud, Dargent 174, 175, 176
The Phantom of the Opera 143–151
Philbin, Mary 147, 149
"The Pit and the Pendulum" 111
Playboy 54
Plummer, Christopher 101
Poe, Edgar Allan 2, 21, 22, 39, 110–113, 127, 129, 163, 204
Polanski, Roman 130–133
Polidori, John 134
Pratt, William Henry 66
Presumption, or the Fate of Frankenstein 66
Price, Vincent 56, 59, 113, 116
Prince Edward 80
Prince Prospero 111, 115–117
Psycho 109, 123, 152–160
Pullman, Bill 173, 174, 175

Quint, Captain 104, 108

Radison, Carrie 54
Raiders of the Lost Ark 175
Raoul, Viscount de Chagny 146, 149–151
Rathbone, Basil 98, 99, 101
The Raven 21, 22, 111
The Realm of the Incas 155
Re-Animator 161–169
Rebecca 22
Ricci, Christina 192
Rice, Anne 128

226

Index

Rice, Jeff 120
Rilla, Wolf 207
Robbins, Tod 70
The Rocky Horror Picture Show 118
Roeg, Nicolas 114
Rosenbaum, Ron 30
Rosenberg, Arthur 10
Rosenberg, Stuart 17
Russell, Ken 9
Rymer, James Malcolm 135

Sanders, George 207, 208
Sarde, Philippe 93
Satan 116, 127, 130, 193
Scanners 58
Scheider, Roy 107
Schifrin, Lalo 17
Schreck, Max 139, 140
Scotty 200
Seigner, Emmanuel 130
The Serpent and the Rainbow 170–177
The Seven Percent Solution 101
Shakespeare, William 130
Shaw, Robert 105, 108
Sheen, Martin 107
Shelley, Mary 2, 62, 65, 134
Shelley, Percy 62, 63
Sheridan, Margaret 200
The Shining 19, 109, 178–185
Silence of the Lambs 174
Simon 73
Sketch Book of Geoffrey Crayon, Gent. 187
Skorzeny, Janos 121, 124
Sleepy Hollow 186–194
Snider, Norman 35
Sophocles 1
Spielberg, Steven 102, 106–109
"Spurs" 70
Stapleton 98
Star Trek 118, 121
Star Trek: First Contact 93
Star Trek: The Motion Picture 12
Stefano, Joseph 156, 157
Steiger, Rod 17
Stern, Sandor 17
Stevenson, Robert Louis 23, 37–39
The Sting 108
Stoker, Bram 2, 135–138, 141, 142
Stop Making Sense 168
Straub, Peter 86–89
Struss, Karl 41
Stuart, Don A.
Sturgeon, Theodore 195
Sullivan, T.R. 40

Susann, Jacqueline 104
Svengali 144

The Taking of Pelham One Two Three 108
Talking Heads 168
Tandy, Jessica 27
Taylor, Rod 26
"The Tell-Tale Heart" 111
Tetrallini, Madame 75
Them 56
The Things from Another World 195–202
Thompson, Hunter S. 84
The Three Musketeers 127
The Time Machine 7
Tiomkin, Dimitri 200
Tobey, Kenneth 200
Tony 179
Torrance, Danny 179–185
Torrance, Jack 179–185
Torrance, Wendy 179–185
Tracy, Spencer 40
Treasure Island 37
Trilby 144
The Trillion Year Spree 195
Twilight Zone 72, 121, 208
Twins 31–33
2001—A Space Odyssey 12, 181, 184
Tyson, Cathy 176

The Unholy Three 71, 74
Urbizo, Enrique 130
Utterson, Mr. 39

V for Vendetta 80
The Vampyre 134
Van Helsing 138
Van Sloan, Edward 67
Van Tassel, Katrina 188, 192
Varney the Vampire 135
Videodrome 33, 58
Village of the Damned 203–210
Vincenzo, Anthony 123
Vlad Dracula 136
von Sydow, Max 50

Walken, Christopher 192
Walker, Andrew Kevin 191
Washington, George 186
Wasson, Craig 93
The Watchman 80
Weber, William 17
Webling, Peggy 66
Welles, Orson 41
Wells, H.G. 7
Westenra, Lucy 138

Index

Whale, James 66
Who Goes There? 196–198
Williams, John 107
Williamson, Nicol 101
Wilson, E.O. 105
The Wizard of Oz 107
Wollstonecraft, Mary 62

Wood, Bari 31
Wyndham, John 204–208

Zanuck, Darryl F. 98
Zellaby, George 208, 209
"Zombie Express Train" 55

www.ingramcontent.com/pod-product-compliance
Ingram Content Group UK Ltd.
Pitfield, Milton Keynes, MK11 3LW, UK
UKHW041946140426
5217IPUK00014B/683